DANGEROUS HILARITY

**The Great Adventures of the
Jackson Twins, Their Family
and the Dogs in Their Lives**

**A Novel for Teens and Young
Adults and All Those Who
are Young at Heart**

by

SIOUX DALLAS

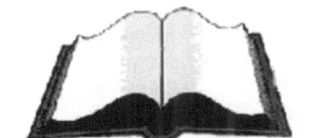

**CCB Publishing
British Columbia, Canada**

Dangerous Hilarity: The Great Adventures of the Jackson Twins, Their Family and the Dogs in Their Lives, A Novel for Teens and Young Adults and All Those Who are Young at Heart

Copyright ©2010 by Sioux Dallas
ISBN-13 978-1-926585-82-6
First Edition

Library and Archives Canada Cataloguing in Publication

Dallas, Sioux, 1930-
Dangerous hilarity : the great adventures of the Jackson twins, their family and the dogs in their lives, a novel for teens and young adults and all those who are young at heart / written by Sioux Dallas. – 1st ed.
ISBN 978-1-926585-82-6
I. Title.
PS3604.A439D36 2010   813'.6   C2010-903153-9

Publisher: CCB Publishing
             British Columbia, Canada
             www.ccbpublishing.com

Dedicated to all of my much-loved students whom I had while teaching public school and horseback riding. I loved all of you and you taught me a tremendous amount.

And to the wonderful people who train and furnish the service dogs and miniature horses for people who need a special friend.

ACKNOWLEDGEMENTS

It gives me great pleasure to say a sincere thank you to two lovely ladies in the Nome, Alaska Visitors Bureau. Myrtle Kinna and Natalie Abrams were not only patient with my many questions, but made sure I received all possible written information on the Nome area.

I'm grateful to the staff of SOUTHEASTERN GUIDE DOGS, INC. in Palmetto, Florida; to PAWS WITH A CAUSE in Wayland, Michigan; GUIDING EYES FOR THE BLIND in Yorktown Heights, New York; and CANINE PARTNERS FOR LIFE in Cochranville, Pennsylvania for their information on care, training and use of service dogs. I've visited numerous times at SOUTHEASTERN and observed as well as handled dogs. God bless all of you for the love and care you give to the animals and humans.

THE GUIDE HORSE FOUNDATION can be found on the internet and will provide valuable information on the use of the miniature horses as guide animals. These precious little animals can be housebroken and are devoted to their human. The pictures of these horses, with their tiny white sneakers, are as cute as can be. The book "Helping Hooves" by Janet Burleson tells of her experiences in training these small horses and helping people who desperately need help - - and a friend.

I visited the training quarters of the Royal Canadian Mounted Police in Ottawa and learned the information which I included in the chapter of the Jackson family encountering them. The officer in charge was very polite and informative. My husband and I had a delightful visit. I'm glad he enjoyed the visit because he died soon after.

On May 23, 2006, the Royal Canadian Mounted Police held the first annual national memorial at its headquarters in Ottawa to pay respect to all members of the RCMP who lost their lives in the line of duty since 1876.

This ceremony does not replace the RCMP Memorial Parade Service held the second week of September, nor does it take away from the involvement in Peace Officer Memorial Day on Parliament Hill in September. May 23rd was chosen to commemorate the creation of the RCMP as a federal police force in 1873. This also gave the Prime Minister an opportunity to pay respect to Canada's National Police Force.

In 1988, my daughter and I took the trip that the Jacksons had. We had a van with a double bed in it and loads of space. We each took a dog and had a great time. One place we stopped for the night, a big man, who looked a little like Teddy Roosevelt, asked us why we were there. We told him just to stay the night at the motel. He said it was a dangerous place. Around three in the morning I heard a strange noise and looked out the window. There sat that big man in the back of his pick-up truck on a chair and holding a rifle across his lap. He was protecting two ladies who were strangers.

PART I
GALENA

Dangerous Hilarity

CHAPTER ONE

No happier dog could be found anywhere. Galena was a strong, healthy German Shepherd, larger than the average dog of her breed. Galena was brown and tan standing a full twenty-six inches at her shoulder which was two inches more than the usual size. She loved her humans and felt that she lived with the greatest family, especially her twin boys. She loved the girl, and the adults, but the boys were special because they had grown up together.

Galena's family was the Jackson family of Fairfax, Virginia. Dr. Herbert Jackson worked for the U. S. Government in the Department of Interior. There was Mrs. Irene Jackson, fourteen year old Anna Maria, who was a high school freshman and twelve year old identical twins, Thomas Harrison and Timothy Michael, who were in the seventh grade. Great boys who made good grades but were mischievous, especially Tom.

Two days before the Christmas holiday, Herb Jackson rushed home with good news. At least he thought it was stupendous news and hoped his family would be as thrilled as he was. Herb came bounding through the front door, bringing a chilly wind with him. He hurriedly shut the door and hopped around on one foot while taking off his rain boots that he had needed that morning. He was so eager to share the news that he could hardly get his gloves and overcoat off. He placed his boots on a mat in the hall closet, his gloves and his rain hat on a shelf and hung his coat on a hangar.

"Hey! Where is everybody?" he called excitedly. "Everyone in the den for a family conference. Hurry. Hup! Hup!"

Galena, feeling the excitement, was running around Herb jumping up to his face and barking. Her tail was wagging so hard she almost lost her balance. She seemed to be saying, "Me, too. I'm family, too." The familiar expression on Galena's face was an open mouth and bright, sparkling eyes making her look as if she were laughing.

"Quiet girl. Yes, you can stay." Herb rubbed her neck and ears and patted her shoulder while he waited impatiently for his family to gather.

Irene came running in from the kitchen with a large, dripping, wooden spoon in her hand. "What is it? Is something wrong?" she asked worriedly. She had grabbed up a dish towel and now put it under the dripping spoon that she had been using to stir the homemade potato soup. She sank down on the couch, relieved to see that Herb was all right.

Galena put her paws on Irene's knees as if to comfort her. "Yes, I love you, too, but be a good girl and lie down." Irene used the back of her hand to wipe her curly, blonde hair off her sweaty forehead. Her hazel-green eyes were anxious and slightly amused. She loved her husband and her children, but at the moment, she thought her husband was acting like one of the children. Her bow-shaped lips curled in a quiet smile. Her fair complexion was slightly flushed from cooking over a hot stove. Galena stretched out at Irene's feet then jumped up when she heard the twins clomping down the stairs.

The twins were running, skipping stairs and landed with a thud at the bottom. Tim nearly tripped over Galena who was jumping up at him and barking. "What is it?" Tim shouted as he took Galena's collar and led her into the den between him and Tom.

"Tell us quickly. Is it a Christmas surprise?" Tom shouted.

"It had better be good. I'm in the middle of finishing a research paper for history class and it counts as one-third of our grade for this semester." Anna spoke around a pencil held in her teeth as she clutched a large open book against her chest. She dropped to the floor with her knees bent and her ankles crossed. Galena promptly came and plopped down with her head and a paw on Anna's lap.

Anna looked up at her six feet two inch daddy and thought he was the handsomest man in the world. His light brown hair was naturally wavy and his green eyes were snapping with thrilling excitement. He was pacing back and forth and running his fingers through his hair. He had run his fingers through so much that his hair was standing up in spikes.

"Please. Everyone. Quiet. Pay attention." Herb grinned and drew himself up as if he were proud of what he was going to say. "I have been requested to take a two to three year assignment to" he hesitated for suspense--

"Nome, Alaska. What a marvelous experience it will be for all of us." he finished with great enthusiasm.

There was a stunned silence so sharp it almost hurt the ears. "Don't everyone speak at once," Herb joked. "I know I'm hitting you with unexpected news, and it will take time for us to think about it and talk it over." He began to look uneasy as the silence grew and he looked from one stunned face to another. "It's a great honor to be chosen for this special assignment." He looked worriedly at his silent family. "Well, someone say something."

"B-b-b but, Dad," Tim wailed, "it would mean leaving our friends and our home and our school and ---"

"Everything," Anna finished weakly.

Tom looked as if he had been punched in the stomach. "No!" he shrieked. "I want to go to winter camp with our scout troop. We're going to learn how to survive in winter weather and how to find directions with a compass."

"My French class is planning a trip to Paris and it'll be during my birthday. We're doing fund raising activities to help pay for the trip. Oh, I have my heart set on going and I've been working hard to earn money for it." Anna moaned.

Irene began speaking so low they could hardly hear her. "I'm working with my Sunday School class to adopt a family for Christmas. I also promised to work with the Chamber of Commerce for our Main Street Art Festival next March."

"Well, we're not leaving tomorrow," Herb snapped, disappointed that his family didn't feel as he did. "I'll have to leave in a couple of months, but all of you can wait until the school year is over and then join me in Alaska." He looked imploringly at them.

Everyone was silent, looking at each other and absent-mindedly petting Galena as she went whining from one to another sensing the distress in the atmosphere.

Herb dropped to one knee in front of Irene, taking her hand and imploring. "Honey, just think about it. Our children will have an opportunity to see a lot of their own country and meet a variety of people. I'm sure you'll find ladies doing interesting, worth while things in Nome." Herb was beginning to worry that his family could not be persuaded to join him in what he considered a fabulous opportunity. He jumped up and continued pacing.

Irene took a deep breath and spoke haltingly. "I don't -- really know. Part of me is as excited as you are and part of me is --- cringing at the idea of such a move and all that it involves. We've lived here for sixteen years and have so many friends.

"What about Galena?" Tom knelt by the dog hugging her against his side.

"What about Galena? Well, I guess she'll have to stay here with someone we trust if they're willing to keep her for us. She's lived here all of her life and, I'm not sure, at her age, that she could make the adjustment." Herb answered without thinking.

"Oh, no!"

"No way!"

"Absolutely not!"

The three children spoke as one.

"Honey, you might as well suggest leaving one of the children behind. You know they will not go off and leave Galena behind. I don't like the idea either." Irene spoke firmly. "She's been with us since she was three months old and the boys were two years old."

"Yeah, Dad. She's one of the family," Tim choked out.

"What kind of work would you be doing, Dad?" Tom questioned with a disturbed expression.

"I'll have a team and we're supposed to investigate to see if there is natural gas under the tundra and maybe coal. There's no oil on the western side of Alaska, but scientists feel they've found evidence to support the theory of natural gas. I'll be working with the environment in many ways for the Department of Interior. There are no roads into Nome because of the snow and constant freezing. We would have to drive to Fairbanks and fly into Nome. Once we get there, we'll find many good roads in the city."

"Is it a done deal?" Tom frowned

"I won't be fired if I don't accept the assignment, if that's what you're asking. I repeat, it's an honor that they considered me. The job will mean a promotion and a much better retirement fund. That'll come in handy with three of you going to college." He gave a nervous little laugh. "I have to be honest. I'm very excited about the opportunity."

"Nah. No kidding. You could have fooled me," Tom spoke facetiously.

Irene got up and started toward the kitchen. "Dinner's ready. Cheeseburgers and potato soup. Why don't we eat and have another talk later."

Anna asked the blessing and ended with, "and give us the wisdom to know what is the best thing for us to do." The meal was eaten quickly with a lot of excited babble, sometimes all trying to talk at once. The children finally agreed to learn more about Alaska and make a decision later--but only if Galena was included. Everyone carried their own dirty dishes into the kitchen. Anna and Irene quickly had dishes done and the room cleaned while the boys carried the trash out. The family then gathered in the den to watch a National Geographic special.

"Let's go to bed and sleep on this. There'll be time to do more talking after we've absorbed information about where our home would be." Irene fluttered around like a disturbed bird as she encouraged her family to go to bed.

CHAPTER TWO

The next day, in their homeroom at school, the students were eager for the holiday and too excited to think of lessons.

"Mrs. Berry," Tim kept waving his hand in the air and even half way standing up. "Tom and I have something to share with you and the class."

"Make it quick, Tim. We have much to cover today."

"Our dad has been requested --" Tim started.

"You know he works for the Federal Government," Tom butted in. "We may have to move --"

"to Alaska." Both boys finished together. "For two or three years," Tim bounced as he talked.

A lot of the students began talking at once with surprise and excitement. Most of them thought it was great and told the twins that they envied them. Hearing the excitement in the voices of their classmates, the twins began to feel that it might not be such a calamity after all, still they were not totally convinced that it would be a good move.

The bell rang to leave the homeroom and go to other classes. The children were clattering about the news and telling others that they met in the hall. The twins were momentarily pleased at the attention.

Herb had been giving each child ten dollars a week for an allowance which they earned by doing chores around the house. Anna earned extra money by babysitting. The twins mowed laws, shoveled snow and ran errands for people to earn extra money according to the time of the year.

Christmas at last and snow. The children loved it, but the people who had to drive to work were not pleased. The twins each got skis and Anna got a motor bike for their main presents. The twins also received a complete set of 'Harry Potter' books. Herb got books he enjoyed written by John Grisham, Ken Follett and Frank Patterson. Irene got a hundred dollar gift certificate to a local spa for a day of relaxation and pampering. The three children had pooled their money and purchased tickets for a stage play and a dinner for their parents. Everyone received smaller gifts.

The twins went to friends' houses to compare gifts. Anna left with two girlfriends to go to another friend's house. She could hardly wait to get their reaction to the possible move to Alaska.

The new year came with a lot of celebrating. The Jacksons celebrated with friends at the Emerald Greens Country Club, and had a great time. The thought often ran through their minds that this might be the last time they'd do this for a long time. The Fairfax Fire Department put on a display of fireworks and ended with a giant rose and the American flag in the sky. The police bagpipe and drum marching band furnished music.

January brought more cold weather and the fulfillment of many plans. "It was so wonderful. We collected enough to adopt two families. It was touching to share in their pleasure," Irene was pleased that her class had a successful project. Her ideas for the Main Street Art Festival were accepted and plans were made to print brochures for distribution to business places and to the public.

"Ya hah!" Tom dodged a snowball thrown by Alex Baughman. Then Tom shot one and hit the scout leader. The twins and fourteen other boys enjoyed the camp-out even in cold January on a long weekend. Fortunately there was only a light dusting of snow. In spite of the bitter weather the boys enjoyed hiking through the safe areas of the Blue Ridge Mountains, plotting different trails according to the maps provided by forest rangers, and learning to find their way back to camp with a compass.

Tom was bouncing around. "Zowee! Isn't this great," he exclaimed. "I wouldn't have missed this for the world."

"Yeah," Danny Garrison stated, "think of all you'll be missing if you go to Alaska and we'll be here doing a lot of fun things. You won't be here to enjoy them," he said with a sneer.

"Stuff it, Danny." Mark Tully said. "You're just jealous that they're going to get a great adventure and you won't have a chance to do as much."

"Ha. Who wants to go to old Alaska with the cold, ice and dangerous animals?" Danny answered with a twisted grin. Privately he **was** envious. Starbursts of anger shot through his mind as he thought of what he considered the injustice of it all. *Why can't I ever have a chance to do something fun or go somewhere so cool?*

"I would love to be going," Benjamin Dyang yelled.

"Besides, they'll have a chance to do more fun things than we'll ever get to do," Jed Winters proclaimed.

"It's going to be a fantastic experience," Ed Warden, the scout leader, said. "We're all glad your family will have this opportunity and we'll be waiting anxiously for you to return and share with us."

Come on, boys," the assistant leader, Ben Sturgill called. "We have to get back to camp so we can prepare supper and get ready for bed."

Tim walked happily on talking to different ones, but Tom hung back walking more slowly and thoughtfully. *How can Tim and I get out of going to Alaska? I have to think of something.*

The boys stuck wieners on sticks and cooked them over the fire. Chili was heated in a big pot. The boys squirted cheese out of a bottle on the hot dogs and sometimes on each other. There was a selection of chopped onions (brought from home in plastic bags), relish, mustard, ketchup and baked beans. They had left white potatoes wrapped in aluminum foil baking in the hot ashes. Two older boys (Eagle Scouts) had stayed behind to watch the fire and the camp supplies. Later the boys roasted marshmallows on sticks over the fire while the two leaders told ghost stories. The boys then washed, brushed their teeth with water from the melted snow and slid down into warm sleeping bags inside tents. Camping lanterns were in each tent for warmth and light and, in some cases, for comfort.

February flew by and then March rolled around with cool but sunny days. People were dressed warmly and happily enjoying the big street festival that had followed a huge parade of fourteen floats, four high school bands and a marching bagpipe and drum band. A great horse group had marched and demonstrated how their hoses danced to music. A few people had decorated their pets and walked with them. One woman had dressed her little black poodle in a doll's dress and pushed her in a baby carriage. The Shriners had funny little cars, clowns and several marching groups.

Two blocks had been roped off so that people could walk freely but vehicles could not drive through. There were loads of arts and crafts booths, a face painting booth for the children, several food booths and various business booths that gave out goodies to advertise their particular business. An artist sat on the sidewalk doing caricatures of people for five dollars which would be donated to the city fund for youth programs. A new bakery was giving out tiny donuts and cookies. The longest line was at the booth selling funnel cakes.

Some of the police demonstrated the agility and obedience of their dogs. The dogs ran through an obstacle course and then showed how they followed commands with hand signals as well as voice.

Irene began to make preparations for their move with a reluctant Anna and even more reluctant twins helping. They conferred on lists of things to do, things to take and things to store until they returned to Virginia. Time passed much too quickly.

Anna gradually began to talk with more interest after finding her friends were interested. The twins only expressed themselves when someone brought up the subject.

With a lot of groaning and excuses from the twins, Irene took all of them for medical check-up and dental care. Even Galena visited her veterinarian. Irene reminded them, "All medical records will be taken with us, but school records will be sent. Now let's go home and see what clothes we can take and what we need to buy. We'll be needing far different clothing than we do here.

Galena busily inspected all of the packed boxes and items left on the beds to be packed while she went from room to room supervising. Irene was exasperated one day to discover that she would place an item in a box and look around to see Galena industriously unpacking by taking the item in her mouth and dropping it somewhere in the house. Well. She was helping, wasn't she?

During March Herb planned to leave to meet his crew and find a house for his family. He promised to call as often as possible and to take pictures so the family would have an idea what to expect. One evening he called the family together.

"Anna, I know I can count on you to help your mother and relieve her whenever possible. Boys, I'm counting on you to take care of your mother and sister and be a help instead of a hindrance. Remember, Galena is old and will need a lot of care and attention. Her age is about seven times that of a year of yours, so take good care of her."

In April Anna celebrated her fifteenth birthday in Paris with her school group. Her family would have a birthday celebration when she returned. After talking to several friends about her move, she began to feel a little better about leaving Fairfax. Of course she would miss everyone, but it would be exciting to make new friends in Alaska.

In May the twins celebrated their thirteenth birthday with a super party. At one o'clock they had a cook-out in the back yard and games galore with eighteen boys that were invited. Tom had vetoed inviting girls with the explanation that girls didn't want to get dirty and they would be playing rough games. They played a tug-of-war, touch football, volleyball and several others.

The boys argued over who would cook the burgers and hot dogs on the grill until Irene just stood back and let them have at it. She smiled to herself thinking that half of them would scream indignantly if they were required to help at their own homes. The potato salad, baked beans, tomatoes, pickles and chips vanished as if a magician had waved a wand. Anna could hardly believe that the boys could eat all they had and still demolish two sheet cakes and four gallons of ice cream with twenty-eight cartons of soft drinks.

Some of the parents had offered to help, but Irene thanked them graciously and said she and Anna could handle it with the help of the boys.

The parents and other neighbors were invited to come later for a grown-up gathering.

"This is super," Dan Baxter said around a mouth full of food. "A cook-out's great, but the skating will be fun, too. Course this isn't the end." He almost choked when Jacob Solomon quickly placed his hand over Dan's mouth and Enrique Cabrera glared at him. The twins were too busy opening gifts to pay attention to Dan.

At five o'clock the boys left to go to the skating rink and Anna went to a friend's house to meet a group to go to a movie. The adults gathered with Irene each bringing food and beverages and lots of curiosity about the move.

The twins ran back to the house at eight-thirty just as a taxi pulled up. Slowly crawling out of the taxi, Herb was smiling as he walked tiredly to the group in the back yard.

After greeting Herb and hearing about his trip, the neighbors went home and the Jackson family were together alone at last. Galena was so happy to see Herb that he could not sit without her trying to climb in his lap. Herb was happy to be back with his family and had a lot of news about Alaska and their new home.

CHAPTER THREE

The next morning Irene had blueberry pancakes and sausages ready for breakfast. Everyone ate, laughed and talked, happy to have Herb back with them. After breakfast Herb waited for the children to brush their teeth and then called the twins to him.

"I bet you guys can't guess what I've planned for your birthday," he grinned, pleased with himself.

"But Dad, our birthday was yesterday," Tom giggled. "It's okay, Dad. You do a lot for us all the year.

"I know it was yesterday, and I'm sorry I couldn't be here. I owe Anna a special day, also. That won't make your surprise any less exciting though."

He grinned at them as he put an arm around each twin's neck and hugged them close. He gave Irene a quick kiss and hugged Anna.

"What surprise, Dad?" Tim questioned as both boys danced around him. Galena jumped with them sure she was part of whatever was going on.

"Let's go outside and you'll see." Herb placed a hand on each twin's back and went toward the front door. Tom and Tim jumped out the door ahead of him and stopped in surprise. In front of the house was a chartered bus filled with friends who were yelling at the twins out of the windows.

"Hurry up, slowpokes"

"You're holding us up."

"Will you get a move on."

"Come on the day is rushing by."

"Why? Are you expecting us to get on that bus with you?" Tim yelled half laughing and half serious.

"Happy birthday," eighteen voices chorused.

"But all of you were at our party yesterday and none of you said anything about this." Tom said looking at his dad with a puzzled expression. Looking past Herb the twins saw Irene and Anna waving at them.

"Ole big mouth, Dan, almost spilled the beans yesterday," Mark yelled out of a window. We knew it but were all sworn to secrecy."

"Get on board my suspicious sons. We're off on an adventure. It's part of your birthday surprise." Herb laughed and urged them to board the bus so he could get on.

"Yip! Yip! Yipee!" the twins clambered aboard the bus calling goodbye to Irene and Anna.

"Come get Galena," Herb called. "She thinks she's going, too."

Anna ran and took the protesting Galena by the collar. Galena cried all the way back to the house and drug her feet trying to convince Anna that she should be on that bus. Once she was in the house with the door shut she calmed down and ran over the place on her inspection tour.

Twenty boys sang, told jokes, wrestled and laughed loudly on their way to Washington, D.C., their nation's capital, fifteen miles away.

"Hey, Timmy, your dad is the greatest. None of our dads would have thought to bring our crowd into D.C. for the day." Jimmy Dodd spoke loudly as he walked through the Smithsonian Museum with their group.

"None of our dads would have been brave enough to try it," Mark Tully laughed and hurried over to see the furniture used in Archie Bunker's house in the famous television show, 'All In The Family' and the set of 'Star Trek'. Fonzie's jacket from 'Happy Days' was there, also.

"The rest of our dads probably couldn't have afforded it," Alan Begley muttered, but no one paid any attention to his comment. Truthfully, he was having a fabulous time.

"Yep, isn't it rad? I've always liked the Smithsonian but never had time to see as much as I wanted to," Tim answered.

"Maybe your dad's doing this to make up for dragging you off to Alaska," Alex said with a crooked grin.

"Maybe," Jason Horn interjected, "but dude! I was totally wiped out to see Lindberg's plane and all that first exploration stuff. And I never thought I'd get to see a real space ship. Besides," he turned to Tom, "you guys are going to have a great life and be back before you know it." In the Natural History section they were all standing beside the huge stuffed elephant looking up with open mouths and wide eyes.

"Dad always does something special for us and our sister on our birthday," Tom explained

Herb gathered the boys and took them out to the sidewalk where he had made arrangements with food venders to have their carts there at noon. A young woman stood with a calculator and totaled the price for Herb to pay.

"Whoo hoo!" Herb laughed with hands over his ears. "It sounds like feeding time at the zoo," he laughed as the boys shoved and shouted their selections. Herb thanked the vendors, and the girl, as he took time to grab a sandwich, chips and a soft drink. He paid the bill and included a generous tip.

The boys wolfed the food down and boarded the bus again for a tour of the city. They were impressed with a big statue of Abraham Lincoln sitting in a chair at his monument. The statue of Franklin D. Roosevelt and his little dog were admired. Some of the cherry trees still had late blooms on them. The boys were surprised to learn that the first trees had been a gift from Japan.

The bus driver talked over the speaker as he drove them around. "On July 16, 1791, Congress approved a location for Federal buildings. As soon as George Washington agreed, Major Pierce Charles L'Enfant, a French engineer, laid out the plans for the new city. L'Enfant was a friend of Washington's and had fought with the Americans during the American Revolution. On September 18, 1793, the cornerstone of the Capitol was laid, but the government didn't move to D.C. until 1800. He drove on and stopped at the Mall."

"Whoa. Are we going to walk all the way up there?" Benji Morrison leaned back, with his mouth open, to look at the top of the Washington Monument.

"You can if you wish," Herb answered. "The monument is five hundred fifty-five feet tall and has eight hundred ninety-eight steps to the top. There's an elevator if you don't want to walk up."

A chorus of, "I'm walking," came from all of the boys.

About half way up Herb had to sit down because he was laughing too hard to continue. About a dozen of the boys were gasping for breath and three of them had gotten down to crawl up on hands and knees.

At the top they were welcomed by a Park police who told them, "The Washington Monument is made of white marble from Maryland. Construction on it began in 1848 when James Polk was President and was completed in 1884, but it wasn't opened to the public until 1888. George Washington had died on December 14, 1799, so, he never knew of this dedication to his memory."

"Why did it take so long to build it?" Aaron Langley asked.

"The marble was mined and polished by hand which took a lot of time. Then it had to be transported by mule-drawn wagons and put in place. This naturally caused the work to go slowly. In 1848 James Marshall discovered gold at Sutter's Mill in Coloma, California. A lot of the workers went west with the dream of becoming rich. Can anyone tell me what happened in 1861?"

"I can," several voices rang out at once. "The War Between The States."

"Right," the policeman was pleased. "There was no work going on during those four or five years."

"Don't you mean the Civil War?" Alex asked.

"No," the policeman said. "They gave the correct answer. Here young man read this card from the Library of Congress. It's official. Please read it aloud."

Alex reluctantly took the card and read. "The Congressional Record of March 2, 1928 reports Senate joint resolution No. 41 wherein Congress recognized the title, War Between The States as proper. A war was waged from

1861 to 1865 between two organized governments. The United States of America and the Confederate States of America. These were the official titles of the contending parties. It was not a Civil War as it was not fought between parties in the same government. It was not a War of Succession because the stated, who had seceded, did so without a thought of war. The right of a state to secede had never been questioned. It was not a War of Rebellion for sovereign, independent states, co-equal cannot rebel against each other. It was a War Between The States because twenty-two non seceding states made war upon eleven seceding states to force them back into the Union. It was not until after the surrender of 1865 that secession was decided to be unconstitutional."

"But I thought it was fought over slavery," Charles Bloomingdale said.

"Oh, no," the policeman answered. "It was never fought over slavery. The question of slavery didn't enter into discussion until the third year of the war when Lincoln decided to use it to force the south to surrender. They overlooked the fact that there were slaves in the north in factories and homes. There were more working in the south on farms and plantations.

And not all of the slaves were black. Some were Asians and quite a few were poor whites who owed money to the plantation owners." He continued, "What most people don't know is that there is an aluminum cap of the tip top of the monument with the words, 'Laus Deo' on it. This means Praise be to God."

"Now if you'll excuse me, I have to go down to my horse and go on duty in the park area," the policeman said.

"A horse! Can I ride him?" several boys yelled.

"Afraid not. Sorry. He's on duty just as I am and he's a working animal. Have a good day, fellows. Thank you for allowing me to be part of your party. Gotta go. My horse is waiting."

"What's his name?"

"What kind is he?"

"What color is he?"

The questions came fast and loud. "How do you know the horse is a he?" Herb laughed.

The policeman laughed. "Yes, it's a he. His name is Ebony Warrior - called Warrior. He's a black Morgan stallion and is highly trained. He can walk quietly through traffic or a crowd of people and he can walk sideways and push a crowd back. There are several others out there." With a smile and a wave of his hand over his head he turned to go down on the elevator.

"Wait," Herb called. "May I send some of the boys down with you? The elevator is not large enough for the entire group."

As some of the boys crowded in with the policeman, Herb cautioned them. "Please don't annoy the officer with more questions. Stand right at the bottom and don't move until I get there."

When Herb and the remainder of the boys reached bottom, the policeman was standing with those who had come with him. He saluted smartly, made a square turn and briskly walked to a jeep. He turned the vehicle and drove toward the stable. The boys looked after him with open admiration.

Herb had kept a very nice surprise until last. On the bus the driver, James Richardson, listened patiently as several boys tried to tell him what they had seen. Herb called for attention. "I have made arrangements for the Senators and the Representatives from Virginia to meet with us at three-thirty this afternoon in the Capitol Building."

A cheer went up. The driver playfully hunched his shoulders at the noise but grinned in the rear-view mirror at the boys.

On the way up Pennsylvania Avenue, Miguel Perez suddenly shouted. "There he is! Oh, look there he is."

"Who?" the boys rushed to one side of the bus. "Where?"

Miguel could hardly speak in his excitement. The boys looked in the direction he was pointing.

"It's him," Danny yelled.

"It is he," Herb corrected. "Oh, well."

"There's the cop on his black horse," Jacob Solomon yelled.

"Are you sure it's the same person?" the driver asked.

"No," Aaron Langley said disappointed. "It isn't him. It isn't even a man. It's a woman," he said disgustedly.

The mounted policewoman smiled and waved at the exuberant boys as they called to her through open windows. The horse looked in their direction but went quietly on his way.

The Congressmen had arranged to meet the boys in a room that was reserved for news interviews. The boys had studied how laws were made and bills were passed, therefore, they were able to converse intelligently with the politicians and to ask sensible questions.

Leaving the room they were walking down a ten feet wide hall when Pat Sinaguglia gave a strangled gasp. "Is that who I think it is?" he whispered loudly. "Look." he shakily pointed to a man coming toward them followed by several people with cameras.

"Is it the President?" Alex blurted.

"No, even better," Dan Baxter spluttered tripping over his own feet and stepping on Herb's feet as he leaped forward. "It's Arnold Swartzie-who's-it."

An embarrassed Tim spoke up. "Arnold Schwarzenegger. Hello, sir. I'm sorry. My friend didn't mean to insult you. It's just that we admire you so much and are impressed to see you in person."

"Young man, you're surely a diplomat." Arnold said with one of his famous smiles. Being a gentleman and one who loves children, he could understand the attention the boys were giving him. He graciously sat on the floor with his back against the wall and motioned for the boys to join him. He talked to them and listened a lot. He answered questions about his movie career, his family and his job as Governor of California. For about fifteen minutes the cameras whirred and reporters frantically made notes. Additional politicians, secretaries and other workers were drawn to the group. The reporters asked Herb for information about the group.

Getting to his feet, Arnold smiled widely and said, "Goodbye, fellows. Have a great time and happy birthday to the twins. Maybe I'll be lucky enough to join you on the birthday next year." He waited patiently while the twins explained where they would be the next year. Herb was pleased that the twins seemed to be feeling better about the move. At least they were telling others about it in an enthusiastic manner.

"Boy," Arnold exclaimed, "that sounds like a lot of fun. I would love to go with you. Good luck to you and your family. I'd like to hear about your adventures. Bye now." He waved to all of them and walked away with the entourage following. Ben Dyang, being a very polite boy, followed him to thank him again. The politicians, who had gathered, were as amused as Herb was embarrassed.

"I need to apologize for taking so much time -- and all this space. Thank you for your kindness in meeting with this motley crew and thank you for your patience. I'm sure the boys enjoyed the visit as much as I did."

"Thank you. Thank you," the boys called out as they trooped off.

"We enjoyed it as much as the youngsters did, Senator Warner smiled.

"Yes, we need to thank you. I can hardly wait to tell my own children about this," a Congressman grinned. "It was a treat for us, too."

Tired, but animated, the boys boarded the bus again and later followed Herb into the Roy Rogers Beef House for dinner.

They rode home, high with the excitement of the day, but as the miles slipped by, they began to feel sad. The day for the Jackson family to leave was so close. Subdued and sleepy boys slumped in their seats as they traveled over Key Bridge and home to Fairfax.

Bursting into the house, the twins talked at the same time telling their mother and sister about the day. Anna was thrilled that they visited with Arnold Schwarzenegger. "It isn't fair," she moaned, "I would have been there all day and wouldn't have seen anyone interesting.

"Don't whine, darling." Irene put an arm around Anna. "You do and see a lot of good things and have met a lot of nice people. Boys, did you go to the White House?"

"No, Mom," Tim answered. "We've been there. We wanted to see places we haven't seen or had not seen enough."

"Benn there, done that," Tom said over a yawn and thought *I wonder if dad really did take us as a bribe to go to Alaska? No. Shame on me. He does for us all of the time. What difference would it make anyway?*

CHAPTER FOUR

Herb sat up in bed with a start. He was awakened by Galena's cold nose stuck against his face. What was that noise? Irene grumbled sleepily but did not open her eyes. Herb got up quietly, put on robe and slippers, and tiptoed down the hall. "Brrr. It's a chilly spring," he whispered to Galena padding beside him. He crept down the stairs trying not to trip over Galena. Passing through the front hall, he took a baseball bat out of the closet in case he needed to defend himself.

Galena was jumping at the dining room window. Was someone trying to break in? Herb couldn't see anything threatening, so he eased out the back door and walked quietly around the house to outside the dining room. Still nothing. There must have been something for Galena to be disturbed.

He whirled with his heart beating double time when Galena began to jump and bark against a gigantic oak tree beside the house. Looking up in the branches, Herb was startled to see a figure moving around.

"Come down right now. I have a gun. I don't want to shoot you," Herb bellowed angry and a little frightened.

"Aw, Dad. Who could you shoot with a baseball bat? Besides, you don't own a gun. You don't approve of having guns in a home."

"Tom! Is that you, Tom? What are you doing up in that tree. Come down this instant." Tom was laughing until he could hardly climb down.

"March yourself into the house, young man." Inside, Tom and Herb were met by the rest of the family.

"What were you doing outside, Tom? Irene was puzzled.

"Dorf brain. It's five thirty-five," Tim grumbled. "It's even too early for the chickens." Anna knelt hugging Galena and waited sleepily for Tom's explanation.

Tom was grinning until he got a good look at his dad's expression in the light; then his face fell and he instantly grew serious. "Well, I woke up a little after five and knew it was time for Jason to deliver the papers. He's one of my best friends, and the other day he suggested that if I ever wanted to talk about our move that he was available to listen. There was something I wanted to discuss with him.

"What was it?" Tim demanded.

"Jason suggested that if Tim and I didn't want to go to Alaska, that maybe we could stay here with friends."

"Right on. Great idea," Tim yelled.

"Wrong. Bad idea," Irene said firmly. "Do you mean you would be willing to stay behind and let the rest of us go off with Galena and not see us for three years?" Irene was astonished and hurt.

"Taking two thirteen year old boys, willful boys at that, and being responsible for them for that length of time is a responsibility that few people would want to try." Herb was angry. "We've always made important decisions as a family. I'm disappointed, no, I'm hurt, that you would be willing to break up the family and talk to someone outside the family about it."

"Tom, I'm not happy about leaving Virginia either, but -- break up our family. Ah, no. We have good parents that have always listened to us and considered our feelings and have furnished everything that is good for us. Sometimes give us things just for fun. Oh, how could you?" Anna spluttered and choked up.

"Well -- I admit I didn't think it through. I just had a thought and flew with it. I didn't even tell Tim. No, I don't want to break up our family, but none of us really want to move and go to that place."

"Thomas Harrison Jackson, I'm sorry you feel as you do. It *is* my work and maybe I got too excited and didn't consider family." Herb spoke softly with bowed head.

"Stop it." Irene ordered. "You **are** supporting us and you have a right to enjoy your work and want something better for yourself. We're proud of you and are grateful for the good life you've provided for us." She turned to glare at Tom.

Tom had cringed in hearing his full name knowing how angry and hurt his dad would be to call him by the full name.

Irene stood in front of Tom. "Why would you go out the window and down the tree? It's so dangerous. Why wouldn't you walk quietly down the stairs and out the front door?" she asked angrily.

"He does that a lot," Tim piped up. "I told you he's a dorf brain.

"It's better than being a mushy pea brain." Tom hit Tim on the shoulder which Tim quickly returned.

"That's enough from both of you." Herb was more angry after hearing the full story and knowing that Tom had made a habit of climbing out the window and down the tree. He glared at Tom. "You disturbed all of us for something that

31

could have been dangerous and certainly could have waited until tomorrow. Suppose you had fallen and broken your back making a cripple of yourself for life. Or you might even have had an injury and caused brain damage."

"You gotta have a brain to damage it," Tim chortled.

"Both of you. **Go to your room -- now.** You can come down for breakfast at the usual time, then you'll return to your room until your dad and I decide what we'll do about this." Irene was frustrated.

"Aw, Mom. That's not fair. I didn't do anything," Tim protested.

"You contributed to the general confusion. **Go.**" Irene glared at them.

The twins stomped up the stairs and slammed the door to their room. Tom threw himself on his back on his bed and hugged a pillow to his chest. Tim backed against the wall and slid to the floor, wrapping his arms around his drawn-up knees and slightly rocking himself.

Tom pounded the pillow with his fist. "I'm so gosh darned mad. Why should I be punished for having my own opinion? I have rights, too."

Tim looked up with misty eyes. "I'm angry, too. You have to admit that you're the one that did the stupid things that caused our parents to worry and be upset. What you did was so dangerous. I didn't do anything and I'm getting punished the same as you. No **that** isn't fair."

"Forgive me for being such a devil in this family when you're such an angel," Tom spat sarcastically sitting up.

"Shut up, Tom. I'm not calling you names. You are so obnoxious sometimes," Tim answered with hurt in his voice.

"Well, Mr. Goody-Goody. You just haven't happened to get caught. You've done bad thing, too, Tim."

"I'm not a goody-goody. Yes, I've done things I shouldn't, and maybe mom and dad didn't happen to catch me, but I've never gotten up in the dark, woke the whole family, and did something so stupid and dangerous."

"Okay. Okay. I'm sorry, Tim. I have no business being mad at you. I'm the one who's guilty and I'll have to take my punishment like a man." Tom rolled on his back looking thoughtfully at the ceiling. "What do you think they'll do to me?"

"That's hard to say. The fact that they're taking time to discuss it proves that your punishment will be a dilly. If I could ever learn to keep my mouth shut, I wouldn't be in trouble, too."

"Thanks a lot. Just what I needed -- encouragement."

Tim stood and went to brush his teeth again, then crawled into his bed. Tom laughed. "Why did you brush your teeth again?" Tim shrugged his shoulders and turned out the light. All that could be heard was the click of Galena's nails as she patrolled the house protecting her family.

Tim came bouncing down for breakfast as Tom walked in subdued and anxious. Neither boy mentioned the previous activity. They sat quietly sliding glances at each other and the rest of the family. Galena sensed the tension and walked around the table whining and pushing her nose against each one.

After a nearly silent breakfast, Herb pushed his chair back and sipped his coffee staring at Tom and making him uneasy. Finally he spoke. "Tom, your mother and I have reached a decision. I don't want any arguing or whining. Do you understand?"

"Yes, sir," Tom answered softly.

Tim was sorry for his twin and tried to lighten the air. "Hey, Dad. Did we tell you how much we enjoyed the day in D.C.? We really do appreciate you taking the time to come all the way back and give us such a neat surprise. You spent a lot of money and we appreciate it."

"Tim, you may be excused. Go straight to your room and don't try to stand in the hall and listen. Anna, you may be excused, also." Herb spoke quietly.

Anna looked as if she would like to say something, but she went with an arm around Tim. In the hall Anna shook Tim's shoulder. "When are you going to learn that flattery doesn't get you everything?" She looked sympathetically at Tim.

Tom wriggled in his chair and looked anxiously from Irene to Herb. Galena put her head on Tom's lap as if she, too, sympathized with him.

Herb sat a few minutes looking down in his cup. He slowly raised his head and looked at Tom. "Son, you know how much I love you -- we love you. What you did was not only dangerous but unnecessary. And you disturbed the family's rest. How would you have felt if a neighbor happened to look out to see a figure in our tree, jumped to the conclusion that someone was breaking in and called the police? They certainly would not have thought it was funny. You must learn to analyze situations, think before you act and accept responsibility for your actions." He drew a long, slow breath.

"Responsible parents give their children guidance while allowing them to grow and learn through personal experiences. Sometimes an experience is not a wise choice. I hope you learn from it, to think before you act, and to consider the feelings of others."

"Yes, sir. I sure have. May I be excused?"

"Not yet, dear," Irene said. "We haven't discussed what you are to do." She patted Tom's back and reached to hug Galena who pushed her head between Irene and Tom.

"Now then," Herb continued, "you will go to Sunday School and church tomorrow as usual. But you'll spend the afternoon in your room while Tim goes skating and eating out with your friends. You need to think about what you've done and be able, later today, to tell me what you've learned from this."

As Tom got up, Irene took his hand, "Don't forget to change the sheets on your bed and bring all dirty clothes to the laundry room. That includes towels and wash cloths as well as linens and clothes. Remind Tim to do the same. Here's the furniture polish and a rag. While you're doing the polishing, Tim can run the vacuum in your room. Anna will vacuum the hall after she has finished her room. I could use some help in the rose garden for a little while after you boys finish. Dad's going to be cleaning out the basement and packing some things he wants."

Tom hung his head and nodded. He drug out of the room and slapped up the stairs. He stumbled to his bed and fell across it. "Parents. Who need 'em?" he muttered.

"Gosh. Was it that bad?" Tim asked in a soft, sympathetic voice.

Tom thought a minute them rolled to his side, propping an elbow on his thigh and cupping his face in his hand. "Truthfully? No, not that bad, and I shouldn't feel badly toward our parents. I did bring this on myself and they do love us or they wouldn't get upset and worry so much. But I'm still mad at the whole situation." He sighed and rolled on his back with his hands clasped behind his head.

"Well for gosh sakes, if you don't tell me quick what they said, I'll --I'll"

"All right. Keep your britches on. It truly isn't all that bad except you have to promise me one thing."

"Sure. What?"

Tom told Tim what his punishment would be. "Promise me you'll not breathe a word of this to the guys. I would just die if they knew how stupid I've been."

"I promise. I won't talk about it. But what'll I tell them when you don't go with us tomorrow?"

"I don't know. Tell them I got sick and had to stay in bed."

"You want me to deliberately lie?"

"Nah. I won't ask you to lie."

"I know. I'll stay home tomorrow, too," Tim said gleefully.

"Uh uh. Mom and dad won't let you," Tom said sadly. "Unless you can convince them you're really sick."

"Now you want me to lie to our parents."

"Shoot," Tom said with disgust, "I guess you'll have to tell the truth. It'll come out anyway. Stuff always does."

I won't tell everything. I'll just tell them about you climbing out the window. I won't tell what time it was.

Don't worry. I won't tell them anything that'll make them tease you."

"Thanks, Tim. You're the best brother in the world. I guess we'd better get busy cleaning our room. We have to do the usual Saturday things. Go get the clean sheets while I take the dirty ones off our beds. Dad's cleaning out the basement and packing. Oooooh!" He fell back on the bed.

"What's wrong? Do you hurt?" Tim asked worriedly.

"Alaska," Tom spat out bitterly. "Every time I think of it, I get sick to my stomach."

"I know. Me, too. When our friends talk about it I think it might not be so bad after all. Then I'm alone thinking and I ---" Tim looked with sympathy at a mirror image of himself. Light brown hair, bright green eyes, lightly tanned face with a few freckles across the nose, a cleft in the chin and full lips that were now turned down. Both boys were tall for their age. At five feet eight inches and well muscled bodies from loads of athletic activities, they could have passed for a couple of years older.

Both boys sank down on their beds with elbows on knees and chin in hands. With a sigh they finally got up to do what they did every Saturday.

CHAPTER FIVE

Tim had made arrangements to meet some of the boys at the city library on Monday after school. He and Tom walked in to find several boys at a table with numerous books on Alaska in front of them. The twins sat and whispered greetings.

"Hey! Here's some interesting stuff." Pat spoke loudly in excitement.

"Shh. Keep your voice down or we'll be kicked out," Tom poked him.

Pat continued to read in a lower voice. "Since 1867 the stars and stripes have flown over Alaska, but it wasn't until 1958 that U. S. Congress approved Alaska being admitted as our 49th state. On January 3, 1959, President Dwight Eisenhower signed the papers. The name Alaska comes from an Aleut Indian word meaning Great Land. Wow! Russia is only one hundred ninety miles from Nome."

"Great. I hope we get a chance to visit Russia," Tim whispered. "I'm looking forward to meeting some real Eskimo and Indians and now some Russians."

Pat looking puzzled said, "I thought Russia was only fifty-three miles from Alaska."

"Well it is at farther northern points where people don't live, but Nome is south of there." John Trivet explained.

Perry Morton struggled to talk quietly, "This is from the material you guys got from the Nome Convention and Visitors Bureau. It says three lucky Swedens, Jafet Lindberg, Erik Lindbloom and John Brynteson, discovered gold on Anvil Creek in 1898. When the news reached Klondike, thousands came and built a camp called Anvil City. No trees to build with so they had to set up tents that covered the thirty miles between Cape Rodney and Cape Nome. From about one hundred people, it grew to over ten thousand. Huge storms and fires left little in that first camp."

"Now me," Benji took the paper. "During World War II, Nome was the last stop for planes flying to Russia. U. S. troops were stationed in Nome in Quonset huts. Today air travel has taken the place of steam ships."

"Listen," Jim read on, "nowhere else is there so many bear and fantastic fishing. Caribou, reindeer, moose, deer, elk, bison, seals, otter and numerous birds are familiar sights." The boys all started talking about animals, and hunting, with camera, of course.

Tim read, "Because of the many people who came during the gold rush, this area became a supply and transportation center. A big Federal building was built, but Juneau became the capital."

Jason started giggling and hissed. "That reminds me of a joke. This boys went up to his teacher and said, "What's the capital of Alaska?" She answered, "Juneau." He said, "No, that's why I'm asking you."

The boys laughed so hard they were asked to leave the library. They walked side by side with arms around each other until they met someone they had to allow to pass. Then they ran and tagged each other, trying to trip each other as they made their way.

This stopped when Alex staggered and fell off the sidewalk. The boys were concerned about the blood that showed through his jeans on his right knee. He assured them it was just a scrape. The boys went on more calmly.

Being normal boys they soon left the memory of Alex's misadventure behind and again ran down the sidewalk chasing, jumping up in the air pretending to shoot baskets and making up games as they ran. Life was good and they were enjoying every minute.

That night Herb took Anna into Washington, D.C. to eat dinner and then attend a stage play at the Kennedy Center. It was late for her birthday, but Herb wanted to keep his promise to do something special for her.

CHAPTER SIX

The eighteenth of June would be the eighteenth wedding anniversary of Herb and Irene. Relatives and friends wanted to give them a party, so, on June fifth there was a big celebration.

"We'll sure miss the Jackson family. They're wonderful neighbors," Mrs. Goodson said to Herb's brother, Henry.

"What will they do with the dog?" Mrs. Parsons asked as she watched Galena winding among the people, wagging her tail and loving everyone.

"Oh, I guess she'll be put to sleep. She's so old." Uncle Henry's wife, Aunt Minnie stated.

"Oh, no." The twins spoke as one. Anna's lips were tight as she rubbed Galena's back. "If Galena doesn't go, we don't either," she said.

"Besides," Tom said through gritted teeth, "we'd stay here if they'd let us."

"You really don't want to go?" Uncle Henry was surprised. "But, why not? Most kids would be thrilled to get to travel and live adventures."

Aunt Minnie spoke forcefully. "You should be thankful that you have parents who are giving you opportunities like this."

"Who wants them?" Tom almost yelled. "Opportunities, I mean."

Irene had joined them. "Stop that," she ordered. "You children are being rude. I'm sorry," she said to the small group that had gathered. "There have been a lot of conflicting emotions concerning the move. I was hoping my children had accepted it by now." She looked so sad that Anna put an arm around her mother.

"I'm sure we'll like it when we get there, Mom. It'll take some getting used to, but we'll be fine as long as we're together as a family -- including Galena." She turned to glare at her brothers.

"Yeah, I guess it'll be okay," Tim mumbled. "Excuse us." He and Tom left to go into the house taking Galena with them.

Fortunately the conversation was just with the small groups and Herb and the remainder of the crowd were not aware of the conflicts. Everyone left saying what a great time they'd had and how much they would miss the Jackson family. The majority of them spoke of their envy of the move.

Herb left the next day to start his work in Alaska. The family would follow soon. When one of the twins would ask Galena, "Do you want to go for a really long ride in the car?" she would bark excitedly and run around trying to figure out where they were going and when.

Ten days later they received a letter from Herb. After dinner they sat around the dining room table while Irene read the letter to them. The children laughed hysterically until their sides ached when they heard about the honey bucket. It was so strange and funny.

Herb wrote, "It's impossible to dig and lay pipes in the hard, frozen ground. Farther north indoor bathrooms are as scarce as hen's teeth."

"Hen's don't have teeth," Tim shouted laughing.

"That's what it means," Anna said, "Now hush and let mom finish."

Irene read on, "We could have a ten gallon bucket, called a honey bucket, to use as a commode." The entire family was intrigued with this lifestyle.

"Yuck! I just thought of something," Tim frowned and shuddered.

"What?" Tom asked.

"That ole honey bucket would have to be emptied and washed."

"Ohhh. Would we have to do that?" Tom wrinkled his nose and waved his hand in front of his face as if to wave away an odor.

"We'll all have chores to do just as we do here." Irene said with a straight face. The twins howled and rolled from their chairs to the floor. Galena was concerned thinking something bad had happened to her boys. She growled and ran around barking looking for the trouble. She was ready to defend her family and make short work of any trouble.

"Get off the floor," Irene ordered. "You're disturbing Galena. She doesn't understand what you're doing. Now let me finish the letter. Daddy says there is a honey wagon which comes around to collect the dirty buckets and leave clean ones." She had to stop again because the twins were making weird noises and exciting Galena. "Puh-leese, may I go on? Daddy says that since it's warm enough now where we'll be that he'll be able to put in a bathroom for us."

"Wahoo! No chance of yucky stuff then," Tom yelled. He saw some pictures sticking half out of the envelope.

"What are those pictures dad sent?" Irene looked at them and then read the back.

"This is one of the front of our house and these two are of our deep freeze."

"Deep freeze? Curiouser and curiouser," Tim grinned.

"But this is a hole in the ground," Irene read on. "Our deep freeze is an underground room about eight feet by eight feet and seven feet deep. A metal door opens at ground level and we climb down a ladder to get whatever we want from the freezer. It's dug deep to keep food cold and the metal door keeps wild animals from getting our food."

"There's even shelves built in," Anna observed. "Well, as my brothers would say, that's neat and rico."

"Irene, how in the world are you going to adjust to such a dramatic change in your life?" Four of her friends were visiting to bring last minute gifts and to say goodbye.

"I'll be happy wherever my husband and children are. I've always wanted to write books for children and now, maybe I'll have time to write. Anna is an excellent artist, so, I'm hoping she'll be willing to illustrate for me." Irene's face glowed with the idea of her dreams coming true.

"I didn't know you were interested in writing," Marion Parks exclaimed. "How wonderful. What type of writing have you done?"

"Just for children in church, a few newspaper columns and for my own interests. I'm trying to write a family history for the children. I've done a lot of research on all four sides of our family. Genealogy is an addiction."

She laughed. "I'm sure there'll be loads of material where we'll be living, especially with the boys into enough to give me lots of inspiration. In fact, knowing them, I'll probably have enough material for multi books."

Finishing their tea and finger sandwiches, the ladies wished the family all the best, gave Irene hugs and tearfully left.

In their bedroom, the twins were still grumbling. "Why does everyone assume we're going for sure?" Tom fumed.

"Because we are," Tim said with a sigh. "Face it. Dad's already in Alaska and has a house for us. Mom's packed and all our records are ready. Might as well make the best of it. We'll just feel worse if we dwell on it."

"That's easy to say. Make the best of it," Tom sneered, falling on his bed. Tim was already on his bed. The twins lay on their backs looking at the ceiling. Suddenly Tom sat up. "Hey, I got it. We'll be explorers. We can put our scout training to use and maybe even explore areas where no human has ever been." His eyes twinkled as he gazed into space, seeing himself with nothing in sight but snow and ice.

"You sound like a television science show," Tim laughed. Then he lay back down and continued to brood. "Yeah," Tim spoke in awe of the thought. "I can see us catching the biggest whale or maybe the most ferocious bear. We both have a love of science. Maybe we'll do something that'll make us famous, something no one else has even thought of."

"Such as?"

"Who knows. Maybe we'll discover a chemical that can be used to clean the dirtiest, most dangerous waters. Lakes and rivers could be purified. Just think, we could clean up our environment and make it a safer, healthier place for everyone to live."

They daydreamed, made plans and became excited thinking of how famous they could be, maybe even written up in history books. They might even be recognized by the President of the United States and given a big ticker-tape parade while crowds cheered.

Anna was in the kitchen helping her mother with dinner. "Mom, I'm sorry, but I still have mixed feelings about our move even though I don't want to have them. I want us to be together as a family, but I hate to leave familiar places and friends. I'll be a stranger in Alaska. All the kids there will have friends, know the teachers and ---"

Irene broke in. "You'll love making new friends and seeing different parts of our country. Your friends here will be eager to hear from you and will envy your experiences. You've always been popular because you're kind and thoughtful of others. You'll do the same there --- just you wait and see."

Irene hugged Anna while looking up at her beautiful daughter. She smiled at the beautiful heart-shaped face framed by dark blonde, curly hair. Her hazel-green eyes were serious and thoughtful. Anna stood five-eight, an inch taller than her mother.

Tom and Tim came clamping down the stairs, their feet hitting hard as they walked. "I'm starved. Isn't dinner ready?" Tom whined.

"Patience, my poor famished son. We'll eat in about five minutes. Have you both washed?" The twins vowed that they had washed, then sat at the table talking low to each other. "What's wrong with me? One day I'm excited about leaving and then I want to hide and not go," Tim confessed.

Tom nodded in agreement and shrugged his shoulders.

On June seventh, the last day of school was exciting and sad. Mrs. Berry smiled as she placed an arm around each twin. "Boys, I have a suggestion. You'll be writing to friends here, but would you please write to me so that I can share with everyone in school? I would appreciate a picture now and then, also."

"Sure. Works for me," Tim stated with a grin and Tom nodded. "We'll send you our address and phone number as soon as we can."

Irene checked boxes again to ascertain that each box was labeled so she would know where to look for their things when they got to Alaska. All boxes were loaded on a big truck. The government was paying for shipping and traveling expenses because Herb was an employee. She watched the truck pull away and breathed a prayer for all of them. *Oh, Herb, I hope I can do this without you. How I wish you were here to travel with us, but you need me to be a helpmate and get us to you safely.* She felt she could count on the children now that they accepted they were moving, or so she thought.

The plan was to take three weeks zig-zagging across the United States.

They would visit historical places, explore and appreciate their own country.

The next morning they were up early to leave. The house had been left in the hands of a real estate agent to rent and care for until their return. Dan Baxter's mother, as the real estate agent, volunteered to strip the beds, wash linens they had used and place items in the linen closet. A cleaning crew would come in and clean everything, as well as wash windows, getting everything ready for renters.

The station wagon was loaded with clothing needed for the trip. Galena's water dish, food dish, jugs of water and a sack of dog food were in the very back. A cooler filled with ice, soft drinks and sandwich meat was placed behind the rear seat. Fried chicken, a small baked ham, potato salad and deviled eggs were placed in the cooler with carrot sticks and tomatoes. Bread, peanut butter and various jellies and additional snacks were in a huge contained beside the cooler.

"Anna, place this first aid kit where it can be reached quickly. I hope and pray we won't have to use it," Irene instructed.

"Mom, you've got enough here to feed a small army," Tim laughed.

"It won't last long. We'll eat this before we have to start eating out. This will help a little and save time, too. Tim, please check and make sure there's a sharp knife and enough tableware for all of us. Oh, get the napkins off the kitchen counter. Are the plastic plates and cups in there, and the jugs of water?"

"Check and check, Mom. Your order has been obeyed." Tim saluted just as Tom tackled him from behind. They dropped to the grass to wrestle.

"Don't get dirty before we start," Irene ordered.

"I bet nobody else is up as early as this," Tom observed as he stood up. "The sun isn't even fully up yet."

"Starting early will get us out of the heat for a while and give us time to stop for rests without losing time. Galena will need pit stops, too." Irene explained.

They were surprised to see neighbors sleepily coming still in their night clothes, slippers and robes. The Jacksons were touched. After dozens of hugs and well wishes, the family tearfully, but bravely, waved and drove off.

Herb had toured most of Virginia with the children since they were young, so, Irene drove at an angle from northeast to southwest, Virginia without stopping to sightsee. It took six hours to make this part of the trip. She drove across the line into Kentucky before stopping for the night.

"We more than likely won't cover this many miles in one day again. I'm not accustomed to driving a lot and I'm ready for a rest," Irene sighed. "But there was no need to stop since we knew a lot about the part we covered."

The next day they drove into St. Joseph, Missouri to one of the first Pony Express stations. It was thrilling to see the small room, artifacts, pictures and even a copy of the newspaper of that day.

Irene finally admitted that she was tired and developing sore muscles because she was unaccustomed to driving so much at once.

"Mom, please let me help you. I can drive as long as a licensed driver is with me. The boys will help me watch for signs and you can rest. You can't go on this way." Anna looked imploringly at Irene.

"I don't know, honey. You're still awfully young."

"I've driven several times with dad and he thinks I'm a very good driver."

"Well, as soon as I get out of city traffic, maybe you can take it on the open highway." Anna drove well and Irene gave a sigh of relief for the help she now realized she could count on.

The next morning early, Anna started the drive before traffic picked up.

"Anna, we'll angle south and go through Oklahoma."

"Where you headed, Mom?" Tom asked through yawns.

"I thought you might like to go to Arizona and see the Grand Canyon."

"All right!" Both boys were wide awake now.

Herb had gotten AAA tour books for all the states they would go through. They had enjoyed reading the information and checking what they would like to see. Tom picked up the tour book for Missouri. "Mom!" he yelled.

"There was so much good stuff to see in Missouri and didn't stop for anything. President Harry Truman's house is in Independence."

"Sweetie, we can't possibly stop at every place of interest or we'd never get to Alaska, at least not for about a year. You know dad is anxious for us to get with him and we've missed him."

"Yeah, mush brain, we'd never get anywhere." Tim punched Tom on the shoulder not saying **he** would have liked to stop at several places. The twins began to wrestle on the back seat which excited Galena to a barking fit. She climbed on them snapping at their arms.

"That's enough," Irene ordered firmly. "I know you're tired and bored, but remember we're driving up here and watching traffic. You're getting on my nerves and upsetting

Galena." The twins would have stopped several times an hour. They thought the time was going too fast, but Irene felt the time was dragging.

"You keep forgetting, guys, dad's waiting for us and he expects us to arrive on the day we agreed upon. Try to think of mom's feeling and cooperate, please," Anna reasoned.

Much to the twins' delight, Irene did agree to stop in Tulsa, Oklahoma. There were many historical places to see; one being the home of Will Rogers just on the outskirts of Tulsa. Tim read aloud from the AAA tour book. "This is the last home for several Indian tribes, those that came from the east as well as those that lived in the area. Oklahoma got its name from the Choctaw Indians word meaning 'red people'. The nickname Sooner State came from people who illegally tried to make land claims in designated areas sooner than the people who obeyed the government date of April 22, 1889."

"Well, it was illegal, but you can't blame them for wanting land and homes for their families," Tom stated. "I wonder how the Indians felt. After all this was the land they had lived on for hundreds of years."

"The Indians were betrayed by people they trusted," Irene explained. "They were hurt, confused, bitter and despondent. Some were old and tired and didn't want any more trouble, so they gave in."

Tim nodded, looking sad, but continued to read. "Sequoyah, the Cherokee who wrote the first written alphabet for his people, came to Oklahoma in 1828 to live. He taught his people to read and write their language. Oklahoma was admitted as the 46th state in 1907. Since then Indians have been elected to both the state and national legislatures." the twins settled down to read the remainder of the information silently.

"Can we go to Oklahoma City? We'd like to go through the National Cowboy Hall of Fame and Western Heritage Center," Tom said.

"Yeah, and while we're there, we can go through the National Softball Hall of Fame and Museum, but I don't want to go by the building that crazy man bombed. I'd cry even it was a long time ago. That was back in 1995, but the fact that so many innocent people died, including babies, makes me sad," Tim finished.

"I know what you mean, "Anna answered him, "but we won't have time to spend in so many places in each state. We're going to have to sit down with the tour books and decide what we, as a family, truly want to see."

"Makes sense to me," Irene said. "When we stop tonight, we'll all go through the books together and decide what we can do."

Driving as much as they could, and not wanting to waste time, they pulled into Oklahoma City around eight that night. The twins took Galena for a quick walk and then returned to their motel room to feed her and leave her a fresh bowl of water. The family went across the street to a restaurant and were back in their room by nine thirty. They spread the AAA books out on one of the beds, with a map of the U.S., and read through the ones for Oklahoma, Texas and New Mexico.

As usual they had a room with two double beds. The twins slept in one bed and Irene and Anna slept in the other. Galena slept on the floor between the beds. The next morning they were eager for sightseeing. Galen was taken for a walk and fed. They went across for breakfast and took a tour bus to see the city.

A little after one that afternoon, they were tired and ready to rest, but very happy that they had seen all they did. Galena was taken for another walk and the family went across the street for lunch. They came back to the motel and settled for a short rest.

The twins did agree to go to the City National Memorial on Fifth and Harvey. It was built in memory of the victims of the 1995 bombing. They were impressed that there was a stone chair for each of the 168 people killed.

"I wonder how Timothy McVeigh felt when he bombed the Alfred P. Murrah Federal building and discovered he'd killed so many babies?" Tom mused.

"People like McVeigh have no integrity or remorse and he probably didn't feel guilty at all," Tim answered.

Their next stop was the Red Earth Indian Center. After all the walking they were ready to go back for dinner and to an early bed. The next morning they were eager to continue. Galena had been a good traveler. She had cooperated with every mile and every stop, but she was getting tired of being cooped up in the car and in motel rooms. It disturbed her that the twins were reading the books and ignoring her. With no warning, she jumped from the back of the wagon to the back seat and tore the tour books from their hands to shake and tear them. The twins yelled so loudly trying to get the book from her that Anna pulled over and stopped. Irene ordered everyone out of the car. "Take Galena for a walk, but stay right on this side of the highway where I can see you.

The twins walked Galena and then ran back to the car. When they returned, Irene and Anna had made sandwiches. There were also fruit, chips and soft drinks. Galena was given fresh water and let lie in the shade of the car. They were afraid to go far off the road for fear of snakes.

Back in the car Anna continued the drive into Texas. Their stop for the night was between Dallas and Fort Worth. The twins were thrilled to be in Texas because of the movies they'd seen and the books they'd read. They expected to see cowboys, cattle and gunfights just as they'd seen in movies. They were disappointed that the cities were as modern as they had in Virginia.

The next morning they were up early and eager to sightsee. The first stop was the John Fitzgerald Kennedy Memorial to remember the assassination of the president in Dallas in 1963. They then went on to Fort Worth to the Stockyard Museum. They rushed through the Stockyards Station Historical Walking Tour.

"Oh, Mom, let's go to San Antonio and see the Alamo," Tom begged.

"Please," Tim whined. "We want to see it for ourselves. You don't know when we'll ever get this opportunity again and we are so close."

"Oh, year?" Anna stated. "You're not the ones driving. Mom, shall we?"

Irene thought for a few moments and finally agreed. The twins cheered so loudly that Galena began to jump from one seat to another barking. Irene and Anna both spoke loudly at once ordering them to be quiet and get Galena settled.

CHAPTER SEVEN

Anna drove on south to San Antonio secretly pleased that they were going to see the Alamo. It was late afternoon when they arrived, so, Irene decided that they would eat, take Galena for a walk and rest.

"Let's call your dad and tell him where we are. He expects to hear from us every day and I'm sure he's concerned about us doing all this traveling."

"This cell phone bill is going to be horrendous," Anna observed. "We do need to talk to dad and let him know how far along we are."

After the call they went out to dinner and to look around the area. This was their first time in Texas and they wanted to see as much as possible in the time frame. Irene decided they had enough time to go through the Buckhorn Saloon and Museum. The admission was eight dollars each. The 1881 museum was a step back into the old west. The twins reluctantly went to bed but were eager to get up early and see the Alamo.

"Well, where is it?" Tim asked excitedly.

"You're looking at it, "Irene answered. "I told you it wasn't what you see in the movies. They had to build a wall around it to protect it from souvenir seekers. The building is smaller than we expected." She read from a pamphlet. "Established in 1718 by Father Antonio Olivares, this was originally a Spanish outpost called Mission San Antonio de Parras. When the Mexicans took charge, it became known as Pueblo Alamo. In 1835 Mexican General Santa Anna came to the Alamo with the intention of destroying it. Texas General Sam Houston ordered Colonel James Bowie to destroy it and get his men out of the area to safety. Instead Bowie, determined to fight for Texas independence, stood his ground. In

February, 1836 Col. William Travis and David Crockett joined Bowie with only a little less than six hundred men to fight Gen. Santa Anna's four thousand plus. The patriots fought valiantly but the battle was soon over. One hundred eighty-nine Texans lay dead. The Alamo remains a symbol of Texas' pride and independent spirit."

After the tour, they all agreed that it was worth it to see the Alamo and learn more about the history of Texas. They now had a better understanding of what the early people went through to gain independence. It was past time for lunch, so they went to a restaurant. The twins learned there was to be a rodeo in Lubbock. They begged to attend because they'd never been to a rodeo. Irene agreed and they went back to the motel to get Galena and drive on up to Lubbock. They were lucky to find a motel room with the crowds coming to attend the rodeo.

The rodeo opened with riders carrying flags, trick riders, singers, chuck wagon demonstrations and draft horses pulling weights to show their great strength. The twins were almost in tears thinking the animals might be treated so badly. A man seated beside them explained what was going on and the Jackson family began to enjoy what they were seeing. They admired the spirit and determination of the animals to fight for the freedom from restraint. The bucking horses and the bucking bulls were awesome. Near midnight, they were tired and ready to crawl into bed. First they called Herb to tell him of their day.

Anna was driving through northern Texas on the way into New Mexico when Irene decided they could stop in Amarillo.

"Holy cow, Mom! Look! Are those real cowboys? There's horses, too," Tim yelped. "Did you see that cowboy get on his horse with one jump from the ground?"

Anna smiled. "Guys, you've been watching too much television. Sure those are real cowboys, but nothing like you see in movies. Most of these men have college degrees and live in beautiful, modern homes. They probably carry walkie talkies for places where a cell phone won't get a signal. They're as modern as you are."

"Aw, don't spoil it for us, Anna," Tom answered

They stared at horses tied on a side street while traffic and modern buildings were all around. Anna pulled to the curb and stopped. The twins quickly opened both back doors to get out, but Galena beat them. She ran around the corner toward the horses making funny whimpering noises.

"Get Galena," Irene yelled. "She's never seen a horse and probably thinks they're big dogs." These were well-trained working horses that were accustomed to ranch dogs and all sorts of animals, but Anna was not aware of that. Irene ran after Galena and burst out laughing as she came around the corner. "Tom," she called, "bring the camera -- hurry."

Tom ran back to the car as Tim slid to a stop beside his mother. He, too, burst out laughing. Galena was running to each horse giving doggy kisses on each nose. The horses were nosing her and being friendly.

"What's so funny?" Tom panted as he ran back with the camera.

Irene focused the camera and took pictures. "Something to remember about our trip to show daddy. Galena's first introduction to horses."

Gathering her troop back into the car, Irene drove to the edge of town to a motel. "Like us, Galena is bored and tired. Walk her and then we'll eat dinner. All three of you go and stay together. I don't want anyone getting lost or distracted by something."

The next morning the twins walked Galena while Anna filled her food bowl and put down fresh water. Galena was left in the room while her family went for breakfast at the same restaurant they had dinner the night before. The twins were ecstatic to find cowboys eating breakfast. The men were glad to talk to them and answer questions. After eating, some of the men went outside to stand by the children for Irene to take pictures. They thanked the men and reluctantly prepared to travel on.

Irene drove on to the west. In less than an hour they were crossing into New Mexico. Galena was sitting happily in the front seat looking out the window while Anna massaged her neck and ears. Tom and Tim eagerly opened the AAA book of New Mexico.

Reading to himself, Tom blurted. "Hey, I didn't know this."

"What? Why brother mine, I thought you knew everything," Tim teased.

"Laugh, you fool, and show your ignorance, but listen to this." Tom read aloud. "New Mexico is the site of the oldest white settlement in the western U.S. In 1609, two years after the funding of Jamestown, Virginia, Spanish colonists established the city of Santa Fe. For more than two hundred years the Spanish ruled all of the southwestern part of our country."

"Wow. Are you sure?" Tim questioned. "I thought whites settled in the east and moved to the west. I know Indians and Spanish were here together, but I've never heard of the white settlement."

"Actually," Irene told them, "I read somewhere that the Norsemen were here long before that. We'll probably never know how many and who landed in our country before written records. I do know that Jesuit priests came down from Canada to work with the Indians during the early 1400s. The priests left meticulous, beautifully hand-written notes."

Tim continued with the reading. "Ancient pueblo ruins and cliff dwellings show that the area was inhabited long before the discovery of America. Acoma, the sky city, is a village built on a sheer cliff that rises 357 feet above the plains. One can still visit by climbing a ladder and going into the three-story adobe houses dug into the cliffs and reinforced with mud carried on human backs in hand-made baskets. Lots of Indians return today for ceremonies and festivals on the spot."

They discussed the difficult life of these early people and then read on. "A part of the Pueblos, the Zuni, live on a reservation west of these ruins. A smaller group, the Navajos, are on a reservation in the northwest of the state. A third is the warlike Apache who caused people to build high in the sides of the cliff where they could climb up and then draw the ladder up after them to be safe from attacks."

"Mom, can we visit one of these reservations?" Tom asked.

"Sorry, we can't stop. You've been to the Cherokee Reservation in North Carolina."

"Aw, well, we'd better stop and give Galena a potty break. She's acting antsy." While Galena took a potty break, they got out and stretched a few minutes. Back in the car Anna took the wheel to drive.

"Aw, gee," Tim mourned, "if we were farther south we could see Fort Selden, the remains of a frontier military post built to protect travelers and those settling in Mesilla Valley from Indian raids. Later railroads were built and travelers used Fort Selden to rest and make connections to other types of travel. From 1884 to 1886 young Douglas MacArthur lived on Fort Selden with his father who was the fort commanding officer. Today Rangers, in costumes, show people over the museum and give talks."

Irene was enjoying her sons reading about the history of the country. "I'm glad your dad got us the tour books. You've learned a lot of interesting facts and they've given you something to do on the trip."

All three children voiced their opinions and agreed that they appreciated the books. Later in the afternoon, they crossed the border into Arizona. Irene thought they were doing well and suggested they stop early. Galena jumped out of the station wagon and began to run in circles.

"Poor old girl. She's tied in knots. I bet her muscles are stiff," Anna observed. "She's not used to being in an enclosed space as long as she has on this trip, even though she's been a good traveler."

"Let her run, but keep an eye on her so that she doesn't get hurt or into trouble," Irene cautioned. She left the children and dog in a grassy area and went to a nearby motel to register and ask about a restaurant. Coming outside she was dismayed to find that Galena was running loose while the children talked to riders with their horses. Not wanting to embarrass her children in front of strangers, she hurried to the wagon and got Galena's leash.

"Howdy, ma'am." One man touched two fingers to his hat brim. "All four of us men, and one of these women, are deputy sheriffs. The other three women are wives to these galoots," he grinned.

"Hello," Irene answered pleasantly. "How nice of you to stop and speak to my children."

"Happy to do it, ma'am," a second man spoke and gave the same two finger salute to his hat brim. "That's partly why we're here. We mostly work with the Tribal Police on the Navajo Reservation to help tourists, especially lost tourists. We're also guides for horseback sightseeing and whatever else is needed."

"How far away is the reservation?" Tom asked excitedly.

"See those posts on either side of the road about a hundred feet back there?" the third man pointed.

"Yes, sir," both boys spoke.

"That's the gateway to the reservation on this road. In fact, here's Chief Straight Arrow coming now on that pinto. Howdy, Paul," he turned his horse to face the chief. "I'd like to introduce you to these nice people. This is the Jackson family from the state of Virginia. They're traveling to Alaska to meet Mr. Jackson and live there while he works for our government."

"Pleasure, ma'am. Young people." The chief smiled and removed his western hat to bow slightly to them. "I hope you've had a good trip."

"Yeah, but we haven't been able to stop and look at a lot of things we wanted to," Tom blurted.

"But we've had a great trip and enjoyed being together as a family. Hey, you haven't met the other member of our family. This is Galena." Tim, the peacemaker squatted by Galena and threw his arm over her.

"I've been noticing what a beautiful, and big, dog she is," one woman said.

"Yes, thank you," Irene chuckled. "She is a good girl but if she feels that either one of us is being threatened, then she's a tiger."

"That's the kind of dog to have," the chief smiled. "Forgive me, but I need to speak to the deputies on a business matter." the chief and the deputies tipped their hats and rode off to have a private talk. The three women dismounted and came closer to talk to the Jacksons.

"Hi, I'm Pam. This is Sandy and that's Ginger." All were attractive women and about the same size. Irene judged them in be in their late twenties. Ginger seemed to be the jolliest one of the group. All were in jeans, western shirts, western hats and boots.

"Can we ride your horses?" Tom blurted impatiently.

"May we, not can we," Irene whispered.

"Do you know how to ride?" Pam questioned.

"Not really, but it can't be too hard," Tom answered anxiously.

"I promised to let them have lessons as soon as possible," Irene was embarrassed. Pam looked at the other two, raising her eyebrows in a question. They nodded.

"Would you consent for us to sit a youngster on our horses and lead them around?" Sandy asked.

"I don't want them to be a bother to you," Irene answered.

"No trouble. Okay kids. Up you go. Now listen up." Pam took Tom's arm and led him to her horse. "This is a western saddle which is basically a working saddle. The front piece is called a horn. That's the place for a coiled rope. Good riders don't hold the horn unless they're in trouble."

Sandy placed an arm around Tim. "I won't take time to fill your head with a lot of information today. Just listen. Stand with your left shoulder by the left shoulder of the horse, facing the rump. Take the stirrup in your right hand and turn it to face you. Place your left foot in the stirrup on the ball of your foot and step up. Lift your right leg high enough so that you don't kick the horse. Don't bang your full weight in the saddle because it might hurt the horse's back. Their kidneys are under the back of the saddle. Sit up straight. Ready?"

"Sure." the twins were eager to start while Anna just grinned happily. Galena was whining and wondering what her humans were doing on top of those big animals.

"Shh. It's okay, girl. They're doing fine." Irene patted Galena and sat on a big stump to watch. Galena was trembling with worry and excitement.

All three children enjoyed walking the gentle horses. They made a large circle under the trees. Pam, Ginger and Sandy walked beside their own horse. The women were pleased with how well the children did at a walk and had them practice turning left and right still sitting straight. The ladies gave them valuable pointers about starting, turning and posture. "Are you ready to jog?" Pam called to them.

"Aren't we going to trot?" Tom asked.

"Trot is English and jog is Western," Sandy explained. "The jog is slower than the trot. You have to sit up straight, lower your heels just a fraction because the heels act as a brake in the air. Let the muscles on the inside of your thighs absorb the shock. Now squeeze the calves of both legs and lightly touch the outside heel to the horse. The outside being the one on the outside of a circle. Ready? Jog."

As the horses obediently started to jog, Tom leaned forward and let his toes go down. Before he could think, he was leaning over the horse's neck. "Help! What am I doing wrong?"

Sandy took charge. "Everyone sit up straight, place pressure on your seat muscles and gently pull back on the reins, then release the reins." All three horses came to a full stop.

Pam patted Tom's leg. "Honey, you didn't do any worse than most people do when they start riding. You let your toes go down and leaned forward.

Always either keep your foot level or lower the heel slightly. Sit up. On horseback, as the head goes, so goes the body. Leaning forward not only throws you off balance, but it can be a body command to the horse to go faster. Let's try again. Turn to the left and walk on."

When Tom had cried out, Galena barked furiously and strained to go to him. It was all Irene could do to hold her back. Ginger walked to them smiling. "Is this the first horse she's seen?"

"No." Irene told of seeing the horses in Amarillo. She's just concerned that one of her family needed her."

"That's sweet. She loves all of you and obviously you love her."

"That's true. She's been with us as a weanling since the boys were two years old. It's a mutual admiration." Irene laughed.

The deputies returned and were surprised to see the children riding.

"Hey there, partner. How long have you been riding?" Ginger's husband asked.

Tom made a big deal of checking his watch. "Oh, about twenty minutes."

"No," he laughed, "I mean in months or years."

"Like I said, about twenty minutes."

"Well, buddy, you're all doing well. Sorry to break up the party, but we have to move on."

The three children called out, "Thank you," over and over. They were grateful for a chance to ride with instructions. After dinner they took Galena for a walk. "Isn't the air nice?" Anna sniffed appreciatively.

"Yeah," Tom agreed. "You know I've enjoyed the trip more than I thought I would. If we just didn't have to live in Alaska," he sighed.

"Ummm. The air does smell fresh and clean," Tim hurriedly spoke before Irene could admonish Tom. "What a difference. I don't smell exhaust fumes or neighbor's cooking or any city odors." They walked slowly back to the motel enjoying the fresh air.

Back in the motel Irene pretended to be interested in the TV Guide so her children couldn't see her smiling. A lot of groans were heard as muscles spoke their piece about being used so differently during the day. Tom complained the most. Galena looked at Irene and comically rolled her eyes as if she understood the conversation. She gave a big sigh and collapsed on the floor between the beds.

As they walked to breakfast the next morning, Tom scowled. "Why are my thighs so sore? My seat's even sore."

"Because, bird brain, you don't ride a horse every day. If we rode often, our muscles would toughen." Tim winced as he walked with legs wide apart.

"Mom. He's calling me names again," Tom tattled.

"No one is to call anyone names. We must be considerate of each other's feelings or our trip will be miserable." Irene walked between the boys.

Later, on the road, Tom suddenly yelped loudly causing Galena to jump up and bark. "We were right by --right by the Navajo Reservation and didn't even stick our noses in."

Anna, sitting on the back seat with Tim, reached forward and patted Tom's shoulder. "Just think how much more fun it will be to see the Grand Canyon. Besides you wouldn't see anything but small houses and poor animals."

CHAPTER EIGHT

Around one thirty they arrived at the Grand Canyon. "Stay together, please. This is a big area and there are a lot of people milling around. I don't want to be worried about any of you." Irene looked sternly at them. "We'll save the gift shop for the last."

Men were on mules riding around answering questions and acting as guides.

"Mom, may we ride a mule? We know how now."

"Tom, how often have I told you that it isn't becoming to whine and it doesn't get you anywhere? Those mules are only for the people riding down into the canyon. Didn't you hear the guide say the last group had gone down for the day? We're leaving in the morning."

Irene turned around to continue taking pictures. When she turned back around, Tim was beside her and Anna was slightly behind her. "Where's Tom? Where's Galena?" she asked anxiously. Tim shrugged his shoulders. Anna called Tom's name aloud and then called for Galena. Irene gazed down into the canyon and began to fear the worst.

"Tom!" she called loudly. People turned to look hearing the panic in her voice. "Has anyone seen a boy who looks just like this one" And a German Shepherd?" By now she was babbling, fighting to keep from crying. Minutes went by while she hunted frantically dragging Tim and Anna along.

A Park police roared up on a motorcycle. "Ma'am. I got a call that someone needed help. How can I help you?"

"Yes, sir," she gulped on a sob. My son is missing along with our dog.

He looks just like his twin here except he was wearing jeans, a red and white striped shirt and sneakers. You can see this one has a blue shirt on. She was trembling and crying by now. Anna hugged her mother and tried to comfort her even though she, too, was crying. Tim was silent with a white face and a grim mouth.

"Ma'am, we have plenty of officers to look for lost people. We're experienced in this. You'd be surprised at the number of people who are thought to be lost and have just wandered away from their party. Why don't you wait in that building so I'll know where to find you. We can't have all of you running in different directions. When we locate your son we need to know where to bring him."

Reluctantly Irene, Anna and Tim went to the building adjacent to the gift shop. Constantly looking back, Irene, with a heavy heart, led the way through a glass door and into a room about thirty by forty feet. Four desks with telephones and a computer on each one and a large wall map of the area proved to be the command area for the officers. A couch, four lounge chairs and restrooms were available.

Two officers soon came in and tried to comfort them with soft drinks, tea or coffee and showing them a water fountain back by the rest rooms. They also assured Irene that her son would be found and well. They soon realized that Irene was not interested in small talk and went to their desks to work.

For once Tim was so frightened, he was speechless. He and Anna sat on either side of Irene and held her hands. Tim's heart melted as he felt his mother's hands shaking and knew how worried she was. He told himself that he would give Tom what for when he returned. At the moment he forgot all the times he had caused a worry. "Mom, I hope Tom's all right."

Anna shook her head at Tim. "Apparently Galena is with Tom. She'll take care of him. The policeman did say there were loads of people ready and willing to search. They've had training and experience."

After about half an hour, Tim had shredded tissues around where he was sitting and Anna had silent tears streaking down her cheeks. Irene was rocking her body back and forth. Every few minutes she would moan aloud, but she wasn't conscious she had made a sound. Tears had dried in gray streaks on her face that had lost color.

The door opened and a joyful bark penetrated their sadness. "Galena!" Tim and Anna both cried out at once.

"Did you find Tom? Did you find my son?" Irene asked anxiously as an officer entered with Galena.

"Well, ma'am, here's your wandering son." An officer answered as he came in with a hand on Tom's shoulder.

"Oh, Tom," Irene sobbed as she hugged him tightly. "I don't know whether to beat you or hug you. Where were you? I told everyone to stay together. We'll discuss this later after I've had time to calm down." She turned to the officers. "Forgive me. I do thank you with my whole heart. I'm so sorry a child of mine caused you trouble. Thank you for finding him. Where **did** you find him?" She was shaking and babbling with tears streaming down her face. The officers smiled.

"We had a radio call from the guides that went with the last riders in line. By the way, that group is staying overnight. The guide said he thought he saw someone trying to walk down. They turned a bend and he didn't get a good look, but he radioed us to check it out," one officer said.

"When we got to him, this young man was on a narrow part of the trail, backed up against the cliff and looking down into the canyon as if he were frozen in time. The dog wouldn't let us near him. We had to stand back and keep talking until he responded and could reassure the dog that we were friendly," the second officer laughed.

Tom looked at Irene with a trembling lip and a catch in his voice. "Mom, I'm truly sorry. I didn't think how far down it was. I thought I could go down and be back before you'd miss me. It's only a mile."

Tim snorted. "Goofy. It's a mile straight down. The trail curves around so that mules can walk without falling off. I don't know how far down it really is. You're not indispensable, you know. Why did you take Galena with you and risk her life?"

"I didn't **take** her," Tom sputtered with tears in his eyes. "She followed me. Boy, you should have seen her. She wouldn't let the officer close and she stood in front of me for fear I'd fall off. She's a real good guard dog." Tom fell to his knees hugging Galena, but truthfully, he wanted to hide his red face and tear-filled eyes against her fur. She wriggled in happiness.

"You're fortunate to have her," an officer said. "It's true, she wouldn't let us near the boy until he roused enough to talk to her. He was a little green around the gills. I hope this young man has learned a valuable lesson that things aren't always as appealing as they seem." He put an affectionate hand on Tom's shoulder. "Promise me you'll stay with your family from now on and let your mother know where you're going if you do separate from them. Your family loves you and your mother's heart was in great pain when she lost track of you. They didn't know whether you were badly hurt or abducted by a dangerous person."

"Oh, yes, sir. I promise. I've learned my lesson."

"For how long?" Tim muttered as he knelt to hug Galena.

"Ooooo Tom. I could shake you until your teeth rattle," Irene scolded. "I was so frightened not knowing what had happened to you."

"But, Mom. I knew you wouldn't let me go down and we didn't get to ride the mules. Some how it was more frightening to look down from where I was standing than from the top."

Anna spoke through gritted teeth. "Thomas Harrison Jackson, you left us here worried sick and all you can say is you thought you'd be back before you were missed. For all we knew some evil person could have knocked you out and kidnapped you. Or you could have fallen off and been killed, and **you know** Galena would have jumped off after you. How could you have put her through that? I thought you loved her and us. How thoughtless and selfish." She began to cry.

"Anna," Tom sobbed, "I do love Galena and I do love all of you. Yes, it was thoughtless. I wanted something and was going to get it regardless of the outcome. I'm truly sorry. What more can I say?" He was now sobbing uncontrollably.

"Stop it," Irene spoke firmly.

Tim was standing looking at Tom in amazement. He never thought Tom would break down like this, especially in public. Maybe -- just maybe Tom was truly sorry. After all, Tom was his twin and they had always been close and stood by each other through everything. Tim placed an arm across Tom's shoulders. As tall and big as they were, they were still young boys.

"We're all emotional and might say things we'll regret," Irene said. "Let's keep quiet and go on." Her eyes were sad, but as the mother she had to take charge and keep her family together.

Irene placed an arm around Tom as they walked out to the station wagon.

They were trying to get to the vehicle and not look at the people who were staring curiously at them.

Tom looked at his mother. "Mom, I'm ---"

"Shh. Don't talk. Again you've caused needless worry. Your dad will be so disappointed when he hears of this."

"Mom! Please don't tell dad," Tom begged between fresh sobs.

"We don't hide anything from each other. That would be like lying. Let's put it to rest for the time being. Please, please don't wander off again. Try to be more mature and consider how others might feel as a result of your decisions and actions."

Tom nodded and crawled into the back seat. Anna prepared to drive. Tim came back from walking Galena and got into the front seat. Irene put Galena into the back of the wagon and got in beside Tom. The silence hung as heavy as a thick curtain while they returned to the motel.

They went to dinner and little was said. When they returned to the motel Anna and Tim took Galena for a walk. Tom was uncomfortable because his mother was silent and his siblings were not talking to him. Tom jumped into the shower and crawled into bed, waiting silently while Tim and Anna took turns showering and dressing for bed.

Galena sensed sadness and whined until Tim encouraged her to get on the bed and cuddle a while. Tom's chest felt as if something heavy was sitting on him. With a great sigh Galena slid off the bed and took her spot.

The next morning the twins walked Galena saying only what was necessary. Galena was left with her breakfast and clean water while the family went silently to their breakfast.

CHAPTER NINE

Anna was driving as they headed north toward Utah. In northern Arizona there were signs saying, "dust blowing area." The wind whipped the red dust around and across the road until Anna was forced to drive so slowly she almost stopped in places. Visibility was limited.

All of them exclaimed in sorrow to see the skinny, hungry horses with all ribs showing as they staggered beside the open road. There were even starved sheep and goats. There was no grass to eat and no water where they were. The twins hoped someone owned the animals and would take care of them. Irene reminded them that the people were also poor and most of them didn't get enough to eat. The animals were either turned loose to fend for themselves or had been abandoned.

Tom tried to take their minds off the sadness by reading aloud from the Arizona tour book. "Aw, we can't go through Flagstaff. It says that Flagstaff got its name from a flagpole made from a Ponderosa Pine. In 1876 a group of people stripped the branches from a pine that was growing beside the trail. It remained as a landmark for wagon trains traveling to California. The fort built here became known as Flagstaff. In time a town developed and was given the same name. Boy! That's interesting."

Galena became worried again because she could not understand why her humans were so quiet and seemed so sad. She moved from person to person whining and licking any face she could reach.

Irene finally chuckled. "Everyone, including me, lighten up. We're worrying Galena."

The temptation was too much for Tim. He picked up the Utah tour book and read aloud. "Hey, listen. In Marysville, Utah is the Big Rock Candy Mountain. I always thought that was just a cute song Burl Ives sang, but it's true. Wow! There's even a lemonade spring."

"Will we be there?" Tom asked hesitantly.

After a moment of silence Irene answered, "I think we might be able to stop." Looking at the Utah map she said, "Yes, we'll be near there in time for a late lunch."

"Hurray!" both boys exploded.

The family was in awe of the scenery. "My goodness," Irene observed, "the rocks do look like giant pieces of candy. It must be different chemicals in the rocks that show various colors when the water settles in them. Let's try the lemonade spring. I'm ready for a cool drink."

They paid for their cups in the gift shop and hurried out to try the lemonade in the spring. "May I buy a bag of that real rock candy to take to dad?" Tom asked almost shyly.

"Of course, Tom. That's nice that you thought of your dad. I don't know if he ever came here or not." Irene said as she smiled and patted his back.

"Yeah, suck up to dad. Maybe he won't be too mad at you for scaring us and giving mom such a hard time on the trip," Tim sneered.

"You're just jealous because you didn't think of it," Tom shot back, "Both of you--outside this minute. I am so embarrassed that you would cause a public spectacle. Tim, I'm astonished at your attitude."

Tim snorted and whirled around to walk toward the car beside Anna. She looked at him with a sad expression. "Tim, I love my brothers and have been truly proud to be your sister, but I don't understand you. Both of you know that mom is under a strain being responsible for everything, and us, on this trip. Remember, she wasn't too enthused either about the move.

After all, dad is making the money that you gladly spend. We're all tired and, yes, you're probably bored most of the time, but you're making it worse for you and for us by your attitude."

Anna turned to look at Tom who had caught up with them. "That goes for you, too, buddy boy. Let's make a pact that we'll think before we speak. We have to be together, in a small space, so let's strive to make it easier for mom and ourselves. It doesn't feel good to have someone we love say hurtful things or try to belittle us. Can we make an agreement to be more considerate and think before we speak?"

The twins looked at each other and then shamefacedly nodded at Anna. "Okay. Let's build on it." She held out her left hand and each boy placed his left hand on the stack followed by their right hands. "Now. We have a firm agreement." Anna grinned.

"What's all this?" Irene asked as she walked to them.

"Just something we promised each other," Anna smiled as she took Galena from the station wagon. "I'll give Galena a break and then I'll drive, Mom." Galena obviously enjoyed the break. Irene privately thought the dog was better behaved and less trouble that her sons.

On the road again, Tom began to read from the book on Idaho. "Gee, Mom. This is one of the less populated states in the west with a lot of uninhabitable land. We'd better fill the gas tank every chance we get. I'd sure hate to be stranded out in some of this wild land."

Continuing his silent reading, he burst out laughing. "It says the name, Idaho, comes from a Shoshone Indian word , Ed-dah-how, which means, 'look, the sun is coming down from the mountain'. Isn't that a hoot. Others say it really means gem of the mountain."

He read on silently and then spoke, "Gold was discovered in 1860 which brought the state's population up to 15,000 people. In 1877 General O. O. Howard, with his troop, defeated the Nez Perce Indians led by Chief Joseph. In 1890, Idaho was admitted to the Union as the 43rd state. During the 1900s, Idaho had a steady increase in irrigation and hydroelectric power. Since 1951 atomic power has been produced by the National Reactor Testing Station near Arco."

Tim had been thinking and broke in, "Wasn't it Chief Joseph who said, "I will fight no more forever"? We saw the movie, remember? I felt so sorry for the Indians. They sure got a dirty deal."

Anna and Irene looked at each other knowingly and laughed when Galena looked at the boys, gave a grunt and a deep sigh, and stretched out to fall asleep. "She's relieved," Anna chuckled. "There's peace for a while."

Late in the afternoon, Anna drove across the border into Idaho. She had to go to Rockland where there was a gas station, restaurant and motel together. Galena was so happy to be stopped that she walked across the boys to get outside where she ran around and around the station wagon.

Irene stretched, "Ummm. We're all tired, so why don't we eat soon and go to bed early. You can watch television if you're not sleepy. At least our bodies can rest."

The next morning Irene drove across the border into Washington. It rained for hours, but they didn't complain much because it had been a decent trip so far. "Why don't we stop in Spokane for a lunch break?" she suggested.

The rain had stopped for a while and the air was fresh and clear. "Mom, over there's a great looking park. We can buy food and go over there for a picnic." Tom looked at Tim. "Wouldn't you like that?"

"Sure," Tim replied eagerly. "I know Galena will like it. Let me get the Frisbee and play with her. Seeing Tim take the Frisbee out of the car, Galena was wild with joy.

"Catch her! Galena! Come back here!" Irene yelled as Galena ran across the street toward the park. A car screeched and turned sideways. An eighteen wheeler driver, following the car, blew his air horn and yelled as his truck went sliding out of control because he had to throw on his brakes. Galena came back with her tail between her legs knowing she had down something wrong. The Jackson family looked on in horror expecting to see a terrible wreck, but the truck driver was able to wrestle his truck back on the highway and stop just short of the car.

The frightened and very angry truck driver climbed down from the cab ready to do battle. "Where in the blue blazes is that mangy mutt and who does it belong to?"

"Mangy mutt?!" Tom shrieked stomping up in the man's face with his chin out. Anna grabbed him by the back of his shirt and pulled him back as Irene hurried to talk to the two drivers. Tim dropped to his knees, hugging Galena and still shaking from the fright.

Irene was also shaken and with a catch in her voice apologized. "Oh, sir, I'm so sorry. I'm thankful no one is hurt and apparently there's no damage. There isn't any damage is there?" she asked fearfully. "We've been traveling for over two weeks and the dog is so tired of being in the car she ----"

"Lady! That's no excuse for letting a dog run loose." The driver of the car blurted pugnaciously. He then took a deep breath and ran a trembling hand through his hair. "Okay. I have three boys and two dogs, so I understand how these things can happen. I was so sure I'd be flattened by that semi." He took another long breath. "Is the dog all right?"

"She's fine. Thank you, sir," Tim answered quickly. He stood up in front of the men. "I can understand how angry you are." He turned to the semi driver. "That's a lot of weight to have to stop so quickly, and you probably have a load on board that could have been damaged. My mother told you the truth. We've traveled so long and the dog was very happy to see the park on the other side that she took off before we could catch her. Believe me, she is well trained. You noticed she came right back when she was called."

"She had no business being loose. Why didn't you have a leash on her?" the driver stated.

"There's some people that need a leash more than this dog does." Tom looked as if he would gladly do battle.

"Tom!" Irene spoke firmly. "It **was** our fault and I'm truly sorry. "Is your truck okay?" she looked appealingly at the truck driver.

"Yeah, I guess," he answered gruffly. "I almost jack-knifed and it scared the -- uh -- it scared me." He turned to the car driver. "Can you pull out and give me room to straighten out?"

"Certainly," the man replied and hurried to his car. He turned to the Jacksons. "I hope your family has a pleasant and a safe trip." He got in his car and maneuvered around until he straightened and left with a toot of his horn.

The truck driver walked over and looked closely at Galena. "Is she a full-blooded German Shepherd?"

"Yes, sire," Tim answered proudly.

"Humph. That's the biggest one I've ever seen. Is she trained to be an attack dog?"

"No," Irene said hurriedly. "She does protect us because she's been with us all her life. She would only be vicious if one of us were to be threatened and she felt she was needed to protect one of us."

The truck driver grunted. "She's a beautiful dog, and so big," he said again. "I sure would love to have one like her to travel in the cab with me."

"Sorry," Anna giggled, "the mold was broken when she was born, and she'll be with us as long as she lives." the man shook his head and walked to his truck. It took a lot of pulling forward, backing and turning to get his cab and

81

trailer straightened to drive. He blew his air horn at them as he left.

"He'd better get out of here while the getting's good," Tom snarled.

"Tom! When are you going to learn to control your temper?" Irene spoke sharply. "You could have gotten us in serious trouble if you had angered those men enough to call the police on us. It **was** Galena's fault and we should have had her on a leash. It's the fault of all of us. Now get a leash on her. We'll get our food and cross in safety together to the park. Those beautiful shade trees are calling to me. I can hardly wait to get my shoes off and walk in that lovely grass."

Irene walked to a nearby fast-food counter to place their order. "I would like four deluxe cheeseburgers, two plain cheeseburgers, four orders of fries, two chocolate milk shakes, one strawberry and one vanilla shake. The vanilla one made with butter pecan ice cream, please." She paid and joined her family. Tim helped carry the food while Tom took Galena. They carefully crossed the street and found a table with benches under a huge shade tree.

"Here, boys. Give Galena the two plain cheeseburgers. It really isn't good for her, but I'm sure she'll appreciate a change from her usual dog food. We mustn't feed her like this too often though. We leave in one hour. Don't wander off and get into trouble or get lost."

The twins hurriedly ate their food and grabbed the Frisbee, calling to Galena and ran farther into the park. Irene gave a contented sigh and dropped to the grass under the tree. She lay back with her head on her sweater and one arm over her eyes.

"Umm, Mom. Thanks loads. This strawberry shake is really good and hit's the spot." Anna gave a last slurp and slipped down beside Irene. She smiled to see that her mother was starting to doze.

Irene woke when the boys came yelling back to them. "Hour's up. Whew. Galena really had a good time. She'll be ready to settle down for sure in the car this time," Tim smiled.

"I'm afraid you boys are on a sugar high. I don't know what Galena's excuse is," Irene laughed. "Let's use the restroom in the restaurant and hit the trail. We mustn't waste time."

Galena promptly went to sleep. The twins were soon slumped over and snoozing. Anna drove all afternoon stopping once for gas. She drove across the Canadian border into Vancouver, British Columbia. Irene had their birth certificates and all necessary papers to cross the border. They were glad to stop for dinner and the night.

Irene sighed tiredly. "We should see dad in two days." The twins got out of the car and turned handstands causing Galena to bark excitedly. Irene hugged Anna. "Honey, you've been so much help to me; a real rock that helped steady me. Thank you, darling. Your dad will be very proud of you."

Irene gathered her family and said, "Let's call dad and tell him where we are. We should be in Fairbanks, Alaska day after tomorrow. I hope we can drive straight out to

Nome, but we might have to stay another night and leave the next day."

The twins groaned and fell on the bed pretending to be sick at the stomach. They cheered up when they were allowed to speak to Herb first. Tom spoke first because he claimed to have the privilege of being the oldest---all of four minutes. Galena barked into the phone when she heard Herb's voice and nosed all over the phone trying to find him.

Herb was anxious to see his family. "Hey! I'm so excited. It seems like a year since I've seen all of you and I sure have missed you. I've made new friends but nothing takes the place of family. Just hurry to me safely. You've come this far. Don't spoil your trip by carelessness. I love all of you and am so lonely without you."

They were all rejuvenated to hear Herb's voice and know he wasn't as far away. Galena ran to the door telling them she needed a walk. The twins took her and when she returned she gratefully sank to the carpet. She groaned when she was roused to eat her dinner. They left her eating while they went to find dinner for themselves. Anna was thrilled to practice speaking French to the waitress.

The next morning Anna walked Galena and then left the car to be checked and filled with gas while they had breakfast. Even though they were excited at the near completion of the trip, they told Galena they understood why she was groaning. They were getting tired of climbing in and out of the wagon and sitting so long at a time.

Anna begged to drive because she could travel over roads that were different than any she'd been on. The surface was not smooth and the road wound through forest areas where wild animals were frequently seen.

'We're stopping already for lunch?" Tom whined. "Shouldn't we drive as far as we can?"

"Don't be selfish," Tim scowled. "Mom and Anna have been doing the hard work and they deserve a break. Truthfully, I'll be glad to get out of the car for a while."

Irene smiled at them and reached to ruffle Tom's hair. "We'd better eat while we can. We don't know what we'll find north of here. Look for snacks to take with you."

When they left the wagon to walk toward the restaurant, Galena pawed at a window and howled. Tim ran back to her. "Go on in," he called over his shoulder. "I'll walk her a little. She might think we're leaving her in a strange place." Tim walked Galena, put her back in the car with a chew toy, and ran to join the family.

All afternoon they stopped to take pictures of the gorgeous scenery, and some of the wild animals. Irene cautioned them about getting too close and maybe causing the animals to think they had to protect themselves. They were later stopping for dinner than they had planned. Everyone crawled out of the car, stretching and yawning. For once Galena crawled out and stood quietly beside the twins. They walked her and returned to the car. As Tim put her back in the car, Tom looked around and suddenly spoke excitedly. "Look! Over there!"

CHAPTER TEN

A Royal Canadian Mounted Police rode up to them on a proudly, prancing horse. The twins ran toward him talking at once. Catching up with them, Irene apologized. "I'm sorry. We've always loved movies about the Mounties and love your red coats."

"That's fine. My horse is well trained to deal with people and noises. Ordinarily I wouldn't have this red uniform on. We wear brown and look much like many of your state police do. Today we had a visit from one of our superior officers and we wore the red uniform in honor of his visit. Too, we were on television and the yanks expect us to be wearing red," he laughed.

"Yanks?" Tom looked questioningly.

"Americans. From the United States."

"Oh. I didn't know that you don't wear the red uniforms normally," Tom was disappointed.

The Mountie chuckled. "My name is Reginald Churchill, Lieutenant Churchill, but the people around here call me Officer Churchill."

"Sir, would you please tell me how you train to be a Mountie and how your beautiful horse is trained," Tim pleaded.

"It would take too long to tell all of it, so, I'll just say we first train a lot like the military requires. Then we go through another training period of how to make an arrest without hurting the suspect more than absolutely necessary. And of course, keep ourselves safe. We even have pepper spray sprayed into our own eyes so that we can understand how a person being arrested feels and how to deal with it. It sure isn't pleasant."

"How is your horse trained?" Tim asked. "We met a Park Policeman in Washington, D.C. and he told us how his horse was trained. Your horse sure is gorgeous."

"Gorgeous," Tom teased. "You sound like a girl."

"Whoa. I call her gorgeous frequently." The Mountie's blue eyes twinkled as he dismounted and patted the horse's neck. When he removed the broad-brimmed hat, his straw-colored hair stayed in place. The twins were impressed with his height.

"Wow! How tall are you?" Tom asked with wide eyes.

"I'm six three, but most of the men are six feet."

"You called your horse her," Tom said in astonishment. "I didn't know you could use females."

The Mountie laughed. "Sure. She's a good ole girl. Many times my life has depended on her and she comes through."

"Well, how was she trained," Tim persisted.

"She was given a thorough training by professionals. Again it would take too long to tell the entire process. Just as some dogs don't pass the test to be a K-9 dog, some of the horses don't pass the test. When we're introduced to our horse, they have no saddle or bridle." He smiled at the children's surprised faces. "We have an instructor who tells us what to do. We have to ride, as the old saying goes, by the seat of our pants. Bareback. We learn to guide the horse with our body movements, seat muscles, legs and voice. Then if we have to use a gun or rope, our hands are free to do so."

"Don't you ever fall off?" Tom asked in winder.

"Of course, at first. Fortunately I never got hurt more than bruises and a badly damaged ego. I grew up with horses, but, boy did I learn more. Some of the trainees have had broken arms, shoulders out of joint, one even had a broken jaw."

"Cool," Tim said softly at the same time that Irene said, "Good grief. Don't either of you dare to ask to train to be a Mountie."

The talked briefly, thanked the policeman for his time, and started to walk away. Irene whirled around. "Excuse me. Do you know where we can stay for the night? I haven't seen a hotel or motel."

"No," the Mountie answered in a clipped Canadian accent. "You won't find them here. You will find bed and breakfasts in homes. There are women, mostly widows, who will keep you for the night and even feed you. Follow me and I'll show you one of the best."

He left the reins on the horse's neck and walked off with the horse following at his shoulder. They were on a short street where a white house with green shutters stood at the end. They walked through a white gate with a high arch over it, supposedly for flowers to trail across.. A clean, white fence stretched around a neatly clipped lawn with a flower bed beside the front porch. The wide porch had a swing and four rockers on it.

Officer Churchill knocked on the door, opened it and called, "Hello, Mrs. Storch. It's Officer Churchill."

A short, plump, pink-cheeked, white-haired lady hurried to the door. Anna smiled to herself thinking she looked like a sweet grandmother.

"Hello, love," she said in surprise. "It's my lucky day to have the most handsome man in town come calling." Her head came to the middle of his chest as she put her arms around his waist to hug him, then turned twinkling blue eyes on the Jackson family. "Now who are these nice people?"

"Mrs. Storch, I'd like to introduce you to these nice people who have come all the way from the state of Virginia across the United States and are on their way to Alaska."

"Saints alive," she exclaimed.

"This is Mrs. Jackson, her daughter Anna, and her sons, Tim and Tom."

"What a beautiful young girl and twins. How lovely. Such tall, handsome boys. How do you tell them apart?"

"I'm the oldest," Tom boasted.

"Yeah, by four minutes," Tim grumbled.

Irene hurried to speak before the boys could get into an embarrassing verbal battle. "When they were small it was sometimes difficult. Of course, their father and I knew which was which, but they pulled some stunts on teachers and friends. Now they dress differently. Tom's face is more oval while Tim has a square jaw line."

"Where is your mister?" Mrs. Storch asked as she led them into the living room, or as she called it, the parlor.

"I'll leave you folks to get acquainted. I must leave because I **am** on duty," Officer Churchill stated. He wished the family a pleasant trip, saluted and left. He whistled to the mare who had wandered a few feet away eating some flower tops on the outside of the fence. The twins ran to the window as the horse came trotting obediently to him.

"Gee whiz! Did you see that?" Tom yelped.

"Tom, none of us are deaf. Inside voice, please," Irene glared at him.

Mrs. Storch chuckled. "I know how he feels. We, in this town, love to watch the Mounties and the horses. We never tire of seeing them. It's unbelievable how those animals behave better than my wee ones ever did."

She started walking out of the room. "I'll show you the rooms. If you want to share by twos, it'll be fifty-five dollars which includes breakfast. If you want dinner, I'll have to have three dollars each. I hope you have Canadian money. It's not always easy to change money by the rates."

"Oh, yes," Irene answered. "I changed when we first came across the border."

Anna smiled at Mrs. Storch. "We've been lucky this entire trip to get a motel room with two double beds so that we could stay together. We also have a dog."

"Have you kept the dog in your room each night?" Mrs. Storch asked in astonishment, "I didn't think motels would allow animals,"

"Our dog is well trained and kept clean," Tim stated proudly. "We take good care of her and think of her as one of the family."

"Why don't you bring her in then. I'd like to meet her."

The twins happily raced out to the car to get Galena. She walked sedately through the doorway as if she were a royal lady.

"Mercy me." Mrs. Storch took a step back. "What a big dog and so beautiful. I never knew Shepherds got this big."

Tom walked to Mrs. Storch with Galena by his side. "Sit." Galena obediently sat and looked sweetly at Mrs. Storch. "Hello, Galena." the dog raised one paw and seemed to be smiling up at Mrs. Storch. She bent and took the paw. "Down." Galena went all the way down to lie on her stomach. Mrs. Storch's plump figure shook with laughter as Galena gave a deep sigh and stretched out on her side.

"She's a tired miss. It's been a long journey for her. I think she will be glad to spend the night in my home. Come along to your rooms."

She led them upstairs to two rooms connected by a large bathroom. The lovely oak floors were clean and polished, covered by hand-crafted scatter rugs. The twin beds in each room were made of sturdy red cherry and covered with hand-made quilts and matching pillow shams. The quilts were white with appliquéd multi-colored flowers sewn on. There was a table between the heads of the beds with a lamp on it. An armoire in one corner served as a closet. A wide window, in each room, with white, fluffy lace curtains, looked out over beautiful trees and a pond.

"Galena stays with me," Irene said firmly.

"Aw, Mom. She likes to be with us," Tom begged.

Galena trotted into the room behind the boys and promptly stretched out between the twin beds.

"See, Mom. That proves she wants to be with us," Tom wouldn't give up.

"Sorry, boys. I want to make sure she isn't made excited during the night and start barking." Irene snapped her fingers and Galena immediately got up and followed her through the bathroom and into the room Irene and Anna would share.

"There's only you and me here tonight," Mrs. Storch said. "My room is downstairs on the other side of the house. I'm sure she won't bother me. By the way, did you tell me where your mister is?"

"Oh, I'm sorry. I wasn't dodging the question. The Mountie left and we kept talking. Mr. Jackson is in Nome, Alaska and we're going there to join him. He's waited anxiously for us and we've sure missed him."

"Yeah, he works for our U.S. Government and we'll be living there for at least two years, maybe three." Tim hurriedly explained.

"I beg your pardon, son. Do we speak to adults with yeah?"

"I'm sorry. My parents have taught me to say yes, ma'am." he apologized.

"I can't blame you for being excited. I would be, too. What a great adventure you'll have," Mrs. Storch smiled.

"Mrs. Storch, I don't mean to be rude, but where are you from originally? I love your accent."

"My mister and I came from Sweden when we first married over sixty years ago. He hoped to find gold, but there were too many doing the same. He got a job cutting timber and died two days after he retired. My five children are all grown, married and live away. Two are down in the states, one in Washington and one in California. Three are still in Canada, but on to the east, two near Toronto and one in Nova Scotia. They are all well educated and have fine jobs."

The family had an enjoyable visit with Mrs. Storch. She took them on a walking tour of her neighborhood after dinner. They eagerly called Herb to tell him how close they were.

The next morning after breakfast the Jackson family reluctantly said good-bye to Mrs. Storch.

"I wish you could stay longer. You're such a nice family and easy to know. I'd love to take you in as my family. Oh, I have many blessings and wonderful neighbors, but I do miss having people in the house with me."

"Mrs. Storch, the short time we've been together, I've become quite fond of you. My children admire you and Galena sure likes you," Irene said as she hugged the dear lady.

"She's a good girl and one dog that anyone would be fortunate to have." Mrs. Storch sat on a low stool to hug Galena. Everyone laughed when Galena leaned against her and made cooing noises.

They left looking back and waving as long as they could see Mrs. Storch. On the road again they were becoming more excited about seeing Herb. "Dad will be meeting us soon," Tom joyously informed Galena. She barked and wriggled all over as if she knew what was being said.

The four of them sang and laughed with joy as they traveled north into Yukon Territory. The last part of the journey seemed to be the slowest and longest of all. They stopped in Dawson too late to sightsee. They stopped for gas and to ask where they could have dinner and stay for the night. Again they stayed in a bed and breakfast home. The couple who owned the home, Ian and Rianne Rymer, were very nice, but not as jolly as Mrs. Storch.

They made their nightly call to Herb. It was difficult to tell who was the more excited, Herb or his family. Even Galena sensed the excitement and jumped around. She seemed to understand that Herb was closer.

After a good, filling breakfast of cereal, sweet rolls, fruit and milk, they were eager to continue. The afternoon found them in Fairbanks. Irene drove to the airport and all of them jumped out of the station wagon full of joy.

"Hey, look up there. There's snow on the mountain and it's nice down here," Tom shouted.

A smiling man walked toward them. "Hello, I assume you're the Jacksons."

"Yes, I'm Mrs. Jackson," Irene answered puzzled. *Who is this stranger?*

"My name is Paul Grigsby. Mr. Jackson hired me to fly you to Nome. I hope you've had a pleasant trip."

"Tiresome but very good," Anna answered.

"Great. Let's get the plane loaded." Paul picked up suitcases.

"And Galena?" Tom questioned fearfully.

"Of course Galena. I've heard all about her and am anxious to get to know her." Paul looked behind the twins where Galena was sitting quietly.

"Here, girl," Tim spoke to Galena and showed her to walk to Paul. "Friend, Galena. Sit. Hello." Paul laughed and knelt to take the paw she held up, rubbing her behind her ears and down her neck.

"What a beautiful girl you are," Paul said. "I hope you'll adjust well and enjoy living here."

"She'll be happy as long as she's with us," Irene told him.

"It's good you're here at this time of the year. She can become accustomed to the climate as the weather changes and before winter hits us."

Irene looked puzzled and looked around. "I thought I heard someone call my name." she cried, "Yes!" and started running.

"Yes what, Mom?" Anna asked as she saw her mother running. "Yes!" Anna yelled and ran after her mother.

The twins were puzzled to see a tall man coming toward them with one arm around Irene and one around Anna. Galena gave an excited bark and broke away, trailing her leash, as she ran to the three people.

By the time the twins recognized Herb, he was kneeling and hugging Galena. She was giving him doggie kisses all over his face. The twins ran and threw themselves at their dad. None of them had expected to see him here at the airport.

"Oof." Herb sat down hard with both boys clinging to him. They were too big and strong to be held like he held them when they were little. Herb fell backward to the tarmac hugging both boys to his chest. Galena was barking and jumping on them wanting to join in. Finally, able to stand, Herb had to hug everyone over and over.

"Oh, you guys. You don't know how good it is to be with my family again. I sure missed all of you." He laughingly took his handkerchief and wiped the tears of joy from

Irene's face. He kissed her over and over. "My darling, my darling. I don't ever want to be away from you so long again."

"Hey, Dad. What'er we going to do with the station wagon? Will it go in the plane?" Tim asked.

"No," Herb chuckled. "I've already sold it to a man who works here at the airport. We'll have two other cars, four-wheel drive, that we'll need to get around in Nome. Now check and make sure you've taken everything from the wagon."

"Dad," Tim said, "wait until you hear what a good driver Anna is. She helped mom a lot." He complimented his sister with pride.

"I'm eager to hear all about your trip across country when we get settled. Yes, I'm proud of Anna, and -- of you boys." He then turned to place a hand on the back of Tom's neck. "You, I'll talk to later." He hugged Tom to show that he still loved him even though he was a rascal.

Soon they were ready to take off. Paul taxied to the end of the runway and turned facing the wind. He spoke to the control tower on his radio. Galena looked anxiously out of the window and then to each member of her family. It was the first time she'd flown,

"It'll be scary to her at first, but she'll settle down if we stay calm and reassure her," Herb told them. Galena sat beside Anna with a seat belt through her harness. She whined and tried to get off the seat. Anna soothed her and told her everything was okay.

They were soon gliding over the wide expanse of snow, frozen water and snow-covered mountains. They hadn't realized how time had flown when Paul said, "Look below. There's your new home."

Everyone crowded to the window to be able to see. Even Galena pushed to look out just as if she understood what was said. On the outskirts of Nome, they cam in smoothly and coasted to a stop.

"We're here at last!" Tom cheered.

"Why are you so happy? I thought you were against making this move," Tim teased him.

"I was -- or I am against leaving Virginia, but all the traveling wore me out. I know all of you, and especially Galena, are tired. Since we had to make the move, yes, I'm excited to be here."

Herb had left one of the cars at the airport. A man, who worked with him, would come with another car and bring the luggage to the. Galena and her family rode gratefully to their new home.

Delighted to have his family with him, Herb proudly showed them the house he had purchased. "The porch was a short one across the front, but I had it extended all around this side. This way if anyone has dirty shoes, they can come in the kitchen and leave the dirt outside. Later I'm enclosing it to make a mud room,"

"Dad, you're so smart," Anna hugged him.

"If that were Tom making up to you, Dad, I'd say he thought he was in trouble, but Anna doesn't get into trouble," Tim teased.

Herb quickly reached out and grabbed Tim around the back of his neck. "Smarty, but oh, how glad I am that you're here. Come on, everyone. See the rest of the house. The kitchen then a dining room and into the living room. There is a half bath by the kitchen. Down this hall we have four bedrooms and two bathrooms. I had a bedroom and a bathroom added. At the back is a storage shed. Outside of the kitchen is a concrete pad that I had laid for the vehicles to be parked. I'll enclose it before winter hits us."

Irene had silently followed, looking at her new home. "Herb, I think it's wonderful. You're to be congratulated. It's beautiful; not as large as our home in Virginia, but it's great and all on one floor. Hooray! No more stairs to climb. Thank you, dear."

He smiled and placed an arm across her shoulders. "You can leave these hard-wood floors as they are or order carpet. If you're going to order, or change anything, do it soon. Winter hits quickly here and it is almost impossible to get anything delivered."

"Why don't we leave the floors as they are for a while. We'll use scatter rugs and potted plants to dress up the rooms. Where can I buy potted plants, Herb?"

He laughed. "I'm afraid you'll have trouble with house plants. You can talk to some of your neighbor ladies and ask them. Who wants to ride around with me and see the town?"

Everyone laughed when Galena barked and ran toward the door before any of them could speak. They all piled in the car and toured the town.

"Hey, Dad. Everybody seems to know you. They're sure friendly. I think everybody we've seen has waved and grinned," Tim observed.

"Yes, all the people depend on each other to survive. The town becomes like one big family. You'll see. You'll fit right in."

They went to Fat Freddies for dinner and the Jackson family was impressed with the people who came to welcome them and offer help when needed. They went home and happily prepared for bed.

CHAPTER ELEVEN

The children in the neighborhood were enthused with Galena. Some had dogs as pets but all the dogs were working breeds and none had the personality that Galena did.

After they had been there two days, the Jackson family visited Jon and Marie Kalvinchaki who had a large vegetable garden on the coast. Herb wanted his family to see the size of the vegetables.

"Holy cow! Look at this!" Tim yelled. "This head of cabbage is bigger than my head."

'Sure, pinhead. Anything is bigger than your head; your brain that is," Tom couldn't keep from teasing. "You're right though. All the vegetables are much bigger than we're used to seeing. Hey. What is this?"

"Rhubarb," Jon chuckled. "Where you come from rhubarb is about eight or ten inches long with little green leaves. Here they are almost two feet long and over a foot broad." He then explained about the warm water currents that ran by the coastline and helped vegetation grow well. The Jacksons enjoyed meeting the Kalvinchakis and seeing their home and garden. They drove around sightseeing.

Summer in Nome was not too different than spring in Virginia. The average temperature was from 55 to 70. The family quickly met most of the people in town and liked everyone. Even though they met many children from several states, the biggest thrill was in meeting real Eskimo and a few Indian children known as First People.

They were shocked to discover that there were over one hundred different tribes represented in Alaska, the major one being Inupiat. Their research had shown lots of Indians on the eastern part of Alaska around Fairbanks, but few in or around Nome.

One day Anna was lethargically cleaning house and day dreaming. Irene bustled into the room arranging flowers. "Are you okay, darling?"

"Sure, Mom. Why do you ask?"

"When I came in you were so wrapped in your thoughts that you appeared to be -- kind of sad."

"Oh, no, Mom. Not sad. Just thinking of school, new friends and well--"

"Are you still worrying about all that?"

"Not really. Well, yes, some. The kids here already have friends, know the teachers and are secure in their life."

"That's enough, Anna," Irene said firmly. "We've been over this adnauseam. You are a top honor roll student and you've always been popular and well liked by teachers and lots of friends. I have a lot of faith that you'll do well and be happy. Just wait and see."

"You're prejudiced, Mom," she laughed. "I know I'll have stiff competition. The ones I've met are intelligent and popular."

"Don't be silly," Irene chuckled. "I've heard you say many times that stiff competition drives you to do better and it's stimulating to you. A good challenge is right up your alley."

"Okay, okay, Mom," she laughed. "Would it be better if I whistled while I work?"

"Ho, ho. Remember what your grandmother Morrison used to say. "A whistling women and a crowing hen never come to a good end.""

"That's nonsense," Anna giggled. "I always wondered what she meant by that. A crowing he," she said with a huff.

"The old folks were superstitious. Sometimes, no one knows why, a hen would crow. They believed she was announcing bad luck, so, they hurriedly twisted her neck and made chicken and dumplings, thinking that would eliminate any bad luck. Too, in those days, a young lady would never think of whistling. That was too mannish.""

Putting their arms around each other's waist, they laughed and walked into the kitchen to start dinner.

The remainder of the summer passed too quickly for the twins and Anna. Time for school. August twenty-eighth was the first day for students. Eighth grade for the twins and tenth for Anna. It was slightly cooler than it would be in Virginia.

During the summer the twins were delighted to learn how the natives used to hunt and fish. A few still hunted in the old ways. Both boys had become skilled in paddling kayaks and canoes. Anna had loved learning to cook with native foods and to decorate with natural items. The three children learned that people are basically the same wherever they are.

Tom and Tim met lots of children that they liked. Four boys had become their best friends and the six of them were inseparable. Two Eskimo boys, Benjamin Oakno Eskise and Samuel Motado Cramus lived near the Jacksons. Two Indian boys, Alan Brave Bear Tormas and Charles Running Horse

Berrea lived near enough so that it was no trouble to get together.

Benjamin, Samuel, Alan and Charles were all pretty much the same height (five-three) and weight ( ). All had coal-black hair and black eyes. Benjamin was a couple of inches taller but no heavier. Samuel had a small scar on his forehead from a sled accident. They were all pure boy, full of vim and vigor. They were all a few months younger than the twins, but the six boys had built a solid friendship.

One day, while walking around town together, Tom stopped and pointed excitedly. "Hey! Will you look at that! Someone is building a house out of wood and in the shape of an igloo on stilts. The house is round."

Ben turned to see what Tom had seen. "Yes, you'll want to see this for sure, but we can't get too close. We might get in the way and the workers have such a short time they can work outside that time does count. They work many hours when they can."

Charlie took up the explanation. "Don't forget that everything has to be shipped in which makes materials very expensive. Our climate doesn't allow trees to grow so we don't have natural wood for building. Shipping adds to the cost and construction crews have to charge what their service is worth. A house like this will cost a minimum of three hundred thousand."

"Gee, I just didn't think about it." Tim was impressed. "Is that why food is so expensive because a lot of it has to be shipped in."

"That's true," San answered. "Six dollars for a gallon of milk, five dollars for a loaf of bread, five dollars for a dozen eggs and fruit is very, very expensive."

"You have to remember that we were born here and have lived here all our lives, so, it nothing unusual to us," Alan added.

"We'd better get home," Tom interrupted, looking at his watch. "Galena was upset that we left without her and she'll need to go for a run."

"Your family takes better care of that dog than a lot of people do their children," Ben observed. "I don't blame you. She is a sweetheart, and, you'll have to admit, a little spoiled."

"Race you," Alan yelled and took off running with five boys close on his heels.

The weather gradually became colder. There was now about six hours of sunlight during the day. Icy ground and snow made it difficult to get around except for short distances on foot. Dog sleds were used daily. School, work, worship services and community gatherings were the only places people could be found.

Anna and the twins walked together to school. Anna left the twins in one wing and went to another side of the building for her classes.

The four best friends got a charge out of Tom and Tim learning to walk on snowshoes and waddle along in heavy clothes without tipping over. The six boys began to walk together with Galena herding them along and then returning home after she saw them safely in school. She was waiting outside every afternoon for them to walk them home. All the children learned to love Galena. She seemed to be more "in tune" with humans than the average dog.

The people in the community were drawing closer together in friendship and in caring about what happened to each other.

Police Chief Causuc Houmay really took getting used to. He was not unfriendly, but was not friendly to the majority of people. It was clearly evident that he didn't care for animals, especially pets. He was about five-eleven, stocky build, with black hair and black eyes. He rarely smiled. Tom told his family that the way the Chief look at him made it look as if the Chief had X-ray vision. "Dad, he's the biggest grouch. Galena only walked toward him to greet him, like she does everyone, and he actually screamed."

"He jumped back as if she were a snake striking," Tim laughed.

"Yeah," Tom laughed loudly, "we couldn't keep from laughing and he chased us."

"Boys, I'm ashamed of you. Didn't you stop to think that maybe, when he was little, a dog bit him and that makes him afraid?"

"We thought of it on the way home, but it was too late then to say anything to him," Tim explained.

"Well, it would be nice if you would apologize to the Chief. At least don't take Galena near him again," Herb reasoned with them. "Do be respectfully to the Chief. Try to be compassionate and friendly with him, and maybe you'll win his trust. He might have personal problems that people don't know about. Never be quick to judge people until you know more about them. Remember the Indian saying,

"Never judge a person until you've walked a mile in their moccasins."

"What does that mean, Dad?"

"Just what I said. You need to get to know a person and what their life is really like and try to understand them."

Irene opened her day care center and thoroughly enjoyed the younger children. They loved her, not only because she was kind to them and played with them, but she made up stories putting their names in as characters and encouraged them to make up and write their own stories. She also taught them to appreciate art.

One day they would pull fresh cooked taffy. After rubbing their hands with butter so the candy would not stick, they would pair up and laugh and pull; then eat and enjoy. Another day they would make salt maps, wait for them to thoroughly dry, then color them. At another time a child would lie down on a big sheet of butcher paper and a buddy would draw all around their form. The buddy would then draw in the face and clothing. They made snow ice cream and snow angels as well as snow people. Irene took notes to write a book for children and Anna drew whimsical pictures.

One morning in October, the clouds were heavy and threatening. Big, soft flakes of snow began to fall on what was already there as the children got ready for school.

Irene called to the twins, "Boys, bring Galena back to the house. It's too dangerous for her to be out in this storm. She's still not accustomed to being out in this weather. I know she'll be disappointed, but it's safer for her to remain inside."

"Aw, Mom. She'll think we don't love her anymore," Tom grumbled.

"She'll be all right after you leave. Bring her back in and go."

Galena protested, but they brought her back inside. She howled loudly as the boys shut the door and left. Ben and Sam were waiting for them in front of the house. The twins ran to join their friends. Alan and Charlie joined them at the end of the street. The six boys ran joyously and enjoyed the falling snow in spite of the fact that it meant problems for adult workers.

Irene put Galena in the twins' room until she could stop wailing. She howled and threw herself against the door until Irene finally let her out for fear she would injure herself.

"Heigh ho!" Tom proclaimed while trying to turn flips while wearing his snowshoes. He landed on his back with a thud which was hysterical for the others. "Now we can learn to drive a dogsled. Do you think Galena can learn to pull us? She used to pull us on our skateboard in Virginia."

"I don't think so," Tim said slowly. "She hasn't been trained to pull weight and the weather is much colder here which makes it more difficult for the lungs to breathe. Besides, she's too old."

"Hey, listen. I know something we can do and you'll like it," Ben attempted to console Tom. "We'll teach you ice fishing."

"Wow! Cool!" Tom was excited. "When can we go? What equipment do we need? What do you mean, ice fishing?"

"It isn't hard," Sam spoke. "First you dress warmly. Then you get a fishing pole and a bucket."

"Okay, old man," Charlie teased. "You're taking too long. What you do is cut a hole in the ice, sit down and prepare to have a cold seat, drop your line through the hole and wait --- and wait."

"You wanta know the truth?" Tim frowned. "It sounds boring and very cold."

"Well, we can go walrus hunting on the ice flows," Ben boasted.

"No way," Sam said quickly. "That's too dangerous. My dad is a grown man and he'd never go after walrus without several adults with him. Grown men go together and carry guns to protect each other. The bull walrus is aggressive and dangerous. It doesn't take much to cause him to attack. They are very strong. Just hope one doesn't fall on you. Too, they have those big tusks."

"Yeah," Alan added. "The males, bulls, can weigh over three thousand pounds and be ten to twelve feet long. A cow can weigh a little over two thousand pounds and are eight to nine feet long. A calf usually weighs one hundred eighty-seven pounds when born. So you see how dangerous they can be. Let's plan things to do that we know we'll be given permission to do. That way we won't get in trouble with our parents and we'll enjoy it more."

The twins grew tired fighting their way through the rapidly falling snow and strong winds. It took them longer to walk to school. Hearing a strange noise behind them they whirled with their hearts in their throats. What was it? Was it something attacking them? Was it a wolf? A polar bear? What? They were so frightened they could hardly breathe.

Squinting through the darkening snow, they saw a shape jumping high through the deep snow and running toward them.

"Galena!" All six boys bellowed as one with relief.

"Oh, no. Now we're in trouble with mom," Tom groaned.

"It's not our fault," Tim protested. "We did take her back to the house. How in the blue blazes did she get out?" their friends thought it was funny and all hugged Galena praising her with, "Good girl."

Tim tried to sound stern while pointing to the house. "Go home, Galena." She looked as if she were grinning at them, but she turned to trot away, looking back over her shoulder in hopes they would call her back. The last they saw of Galena was her tail wagging like a conquering banner as she bounded through the snow.

CHAPTER TWELVE

The weather was too bad for outdoor play and everyone couldn't use the gym at the same time. Tim asked the teacher if they could teach spelling baseball. She agreed and Tom decided to pitch while Tim kept score.

"I'll explain the game," Tom started. "The class will divide into two teams. I guess the fair way is for everyone to write their name on a scrap of paper. First choose two captains. The captains can then take turns drawing names. That way no one will feel that they were chosen, or not chosen, for personal reasons. We'll set certain parts of the room as bases."

Tim continued the instructions. "One team at a time will play. Tom will pitch a word to the first player. If the player spells the word correctly, he or she will then go to stand on first base and the second player steps up to the plate. If the word is spelled correctly, that player will go to first and the one on first goes to the second base. If the word is misspelled, the player sits down and that's one out. Three outs and the team sits down and gives the next team a turn. To score, a player must advance all the way around and back to home plate. Any questions?" After both teams have a turn, that's an inning."

"What happens if a speller doesn't get a chance to spell in the first inning?" Jimmy Lone Eagle asked.

"The same in real baseball. The next player, whose turn it is to spell, would step up to the plate and proceed as those before. We can decide on three innings."

The teacher enjoyed the game as much as her students did. She clapped and thanked them. "That was delightful. How would you like to teach other rooms to play and then we can challenge each other. Two strong teams can be selected to demonstrate for the parents at the next parent day."

"Can we play it every day?" Anita Cumberland was enthused.

"I'm afraid you'd get bored and not like it if you played too often. How about once a week? Maybe on Fridays." The teacher suggested. The class grumbled but agreed.

Snow fell heavily all morning. By noon the sky was dark and the thick snow made it difficult to see more than a couple of feet. School was dismissed early. Anna came to walk home with her brothers.

"Jim Garrison gave me a rope," she explained. I'm to tie it around my waist and around you boys. That way we won't get separated and lost. It's dangerous to not stay together." She looked at the four friends of her brothers. "I'm sorry. There's not enough rope, but if each of you will hold on to one of us, we should all right." Struggling through the snow and screaming wind, made it difficult to even breathe. Their scarves were wrapped around their faces except for their eyes.

The group was grateful to finally reach their homes. They were all tired and hungry. "Galena, we're home," Tim called as soon as he could get out of his heavy clothes. "Galena, where are you?" No dear dog. Why hadn't she run to meet them as she usually did?

"I bet she's under the bed asleep," Tom reasoned. "I'm so glad she's in where she's safe and warm." He shivered as he took the last of his cold, damp outdoor clothing off.

Irene was in the kitchen. She placed a grilled cheese sandwich and a bowl of tomato soup in front of her three children. A plate of fresh-baked cookies waited at the end of the table.

"Thanks loads, Mom," Anna sighed.

"Mom, you're the greatest." Tim hugged her thankfully.

"Words have not been invented that say how marvelous and how appreciated you are," Tom didn't want Tim to outdo him. "I sure am glad you didn't let ole Galena out. The snow and cold are murder. Where is she? Here, girl. We're home, Galena."

There was a strange silence as Irene turned slowly from the sink to face them. Icy tingles ran up their spines when they saw the expression on her face. "I hoped she was with you since she ran out of here." She spoke softly in the stunned silence.

"Galena demanded to be let out when she heard some younger children outside. I kept her in, but when Mrs. Parsons came in, a little before twelve, she was slow getting in. Galena took advantage of it and charged out before I could stop her. I thought she'd come to meet you."

Four pairs of eyes turned to the kitchen clock showing five minutes before two. The twins sat with tear-filled eyes while Anna ran to the door to call for the dog. The cold fury of the biting wind drove her voice back forcing her to give up and shut the door.

"Don't even think of putting on those clothes," Irene ordered as the twins ran to their outdoor wear. "You absolutely will not go out again."

They were all feeling miserable and wondering what could be done when Herb stumbled in frozen and hungry. He had to lean firmly against the door to get it shut.

"Dad," Anna ran to him sobbing. "Galena is out there and we don't know where she is. She's been gone all afternoon. Dad! Do something."

"Mom won't let us go out and look for her," Tom wailed. "We can't just sit here and do nothing."

Irene put her arm around Anna. "Honey, dad has to get some hot food in

him and warm up. We can't risk a human life out there even for Galena."

"Mom!" all three children shrieked.

"Galena is one of the family. We brought her all these thousands of miles away from the comfort and security of the only home she's ever known and now something horrible has happened to her. Don't you care?" Tom cried.

"Would you be this calm and say all that stuff if Tom or Anna, or me, were lost out there?" Tim choked.

"Children, don't you dare talk to your mother like that. Of course she's as worried as you are." Herb stood up and hugged his wife. "Sweetheart. They're upset. Let me finish eating and warm up a little and I'll see what can be done."

Herb called other families in his work crew. "Galena is missing. Please watch for her and pass the word along so others will be on the alert, also. She'll need shelter for sure. Let me know as soon as you see her or even if someone thinks they've seen her. Thanks a lot. I'm going out to look as much as I can."

Eleven men braved the storm to help in the search, but it was too cold and dangerous to be out long. Each called for Galena, but the cold wind swallowed their voices. Word quickly spread through the entire town.

Two miserable days passed slowly. The third morning Anna opened her eyes to darkness. She knew the sun would not peep through until nearly noon. Thankfully it had stopped snowing, but was still bitter cold. There was an eerie stillness in the air. The twins bounded out of bed eager to search for their dog. Several days turned into weeks while friends and classmates helped search. A couple of bush planes went over the area as much as they could safely fly.

Chief Houmay growled. "It's stupid to go to all this trouble for a no account dog. She's probably been killed and eaten by now by a wolf pack or a polar bear." All of the children thought he was cruel and insensitive.

"Stupid jerk," Tom snarled.

"Ignorant heathen," Tim followed Tom to go to the Chief. Herb saw them and immediately ordered them to come to him.

"Come here this instant. You're not going to help the situation by being rude to the Chief. No one agrees with him, so just ignore it and go home."

The twins reluctantly struggled home, weary, heart-broken and unable to eat or sleep. Listlessly they showered, brushed their teeth and prayed.

"Dear Lord, protect Galena. Keep her safe and help her find a warm place to go and something to eat. Bring her back home to us soon."

So many weeks went by, the Jacksons almost lost hope. Anna, Tom and Tim went to school with heavy hearts and didn't feel like doing the excellent work they usually did.

CHAPTER THIRTEEN

"Hey, Herb," Ben Gregory called to him at a work site. "I could have sworn I saw Galena with three wolves last night. I called her name and she stopped to look at me. One of the wolves circled back and pushed her on. She trotted off after them but she did look back once and hesitated."

"I was afraid of that. Even though she was raised from a weanling by us, her ancestors were wolves. It's only natural that they might be drawn together. I hope, for the children's sake, that she'll not forget us and will make her way back home. Thanks for letting me know. Do me a favor. Don't mention this to anyone else. I don't want my family to raise false hope. You know how upset they are."

"Sure. I understand."

Although school was out for the holidays, the Jackson children were too sad to think about tomorrow being Thanksgiving. During the night Tom awakened thinking he heard a baby crying. He frowned and snuggled deeper under the warm covers. Suddenly he shouted as he jumped out of bed and went flying to the front door. He could hear now that the scratching and whining could mean only one thing.

"Galena!" He shouted so loudly that the entire family came running. Tom opened the door to be knocked down by a wet bundle of cold fur licking his face and wriggling all over. They all kissed and hugged her not minding that they were getting damp and cold. She was so happy giving doggy kisses on each face. Herb had to stop the twins from calling friends with the good news at three in the morning.

What a wonderful, marvelous, scrumdunktious Thanksgiving. When the blessing was asked at the dinner table, each one had things for which they were thankful, the main one being that Galena was home.

Two weeks passed. One day after school the twins rushed home to show that each had made an A on both Geometry and Science tests.

"Mom! Come see what we have. Where's Galena?" Funny, but Tom could never seem to use an indoor voice when he was excited. "I sure am glad she stayed in where it's warm and she's safe. I'd have a heart attack if she got lost again," Tom spoke through chattering teeth.

Irene smiled and motioned for them to follow her quietly. They went into the kitchen where she pointed to a pile of old towels and a small rug in the corner. Galena lay there, grinning at them, while her tail drummed a happy tune. By her stomach were two little balls of silver and grey. One was a fat little character trying to root around to nurse. Their eyes were not open. With trembling knees, the three walked closer and almost reverently knelt to gaze in wonder.

"Galena must have mated with a wolf during the time she was lost. I'm surprised she even tried. She's too old to have little ones, so we must be extra careful with her." Irena looked lovingly at the dogs.

"Two of them," Tim whispered with tears in his eyes.

"There were more, but only two survived. I'm not sure one of these will make it. Don't expect Galena to romp as she has in the past. I want a veterinarian to look at her as soon as possible. Dad will know how to contact a doctor."

No dog was ever cared for with more tenderness and love. During the night the little weak one died. Galena cried as if she were human.

"Oh, Mom. I hope Galena will be okay. Do you think she really is aware that her baby has died?" Anna petted Galena and hugged the tiny remaining baby.

The next morning the twins came rushing into the kitchen then skidded to a stop. "We've been discussing names for the puppies," Tom stated. "Super brain here thought we should name them by the alphabet; like Abaigail, Bianco, Caleb, and so forth. Isn't that a riot?" He finished dropping to a chair slapping his thigh and laughing loudly at Tim.

"Attention," Anna said firmly. "Have you noticed that there is only one baby now? The weaker one died during the night."

"Oh, no," the twins chorused. "Mom, is this one going to die? Will Galena live?" Tom was almost crying.

"I don't know. Galena **is** old and was out in the blizzard a long time. We don't know if she got enough to eat or whether she picked up bacteria of some kind from the wild animals. This is the wrong time of year for her to have babies and ----" Irene sighed, "the baby looks strong enough to survive, but we'll just have to wait and see."

"Maybe we shouldn't handle the baby until she's bigger and her eyes are open," Tim reasoned.

"That an excellent idea," Irene agreed with him. "In the meantime, give Galena your usual love and attention. We need to see what a veterinarian has to say."

Tom jumped up and ran to the phone. "Dad! Only one of the babies has lived and Galena needs a veterinarian as soon as possible. Do you know where we can get one? Right now!" He said all this on one breath.

Irene took the phone. "Herb, I'm sorry we're bothering you at work. We'll talk about this when you get home tonight. Take care. Get home safely."

"Mom! Why did you hang up? We need to get Galena and the baby checked before it's too late," Tom almost cried.

"Tom, I'm not sure there's a veterinarian in Nome. We may have to wait until one can fly in. We'll get something done when dad gets home."

"We're in luck," Herb called as he walked in the door. "Mr. Durango has his veterinarian on call and the doctor flew in yesterday to check the sled dogs. He said he would come by tonight and give Galena a check-up. Yes, I know, in Virginia we would have had her in an animal hospital long before this, but we're doing the best we can."

Tim sat on the floor and encouraged Galena to lay her head in his lap. "Galena's going to be fine. We love her so much that nothing can happen to her."

After supper there was a knock at the door. Herb answered the door and came back with a tall, good-looking Indian. "This is Doctor Condova. He's going to check the dogs. We can't thank him enough."

"Hi, folks. I sure am glad to meet you and I'm real glad to meet this nice girl." He squatted down to talk to Galena. "I've heard a lot about you ole girl. You have a huge fan club in town. Let's see what's going on. By the way," he said to the family, "my name is Matthew. Most folks call me Matt."

He reached toward the baby and Galena immediately growled and hunched over her baby.

"Calm down, little lady," Matt said soothingly. "I won't hurt your baby. What a pretty baby. Let's forget the little one for a while and check you out. Maybe then you'll let me see your baby." He calmly touched Galena and moved slowly so she wouldn't feel threatened.

"Other than her age, she seems to be doing fine. You've taken excellent care of her. Of course you understand she's been through unusual events." He looked up at Anna. "Maybe if you picked up the baby and handed her to me the mother would be more accepting."

Anna picked up the baby and handed her to Matt. Galena watched carefully and even stood up to look closely. "This is a healthy little girl. I think she and her mother will both be fine."

"Galena is all right, isn't she," Tom was worried.

"Galena's fine. She won't have more babies though. I'm shocked she had this litter. I don't want to worry you needlessly, but you need to hear the truth. Even though she's fine now, she's too old and this may cause her life span to be shorter."

"We love her so much she'll be strong," Tim assured him.

"Strong, sincere love has been known to work miracles for both people and animals. I'm sure you'll take good care of her." He stood up.

Herb shook hands with the doctor. "How much do I owe you, Matt? We can never pay you enough. I wasn't sure how to get in touch with a veterinarian. You've given us hope and we appreciate you coming out in this weather and this late at night."

"When you've lived her for a while, you'll find it easier to travel in bad weather and at night. You don't owe me anything. I was in town anyway. It's my pleasure to meet all of you."

Irene offered him a hot drink and even food, but he declined. They each thanked him and told him he would be welcome in their home whenever he was in town.

Christmas is going to be the best ever," Tim sang out. "Something special has happened at all the holidays since we came to Alaska. I'm glad I've been keeping a journal. What great memories we'll have to share with everyone back home."

All thirty-seven of the children in town helped to decorate the ten feet tall tree in the Community Center. Several juicy, plump turkeys were furnished by the government to their workers. Each family brought a covered dish, a dessert or bread and they all shared. Herb, Ben Gregory, Dan Eskise and Juan Berrea worked in the kitchen doing most of the cooking that was necessary. They had cleaned, stuffed and baked the turkeys. Irene and some of the women prepared coffee, hot spice tea and hot chocolate.

The elementary school children had made the decorations for the windows, doors and walls. Even the ceiling had long ribbons hanging with dangling decorations. Three long tables were set up in front of the kitchen window to hold the dishes of food that everyone had prepared. The twins helped when other long tables were set up with white paper covering and folding chairs placed for people to sit while they were eating.

"I don't know when we've had such a great Christmas. We miss relatives and friends in Virginia, but you folks have become so dear to us that we are like one big happy family," Herb spoke. "Thank you for making us feel so welcome and taking us to your hearts. Regardless of how long we'll live here, or where we'll go after we leave, all of you will be in our hearts."

"It was a blessing to us when your family came here," Jed McKinley stood to be heard. "You have made us feel important to you and we're all working together better than we ever have."

"Yes! Yes!" the crowd roared and cheered.

"I see Santa has left some early presents under the tree. My goodness. Look at this. It says this is a present for Seneca Brownley," Mr. Eskise said.

The children were jubilant as gifts were given to every child ten and under.

The high school glee club entertained with song and skits. The evening ended with everyone singing carols. Pastor Orus Jabeway read the Christmas story from the Bible and prayed a dismissal. Everyone was reluctant to leave, but it was getting late.

Outside, even though it hurt the lungs to draw a deep breath in the cold air, most of the people paused to look at the sky with bright stars and snow glistening like jewels in the moonlight.

"I feel as if I'm inside a beautiful Thomas Kinkade painting," Tim said softly with awe.

CHAPTER FOURTEEN

Everyone referred to Galena's pup as 'the baby'. One day, late in February, Anna cuddled the three and a half month old chubby puppy who was busy giving her puppy kisses. In the kitchen, after breakfast, Irene was wiping the table while the twins sat on chairs stretched out as if they were lounge chairs. The backs of their necks were on the back of the chairs.

Stepping over Tom's long legs, Irene chuckled. 'Good grief. I do believe you boys have grown a foot since we moved here. You're already much taller than I am." The twins laughed delightedly.

"It's past time we gave this little scamp a name," Anna spoke. "We shouldn't keep on calling her Baby. She deserves a name of her own. Maybe we could call her Stormy because she was born during a blizzard."

"No," Tom laughed, "Butterball would be a better name for the tubby tummy."

"A name is important and should mean something," Irene remarked. "Think about it and we'll have a family council to discuss a name."

The twins grabbed down-filled coats and fur lined boots and ran out the back door calling that hey were going ice fishing. They had been warned by their parents, and by neighbors, about thin ice. Everyone cautioned that they should have an experienced adult with them. Polar bears had been sighted nearby. These animals could run fast it would not be easy to get away if the boys wandered into an area where the bears were searching for food.

"I sure enjoyed the package we got from Mrs. Berry and our friends in Fairfax. She sure has been nice to include notes from our friends in her letters to us." Tim talked as he struggled to walk upright on the slick path.

"Yeah. Jimmy Dodd is staying on the top honor roll and Mark's grandfather from Scotland is visiting. That's super. The Sloans have a new baby girl. Have you ever thought how it would be to not be the youngest? I wonder if our parents will ever have another baby?" Tom mulled quietly.

"I guess we'll stay the youngest. Mom and dad are probably afraid they'd get another one like us," Tim laughed.

They wandered down to the edge of the ice-covered water behind the grocery store and looked over to an ice island. They couldn't see Mr. Merkle who owned the store, therefore, he couldn't see them.

"Hey, there's a canoe. The ice is thin here beside the shore. We can break through it. Let's paddle over to that ice float," Tom was enthused

"Oh, no. We're not supposed to do that. You know better," Tim answered with a stern look. "Further more, it's not our canoe."

"We're in sight of the store and any adult could see us," Tom spoke indignantly. "Come on. Don't be a chicken. I'm going even if you won't."

Tim hesitated. "Well --- maybe. I can't let you go alone. Promise you'll just go out and then straight back. Okay?"

"Sure. Sure." tom gleefully stepped in the canoe.

As they paddled through the icy water and around small ice floats, they pretended to be Arctic explorers. Tim continued to feel badly about disobeying and truly wasn't enjoyed the adventure. They left the canoe tied to a big ice ball and Tom persuaded Tim to walk on the ice with him.

In the distance they could hear walrus bellows. Creeping closer they pecked around a mound of ice and came face to face with a big, angry bull walrus. He charged at them so fiercely they tripped over their own feet running away.

Intending to jump into the canoe, Tom gave a mighty leap and landed in the icy water. Tim got in the canoe and leaned over to pull Tom out. Frightened, Tom grabbed Tim and, in the blink of an eye, both boys were in the water. They knew they would die quickly from hypothermia if they didn't get help immediately. They each had enough breath for one big scream.

Irene opened the backdoor to set out a garbage pail. Galena's head jerked up and she lunged at the kitchen door just as Irene shut it. Galena clawed frantically at the door and howled as if her heart would break. The puppy attempted to hide in fright because he'd never heard her mother like this. Galena kept throwing herself against the door and screaming.

Hurrying to let Galena out Irene scolded, "All right already. Sheesh. If you have to go that badly, let me open the door before you break it down."

Galena rushed out so quickly that Irene stepped out on the porch to see Galena down at the water's edge still howling and looking out over the water. Several men ran from the store when they recognized the fright and urgency in Galena's voice. With a sinking heart Irene could see faintly in the distance what she knew were her boys.

A man ran by her into her house to grab the phone and call for help. None of them saw the brave, faithful dog plunge into the icy water and strike out swimming to her beloved boys. Men were running to get power boats.

Galena reached the ice island and pushed Tim up on the ice with her head. Tim was numb and almost unconscious. Galena tried to push the now unconscious Tom up but she was too numb. The men reached them just in time to get all three to safety. Five minutes more and all three would have been dead from hypothermia.

Anna briskly rubbed Galena dry and wrapped her in heated blankets. She was fed warm milk and warm wet food and placed on a bed with a hot water bottle beside her. That corner of the kitchen belonged to Galena. Anna insisted on staying up until midnight that night to keep Galena company. She whined a lot but finally went to sleep.

In the meantime the twins had been lowered into warm water by the paramedics and the heat was gradually increased. Dry and wrapped in heated blankets, they were given hot soup and tucked into bed.

The next morning the twins awakened to hear Anna sobbing loudly. They got up and made their wobbly way to the kitchen. Anna was cuddling the puppy and sobbing as if her heart would break.

Irene and Herb stood with arms around each other and both were crying.

They each reached to hug one of the boys. Fearfully the boys looked in the corner to see the still form of Galena lying peacefully on her favorite quilt. Brave, faithful Galena had given her life in her efforts to save the boys she loved.

"It's all your fault, Tom," Tim sobbed in anguish. "You killed her and almost killed both of us."

Herb spoke quietly, "No, Tim. You'll both have to take equal blame since the episode yesterday caused her death. Be kind to each other. We're all suffering the loss of a dear friend. Being cruel to each other will not bring Galena back."

"Children," Irene spoke softly. "Galena was old and we've had her for a long time. Having babies weakened her and then the swim in the icy water was too much for her weakened condition. We'll hold on to the beautiful memories and be thankful she was a part of our family. Too, she left us something of herself in this precious little girl."

The community grieved with the family. Galena had won a place in each of their hearts with her gentleness, her bravery and her love for people. All of the children insisted on a people type funeral for Galena. The ground was still too frozen to dig a grave, so, she was cremated and her ashes kept in a beautiful urn. A Royal Canadian Mounted Patrolman played Amazing Grace on the bagpipes while the children held hands and cried.

Two days later the house was still dark with grief. "Tim, do you till blame me?" Tom asked, his head hanging down with a miserable expression on his face.

Tim thought a moment. "No. Not really. I'm sorry that I made you feel worse. All of us have been heartbroken. I know you loved her as much as I did. Friends, back in

Virginia, are going to be sad, also. We need to write and tell them."

The four boys, who were close friends of the twins, had a color picture of Galena enlarged and framed. By special request the picture was hung in a place of honor in the Community Center for a few weeks.

In April, for Anna's sixteenth birthday, Irene got permission to have a pajama party on a Saturday evening in the Community Center. She learned that three other girls had birthdays during the same week.

"Darling, I have something to ask you." Irene spoke to Anna after school one day. "I learned today that Judy Wampus, Deena Leminus and Shoopo Gormas also have birthdays this week. Would you be agreeable to include them in the party? Their families will have gifts for them, but I think it would be nice to share."

"What a super idea, Mom. I think it would be colossal. Have you talked to their parents?"

"No. I wanted to talk to you first. Maybe you would like to call them and invite them to share with you."

'Sure, Mom." Anna excitedly made the calls and was delighted that each of the girls was surprised and pleased to be included.

On Saturday morning, Anna, Shoopo, Deena and Judy met in the Jackson kitchen to cook delicious food and great desserts. They talked and giggled and shared memories of previous parties.

Fourteen teen girls and five mothers spent the night in the Center. They ate, line danced, sang, played games and had a fantastic time. Others had provided a variety of snacks, so, there was no shortage of food. Each girl had brought a sleeping bag and a pillow. Needless to say, there was little sleeping. They all rushed the next morning to get to church on time.

"Poor Baby." People continued to call her as they petted the puppy. Not realizing what had happened, she was thrilled with the attention. Pretending to growl fiercely, she chewed on shoes, clothing and even fingers.

"Poor wee one," a neighbor sighed as she cuddled the puppy.

Anna kissed the top of the fuzzy little head and said, "Call her Greatheart. Her mother was so brave and had such a great heart. I just know she's going to be as dear to us as her mother was."

At last the puppy had a name. Would she be a family member and be as faithful as her mother had been? After all, she was half wolf. Would she be loving and brave?

Dangerous Hilarity

PART II
GREATHEART

Dangerous Hilarity

CHAPTER FIFTEEN

"Oh, don't stop. That feels so good. I am so happy. I do love you." Greatheart seemed to be saying a she wriggled and whined with pleasure, looking at Tim with eyes full of love. He was rubbing her tummy and tickling in just the right spots. He then gave her neck and back a massage.

In May, the twins had their fourteenth birthday. Greatheart was almost six months old. While the twins were happily planning what they wanted to do, Herb was planning a surprise for them.

"I would love to do so many things, I can't decide which is the most important," Tim spoke thoughtfully.

"Dad can't top the one last year when he took twenty of us on a bus trip around Washington, D.C." Tom slumped in a lounge chair and began to daydream about that wonderful trip.

"Hey, Anna," Tim called as she came down the hall preparing to leave the house. She hurried into the living room. "Anna, do you know what dad and mom are planning for our birthday?"

"Sorry, dear brothers of mine. I haven't a clue. What makes you think they're planning anything? After all, we've had a lot of expense with our trip out here and it took a lot of money to buy this house and two car and all that we have needed. They might just think all you need is a special dinner and a cake," she turned and smiled as she went on out.

"Bad news," Tom worried. "Do you think that's all it'll be? Dad has always done special things for all of us."

"Look at it this way, "Tim answered. "We need to count our blessings. We're getting big enough that we don't need a treat of any kind. Just be thankful we have the family we do. We have lots of good friends and, above all, we have the best dog in the world." Tim wrestled Greatheart on the floor.

"Boys," Irene called, "please come help me. I'm going to clean house thoroughly today and I need muscle."

Tom was ready to complain, but Tim reminded him that they should be thankful for the family they have. The twins worked industriously, if not eagerly, and before long the house looked as if it could be in a magazine.

The four of them worked hard with only a small break for sandwiches and hot chocolate at lunch.

When Herb came home that night, Irene met him with a hug and a big smile. "I want you to know that we have the best children in the world," she bragged.

"Tell me something I don't know. I've known that for many years." Herb grinned as he hung up his coat and prepared to settle down after a long day of exhausting work. "Is there something special I missed?" Irene explained how they had helped her all day, she and Anna cleaning and the twins moving furniture.

As Herb hugged each of his children, he said with a solemn face, "I guess they've earned their trip."

"Trip! What trip?" As usual Tom was the one shouting.

"Ooooo, lower the volume," Anna giggled with hands over her ears.

"I'm not sure you'd be interested. Nah. I don't think you'd care to know," Herb teased as he placed an arm around Irene and walked into the dining room.

Tom was on his heels, full of questions, but Tim held him back. "Cool it, man," Tim whispered. "We'll know soon enough. Dad's teasing. Let's don't play his game and pretend that we don't care to know what he's talking about. We can be as good as he can about this."

"If I can," Tom hissed. "Pinch me if I start to say something I shouldn't."

"I shall be delighted to do that," Tim laughed as they took their seats at the dining table and bowed for the blessing.

Herb looked at Irene with a quizzical expression. She shrugged her shoulders and shook her head. Dinner was eaten with less than usual conversation. As they left the table, each child thanked their mother for preparing a good meal. Herb had taught them to do so at an early age. Each one took dirty dishes to the kitchen and cleared the table. It was the twins turn to wash the dishes and clean the kitchen. Anna took out the garbage.

Later in their bedroom Herb chuckled. "I know they're dying to know what I'm talking about, but the rascals are determined to make me think they don't care."

"Good for them," Irene smiled. "Maybe they're maturing at last. At least they're mature enough to make you squirm."

"Me? Why am I squirming?"

"Because they won't play your little game and beg you to tell them what you're talking about."

"Ha! Well, I can hold out as long as they can," Herb grunted as he crawled into bed. He punched his pillow and flopped back.

A few days later several boys asked the twins if they were coming to the party at the Community Center on the following Saturday. They were whispering in church so more than one adult frowned at them and shook their head. The twins could hardly wait until after church to ask about the party.

"Is it for anyone special?" Tom grinned hopefully.

"Not really. Old man, Garrith, found some gold and said he wanted to give a party to all those who had supported him. He had tried, to quote him, for over forty years and now that he's almost too old to enjoy it, he finds it." Sam laughed. "He's a likeable old fellow though."

The twins left their friends at the gate and walked slowly in the front door. "You thought the party was for us, didn't you?" Tim questioned Tom.

"Yeah, I guess I was hoping. I sure would like to know dad's secret."

"Aw, Tom. Don't you dare let him know you're curious."

The boys walked on into the house and went to their room to change their clothes. After lunch they ran out of the house without thanking their mother as they had been taught.

"Let them go," Irene cautioned Herb. "They're at the age when friends are more important. They haven't forgotten. We've taught them well."

The week passed slowly for the children. The twins were amazed to see so many people coming together to help Mr.

Garrith celebrate. Boisterous children, toys that whirred making strange noises, and bursting balloons made Greatheart so excited that she caused more than one person to trip over her as she ran around barking and jumping in so many directions that it was impossible to dodge her.

The children naturally thought she was lots of fun, but the adults were far from thrilled. Poor Greatheart was finally banished to a tool shed at one end of the building.

The twins, and their friends, were so sad to hear Greatheart howl her displeasure, that they decided to stage a sit -down. After whispering among themselves, there were soon twenty-nine children sitting silently in the middle of the room. Anna was embarrassed at her brothers. Some of the mothers reminded them they were only hurting themselves. They were missing great desserts sitting in the floor.

The women gathered at one end of the room and ignored the children. They were anxious to hear about the book Irene was writing and to ask if they were in it. Irene was pleased to talk about her hobby. The women laughed heartily when Irene told them of some of Tom's escapades.

Herb, and some of the fathers, were annoyed with the children. Herb was especially embarrassed at his sons. After all, he was the boss and most of these men worked for him. To keep from having an unpleasant situation between the men and children, Irene agreed to let Greatheart out of the shed.

After a half hour in the shed she was still howling forlornly. She happily bounced out to immediately knock down some laughing children and to cause a couple of the adults to teeter and totter to keep from falling. "From now on, she stays home," Irene ordered.

Greatheart was fed a disgusting amount of food hidden from the adults. Cake, candy and even soft drinks. Anna was angry when she found the young dog, in the corner, groaning and trying to lay so that her extremely full stomach would not be more uncomfortable than it was. The dog was in agony.

Irene was furious. "Take Greatheart home and make sure she can't get out and follow you back. Put her on the mud porch in case she throws up. And come straight back," she ordered the twins.

Greatheart was hugged, petted and promised a lot of good things for the next day. Frankly she didn't care; she was too full and miserable.

The following week was a school break. Herb called the family together on Saturday night to tell them his secret. He sat silently and grinned at them until the twins landed on him to tickle him and make him talk.

"Okay. Okay. I surrender. Sit down and I'll tell you. Your mother and you three children will be going on a combination vacation trip."

"Combination vacation! What in the world is that?" Tom blurted.

"If you'll be quiet, mush brain, he'll tell us," Tim answered.

"Don't start, boys. I want to know what your dad is telling us. I don't know all of his plans either," Irene told them.

Herb settled back on the couch with an arm around Irene's shoulders. "First, how do you feel about each of you asking one friend to go with you?"

The twins looked startled at each other and then at Anna. "Just one each?" Tom asked anxiously. "That's it?"

"Excuse us a few minutes. Anna would you please come into the kitchen with us?" Tim asked.

Irene and Herb looked puzzled at each other, but waited patiently until their children returned. Meanwhile they watched news, especially the weather. Herb turned the TV off as the children came back and sat on the floor in front of their parents.

"Dad," Anna started, "we've talked it over and decided that we have too many friends to choose just one without hurting other's feelings. We've decided that we get along well and would love to go on a trip with mom. But, aren't you coming?"

"I have to stay and work. Besides I need to stay with our dog."

"Fine. No more interruptions. Speak, O lord and master," Anna giggled.

"Great. Here it is. First you'll fly from Nome to Anchorage. Then you'll board the McKinley Explorer with glass-domed railcars. You'll go through Mt. McKinley National Park and see animals you've only seen in pictures.

Then you'll go through Denali National Park and maybe see a real gold mine. You'll go on north to Fairbanks. There you'll sightsee, stay overnight, and then go west to the Yukon River. You'll board a boat and travel south for a short way on the Yukon and see historic sights. Before you get to the white water, and the big falls, you'll get off and fly back to Nome. That will cover five days unless you decide to stay over somewhere. How does that sound?" He looked at them with a big grin.

"For once I'm speechless," Tom gulped. "Is that to be our birthday present?"

"Good grief." Tim groaned, "Can't you just for once accept the trip, enjoy going to new places and see things we would never see in Virginia? I'm going to take my camera and plenty of film; take my tape recorder so I can record everything without forgetting interesting facts and I'm going to eat all kinds of new foods." Anna put her hand over Tim's mouth or he would have rattled on in his excitement.

"I can't top that and I'm getting sleepy. Good night one and all," Tom yawned hugely. "Oh are we taking Greatheart?"

"Boy, you are sleepy. Dad told us he was staying here with her."

"Tomorrow we do things we never do on Sunday. We'll wash clothes, pack and check on everything we'll need. Please don't be running off and goofing off," Irene said.

"I'll be too excited to sleep," Tim was jumping around the room whooping like he thought an Indian sounded on the warpath.

"You'd better try to sleep," Anna advised. 'We don't want to waste time sleeping on the trip because there'll be too much to see and do."

CHAPTER SIXTEEN

The next afternoon Herb drove his family to the Nome Airport. He flew to Anchorage with them to spend the night and do some sightseeing. Tim was writing as fast as he could in his journal. The Eskise family had agreed to take care of Greatheart while Herb was away.

Tom looked at Tim writing in his journal. "Why are you wasting time with such foolishness?" he snickered.

"Are you going to remember everything we see and do? Are you going to remember all the people we've met and what they said; the odors in the markets and your feelings? Five years from now, or sooner, are you going to remember all of this?" Tim answered calmly. Tom shrugged his shoulders and walked off.

There were mixed feeling the next morning when Herb had to see his family aboard the train and leave them.

Tim wrote, "Not far out of Anchorage we stopped to see a real gold mine. We were allowed to pan for gold and keep any we found. Anna found a nice-sized nugget and mom found several small nuggets. Tom and I each found a handful of small nuggets. What a thrill! We saw beautiful countryside and more snow and ice than I ever want to see again. As much as I've learned to love Alaska and the people, I guess you have to be born here to truly want to stay forever. The Portage Glacier was magnificent. It isn't hard to imagine how much of the earth was covered by glaciers thousands of years ago. No wonder the early people followed the animals as they moved farther south into what we now know as the United States."

There was so much to see and do that Tim had a hard decision to make. He couldn't possibly write about everything, and, while he was writing so industriously, he was afraid he might miss something exciting. He would have to choose what might be more interesting as he would read it five and ten years in the future.

He continued to write. "What great fun to go through Denali National Park. We saw lots of Dall sheep, Moose, caribou and all kinds of wild animals in natural habitat roaming free. The babies of the moose and caribou were so cute, and I now understand the saying 'a face only a mother could love'. The biggest thrill was seeing a family of grizzlies. There were two mothers, one with two cubs and one with one cub. The mothers were teaching their little ones how to find food and how to be alert for danger.

"Oh, yes, I forgot to mention that Mt. McKinley is the tallest mountain in North America. It is six thousand feet higher than Mt. Whitney in California. I lost count of the number of bears we saw. The Alaska brown bear is the biggest of the bears. It can weigh as much as sixteen hundred pounds. Thank goodness they live over on Kodiak Island. We didn't see any polar bear today."

The next morning the McKinley Explorer took them into Fairbanks, Alaska's second largest city. It began as a mining camp in 1902 and is still a gold-mining center.

"Hey! I bet that's an Indian boy. We haven't seen many Indians on the west coast where we are," Tom exclaimed. He rushed toward the boy, not meaning to be rude; he was just curious. "Hi! My name is Tom Jackson. I really live in the state of Virginia, but my dad is in Nome working for the Department of the Interior. Do you live here?"

"Tom! Don't be rude," Irene was embarrassed.

"I don't mean to be rude. I'm just glad to see him."

"That's okay. I understand. My name is Daniel Little Bear Weskin. Yes, I live here. At least, I go to school here. I live just outside of town."

"Please tell me about your Indian heritage. I love knowing about different people," Tom persisted.

"Glad to. I'm an Athapascan Indian."

The twins and Daniel walked around together and exchanged stories about themselves. They hated to leave Daniel, but the trip was planned and they had to follow the plans Herb had outlined for them.

The Jacksons ate dinner and went to their rooms. The next morning they were so excited that it was difficult for the boys to breathe. They boarded a boat to travel down the Yukon River. Even though they dressed warmly, they found that, on the river, they needed a jacket with a hood. On land the temperature averaged in the low fifties, but on the water the moisture made the air seem colder and they felt as if it went straight to their bones.

"Hey, pinhead, why are you writing so furiously when you could be talking in your recorder?" Tom teased Tim.

Tim's face grew pink because he knew Tom would tease him and not let him forget. "I forgot to bring tapes."

Tom hooted and tried to get Tim upset, but it didn't work. When Tim made a mistake, he was mature enough to accept the teasing and go on.

"Look!" As usual Tom could not speak quietly when he was excited. "Look at all the seals lounging on that iceberg. I've read that the bears consider them delicious."

Tim's camera was ready for a great shot. He got pictures of many animals and of fish and fowl. With great glee he took a picture of Anna catching the biggest fish off the boat so far. The fish, that the people caught, were cooked for their dinner at the next hotel where they stopped.

When the boat stopped at Nulato, the Jackson family got off. Others stayed on to ride down the rapids.

Irene saw Paul Grigsby first and told her children he was there to pick them up. They were so glad to see Paul, even though they had enjoyed the trip. Home to Nome, and they were sure ready to go home. They could hardly wait to see Herb and tell him of their adventure.

"If Greatheart jumps and twists anymore, she'll turn herself wrong side out," Anna giggled. The dog was so thrilled to have her family together.

Tim could hardly wait to have his pictures developed and put his journal in order. When he would be an old man with a family and children of his own, he would have the pictures and journal to share with them.

Mr. Eskise began to teach the twins how to throw a spear for hunting and one for fishing. He taught them how to cast a net for fishing. Weeks later he taught them how to guide a dog sled and started them on Greatheart's training for pulling a sled.

Eight months old Greatheart was happy but puzzled. Now her beloved boys would say, "sit" and she would sit as trained. But, instead of playing, they would say, "stay" and walk away from her. She was confused when they scolded her for bounding after them. Why didn't they wrestle and play like they always had done? She was highly intelligent and soon learned that she received praise and lots of hugs if she obeyed their commands. On rare occasions she was even given a tasty treat to eat. She trusted her boys. After all, the boys never went off and forgot about her.

Irene and Herb decided not to celebrate their nineteenth wedding anniversary except with a special family dinner. Irene suggested that they wait to celebrate on their twentieth and then every five years thereafter.

"I'm not surprised Greatheart has learned so quickly. Her mother was highly intelligent and wolves are smart, also." Irene spoke as she watched Greatheart go through her training. Her family got so excited and hugged and praised her when she did the correct things. She loved the attention.

Finally the hardest part was teaching Greatheart to obey hand signals. The twins found it harder than the dog did. This took several weeks, but no one was surprised at the dog's amazing ability to learn. By now, Greatheart thought the lessons were a great game to enjoy.

One morning Mr. Eskise came to the Jackson's home. "I've made a soft, cloth halter for Greatheart. Just let her wear it and become accustomed to it for a couple of days. Then we'll start her training in having something behind her."

"Oh, boy!" Tom yelled, turning cartwheels. "At last we'll have our own sled dog."

"That won't be for several months yet," Tim explained importantly. "She can't pull even light weight until she's at least a year old. I've been talking to other sled dog owners."

"That's right," Mr. Eskise said. "Any training for animal, or human, is more lasting, stronger and safer if it is done safely and thoroughly."

Two long ropes were placed on Greatheart's halter so that she could learn to be driven. The twins took turns standing behind her, holding the ropes and giving her commands. At first one twin would walk beside her to give her confidence. She learned that mush meant to go forward; hiyee meant to run; gee meant to turn right and haw meant to turn left. Ho brought her to a full stop. After a month Greatheart was moving on command like a pro.

"Hey, Tom, Tim," Ben yelled as he ran into the house one morning. "Get your engines going and move on out. Dad is outside and wants to talk to you." they went out quickly to find what Mr. Eskise wanted with them.

"Here's a wagon with rubber wheels. It's time that Greatheart learned to move with an object behind her. These rubber wheels will be easier to pull and won't make noises to frighten her. Too, it will be easier on her back. Remember she's very young yet and we don't want to hurt her."

The light-weight wagon was attached to the lines running from her halter. At first she dropped in the snow and rolled on her back with her legs in the air. Mr. Eskise taught the twins to be firm, but kind. It was hard, sometimes, for them to be firm, but it was a good lesson for them in self-discipline. It took several days before Greatheart would walk forward without turning around to see what was behind her.

146

Greatheart was even more puzzled. Why couldn't she play with her boys as she had always done? Why didn't they want to romp and roll? However, she loved them and trusted them, so it didn't take long for her to learn there was a time to work and a time to play.

Police Chief Causuc Houmay constantly warned them and talked to anyone who was around. "You'll never be able to trust that animal. She's half wolf and the wolf breed will always tell. She's dangerous. You'll be sorry. Just remember I tried to help you." He talked non-stop about stories he heard of people who tried to train wolves and the wolf would turn on them as it matured.

Tom stepped forward, chin lifted and pointed, ready to argue with Chief Houmay. Tim put his fist on his hips and scowled, but said nothing. Mr. Eskise put a hand on each twin's shoulder. "Yes, I've heard of wolf blood turning on people who raised them. But that was because the animals were kept in cages and treated like wild animals. I have also worked with people who found pure-blood wolf cubs and raised them to be great family pets.

Those people were smart enough to teach them to hunt for their own food and turned them loose when they were older. One family told me the wolves would come back to visit them, especially to bring their little ones to meet the people. Kindness and sincere love goes a long way."

He started to walk away and turned back. "One of my best friends had a half wolf, like Greatheart. He didn't try to train the animal and love it as the Jackson family is doing with this dog. The animal is still good with them. They moved from here and took him with them. If there had been any trouble with him I would have heard." Herb had joined the group by now.

Mrs. Eskise explained. "Yes, their wolf dog was a male, very independent, and I guess you could say he was a loner. Greatheart is a female and will protect and care for these boys as she would her own children." Chief Houmay just shuffled his feet and looked angry. She smiled at him. "Don't worry until there is something to worry about."

"Sure," Herb laughed. My grandfather used to say, "Don't trouble trouble until trouble troubles you. He meant that sometimes we can cause trouble by being insecure and encouraging it to happen."

The twins, feeling more at ease, determined to love Greatheart and treat her gently so that she would be a safe, loving pet. Galena had been larger than the average Shepherd. Her daughter, being half wolf, was going to be even larger than her mother. She was also stronger.

"We loved your mother so much and, until you, she was the greatest dog ever." Tom told Greatheart. "We don't know who the wolf is that's your daddy, but I'm sure he's big and handsome because you're such a strong, beautiful girl. Even if we don't know who your daddy is, we love you because you're our own sweet, precious girl."

Greatheart was so happy. She didn't really know what her boy was saying, but she knew it was good by the tone of his voice. She grinned at him and wriggled all over.

It was now in the sixties and dirty slush covered the roads. The snow and ice had melted in town as the weather gradually warmed.

On July third, the Jackson family went to Anchorage to be there for the fourth of July rodeo and a big celebration. The twins were excited because the sun would be up for about twenty hours and, even then it wouldn't be completely dark. The longest day would be on July fifth.

For the first time in her life Greatheart had been left behind for several days without a member of her beloved family, and her heart was broken. Benjamin Yoakno Eskise and Alan Brave Bear Tormas, living the closest to her, were left in charge under the direction of Mr Eskise.

Ben and Alan decided to take Greatheart out for a practice run on a road with a lot of holes and bumps. They used an old rusty wagon that they had found on a trash heap at the edge of the city. This wagon made lots of noise as it rattled and bumped behind her.

Greatheart was upset because it wasn't her boys handling her and the wagon frightened her. It was so scary. She gave a loud howl and ran as fast as she could trying to get away from that horrible, frightening thing. The wagon flipped on its side and really rattled then. She ran too fast for Ben and Alan to catch.

Ben Gregory, driving home from work, looked in the side mirror of his truck, and saw a dog running frantically behind him with a rusty, red object on its side behind her. Ben turned his truck quickly to cut her off. As he stopped his truck, he jumped out and caught her. For the first time in her life, she growled and snapped at a human.

Unfortunately Chief Houmay had been drawn to the frantic flight and saw what happened. "Stand back!" he yelled, drawing his pistol. "I've been expecting something like this. You can't have wolf blood and expect her to be safe to be around humans." Aiming his pistol at Greatheart, he yelled again. "Stand back and I'll take care of her."

"No!" Screamed the breathless Ben as he caught up with them. "You'll have to shoot me first," he cried as he fell on his knees and hugged the dog.

"Me, too," sobbed Alan as he fell on the other side of her. The two boys threw themselves between the Chief and the dog.

Mrs. Eskise and Alan's daddy came running. Alan's daddy was yelling as he ran. "Causuc, put that gun away. That dog is no more dangerous than I am. At least no more than I'm going to be if you don't put that gun away ---right now!. You're more dangerous waving that gun around than the dog is." He spoke firmly while trying to catch his breath.

Mrs. Eskise calmed everyone and told them why the dog was upset. Alan's daddy, Robert Tormas, turned to Ben Gregory. "Did she bite you?"

"No. She truly wasn't trying to bite. She was just asking me not to hold her. I think she's more frightened and confused than she is angry. Please don't think of hurting her," he said to Chief Houmay. "She's upset enough and further more, she doesn't know me. I'm a stranger trying to lay hands on her when she's already frightened."

"Well---" the Chief said slowly. He sure didn't want to look like the bad guy, but still he hated dogs and especially this half dog. Too, he didn't want the people to catch on that he was afraid of her. "Okay, but I'd better put her in a cage for observation."

"No! She's never been in a close place like a cage. Dad! Do something," Alan begged.

"Mother!" Ben turned to his mother at the same moment that Alan spoke to his dad. "We're supposed to be taking care of her."

Mrs. Eskise looked sternly at her son. "Supposed to be and doing it are two different things. You and Alan can still take care of her, but from now on don't ask her to do something she's just learning. Take care of her and leave the rest until Tom and Tim are back to work with her."

Robert and Ben asked the Chief to overlook what had happened and let the two young boys take the dog. "Please," Robert spoke. "I would appreciate it because it really wasn't the dog's fault. She's very young and just starting her training. The boys asked her to do something that she's only done with her family. Too, the wagon is different from the one she's been training with." By now a small crowd had gathered pleading Greatheart's case.

Chief Houmay, wanting to win public favor, reluctantly agreed to allow the boys to take the dog with them. Glaring at them he said, "The Jacksons will have some explaining to do when they return. It wasn't smart at all to leave a dangerous animal with two young boys." He left muttering to himself as he strode off.

"Pay no attention to him. Let's hurry and take Greatheart home before something awful happens. I'll be so glad when Sam and Charlie get home and the Jacksons get back." Alan spoke softly.

Samuel Motado Cramus was visiting with his grandparents in Montana for a month and Charles Running

Bear Bering was on a family trip for several weeks in British Columbia.

The two boys hurried to take the ropes and the wagon off Greatheart and took her to Ben Eskise's house. Greatheart could not understand why that big, scary human had yelled at her and sounded so angry. She wasn't angry at him. Strange things were happening to her without her family. All good things happened when her humans were with her.

The next evening, when the Jacksons returned, they were upset to hear what had happened. Herb and Irene gently, firmly, but lovingly, spoke to Ben and Alan about the boys offering to take Greatheart and assume responsibility for her.

The twins were not angry with Ben and Alan, but they wanted to go immediately and tell Chief Joumay what they thought of him. Anna reminded them that the fault was not the Chief's. The twins were adamant about telling him off.

"Oh, no," Irene exploded. "You will not. Instead, you are both going to Chief Houmay and apologize for your dog causing problems and sweetly thank him for being so understanding."

"Mom!" both Tom and Tim spoke at once.

"You can't mean that," Tom was shocked. "Why would we be hypocrites to apologize to that moron and thank him for being the jerk that he is?"

Herb looked shocked at Tom. "And I can't believe a son of mine is having thoughts like that about another human being. You only mature and truly become a man when you rise above the less than desirable actions of others. Face facts. It **was** your dog and the incident **did** happen. We have to live here for several months yet and work with these people, including the Chief. He can sure cause a lot of unpleasant situations through my work if you continue to make him angry. I don't mean to bow down before anyone and play up to them just to keep them from not liking us. But I do believe in being a bigger person than the one who is voicing thoughts I don't agree with."

"In other words," Tim spoke disgustedly, "suck up to them."

"Tim!" Herb and Irene spoke at once. "I never thought you would be the one we had to reason with over this," Irene said sadly.

"Oh. So Tim is the goody-goody and I'm always the bad guy," Tom said with hurt in his voice.

"This conversation is getting out of hand," Herb said. "In fact, it's no conversation at all. Let's go into the kitchen, sit down at the table, and have a discussion as we've always done. Come on, Anna," he said as the twins stalked out of the yard and into the house.

Anna had been standing with tears in her eyes and saying nothing. None of the children had eve thought of arguing with their parents and, even though she felt as her brothers did, she didn't approve of them responding to their parents in that surly tone of voice. She turned as if in a trance and slowly walked into the house.

Herb thanked the Eskise family and Allan and his daddy. "I apologize for my sons and hope that you'll understand our family must discuss this."

"Of course," Mr. Eskise assured him, looking a little ashamed. "I'm truly sorry, but it was my thoughtless son who instigated the trouble."

"Please accept my apologizes," Robert said, putting his arm around Alan. "I think we all have to discuss this with our children."

"Neither of you need to apologize. We value the friendship of all of you and don't want you to feel badly. My concern is my sons' attitude toward the Chief. I must talk to them and remind them how to be gentlemen. Please excuse me." Herb walked into the house with a straight back and a determined expression.

He found them sitting around the kitchen table--silent. Anna fought to keep the tears from pouring out. The twins sat with clenched jaws and red faces. It was obvious that Irene's heart was aching. Herb breathed a silent prayer that he would be able to reason with his sons. *I don't fully agree with Chief Houmay either, but there are times that it's better to remain silent and stay away from the person who is causing the anger.*

"Boys, first I want you to remember how much you are loved and how proud we are to have you as our children. I'm not saying that your feelings are wrong, or that you don't have a right to your opinion. You know your mother and I have always encouraged all of you to have an equal say in family discussions. What I am saying is that you have been taught the meaning of self-respect, to use good manners, to keep control of your temper and to try to understand the person with whom you are disagreeing. Quarreling doesn't settle anything; it only aggravates the situation. I do feel that the Chief acted rashly. We don't know why. Did it ever occur to you that deep down he is afraid of dogs for some reason? Maybe he thinks it isn't manly to admit his fear, therefore, he pretends to be angry and bluffs his way with threats."

The twins looked astonished, then thoughtful, but neither spoke.

"I don't know that he is afraid, "Herb continued. "It's just a thought. You think he was wrong to yell and threaten? Isn't that what you planned to do to him? How would your actions be any different than his? What makes your actions right and his wrong? Remember the Indian saying, "Don't judge a man until you've walked a mile in his moccasins. We need to try to get to know him better."

After a short silence, Tim spoke. "What do you want us to do?"

"I'm only going to make a suggestion. I don't believe that a forced apology has any merit. I'm suggesting that you think about all that has happened. Remember the unwise decisions of Ben and Alan. After you come to a decision, let your mother and me know what you've decided to do. Consider the fact that the Chief might be afraid of losing his job and is trying to convince the public that he's on top of any situation. I don't know that any of my suppositions are true. I just want you to think it through and then act as gentlemen. I am asking one binding promise. Please do not tell anyone outside of this family what our discussion has been. It isn't nice to talk about another person when they're not present to defend themselves. Do I have your promise?"

"Yes, sir," Tim answered first.

"Yes, Dad," Tom finally said.

The twins motioned for Anna to join them. As the three left the room, Irene and Herb shared a comforting hug.

CHAPTER SEVENTEEN

Two days passed as the twins asked Ben and Alan to again tell them all that had happened. They even asked Ben Gregory to give his part of the situation. With all the talking, they did keep their promise to not tell what the family discussed. They talked to everyone they could find who witnessed the incident of Greatheart's run-away.

On the third day, Herb looked up from his newspaper as the three children entered the living room. Irene had a sock stretched over a light bulb so she could men a hole in the toe.

"Dad. Mom. May we talk to you?" Tom asked.

Irene immediately put her mending down and gave them her complete attention. Herb folded the newspaper and laid it on a table by his chair. Anna, Tom and Tim sat on the couch. The looked at each other.

"I'll start," Tim said. "We've talked to a lot of people to ascertain the facts of Greatheart's great run-away. Then we talked it over among us three. We've decided that we can try to win Chief Houmay's friendship and do as you suggested. We will apologize as tactfully as possible and let the talks end there. Is that okay?"

"In other words, we're going to kill him with kindness," Tom grinned. Anna turned to glare at Tom. "Okay," Tom said throwing his hands up. "I'll let Tim do the talking and I'll keep my mouth shut."

"I'm truly proud of you," Herb smiled. "But don't do something just to please me. Do it because you know it's the decent thing to do." Irene nodded and smiled to show how proud she was of them.

The next day the twins arranged to meet Chief Houmay on the street. "Good morning, sir. If you have the time, we'd like to talk to you, Chief." Tim stated politely while Tom, wonders of wonders, did keep quiet.

"Sure, kids. Fire away," he answered.

"I'd like to," Tom mumbled.

"What's that?" the Chief asked.

Tim hurriedly began. He apologized for Greatheart's behavior, not blaming the two friends, and promised that nothing like that would happen again. To his credit, the Chief was nice to the twins, but couldn't keep from warning them again about the dangers of having a wolf dog.

That night, at the dinner table, the twins proudly told what they had accomplished during the day. Anna smiled with pride with them. "I have to admit that I feel much better," Tim stated.

"Me, too. I'm not as mad as I was, and can see all sides of the happening," Tom supplied.

"Well, that's a relief," Tim spoke with a twinkle in his eye. "I'm glad you're not mad. Remember what dad said that animals with rabies are mad, but humans are angry?" The laugh that followed helped them to relax.

"Just do me, and yourselves, a favor," Irene said. "Make sure that Greatheart is not out alone for any reason. I think Ben and Alan learned an important lesson, also. They meant well, but they just didn't stop to think."

The last week of July Sam and Charlie were both home. Herb took his family, a friend of Anna's, and the four boys that were the twins' friends to White Horse in the Yukon Territory.

"Dad, what are we going to do with Greatheart?" Tom worried.

"We can't take her with us and we can't go off and leave her again," Tim chewed on his lower lip as he worried.

"Dad and I talked it over," Irene answered, "and I'm going to stay here."

"But, Mom," Anna wailed, "that's not fair. You could enjoy this trip as much as any of us. It's the first pow wow and Indian celebration we've seen. You've got to go."

"Shhh. It's all right. I went on the train trip with you while your dad stayed here. Now it's his turn to go and I'll stay with our girl," Greatheart came for a hug just as if she understood. "I want all of you to go and have a fantabulous time. Take lots of pictures so I'll have an idea what you saw."

When they recognized that she was serious, the three children pitched in to help a lot before they left. They packed all they would need for the five days. Paul Grigsby flew them to Fairbanks where they boarded another plane for White Horse.

The twins were so excited to see so many Indian (First People) tribes from all over North America. Anna and her friend were more interested in the booth making jewelry, bead purses and even dresses. Charlie and Alan were thrilled because it was the only chance they had to visit with so many Indians.

There were large arrangements of wigwams as well as slab buildings and other buildings to show the residences of the people. All wigwams are built so that the opening is facing east to honor the rising sun. Flags of many Indian groups flew over their particular area. One drew their attention that said Sault St. Marie-- tribe of the Chippewa.

Walking on, they saw a sign, maruawe numuukahni which meant welcome to the Comanche Lodge. The flag read Comanche Nation, Lords of the Southern Plains. This flag showed an Indian on horseback carrying a lance with feathers on it. Another sign said that the Shoshone tribe from eastern Wyoming was part of this group.

The Cherokee had a program telling about Sequoyah, an Indian that developed the first written Cherokee language. An older Cherokee teen demonstrated the Eagle Dance with a beautiful costume.

The Choctaw had a sign, Ant Chukoa, which meant come in. they learned that this was the largest group of the Muskogean language. They were the first U.S. Indians to adopt a flag of their own and fought on the side of the Confederacy during the War Between the States. The Chickawaw, Creek and Seminole were also part of this language group. The children were interested to learn that Roy Rogers was part Choctaw.

There were so many Indian groups that it was impossible to see all of them in one day. Too, there were loads of booths and animals.

Herb had a lot of sympathy for the problems the Indians face, diabetes, heart, alcoholism and many others. He was pleased to learn he could work with a group to help them get better education, better medical attention and homes for orphans and the sick and elderly.

The Pawnee sign, As-Say-Taw-Ka meant White Horse. Chief War Eagle taught the children some dance steps so they could participate in a dance later in the day.

Each of them did a sand painting at one booth. There was so much to see that it was difficult to make choices. Each day there would be a different special game. This day a group of Indian women played a game called shinny.

"Wow! They're good," Tom exclaimed. "That's almost like our game of field hockey."

A tall, dignified Indian, standing by them, was amused. "Where do you think you got the idea to play your games? The game of shinny started among the Indians of the northeastern part of the United States and Canada."

"Did we really copy your games?" Tim asked wide-eyed and respectful.

"I was teasing you," the man laughed. "I don't really know who started them. I do know that a lot of gymkhana games you play were started by Indians from the western part of the U.S. They were meant to keep in practice for their daily living. All of us have learned from each other, from the early Aztec to people all over the world."

Herb joined them to check on the six boys. "Hello. My name is Herb Jackson, and I'm responsible for these hooligans. I hope they're not being a nuisance. They're just so excited to be here, as I am, also."

"No. I've enjoyed talking to them. I'm Andrew Bloodraven. I'm an attorney in Saskatchewan. This is the first chance I've had in too many years to attend a pow wow."

"Excuse me," Tom interrupted. "Dad, we're going to that booth over there to get something to drink. We'll stay in sight of you. Anna and Rebecca are on the other side."

"Okay, son. You boys stay together." The entire group loved trying new foods. Later, the boys with Anna and Rebecca, joined Herb. "Dad, these people keep talking about gymkhana games. What does that mean?"

Andrew had walked with Herb and now answered Tom. "Gymkhana means games on horseback. In early days the purpose of the games was to keep the warriors' skills sharp for hunting and protecting the tribe."

The next morning they were up early and had a good breakfast. When they arrived on the show grounds, they saw ten tall poles lined up, in a straight line, about twelve feet apart. The thin, swaying poles were about eight feet tall.

"What are they doing with those?" Tom asked.

A young Indian girl standing near them spoke. "Is it okay if I explain to you? My name is Jennifer Two Crows." All six boys welcomed her in almost one voice and stumbled over each other to tell their names.

"When early Indians rode to battle, they carried a pogganmmogan in one hand. The weapon was made from one strong, solid piece of wood with a ball left on one end. The other end had a hole drilled in it and piece of rawhide through it to fit around the wrist. Riding fast the Indian would hold the weapon so that he could swing the pogganmmogan and hit the enemy with the hard ball. It would either kill the enemy or knock him off his horse and often broke bones if he lived."

"They aren't going to try to kill each other now are they?" Tom gasped.

"No." She laughed. "They'll ride fast and try to knock something off the top of the poles. They'll be judged on accuracy of hitting and timed to see who can go the whole way the fastest."

"That sounds like fun," Tim was delighted.

The girl went on. "Yes, it is fun. They ride bareback, as their ancestors did, with only a war bridle and no bit in the horse's mouth. A good rider guides the horse with body movements and legs."

As a name was called, that Indian would ride as fast as he could to hit the things that looked like small pumpkins on the tops of the poles no bigger than a fishing pole. The poles whipped and swayed so that it took a lot of skill to hit the target.

The girl jumped with glee. "My brother won!" They all told her to congratulate her brother and tell him they enjoyed watching.

Anna and Rebecca were standing behind the boys. Anna showed them jewelry she purchased and a lovely hand-made beaded purse for her mother. They all then went into a building that showed pictures and artists' drawings of past famous Indians. There was also a display of early clothing and weapons.

Outside there were a lot of people singing and dancing. Indian men made a large circle dancing clockwise. The women made a circle inside dancing counter clockwise. Four older men played a large, broad drum while a man explained about the history of the dance. It demonstrated the appreciation of the Creator for giving them a good life.

The next days were filled with a rodeo. The time came too soon to leave.

"Tom, don't you want to write something to Mrs. Berry? I've done all the writing. Come to think of it, you haven't taken a single picture or made notes to share with our friends in Virginia." Tim scowled at Tom

"Aw, you know I don't like to write. Besides you've done a good job, so why spoil it?"

"But Tom, you made a promise, too."

"Okay. Okay. Let me get this piece of paper. I'll use it. I'll write something and put it in your letter. Hey! You won't believe this."

"What? What is it?"

"Listen to what's on this paper. Hi Anna, I know that you know my name, but we've never talked much. I've been watching you and think you are real neat. A lot of kids don't feel comfortable around intelligent girls like you, but I admire you and would like to get better acquainted. Could we eat lunch together at school or maybe meet in the library? Just give me a chance. I'd like to be your friend. Regards, Daniel Morgan." Tom read aloud and burst out laughing. "Isn't that a riot? Old brainy Anna has a guy sweet on her."

"Don't show your ignorance, Tom. I'm not surprised. Our sister is very pretty and she does make top honor roll. Besides, she's a sweet, caring person. She's growing up. I mean she's very mature. Do you even know what that means? Naturally she'll be dating and some day she'll get married."

"Blah. That won't happen, or if it does, it'll be a long time yet," Tom smirked.

"I guess you can't help being stupid. Of course it'll happen and it'll happen to you and me. Then again, maybe the girls will be smart enough to see through you." Tom and Tim began to wrestle on the floor.

Irene hurried into the room. "Stop right this minute. You know what always happens. You start out joking and thinking you're being funny, and it ends up with one of you getting hurt and tempers flying out of control. Aren't you supposed to be working on a history assignment?"

The twins scrambled up punching each other lightly. Anna came in and plopped down, "What is it now, Mom?"

"Just your brothers and their usual shenanigans. Look at this mess. Pictures scattered over the table and floor, papers all over the place and -- what is this?" Irene held a paper out to Anna.

Anna took the paper and then out a strangled squawk. "Why those little rats have been in my personal papers. Just wait 'till I get hold of them." She turned stomping toward the twins' bedroom.

"Don't make another step," Irene ordered. "I want to know what this is about. The boys don't usually bother other people's property. There must be more to it."

"You're right," Anna said embarrassed. "I carelessly left it on top of my books. Did you read it, Mom?"

"No. It isn't mine to read. I just saw that it was a letter from some boy. I'll be glad to listen if you want to tell me about it."

Anna read the letter to Irene and explained about the possible friendship.

"Do you like this young man as more than a friend?"

"He has been a very good friend. He was one of the first to welcome me and show me over the building so I could find my classes. I'm not interested in having a special boy friend, but I like having a lot of friends."

Irene smiled. "Honey, you will have several boy friends before you settle for the one special man in your life. Be nice to Daniel and talk to him as you would any friend. He didn't ask to date you; just to talk. Your father and I trust you to stay with a group and not go off with a boy alone. Enjoy being young while you can. A person is young for such a few short years. Then you're an adult with responsibilities and lots of stress. Bring Daniel and any of your friends home whenever you like. I'll talk to your brothers."

"Thanks, Mom. You're the greatest." Anna walked to her room ignoring her brothers. Tim was standing in the doorway and Tom was in the hall leaning against the wall. As Anna passed Tom grabbed his chest and sighed, "Oh, Daniel." He laughed foolishly as she slammed the door to her room.

CHAPTER EIGHTEEN

Irene told Herb about Daniel and of the twins giving Anna a hard time. He chuckled. "Our little girl is old enough to date. We've taught our children how to be a lady and gentlemen. We can't be with them every minute of their lives. We'll have to trust them to do what is right." he pulled Irene's head on his shoulder and hugged her.

"Herb, it makes me kind of sad. Our little ones are almost adult. It just seems like last week I was rocking them to sleep and telling stories every night. Hearing their prayers was such a sweet moment. Now they hardly need me."

"My love," he chuckled, "just like all mothers, you're starting early to sing the empty nest blues. Anna is almost seventeen and the boys are almost fifteen. Don't you think you're worrying much too early. All three of them still have college."

"Time passes so fast though," she sighed.

You're the one that said no matter how much they grow or how far away from home they go, they'll always be our dearly loved little ones." herb smiled. "It's okay. I feel as you do. The boys are almost as tall as I am."

Irene was in ecstasy planning a school opening party in the Community Center. All the families, who worked with herb, had become as close as a family. She and some of the women agreed on the type of party they would plan and a dance that would include the entire community.

The Community Center was decorated by some of the older girls. Mothers made special goodies and planned a simple menu. Several of the people, who played musical instruments, volunteered to provide music.

The young people enjoyed the modern dances while their parents enjoyed boogie and slow, romantic music. Irene and Herb taught the Virginia Reel and other square dances. A few people demonstrated clogging. A few Eskimos demonstrated native dances.

"Ho, boy," groaned Chief Houmay. "I'm going to have to learn to dance so that I can work off this load of fat," he said patting his stomach. "Why did you ladies have to cook so good and bring so much food?" Everyone laughed with him. Most were surprised because, as a rule, he didn't participate. He not only enjoyed the evening, but had made it more enjoyable for the crowd because he was so nice.

"Whoa, Chief," Manuel Barvere said.

"Hold on, Causuc," Landon Heim said at the same time.

"You're way off base, man," Tom Lucreke laughed.

"What d'ya mean, the ladies cooked such good food? Some of us men did a darn good job," Ben Gregory blurted.

Causuc's eyes grew wide. "You? You men cooked?"

"Sure, what's wrong with that? Are you saying real men don't cook?" Herb teased him.

"No," he answered quickly, backing away a little. "I was just surprised."

Jack Jordon walked quickly to the front and took the microphone. "I have an idea. Folks, how do you feel about a cook-off among the men?"

"What do you mean by a cook-off?" the Chief asked.

"The next party we have, the men will do all the cooking -- that includes you, too, Causuc. And I don't see why the people can't vote for the best foods. That doesn't mean that any of the food will be bad, but some will be good enough to be remembered and talked about."

The crowd thought it was a great idea and they agreed on a Halloween party. Everyone cheered and quickly bundled up to go home.

"I used to watch at the window and pray for snow," Anna sighed. "Now I would give anything to be able to wear shorts and walk in the sun."

"Anna, are you sorry you came here?" Daniel asked anxiously. "I was born and raised here so it doesn't seem bad to me. In fact, I love it."

Anna placed a hand on his arm. "I honestly love it and would not change this experience for anything. You can't blame me though. My friends in Virginia are hiking in the woods, listening to the birds, watching animals teaching their little ones to live safely and going on picnics. Some of my friends will be skating and enjoying sports and school functions. Of course I miss them, but I do love it here and have made some good friends which I consider a blessing." Anna twirled in happiness.

"Do you count me as one of your friends?" Daniel asked shyly.

"Of course you are."

"May I walk home with you?"

"Sure. I would like to ask you in for hot chocolate, but it **is** getting late. Why don't you plan on coming over tomorrow?" Anna smiled at him.

Herb hugged Anna as she started to go to her room to prepare for bed. "Honey, I like Daniel. His father is the doctor in the clinic that treats my crew. They're really nice people."

Irene and Herb went to their room. Irene turned for him to take her necklace off. "I'm ashamed to say that I was a little uncomfortable when Chief Houmay walked in. He wandered around with his arms crossed over his chest and seemed to be glaring. But when he relaxed and being to laugh and enjoy himself, I saw him in a different light."

"I know what you mean, but he turned out to be a lot of fun." Herb jerked around when Tom opened the door and barged in.

"Dad, what are you going to make for the men's cook-off?"

"I haven't decided yet. Maybe it'll be a surprise. Goodnight now. I'm coming in to kiss you kids goodnight."

"Oh, yuck," Tom spoke without thinking. He covered his mouth with his hand and ran to his room.

"You can tuck me in, Dad, but I don't need kissing," he yelled back.

Herb ran into the twins' room, picked Tom up, turned him upside down and dropped him on his bed. He blew a smacker on Tom's neck and then kissed his cheek. Tucking both boys in, he kissed Tim's cheek.

"Dad! Don't you know we're too big for that," Tim yelped.

"My darling sons, you'll always be mine and when you're grown, with children of your own, or even grandchildren, I shall love you, hug you and kiss you. I'm very proud that you're my sons."

Irene followed him in to kiss the twins. "You never get too big for us to love you and kiss you," she smiled.

"No one ever got too big for that," Herb laughed as he picked Irene up and kissed her. "Goodnight, boys," he called carrying Irene to their room.

"Oh, gush. Yuck. Blah," Tom said disgustedly.

"Don't knock it," Tim advised. "At least we have parents who love and respect us, and each other, and care what happens to us. We're lucky. There are too many kids who are abused, abandoned, neglected or have one parent who must work too hard to make ends meet and don't have time for them."

"I know we should be thankful; and I am." The boys silently said their prayers and settled down to go to sleep.

Herb and Irene knocked on Anna's door and entered when he responded. They gave her a goodnight hug and a kiss on her cheeks. Then they went thankfully to their own room for a much needed rest.

October 31st, Halloween, fell on a Sunday, so the men's cook-off was held on Saturday night. A lot of the men, who had cooked, brought their food to the Center to prepare it or to finish. The women, and a lot of men who had not cooked, set up tables and placed white paper coverings on them. A few of the women had prepared an item for food in the event that there wasn't enough. Causuc came in carrying a casserole of buttered candid yams with black walnuts in them and marshmallows covering the top. He would place this in the oven later to brown the marshmallows. There was a lot of laughter and good-natured insults.

After the delicious dinner, everyone was pleased and complimentary of all the food.

"Oh, I'm sinfully stuffed," Tom moaned and then stood. "I sure am glad I'm not a judge. It would be too difficult to select one over another," he said loudly. "Thank you men. You've done us males proud." He sat down among clapping, cheering and more friendly insults.

Irene was busy taking notes for her book. She had so many great ideas. It would just be a matter of time to sit down and type them into a manuscript.

Jack Jordon walked to the front to the microphone and called attention.

"Okay, folks. It's time for the presentations. You've all had a chance to sample everything and cast your votes for each category. Four of our teens have been counting ballots and have made the tallies. Here are the results."

He grinned waving the papers over his head.

"Get on with it," someone yelled good-naturedly.

"Be quiet and let him speak," a woman scolded.

He cleared his throat and started. "For the best stew, venison at that, the blue ribbon goes to ----Yehat Eskise. Come get your ribbon, man. Congratulations." There was a lot of cheering for the popular Yehat.

Runner-up in the main course for his elk burgers is Morgan Wise Owl Osage." Again a lot of cheer as he collected his red ribbon.

"For the best bread, sourdough at that, the blue ribbon goes to Ben Gregory." A lot of cheer and whistles followed. Runner-up with his double yeast loaf goes to Gerald

Buckley. He was a newcomer but the crowd cheered just as loud.

"For the best cake, Velvet Maple, the blue ribbon goes to Herb Jackson." The crowd went wild for their popular boss. " Runner-up with his Ginger

Coconut Cake is Robert Tormas." More cheering and friendly insults

"Now for a big surprise. Of all the vegetable dishes, the one that received almost all the votes, is the one made by --- **Chief Causuc Houmay!**" There was a gasp and then people stood up to, as Tim said, cause the room to rock. Several jumped up to slap him on the back. For once, Causuc was speechless. He beamed with pride and walked to the front clasping his hands over his head in a victory salute. "This is the first time I've cooked anything to share. Thank you all."

"Okay, now. We're not through," Jack tried to get the room quiet. "The runner-up with his Asparagus Delight is Paul Grisby. He, too, received cheers and friendly insults.

Tom leaned over to whisper to Ben Gregory. "Has the Chief ever been married? I've never heard anyone mention a wife."

Ben looked down with a solemn expression and then whispered. "I'm going to tell you about him, but you have to promise you'll never tell a soul what I'm about to tell you."

Tom nodded. "I promise, but can't I tell my family?"

"Of course. Just make sure that no one outside your family talks of this.

The Chief's feelings would be hurt." He hesitated and then continued. "About four years ago Causuc was engaged to a young, beautiful, gentle, very talented school teacher.

She played the violin and had a lovely singing voice. She and Causuc both sang in the church choir."

"The Chief sang!"

Ben nodded and said, "One day his fiancée, and some girlfriends, went out in snowmobiles for fun. They were caught in an unexpected snow storm. The others were found in time, but Marissa Hornesby, was not found for two days. The Chief was with the group that found her clothing and some of her bones which was all that was left. There were wolf prints all over the place. That's why he hates wolves and even wolf dogs. He was in such deep grief that we feared for his mental stability. He has kept pretty much to himself since then."

Tom was stricken. "I'm glad he won tonight, and I'm so very sorry that I didn't know about this earlier. I understand him better now and I will be nicer to him."

Tom told his family at home that night about Causuc's loss. "I'm so sorry for Causuc, but I'm glad Ben told Tom. He seemed more mature when he told us. It really touched him." Irene was brushing her teeth while Herb talked. She nodded to show she agreed.

"At least our children have learned that other people have sufferings that we might not know about, and that we shouldn't judge quickly or harshly."

The men's cook-off party had been a rousing success. The group decided to select a committee to plan for a community Thanksgiving dinner. As there were a few families hat could not afford to spend money, they were tactfully asked to help set up tables and to decorate. They were also asked to check on the gas supply for the two fireplaces in the Center for the evening. Again some musicians were delighted to provide music.

On Thanksgiving day, all the denominations gathered together for a shared service in the Community Center. The sweet old hymns were enjoyed by everyone. Young children sang songs they had learned in school and a skit was given by some Indian children and others to tell about the first Thanksgiving.

The main dish, for the dinner, was geese stuffed with sage sausage, nuts and herbs. There was also venison roast, biscuits and gravy, several vegetables and desserts galore. Everyone was full and contented. Even though there a few singing loudly off key, they all joined in the familiar holiday songs.

Irene looked around and thought how close everyone had gotten. What a sweet friendship there was in their community. They not only worked together, but depended on each other in time of need. Not one person was made to feel less important than another. After the worship service and dinner, the floor was cleared for the entertainment. Singing groups, dancing and a contest as to who could tell the best joke rounded out the evening.

People were still talking about what great times they'd had when December rolled in. Where had the year gone? The twins insisted on giving Greatheart a first year birthday party. The adults thought it was silly to give a party for a dog.

Postmaster, James Morton, said, "What harm will it do? We are in an area of snow on top of snow, and we're pretty much stuck this was for months. If the kids want to do something cheerful, then let them."

Greatheart enjoyed her one year party. Flash bulbs popped, with loud laughter, as she stuck her face in her special cake and came up with a muzzle covered in cream icing. Her happy tail kept smacking people on the legs and finally a dish of nuts flying off a low table.

"That does it," Irene hid a smile. "Take her home, boys, and make sure she isn't able to follow you back."

The twins, and friends, dressed warmly and ran out to harness their dogs to small sled. Greatheart could now pull a sled and a lightweight child. The children set a race course of about two thousand feet with a zigzag and one turn. Tom drove Greatheart. The race was going well until five sleds make the final turn together. Only one dog had racing experience. The other dogs, having fun with their children, got tangled and ended up with overturned sleds and boys rolling in all directions in the snow. The one experienced dog raced to the finish line.

The dogs were carefully inspected for possible injuries as they were unharnessed. The sleds were wiped clean and put away. There was a lot of teasing and wrestling when Tim stated, "I could have done a better job than Tom. In fact, I could have done better than any of you."

CHAPTER NINETEEN

While the boys were laughing and talking, Tom sneaked away to a shed where construction materials were stored. He was looking for something he might use in a practical joke. Surprisingly the door was unlocked. Becky and Miranda saw Tom sneak away and go into the shed, but said nothing.

The shed was dark, and Tom didn't know where the battery powered lamps were. He bumped into a barrel in the dark and knocked it over. He lit a match and held it high so he could see the interior of the shed. The flame burned near his fingers, and, without thinking, he shook his hand and dropped the match. Not finding anything he wanted, he reached for the door handle. An ear-splitting blast shot the shed apart. The powder he had knocked over exploded and fames covered the area. The fire spread rapidly.

The force of the blast knocked some of the children down who were standing nearby. The dogs jumped and ran away in fright, except Greatheart who had been thrown off balance. She went scrambling as hard as she could, on her side, toward the flames. Greatheart was the only one who had heard the surprised scream.

Tim staggered up in time to see his precious dog just a few feet from the flames and looking as if she were going to run into them. "Greatheart," he screamed. "Come, girl. Tom! Tom, where are you?" Tim ran after Greatheart shaking off the boys who were trying to hold him back.

"Tim! Don't be stupid. You'll be killed."

Tim grabbed for Greatheart's collar while trying to shield his face from the heat. She growled and snapped at him. "Hey, girl. Are you hurt? You wouldn't be mad at me if you were okay."

"Tim," Miranda yelled. "I saw Tom go into the shed before it exploded. I think he's still in there."

Parents and neighbors were running, parents frantically calling for their own child. Greatheart's whimpers turned to howls as her fur began to sizzle. Her feet were on burning boards, but she continued to struggle forward. Herb ran to Tim.

"Dad! I think the blast scrambled her brains."

Greatheart stuck her nose in a hot spot and grabbed something in her teeth. She braced on her injured feet and pulled as hard as she could. Tim was shocked to see part of a coat sleeve in her mouth with a human hand.

"Tom!" he yelled. "Dad!" It's Tom."

The fire was too hot to allow the men to get closer. Too, they didn't know if more powder would explode. A man ran up with a twenty feet pipe. The man placed the pipe over some barrels and used the pipe as a fulcrum to lift the burning boards. As the boards came up, Greatheart got a firmer hold on what she was pulling. She kept backing and pulling until the top half of Tom was visible. Herb and Causuc ran in and pulled Tom out.

Tom's hair was singed and his face burned. Most of his clothes had burned and was sticking to his skin. His skin was red and one arm, thigh and side were badly burned. An ambulance came and quickly took the unconscious Tom to the hospital.

Neighbors carefully scooped the brave, loyal Greatheart on a blanket and lovingly carried her to a jeep and then to the clinic. Even though she was hurt, she kept whimpering and trying to get to Tom. Herb and Irene went with Tim while Anna and Tim stayed with Greatheart.

Greatheart had burned fur, burned feet and one badly bruised, burned shoulder. The doctor cleaned her with antiseptics, removed much of the burned fur that would come loose, wrapped salve and gauze around her and gave her a shot to make her rest and sleep. She needed sleep and time to heal. She would probably have a scar on her shoulder, but she was healthy and would heal far quicker than Tom.

After what seemed like a lifetime, two doctors came to talk to Herb and Irene. "Your son is resting, and naturally he's sedated. His hair and eyebrows will possible grow back, and the burns over his body will heal with time. He has a deep burn on his thigh and right side which will require grafting. He'll be a mighty sick boy for months. Be patient and keep his spirits up. The will to get better can help him heal more than most medicines."

Adam Perkins, supervisor of construction, visited to check on Tom. "I sure am thankful that we had used most of the explosives. There wasn't much left or that whole section of town would have gone up. Why was Tom in there?"

"We don't know yet," Herb answered. "He hasn't come to long enough to talk. Too, we didn't want to upset him while he is still so sick. It's only been two days."

Adam shook his head in sadness. "I blame myself. I've always kept that door locked and I don't know why it was unlocked this time. Two girls said they saw him open the door and walk in."

"Please don't blame yourself. I'm sorry but our Tom would have found some way to get into trouble."

Tim walked around almost constantly rubbing his chest as if it hurt. His heart ached for Tom. A brother could be close, but twins were a part of each other. What one felt, the other usually felt.

The Jacksons decided to not celebrate Christmas, but Tom made them promise to go to the Community Center. Everyone was concerned about Tom and were glad that Greatheart was getting better. When people asked about Tom and why he went into the shed, his family was embarrassed. "Tom has always been our adventuresome rascal," Herb smiled sadly.

The new year rushed in with a blizzard. January seemed to creep by with strong, cold winds and below freezing temperatures. Herb got permission to take Greatheart to see Tom one day. The dog had to be held up so that she could see Tom and hold her face next to his. She tried to jump on the bed to get closer, but could not be allowed to do so. She was obviously glad to see Tom and he was feeling better after her visit.

Finally, during the second week of February, Tom was allowed to come home. Greatheart was ecstatic to have her family together again. The following week, the family, and close friends, surprised Tom with a delayed Christmas celebration. There was a tree, gifts, special food and the works.

Anna and Irene tutored Tom so that he could catch up with his school work.

"I don't know what I would do without Anna," Irene told Herb. "She is going to make an excellent teacher and will be a great mother. She is so compassionate, patient and dependable."

The second week of March, Tom was allowed to return to classes. He was warned about wrestling, or any rough play, because of his skin grafts which were still sensitive.

All three Jackson children had always been on the top honor roll, but for some reason the twins' grades began to slip. Instead of A, they were getting

Bs and once in a while a C. Herb offered to let them fly to Virginia for a vacation if they would bring their grades up and apply themselves. Tom was despondent and Tim was sorry for Tom.

In April Anna celebrated her seventeenth birthday with a cake and a special dinner with her family. She assured them she didn't expect anything else. She did receive a watch from her parents and slips of paper from her brothers. On each slip was a promise to do something nice and useful for two weeks. They offered to make her bed, clean her room, take her turn washing dishes and cleaning the kitchen and anything she was expected to do. All of the promises were useful and welcome.

Daniel took Anna, with some friends, ice skating. Irene asked Daniel to keep it a secret from Anna but to bring her and the crowd back home for ice cream and cake. She was surprised and so touched that she shed a few tears when she opened the lovely gifts her friends brought. Many of them were hand-made.

In May the twins asked only that they invited a few close friends for dinner and a quiet day with family for their fifteenth birthday. Afterward the group went to the movies. Tom was continuously cautioned about being too active.

Irene sighed with relief when the boys walked away from the house. "I think our boys are finally maturing completely. Tom's accident really jolted him to awareness of the results of his irresponsible behavior."

"Children do grow up, but with love, and good, firm training they'll never really leave us. Remember **Proverbs 22:6 Train up a child in the way he should go; and when he is old, he will not depart from it.** Oh, of course our children will move away to work or live somewhere on their own. They'll eventually have their own home and raise a family, but they'll come back to us because they know how much they're loved and they love us, too." Herb stated and hugged Irene.

While the boys were walking to the movies, Tom sheepishly apologized for his behavior on the day of the explosion. "I'll never play a practical joke again. I'm so thankful I was the only one hurt and none of you had to suffer for my craziness. I've been upset enough that Greatheart got hurt because of me. I'm just thankful the damage was no worse."

His friends assured him that he was still their friend and they were also glad that he had learned a valuable lesson. His injuries also taught them a valuable lesson.

Finally school was over for the year. The first week of July Anna and the twins flew to Virginia for a short visit. There was one sad little dog left behind. If she had been able to understand what was happening, she would have been proud of her children. The twins were again making top grades.

The time passed too quickly for the children. They were back in Alaska with suntans, loads of gifts and lots to tell. Greatheart was so thrilled to see them that she jumped as high as their faces to give them doggie kisses.

Benji, Sam, Charlie, Alan and other children, who had traveled, were home again. Their biggest discussion was the coming school year.

Anna was now a senior in high school and the twins were in the tenth grade. For the first time in their lives the twins had divided interests. Tim became absorbed in the science lab and thought he might like to be a family doctor. Tom was interested in oceanography. Anna continued to plan on being a teacher, specializing in art.

School opened and everyone was glad to be with friends and favorite teachers. The twins were on a basketball team and loved sports.

In November, the worst blizzard the people could ever remember blew in. Driving home was a nightmare as Herb gripped the steering wheel and prayed. He recognized that he had to take a snowmobile from now on. Thankfully he pulled into his driveway as close to the porch as he dared. He hunkered deep inside his parka and braced for the frigid blast of the arctic air that pummeled his frozen cheeks. He pushed and staggered against the wind as he made a slow way to the back door. He hesitated to open the garage door against the wind and blowing snow. He didn't feel like cleaning out a garage.

"Herb, darling, I'm so relieved you're home. All I've heard today on the short wave radio is that this is the worst storm for nearly fifty years. Thankfully the children were dismissed early and are home safely."

The storm didn't stop the community from planning another Thanksgiving dinner together. The new families were made to feel welcome and part of the group.

CHAPTER TWENTY

A letter came that took their thoughts from a party. The notice was from Washington, D.C. informing them that a documentary would be made about their area of Alaska. To prepare for this a dog sled race would be held in Nome, The prize for the winner would be five thousand dollars and a chance to star in the documentary the last week of January.

Tim wrote to Mrs. Berry about this race and the famous Iditarod Trail International sled dog race. He excitedly told her to share the information about them training Greatheart and what great hopes they had for her future. After all, she was Galena's daughter.

"I can hardly wait to see what happens. The Iditarod will not be until the first Saturday in March. Drivers, called mushers, are so sure of their own dog teams that they willingly pay the one thousand seven hundred fifty dollars entrance fee. I don't blame them because there is a half million dollars in prize money as well as many great gifts and a chance to be in commercials. One of those gifts is a new truck."

"This is the longest sled dog race in the world because it covers one thousand two hundred miles. The shortest time, so far, to do the whole race was nine days, two hours and forty-two minutes. Isn't that something?"

"A good musher will take better care of his or her dogs than themselves. There are about two dozen check points with a veterinarian at each check point. Each driver has from twelve to eighteen dogs. They often pick up fresh food at some of the checkpoints. They also get fresh bales of straw for the dogs to lie on at night."

"Would you believe the age of the drivers have been the minimum eighteen years to eighty-one years. Can you imagine a driver that old mushing all that distance and facing the dangers of storms and wild animals?"

"The Iditarod Trail used to be a mail and supply route. When gold was discovered, it was transported on this trail. I'm sure you know that in 1925 loads of people were sick and dying with diphtheria. There was no serum or medication and the weather made it impossible for doctors to get to the sick people. Strong, faithful huskies carried the serum to areas where people needed it the most. Some were successful. So the Iditarod is run today to remember the history of that time. Just like people in Virginia dress in uniforms of past wars and historical time, and wear old-fashioned clothes, these people are teaching new generations of brave, compassionate people and even braver dogs."

"They start in Anchorage and will come to Nome. I get excited just thinking about it. How I envy those mushers. I was surprised to learn that in 1985 a woman won the race."

"In 1978 some nice people organized a Junior Iditarod for youth. It only covered one hundred fifty miles, but the rules were the same. It runs a week before the big race. This year a seventeen year old boy won in twenty-two hours and fifty-nine minutes. He got thirteen thousand dollars and some wonderful gifts as well as the publicity."

"Last year a twenty-one year old legally, blind woman won the right to enter the race. She convinced the judges that she didn't want help with anything, just someone to tell her where the flags and markers were. A former WWF wrestling champion rode with her as her eyes. She had run her first race when she was eleven."

"I'll send you a copy of pictures and facts about the race. Tom and I both want to drive, but I know it will be impossible. First our parents would not approve and then we don't have the experience necessary. Besides, Tom is still very sensitive in some parts of his body and I'm sure the freezing cold would not be good for him."

"Oh, yes. Your students might ask about the name Iditarod. The early Athabascan Indians called their hunting grounds, on the trail, Haiditarod, which meant, "the distant place. In later years, when gold miners and travelers were on this trail, they remembered what the Indians called this area and shortened it to Iditarod. Neat, isn't it?"

"Tell everyone hello for us. We do honestly miss all of you and wish you could meet all the great friends we've made here. I'm now glad we had this chance to live here and know more about the people and the land. It won't be much longer until we'll be back in Virginia."

Tim mailed his long, long letter to Mrs. Berry.

The time came for everyone to prepare for the documented race. "Boys, it's foolish for you to think of driving in this race. It's far from demanding as the Iditarod, but it will be hard and challenging. You don't have the experience to drive in all that open country and the wild animal will be a constant danger. That's why each driver carries a rifle and flares. Other drivers can be nasty, too," Herb explained to his sons trying to make them understand they would not be driving without hurting their feelings.

"Dad, you're planning on driving and you don't have experience either," Tom argued.

"I **will** have a lot of experience by the time of the race. This is a three day race, camping overnight, caring for the dogs, being able to shoot a rifle, putting up and taking down a tent, cooking for yourself and the dogs over an open campfire, and many more requirements. I'll be alone most of the time with no one but the dogs."

"Dad, you don't have a team of sled dogs. Where will you get the dogs?" Tim asked worried.

"I've already contacted some professional mushers about renting some of their experienced dogs and will pay them to help me train with Greatheart."

"Greatheart!" Anna and the twins spoke together in shock.

"Dad, you can't take Greatheart out there. She's too young and has no experience. Suppose she get attacked by a polar bear or a pack of wolves?" Anna had tears in her eyes.

"How can anyone gain experience except by doing it?" herb smiled.

Herb rented the dogs and he and Greatheart began serious training. During the first run, Greatheart complained loud and long to have strange dogs behind her and, worse yet, between her and her human. She wasn't sure what was expected of her. Even though she was willing to obey and try, she still complained each time they hooked up for a run. She soon learned she was to lead.

The twins ran as far as they could on either side of Greatheart to encourage her and give her confidence. She quickly learned what was expected and began to show signs of enjoying the training. A sigh of relief went up from the Jackson family, and close friends, when the dogs began to work well together. Greatheart was exhibiting signs of becoming a leader.

The time for the race came much too quickly for Irene. It was cold, and nothing but snow as far as the eye could see. She packed food for Herb and the dogs. Herb had rented eleven dogs, and with Greatheart, making an even dozen. Irene also packed first-aid supplies and extra warm clothing. A tent and bedroll were the last items on the sled.

Irene was worried sick. "Herb, my darling, you're as bad as Tom. You have never done anything like this and you're not a teenager. You're a forty-four year old father and husband."

"And you, my precious sweetheart, are a forty-one year old mother and wife. What does age have to do with it?"

Realizing she had hurt his feelings, and not wanting him to feel badly while leaving, she hugged him and laughingly assured him that she was proud of him even though she was frightened for him. "I will be cheering louder than anyone," she assured him.

Musicians gathered in the cold air of the early morning to give a cheerful send-off to the eleven mushers and their dogs. The instruments could not be played in the freezing cold, so they stood inside the warm Community Center and played loudly to be heard outside.

Chief Houmay lined the drivers up for a final inspection. The representative for the film company gave last instructions and reminded the drivers that they would be filmed. Each driver called aloud as he checked the items on his sled. Food for both man and dogs, clothing, two rifles and ammunition, lanterns, tent, bedroll, portable radio phones, flares and first-aid kit. The rifles were for protection against possible dangers or to signal for help. A snow hook was on each sled. The snow hook acted as an anchor did on a boat. It was dropped in the snow to keep the dogs from dragging the sled past a safe point.

Each dog had been fed well and each driver had a good, hot breakfast, taking a thermos of a hot beverage with them. At last Chief Houmay fired a shot into the air as a signal to start the race. People were laughing and calling best wishes, but Irene was crying inside. Herb was not a man who had participated in sports even though he exercised and kept in good physical shape. She tried to smile bravely, and blew him a kiss, when Herb looked back at her.

Men had gone ahead on snowmobiles and set up markers for camp sites at specific locations. They had placed flags along the required route on tall wooden tripods so the drivers would not get lost. These same men would be spotter judges, meaning they kept in touch with the mushers to assure the well-being of men and dogs.

A lot of the men started out on a run except Herb and one other man. The professional driver had trained herb that the care of the dogs was of first importance. If they were too run too hard from the first, they would not have enough energy to continue. Herb asked for a brisk trot. At first Greatheart tried to run to catch up with the other teams, but Herb calmed her with a quiet, authoritative voice.

Herb rested his dogs for about fifteen minutes several times during the day. At the end of the first day he pulled into the camp slightly behind all the others. He good-naturedly took the teasing about being an old man. As he took the harness off the dogs, he checked their feet for possible injury from ice and snow. Ice chips caught in their pads could be as sharp as a razor blade. He put up his tent, then cooked his food, fed his dogs, then ate and visited with the nearby men.

If the men had not camped together, they might have been in the wilderness alone and facing all kinds of danger. None of these men were professional drivers. The contest was for amateurs. The thick coat of the dogs would protect them from the snow. Herb shook out enough straw for the dogs to lie on. Each dog had a coat which Herb fastened on them for the night. He smiled to see Greatheart's obvious intelligence. The dogs had lain close together for each other's warmth and Greatheart was in the center of the circle of dogs.

The next morning one of the spotter judges complimented Herb. "Dr. Harvey and I noticed how well you've paced your dogs and cared for them. We know how little experience and training you've had. Professional mushers put the comfort of the dogs ahead of their own, but amateurs, such as you and these men, often forget."

Everyone was up early in the cold and dark. There would only be less than five hours of light during the middle of the day. Lanterns were hung on each side of the sled. Tents were taken down and carefully wiped and rolled to be packed on the sled. Dogs were fed and harnessed as a last safety check was made. Herb had rawhide boots for each dog. He was careful to check to make sure the harness was not rubbing the dogs' sides.

Each musher pulled out as soon as his check was completed. A few were careless and only thought of running ahead in hopes of winning, As he slid over the snow, Herb was not upset to find himself alone in the vast wilderness of white. He could see one or two drivers ahead in the distance. He had a good compass, a radio to call for help, his rifle and good dogs.

Herb's lantern began to pick up spots of blood and then bigger spots.

He took out his rifle and brought it up where he could use it quickly. Was a driver ahead of him in trouble? Had that driver's dogs been attacked by wild animals?

Greatheart soon caught up with a team ahead of them, and pulled out to pass. Herb was distressed to see the dogs were limping and apparently in pain. Most of them had feet that had been cut from the sharp edges of ice. The driver, seeing that Herb was passing, urged his dogs to run faster.

As he came beside the driver, Herb called out pleasantly, "Hey, friend, there's lot of blood your dogs are dropping. Some of your dogs are badly hurt. You'd better stop and check their feet. They need wrapping. With that blood on the snow, you might be drawing some unfriendly critters."

"Mind your own business. You're just trying to trick me so you can get ahead. My dogs aren't hurt bad. They're tough and can take it. The snow will pack in their feet and keep the bleeding down."

It made Herb feel badly to know the dogs were in pain and the man was asking them to run harder. *The dogs don't belong to me, and I'm not responsible for his team, and I sure can't force him to stop and wrap the dogs' feet --.* He went on with a heavy heart and was more careful with his own team.

As the hours passed, Greatheart began to catch up with other teams. These drivers had been running all the way and their dogs were tiring fast. Greatheart had kept a steady, brisk trot with short rest stops, therefore she and her team were not as tired as the other dogs.

Just before noon Herb saw the orange flag showing the place where they were supposed to make a turn and return on another trail. As Herb pulled into camp that night there was only one team ahead of him. He saw the driver taking excellent care of his dogs. Herb introduced himself and was delighted to meet James Running Deer, an uncle of Alan Brave Bear. James was Alan's mother's brother.

Other drivers soon came in, but it was a little over an hour before the last team pulled in. It was the careless driver with dogs now bleeding badly and hardly staying on their feet. The dogs dropped in the snow with whimpers of pain and cries of anguish. The drivers could not believe that a human could purposely be so cruel to animals who were being faithful and trying to help him. Men like this would also be cruel to people if they had a chance.

"Those poor animals," Herb said dropping to his knees beside the dogs with a catch in his throat. "I wish you had stopped and called for help when I talked to you."

"And I told you the dogs belonged to me and it's nobody's business what I do with them," Harold Blevins blustered.

"Whoa man. Herb is speaking the truth. What kind of mind do you have to treat these animals like this when they're giving their hearts for you?" David Tuttle was angry.

"We ought to take everything away from you and leave you to go alone on foot through the wilderness," Jim Garrison said through gritted teeth.

Harold answered each man with filthy words and sarcasm. It was obvious that he cared nothing about the animals except to work them for his own use.

Herb prevented a fist fight by suggesting that each of the other drivers take a dog and doctor it. The cut feet were cleaned, treated and wrapped. Each dog was then brushed and fed. Harold, watching them with a smirky grin, said, "Boy, I sure hit it lucky to be with a group of bleeding hearts. You soft-brained guys are doing all the work for nothing. They're only animals and they don't expect better."

Paul Markle whirled, and with his left hand, jerked Harold around while, at the same time, his right fist drew back and slammed into Harold's mouth and nose. Harold tried to swing but was too clumsy. Paul hit him again so hard that he fell on his back and slid a few feet.

Herb and James got between the two men. "A fight won't erase what has happened and won't help the future," Herb spoke firmly with a quiet voice. "I respectfully request that each of you go to your tent and try to remain calm."

A spotter judge came up just at the end of the fight and heard what had happened. The judge checked the dogs and then used his radio to call for assistance for the injured dogs and to report what had happened. Harold Blevins was disqualified.

CHAPTER TWENTY-ONE

The next morning three snowmobiles pulling two flatbeds pulled into camp. Harold's dogs were carefully placed on furs on one flatbed. The second flatbed held Harold's sled and supplies and Harold. The third snowmobile was driven by a federal officer who informed Harold that he would face charges of abuse and animal cruelty.

The drivers were relieved when Harold left. They quickly prepared to continue the race. Anxiety and excitement were high because this was the last leg of the race. Herb and James started off easily, but the remaining drivers took off in a run. Keeping a brisk trot, Greatheart's team caught up with one tiring team after another.

James' team was about two feet ahead when the finish line came into sight. People had lit lanterns all up and down the line. About a half mile from the finish line, Herb called, "Okay, Greatheart. Take 'em girl." With a joyful howl she began to run and her team willingly followed.

It looked as if everyone in town was lined up, cheering and shouting.

Herb and James were neck and neck. Just as they were a few feet from the finish line the dogs, Herb had rented, recognized their master's voice calling encouragement to them. They gave a yelp of joy and turned to run to him. Their quick, unexpected move caused Greatheart to stagger slightly to one side right in front of James' team. Greatheart got her balance and ran across the finish line, dragging her dogs behind her. James pulled his dogs back to avoid a wreck.

Herb felt so bad to be declared the winner. His family and friends were hugging him and congratulating him. Greatheart got a lot of hugs and praise as she was unharnessed and Abram Wrigle claimed his dogs. Herb excused himself and quickly walked to the judges' stand where James was yelling and waving his fist in protest.

Chief Houmay jerked James' arm down so hard that he fell to the ground. Herb pulled James up and apologized. "Don't worry about this sore loser. I'll take care of him," the Chief sneered.

"Let him alone," Herb commanded. "He has a right to be angry. My team pulled across in front of James' team or we would have come across the finish line in a tie."

"How do you know?" James barked hurt and angry. "I could have pulled ahead of you at the last minute."

Herb faced the judges and the film representatives. "Gentlemen, I respectfully request that you declare this race to be a tie. James took excellent care of his dogs the entire time and was always a good sport. We both kept our teams moving well without forcing them. I would appreciate it if you would declare it a tie."

While the judges and the film representatives held a private conference, the crowd cheered for the popular Herb and approved of his request. The officials finally agreed to declare the race a tie with each man receiving twenty-five hundred dollars and both appearing in the documentary. The two men shook hands and grinned for the cameras.

Needless to say, Greatheart was the heroine of the hour. She had proven that she was a valuable working dog as well as a beloved family pet. Chief Houmay grudgingly praised her. "It's not common for a wolf dog to be willing to work in close contact with other dogs and people. I guess you folks were right. It does make a difference when a wolf dog is treated kindly and trained properly." The twins grinned at each other remembering what they had learned of Causuc's past history.

Everyone laughed when Greatheart leaped up and gave Causuc a doggie kiss. He looked astonished and then sheepishly hugged her.

January crawled by with one storm after another. In February polar bears were sighted just outside the town. They were hungry because the seals had been late in coming to the coast. Too, the ice was melting and taking away a place for the bears. The twins were eager to go out with the men to make the bears turn away before they could come into town.

"We're old enough to go with you, Dad. You'll need all the man power you can get," Tom wheedled.

"Yeah, Dad. We'll be lots of help. Besides this is a good time to learn how to handle a situation like this while you're with us," Tim attempted to flatter Herb.

"Hhmmph," Anna cleared her throat. "My dear little siblings. Do you mean you're going to handle the polar bears the same way you did the walrus -- or have you learned a lot about wild animals since then?"

The twins hesitated and darted glances at each other. "Well --- I guess someone should stay in town in case the bears get around the men." Tom spoke slanting his eyes at Anna.

"Sure. You're right," Tim grinned. "We'd better stay here and protect you women." Anna gave a choked laugh and turned away.

About twenty men rode out on snowmobiles with flare guns and rifles. A few of them had old buckets and heavy sticks to beat on the buckets to make a lot of noise and hope to frighten the bears away.

"Yee haw!" Ben Gregory yelled as he came close to one bear. It lowered its head and shook it while circling to try to come up behind Ben.

The people, left in town, were viewing the exciting, dangerous event through binoculars. A gasp went up when herb rode close to a bear and shot a flare gun over its head. His snowmobile overturned and threw Herb out in the snow into danger. Instead of running, the bear reared up and swiped its lethal claws at Herb. Fortunately he was able to duck and run behind the overturned snowmobile. James and Ben dove between Herb and the bear while two other men quickly jumped off their snowmobiles and lifted Herb's snowmobile. Chief Houmay quickly got out and ran to help Herb. A collected sigh of relief went up at Herb's rescue. None of the men were injured. The bears were so persistent that rifles had to be used.

Irene kept watching and saying: "Oh, no, no, no," over and over. She was shaking with fright, but was mesmerized with the action and could not stop looking. "Yes, yes, God bless him," Irene said with a shaky voice when she saw Causuc run to help Herb.

The men drove the snowmobile in circles around the bears making all kinds of noise and then opened a way for the bears to run away from town. "I think they're giving the bears an opening to run away," Mrs Eskise observed.

"It's not working," Mrs. Goughmas shouted. "Oh, just shoot them before some of you men get hurt."

Several explosive noises could be heard. "They **are** shooting," Irene called. A huge cheer went up when the men were seen coming back dragging three bears. Herb, the Chief and Ben were each given a white bear skin. The meat was used to feed the dogs and the fat was used for grease for sled runners and tools.

"Ben, I have no idea how to prepare this skin," Herb confessed. "I'd be grateful for any help you can give me."

"I would be my pleasure, but, believe it or not, Causuc is an expert in curing hides."

"Really! Well maybe I'll ask him if you think he would not mind."

"Herb, if you ask him, he will feel that you've accepted him and have respect for him and ---"

"Excuse me," Herb interrupted. "Chief," he called. "Could you come here for a minute, please?"

"Yes. What is it?"

"I hate to admit my ignorance, but I've never had a hide to cure and prepare." Herb explained. "Ben tells me that you're the best man for that job, and I was wondering if you would be so kind as to give me some help."

Causuc stood tall and squared his shoulders. "Sure," he grinned. "I've done lots of hides. I'll help you make a good rug that you'll be proud to take back to Virginia and show your friends."

"Thank you so much, Chief. Yes, I have many friends in Virginia, but they aren't any dearer than the friends we have here." Herb put an arm across Causuc's shoulder. "I consider you a very good friend, Chief."

Although March came in like a lion, everyone was excited knowing that in about two weeks the Iditarod would be coming into Nome. Airplane services would be busy, restaurants and anything that would draw tourists, would do a lot of business. The mushers would be staying in bed and breakfasts, and some of them would have families joining them. Some homes would have an extra bedroom for rent.

The twins, and even Anna, were thrilled to meet the men and women who were courageous enough to make the long drive through wilderness and wild animals. The mushers were from all over the world.

Toward the last of the month a pod of whales came close enough to be seen clearly from the shore line. The Eskimos and native Indians were permitted to go out and kill some whales. The twins were upset when they were not permitted to even go out in a boat.

A group of people came into town with all kinds of equipment. A few had large cameras on tripods. They were warmly welcomed, and several offered them help because the townspeople thought they were from the film company to make the promised documentary. The twins, and six other boys, followed the group to the beach curious as youth will be. They soon discovered the tragedy.

The boys came running back into town, some crying and all yelling for help. They wanted the men to form a posse and wanted these strangers strung up in old vigilante style. The boys, gasping for breath, and talking at once, told why they were upset.

Sam was the only one who could be understood. "Those men are using clubs to hit the baby seals in the head. They're taking the skins off them and leaving the bodies there. Some of the babies are crying loudly because they're not dead when the men start skinning them. Some mothers were killed and a whole crowd of babies are crying for their mothers."

Herb went with a group of men to investigate and talk to the group. The strangers claimed to have permits, but the townspeople knew better. The Eskimos were permitted to hunt a certain number of whale and other sea life, but special permits had to be issued for outsiders. Herb had taken rifles away from the townsmen before they got into trouble. He reminded them that they, too, would be breaking the law and would be arrested. "We must handle this lawfully."

"I am calling the Governor, newspapers and television stations to expose you," Herb said angrily. "We have pictures of all of you and what you are doing." These strangers were feeling so threatened that they left as quickly as they could get away, even leaving behind expensive equipment. Fortunately there was a television reporter and cameraman in town who filmed and recorded this tragic story. They got this film quickly to their studio so that the public would know what had happened.

The townspeople, and especially the youth, felt like crying when they saw the bodies and heard some babies crying. Some adults did cry. They could do nothing to these people, but they could contact government agencies to pick up the orphan baby seals and give them proper care until they were old enough to be returned to the Bering Sea. With heavy hearts the men picked up the skinned bodies to feed the dogs.

The women used moose milk soaked in cloths to let the babies suck on this. It kept them starving until veterinarians could bring a formula for them.

For several days this pitiful incident made news around the world. Most of the suspects were arrested, some were fined heavily and all of them spent time in jail. The people agreed that good could possible come out of this tragedy because now laws would be enforced to protect the animals.

Two weeks later the real filming crew did arrive to make the documentary. The excitement was not as great as it was planned because the law-breaking hunters had spoiled their joy.

Herb and James each drove a team of ten dogs while the film crew rode beside them and took pictures. Scrub planes circled low to film the two teams and the snow-covered area. Later a narrator would dub in the history, past and present, of Nome, the people and their lifestyle. The narrator's voice and some music would be dubbed by specialists. Millions would be able to see and enjoy the film on television.

Chief Joumay made it a point to welcome the film crew and share information with them that they wanted. Wonder of wonders he told them of the wolf dog and what great things she had done. A lot of people, hearing him, smiled to themselves remembering his first reaction to the wolf dog. The director, Andrew Plassy, was thrilled and excited at the amount of film and information he had gotten.

CHAPTER TWENTY-TWO

Andrew came to the Jackson home. "Mr. Jackson, I've been hearing a lot about this wonderful wolf dog. I know our viewers would love to know more about the dog and how your family raised her. Let me do a special on the dog and her humans. When can I see this great dog?"

Anna looked as if she might laugh out loud. "She's sitting right in front of you looking up at you."

The director turned pale and swallowed several times before he could speak. "Will she attack me? Does she mind a stranger being this close to her?"

Tim walked to the man and knelt by Greatheart. "She's the same as any other dog. Greatheart, shake." Greatheart, with a big grin, raised a paw to welcome the man. He finally took her paw as he took out a handkerchief and wiped his sweaty face.

"Forgive me, but I've only heard about wolves and wolf dogs. I've never been near one, but she seems friendly. Dozens of people have been singing her praises so I guess she's all right."

"You bet she's all right," Tom stated. "She saved our lives once and mine again later. She's been a friend to loads of people in this town. It's all in how kindly you treat an animal and how you make them understand that, even though you're in charge, they're still loved and appreciated."

"I repeat, may I make a story film on her and your family?"

"Yeah, Dad. Wouldn't that be great? Just like Jack London. Yahoo. We'll all be on television." Tom was too excited to calm down immediately.

With a thoughtful look, Tim said, "But it would have to be handled with great care or people would get the wrong idea about owning a wolf dog. They might think it sounds special for them and then either get in trouble or ruin a good animal."

"I agree with you, Tim." Anna said.

"I think what Tim means is that some people have a tendency to go with the herd, so to speak. When there's a movie about a black stallion, the demands for black stallions go up. Not everyone is qualified or emotionally capable of training such an animal," Herb explained.

Irene stepped beside Herb. "The documentary was about beautiful Alaska and the people who settled here. The history of Alaska, and present day Alaska, is important, but we are just one family here and we won't be here much longer. There are hundreds of people who should be given attention for keeping the development of Alaska going forward. We don't deserve it, even with a wonderful dog."

"Well said," Herb smiled. Tom was disappointed, but Greatheart didn't care. The director was disappointed, but he couldn't persuade, or bribe. Them to do a separate film on them and their wolf dog.

After the film crew left, the town was quieter that it had been in several weeks. The townspeople felt a let-down, but everyone was looking forward to seeing their town, and their people, on national television.

Irene warned the children to keep Greatheart on a leash outside. "She is ready to mate and I don't want the same thing happening to her that happened to Galena."

'Why not, Mom?" Tom questioned. "It would be super to have Greatheart's babies."

It could be dangerous," Irene warned again. "If she mated with a wolf, her pups, or cubs, would be almost wholly wolf. It would be against the law to keep them and we would be forced to get rid of them. More than likely they would be destroyed or turned loose to roam with the wild wolves."

"Oh, no, not that," Tim worried. "Let's keep an eye on her. Hey! I have an idea. Why don't we select a good dog and have her mated? Then we'll be sure she's okay."

"No way, Jose," Irene smiled. "My idea is to have her spayed so that she can't have babies. If we take her back to Virginia, our neighbors will be anxious enough about having a wolf dog near them without her having babies."

"Mom's right. We'll have enough problems getting Greatheart accepted," Anna nodded wisely as she continued cooking dinner.

Herb listened gravely. "Let me think about this and check with the home office to see what has to be lawfully done to take her to Virginia."

"Tom, are you awake?" Tim whispered leaning over Tom.

"I am now. What's your problem?" he answered with a big yawn and turning on a light. "You idiot. It's two in the morning."

"Of course it's morning. I've had a supersplendifferous idea. Let's ask Mr. Whitzel if we can mate Greatheart to his prize malamute. Her babies would be safe then."

"You wouldn't be safe when mom and dad got hold of you. Didn't you hear mom? She intends to have Greatheart spayed so she can't be mated. Besides I'm not sure Mr. Whitzel would allow us to use his dog. After all, his dog's a champion. And where would we get the fee? People pay through the nose for his dog's services."

"Well --- if we got the two dogs together and our folks and Mr. Whitzel didn't know about it---" Tim spoke slowly and thoughtfully.

"How are you going to do that? Wow! Mom and dad won't believe this. You're talking more like me than I do."

Tim talked until he made Tom believe it could be done. They were impatient for the hours to pass so they could talk to Ben, Charlie, Alan and Sam and get their help. The next morning the twins rushed out right after breakfast before they could be asked what their plans for the day were. They met the four boys and shared their plan.

"Are you crazy?" Ben exploded. "In the first place Mr. Whitzel will never agree to mate his champion with a half wolf. His dog's puppies sell for an astronomical amount of money. With wolf in them they would be of no use. Your parents will string you both up by your thumbs when they found out."

"It'll be too late to do anything when our parents find out. And we won't talk to Mr. Whitzel. We'll get the animals together ourselves," Tim persisted.

"Crazy for sure," Sam muttered. "You can't mate animals any time you want. They have to be ready. Hasn't anyone ever told you about the birds and the bees?"

"Yes," Tom said with a sneer. "I know about the birds and bees. We happen to know that Greatheart is ready. Why do you think we're talking about this now? I'm just wondering about the final phase of our plan." The six boys walked slowly lost in thought.

"Look!" Charlie hissed. He grabbed the others and pulled them into the alley by the grocery store. Mr. Whitzel is leaving and Koko is in the yard."

"But there's a high fence around the property," Alan pointed out.

"He left in such a hurry that, as far as he knows, he might not have shut the gate securely. We can let Koko out and make sure he meets Greatheart."

Tom was so excited, he was stuttering.

"Hoboy. Prepare to lose our heads," Sam said with a quiver in his voice.

"Where's Tim?" Tom looked around.

"He took off running as soon as Mr. W. got out of sight. Here he comes now with Greatheart," Alan answered.

Tom ran over and opened Mr. Whitzel's gate. "Hi, Koko. Come here. What a pretty boy you are. Have you seen our pretty girl? Her name is Greatheart." Koko ran out and straight to Greatheart. Tim let her off the leash and the two dogs ran off together.

"Catch him," Ben called nervously. 'We'll be in real hot water if anything happens to that champion dog. He's a registered Malamute."

"He won't be hard to catch in a short time," Tim grinned.

The boys walked slowly back toward their homes. They played a game of basketball and talked about the Jackson family going back to Virginia. Much later Greatheart came running to them with Koko close beside her. The boys jumped guiltily when Mr. Whitzel ran up to them.

"I say there, boys. I don't know how my dog got out. Would you hold his collar until I can get hold of him? I'm thankful your dog was here for him to stop and visit. No telling where he might have run off to. Thank you so much." He led Koko off.

"Whew," Alan blew his breath out trembling. "I was sure we were goners."

"That's what a guilty conscience will do to you," Ben said even though he was shaking as he dropped to sit on the ground. "My legs feel like wet noodles."

The twins looked at each other. "Now I feel bad about this," Tim said, "but it's too late. Let's just hope she'll be healthy and have healthy babies."

"We'll know in about sixty-three days," Sam told them.

The boys separated to go to their own homes. Tom and Tim walked with Greatheart between them, now on her leash. They hesitated before entering the house.

"Well, here goes nothing," Tom whispered.

"Boys, what's wrong with you? You're not eating as you usually do." Irene reached to feel Tom's forehead. "Are you feeling sick?"

"Uh--no, Mom, we're fine. We just have a lot on our minds," Tom answered.

"Yeah, a lot on our minds, Tim mumbled. He straightened up and spoke more clearly. "It **is** getting close the time for us to leave. May we be excused?"

As the twins left the room, Herb looked after them with a frown. "Am I getting unnecessarily suspicious in my old age, or did those boys act as if they were guilty about something?"

Anna shook her head. "I don't know what it could be. They've just been in the neighborhood with their friends all afternoon."

"Herb, I do think it's because we are about to wrap up our time here and go back to Virginia. We've all made a lot of friends here and it won't be easy to just walk off even though we're anxious to go home," Irene soothed him.

"Maybe you're right. But something doesn't feel right. I just have a feeling. Oh, well."

"Well, if they're up to something, I haven't a clue as to what it could be," Anna said as she stood to clear the dining table.

April seemed to rush by. The days had more light now that the sun stayed in view longer. Anna asked that nothing be done for her eighteenth birthday. "Just going home will be sufficient."

The first week of May, the twins walked into the kitchen. "Mom," Tim started, "Tom and I have been talking and we don't want anything done for our sixteenth birthday. We don't really feel like celebrating anything. We've made so many good friends that we're going to find it hard to leave."

Herb called his work crew together. "Friends, I first want to tell you how proud I am to have been a part of your group. There just isn't a better work crew anywhere." He paused for the cheering to die down. "We did what we set out to do. We proved that natural gas can be found under the tundra and it will be easy to get out with proper equipment and a lot of care. There is also some coal, but I don't know how much at this time. I won't be here to head the work crew that sets up machinery and does the drilling." Groans and calls of concern were all that could be heard for a few minutes.

Herb continued. "I've made recommendations for administrative positions. This does not mean that I don't approve of the rest of you. Believe me, these are difficult decisions to make. All of you have been honest, reliable, diligent workers and, best of all, you have become close friends. I had to follow government guidelines to make my selections. Of course you understand that my recommendations are not ironclad. The final decision rests with our federal government. At any rate, I'm thankful that I had this opportunity to work with all of you and get to know your families. My family and I will be leaving the second week of June." More groans. "I plan to return for a visit and observe your progress. In the meantime, let's make sure our project is documented correctly and that all required government papers are filed properly." Laughs followed this because filling government papers took time and were a headache.

"I know that whomever is chosen for your administrators will be someone you can appreciate and with whom you'll work as well as you have for me. I can't thank you enough for making my stay here so pleasant. God bless you all." there was a lot of cheers, backslapping and a few tears.

CHAPTER TWENTY-THREE

"Boys!" Irene called angrily charging into the house with Greatheart dragging on a leash. Herb was sitting in the living room and Anna came running from her bedroom.

"What is it, Mom?" Anna asked anxiously as the twins sauntered into the living room.

It was obvious to all of them that Irene was angry. "If you know anything about this, you'd better confess now and save yourselves getting into later trouble."

"Know about what?" Tom asked softly. Tim just stared.

"I've been thinking that Greatheart was gaining weight. I felt something move in her stomach and rushed her to the veterinarian thinking she might have worms. **Well, guess what**?"

"What, Mom. Is she sick or going to die?" Anna asked shaking.

"Do you want to tell her, boys?" Irene snapped

"Tell her what?" Tom asked with a frown.

"For heavens sake, Irene, just tell us," Herb urged.

"It wasn't worms I felt moving in her. It's babies," she said with a sob as she sank into a chair. With gritted teeth she glared at the twins. "I don't imagine you know about it."

Tom fell on his knees, hugging the dog and hiding his face in her fur. "Babies? Really truly? Greatheart, are you really having babies?"

"Honey, maybe she got out sometime or a male came into our yard. It doesn't have to mean the boys know about it, does it, boys?" Herb looked sternly at his sons.

211

Tom giggled. "Babies. I don't know nothing about babies," he said in a falsetto voice as if he were in 'Gone With The Wind'. "Come on, Tim, let's go tell our friends. I'm sure they'll want one of the babies." the twins ran out before their mother could question them further.

"I tell you, Herb. They're guilty," Irene choked.

Herb chuckled reaching to hug her and calm her. "If they're guilty, they sure cover it well. Greatheart, old girl, we'll have to take better care of our little mother. Wish you could tell us the true story. Did you get special vitamins for her?" he asked Irene.

"Yes. She also has to be walked for a specific time each day and fed on schedule."

"When will we have her babies?" Anna asked.

"About fourteen days."

"Man, how did you get out of answering your mother?" Ben asked. "My mother may be little, but she would have had me in a wrestling clinch if she thought I was guilty." the boys laughed at the idea of his small, very kind mother holding him in any kind of clinch.

The days flew by. The three children made excellent grades on their exams. They came home from school to be met by Irene motioning them to be quiet.

"Déjà vu," Tim shuddered. "Is this familiar? Remember when Galena had her babies?" he asked fearfully. "What is it, Mom?"

"Come into the kitchen."

They trooped into the large kitchen. There in the corner, on soft rugs, was Greatheart with four fat, healthy babies. One male and three females. "We can't tell yet how they're going to look," Irene said. "As soon as they mature a little, we'll be able to guess who the papa is."

"Wow. They look fat and healthy," Anna stated in awe. "It doesn't look as if we'll have problems with them like we had with Galena's babies. I'm so relieved." she giggled. "It's a good thing we have a large kitchen with this corner going to the dogs, else people would think we're terrible unsanitary."

"Who cares what other people think." Tom stated. "We take care of our animals." He reached to pick up a puppy and jumped back in surprise. "Did you see that?! Greatheart growled and snapped at me."

"This is her first litter and she's protective. And her last," Irene said firmly. "Let her get used to having them and then she'll let you pet them."

One night, after dinner, Herb called a family meeting. "Our clothing and household items need to be packed and ready to ship to Virginia. Just keep a small case of items you'll need for about two days. Paul will fly us to Fairbanks, where we'll make arrangements to fly to Virginia. We'll actually land at Dullus Airport."

"Will Greatheart fly with us?" Tom asked. Silence.

"Dad?" Tim was concerned.

Herb dropped his head. "I've been a coward. I haven't been able to tell you what I know you'll be anxious to hear." Herb took a deep breath and straightened his shoulders. Irene already knew what he was having trouble saying. Anna dropped to the floor at his feet and waited.

"Well. Go on, Dad," Tom urged impatiently.

"I told you I'm a coward and I'm truly sorry." Herb answered with a shamed expression. Tim sat silently and waited. "I checked with my office in D.C. and with the airlines about Greatheart. My boss informs me that they're reluctant to have a half wolf brought into Virginia. Too, she would be placed in quarantine for a month to make sure she is healthy and safe."

"What's the bottom line?" Tim almost whispered.

"The bottom line is that Greatheart would be placed in unfamiliar situations without us to comfort her. The stress would be unpleasant for her and ----"

"And what?" Anna encouraged him.

"There is a possibility that the stress might bring out the wild side of her causing a reverse in her personality. In that case she would have to be destroyed."

"What you father wants you to do is consider what is best for Greatheart. Forget our feelings. She would be the one feeling as if she were being punished without knowing why. Too, she would feel that we no longer loved her." Irene told them.

Herb continued. "We can put her through a very successful situation that will be alarming for her or we can leave her in familiar surroundings with someone who knows her and will treat her as we have."

"What about the babies?" Anna asked softly.

"It might be possible to take one with us. We have to obtain a health certificate and an okay from several departments both here and in Virginia. She might have to be put in quarantine for a very short time."

The three children looked at each other with agonized expressions. "May we talk it over and let you know what we decide?" Anna asked.

"Of course. It is a serious decision and your mother and I want you to be happy. We also want the dogs to be well cared for and happy. I know we love our girl for her own sake and because she's Galena's daughter. Your decision must be for the good of the dogs."

The next morning, after breakfast, Tom told Irene and Herb that they were ready to discuss their decision, however, they wanted to wait until they had talked to some friends.

The twins asked Ben, Sam, Charlie and Alan to meet them at the Community Center. Anna asked Daniel and several friends to meet with them.

None of the family felt much like eating dinner, but they pushed their food around on their plates. Anna and Irene quickly cleaned up while the twins sat on the front porch waiting for the family discussion. They were surprised to see Mr. Whitzel coming up their driveway.

"Hello, boys. I've heard that you have some mighty pretty puppies. May I see them?"

"Uh -- sure," Tim stuttered. "Yes, sir. Come in." He jumped up and held the door open and then followed Mr. W. into the house. "Mom. Dad. We have company. Please have a seat, sir. My parents will be right in." Tim was nervous and he knew Tom, standing behind him, was about to explode.

"Mr. Whitzel, what a nice surprise," Irene walked in as Mr. W. stood.

"Please, sit," she said. "My husband will join us in a mom--- oh, here he is."

"Hello, Mr. Whitzel. How nice of you to visit us." The two men shook hands and then Herb sat beside him on the couch.

"Forgive me for coming in uninvited. As I told your sons, I heard about the puppies and wondered if I might see them."

"What for?" Tom blurted.

"Tom!" Irene scolded. "I'm sorry, Mr. Whitzel. I cant imagine what has come over my rude son. You're always welcome in our home."

"Never mind," Mr. W. said with a twinkle in his eye. "If what I think is correct, I can guess why he is defensive."

"What do you mean?" Herb asked confused.

"First, may I see the puppies and then I'll answer your question."

"Of course you may see them," Irene said quickly as she stood. "Follow me. They're in a corner in the kitchen."

Greatheart gave a small, warning growl. The babies rolled like fat little balls over the floor. Mr. W. squatted down so that Greatheart could see he was not harming her babies. They bounced around and came to inspect him.

"Just as I thought," he said with a big grin. "That little male is a duplicate of my Koko. And one of the females looks a lot like him, too. He is the sire, isn't he, boys?" he looked at the twins. Silence

"Boys," Herb spoke firmly, "answer Mr. Whitzel."

"Frankly, it is a relief to answer you, sir," Tim hung his head. "I have felt so guilty that it's made me sick. My parents said we could not breed Greatheart because of the wolf blood, but we, Tom and I, thought she would have beautiful babies with the right dog. We know your Koko is a champion and is very handsome, so, we decided to get them together. I know we didn't think before we acted. I'm sorry. I know we should have been more mature and discussed it with you first. But we wanted her to have at least one litter. If you want a fee for breeding, we'll pay you." he finished with a red face and looking very ashamed. Tom still said nothing, just stood getting red in the face and clenching his fists.

"Ordinarily I do charge for Koko's service. However, these puppies can't be registered because of the wolf blood." He looked thoughtful for a moment. "My six year old grandson is coming for a visit soon. His mother tells me he is now ready to care for a dog. If I might have the male to give to my grandson, I'd consider it payment in full."

"Mr. Whitzel, I can't tell you how horrified and ashamed I am. Boys, do you realize that you've broken some laws? If Mr. Whitzel so desires, he can bring charges against you and it won't be something you can get out of easily."

Tom slid down the wall to sit on the floor looking faint. Tim staggered as if his legs would not hold him. He shakily sat heavily in a chair.

Tom finally spoke, "I know saying I'm sorry won't be enough. Our parents raised us to be honest and to take responsibility for our actions. We disobeyed our parents and stole the service of your dog. What we did was wrong and we would like to make it right."

"It's entirely my fault," Tim said. "I was the one who talked everyone else into getting the dogs together. I'm the one who should be punished."

"Everyone else," Herb spoke surprised. "Who else is involved?"

"I'm sorry, Dad, but I respectfully decline to give their names at this time. I'm the one who instigated the whole thing and I'm taking responsibility," Tim spoke softly.

"You keep talking about punishment," Mr. W. said. "What you did **was** wrong and you should have consulted me first, at least talked it over with your parents. What's done is done and there's really no harm. With your parents' permission, I have a suggestion."

Herb nodded while Irene twisted her hands and looked as if she might cry. She could see how angry Herb was and embarrassed and so was she.

"I've given Koko basic training, but he needs more and I don't have the time. He's a restless dog because he isn't being challenged enough. Would you boys be willing to work with him and teach him as you have your dog? If you would be willing to give him the time and give me the male for my grandson, we'll forget all this happened. Deal?" He held his hand toward Tim who thankfully shook hands with him as Tom jumped up to do the same. The twins then excused themselves and went to their room.

CHAPTER TWENTY-FOUR

"Thank you, Mr. Whitzel. You've been very understanding and more than fair," Irene gave a relieved sigh. "I had no idea it was your dog."

"If your sons knew what I got into when I was their age, they'd think I have some nerve," he laughed. "By the way, as long as we have a gentleman's agreement, why not call me Jason." he chuckled because Greatheart walked up to him, sat and gave him a paw. He shook her paw and she leaned against his leg. "See. She's thankful that her young masters are going to be okay."

He leaned over to pet Greatheart. "May I see your fine boy, little mother?" He slowly leaned over and picked up the male who immediately gave him puppy kisses and wriggled so hard it was difficult to hold him. "Oh, yes, this will work out fine. Thank you for letting me see the dogs," he said as he carefully placed the little fellow beside his mother.

"I'm ashamed that you had to visit for this reason and thank you again for being so kind." Herb shook hands with Jason and walked him to the door.

"Please come any time."

The next evening Herb called the family together. "We are being forced to make decisions. Time is getting short. Boys, I'm still upset with you for acting without thinking. I hope you'll honor your agreement with Mr. Whitzel and leave here with good thoughts about you. I want to know who else was involved."

"I'll tell you if you promise not to say anything to the others or their parents. It was my plan and they just helped as friends," Tim answered.

"I won't say anything if you promise to talk to them and explain where you committed a crime and inform them of the outcome."

"We promise, Dad," Tom spoke. "Now can we discuss our plans for Greatheart and her babies?"

Anna spoke first. "We've decided that we love Greatheart for herself as well as being Galena's daughter. We love her enough to let her go. She was born here and is acclimated to this climate. Too, she would have a rough time being accepted in Virginia. City living would be stressful for her. Our final decision is where she should go."

Irene raised a hand. "Your dad and I have talked about where she should go. I must admit I talked to several people and everyone was willing to take her. However, we think you'll agree that the Eskise family know her and helped with her training. She knows them and they love her, therefore they are the best choice."

"That's who we have chosen," Tom was jubilant.

"What a relief. Now about the babies," Irene said.

"We've decided on that, too," Tom answered. "Mr. Whitzel is taking the male as soon as they are weaned. Sam wants one female and Daniel wants the other."

"That leaves one girl," Herb reminded them.

The three children looked at each other. "We were hoping you could make arrangements for us to take her. That way we'll keep a part of Galena and Greatheart," Anna explained.

"Yes, we've named her Hope," Tom spoke hurriedly.

Herb and Irene looked at each other in the way people do who have been married a long time and know each other. "We thought you might want one," Herb smiled. "We didn't know you'd named her though. I like the name. Hope. It says a lot for her future and for ours.

As soon as the babies are weaned and taken care of, we need to take Greatheart to the Eskise home so she'll know it's hers before we leave. She'll feel more at home and won't feel abandoned." Tom hung his head and walked out of the room. Tim and Anna followed in silence as they each went to their rooms.

Happiness in going back to Virginia and sadness in leaving Alaska caused many mixed feelings that changed daily. At the end of the week, Anna was almost dancing as she came gleefully in with the mail. "Look! I've been accepted to enroll in James Madison University in Harrisonburg, Virginia. I was accepted in a couple of other colleges, but my heart has been set on Madison, and I'm going there," she sang it out as she danced around.

"Yea! Good for you. We'll be in the eleventh grade in Fairfax High," Tom proudly stuck his chest out.

"We all have something to rejoice about. I sent enough stories to my publisher and they'll be in three separate books because he's accepted them all," Irene sang out. "Anna, your illustrations were wonderful and your name is given as the illustrator."

"Wow! Great, Mom," Tim ran to hug her.

"Oh, Mom. I'm so proud of you and I don't care whether I get credit as illustrator or not. I'm just happy for you." Anna cheered.

"Group hug," Tom yelled and pulled everyone together.

The next day the babies went to their new homes. The twins dragged their feet as they walked Greatheart to the Eskise home, "We'll bring her things later. We wanted her to get used to her new home before we leave," Tom knelt to hug Greatheart and hid his red face and tear-filled eyes in her thick fur.

"You are the best friends," Ben grinned, "I'd have been crushed if you hadn't left her with me. I love her as much as you do and she's known me all her life. I'll write and tell you how she's doing."

The twins walked home in silence. They gathered Greatheart's food, her dishes, toys, harness and everything she would need. "Don't forget her sleeping pad." Tim wiped his eyes. They took all the supplies to Ben and gave Greatheart a last hug. They ran out hearing Greatheart whining and struggling to follow them. Tears were streaming down their faces as they burst into the house and ran to their room.

The twins asked so many questions worrying about their future that Anna finally lost patience. With hands on her hip she glared at them after had asked a list of questions. "Not knowing definitely, I cannot state with any degree of accuracy for fear of deviating from the chosen paths of aptitude, and not wishing to make a prevaricator of myself, I shall refrain from comment." With that she turned and left the room.

"Huh?" Tim looked after her in confusion.

"Don't pay any attention to her," Tom spoke with disgust, "her head's so big, she thinks she's the whole parade."

Anna came back. "My head big! What gave you that idea?"

"You did the illustrations for mom's books. You have a 4.0 grade point average and will graduate as the Valedictorian and you've been accepted in one of the best Universities in the country."

"You're impossible," Anna stomped out.

The next night people gather in the Community Center to watch the documentary together. The film was shown the first week of June. There was enough food for everyone and enough for the Jacksons to take home with them so Irene wouldn't have to cook and dirty her kitchen.

"Hey, look!" Alan screamed. "There's Uncle James. Isn't her neat? He's a star. "The twins smiled knowing that if their dad had not been such a good sport, James would not have been in the documentary at all.

"That was great." Ben Gregory jumped up to lead clapping. "We are proud of our state and now the whole world will admire it."

"And be envious," Chief Houmay finished. He stood up. "I want to tell everyone how much I value the friendship of the Jackson family. I have to admit that I thought they were irresponsible at first with the wolf dog. But after getting know them, I really like them -- all of them," he grinned at the twins. He waited for the cheers to subside and then continued. "Truthfully, I'll miss you boys. You've kept all of Nome on its toes. Maybe you'll come back and visit."

"You'll come to Virginia to see us, Chief," Tom called out.

"What are you going to do with your house?" Jack Jordon asked.

"We've left it in the hands of a real estate agent," Herb answered.

"My cousin and his family will be arriving here in about two weeks and I'm sure they would love to buy it."

"That'll be great, jack."

"Tell us about your books. When can we read them?" Several people asked Irene urging her to talk.

"They're about my family, your families, especially the children and what a great time we've had here. There are stories about Galena and Greatheart and some of your animals. There are some folk stories and myths of your state. I hope you'll approve and enjoy them. I'll send copies to the city library and to the high school."

"Did you include the race?"

'Sure did. And about my twins' adventures with the walrus and Tom's experience with the dynamite. I also included the battle with the seal killers and the polar bears. Best of all, I've included how dear all of you are to us."

The group cheered and people crowded around to hug them.

Paul Grigsby came to them. "I'll pick you up at six thirty tomorrow morning. I have your cars sold for you."

Mr. Eskise told them they had decided to have Greatheart spayed to avoid the possibility of more part wolf cubs. The

Jacksons left everyone with tears in their eyes. Three days and they'd be in Virginia.

Paul flew them to Fairbanks where they were to make connections to fly out that afternoon. "I'm glad you're going to be able to keep your puppy on the plane with you. She won't be so frightened then."

"Isn't it great? Dad had to pay extra, but we're happy that she doesn't have to go into quarantine. We have a veterinarian certificate with us to prove she's healthy and not dangerous."

"We're all relieved. Paul, we've sincerely appreciated your friendship and your help more than I can express. Do come to see us." Irene reached to hug him.

"Well look who's here," Herb said in pleased surprise. Chief Houmay had come to tell them goodbye and wish them well again. They were even more surprised when he hugged each one.

They took a taxi from the airport into town. "We have almost five hours to fill. Might as well look around and have lunch before we go back to the airport. Stay together. If I have to search for anyone, I might be tempted to leave you behind," Herb grinned.

"Mom, I'm glad you were able to leave most of the furniture for the family who bought the house. They have two girls our age who can be friends with Ben and Greatheart," Tim said.

"Sure. Now that we're moving out, cute girls come in," Tom moaned.

"There'll be plenty of cool, cute girls in Fairfax," herb reminded him.

"Anna, let's go down to the ice cream parlor and sandwich shop," Tom invited.

"I'd love it," she answered stepping between her tall brothers and taking an arm of each one.

"We might as well join them," herb placed an arm around Irene.

Walking behind their children, Irene looked lovingly at them. "I'm glad our children love each other and are friends. Too often siblings don't get along."

As they sat down in a large half-circle booth, Anna took Hope from Irene. "Sweet little Hope. You're going to have such an adventure. Your first plane ride, a different climate and lots of new people to know. It's a good thing we're taking her while she's so little. She won't miss her mother and Alaska."

"Yes. We'll always have Galena and Greatheart in our hearts. This little fuzz ball can't take their place, but she had made her own place in our hearts. You've learned so much about training dogs. Now do a good job on this one and make her into a champion." Herb looked fondly at Hope and rubbed her back. She struggled to get to him hoping to get a stomach rub.

What adventures will Hope find in Virginia? Will she make a good family pet and a good working dog as her mother and grandmother had done?

Will the twins have as many adventures, especially dangerous ones?

PART III
HOPE

Dangerous Hilarity

CHAPTER TWENTY-FIVE

"Oh, my gosh. Look at you two." James Dodd, Mark Tully and Alex Bauman had come to welcome the Jacksons back to Fairfax. "How tall are you guys?" Jim was astonished at how much the twins had changed while they were in Alaska.

"Wow! It's so great to have you back." Mark and Alex echoed Jim's enthusiastic greeting.

"We're six-two," Tim answered proudly. "We're as tall as dad now, so we expected to get tall. Mom thinks we'll be taller."

Tom slapped Jim on the back. "I can't get over how much you three dudes have changed. Talk about us. You're all taller than you were when we left." Jim Dodd had been Tom's best friend while going up.

"Did you take a lot of pictures on your trips and around where you lived?" Alex asked with interest. "Tell us about your time spent in Alaska."

"Time spent?" Tom laughed. "Alex, you make it sound as if we were in prison."

"Nah. You know what I mean. Quitcher teasing. I really am interested in what's been happening to you since you left here."

"Wait until you hear the best news. Mom wrote three books about our adventures as well as about the people in Nome. Anna illustrated them and they're all three going to be published. You'll enjoy reading them because they're about us, our dogs, the people we met including folk's stories and myths." Tim was so thrilled for his mother that he had spoken without taking a breath. He was now gasping causing the boys to laugh.

"Wow!" Mark drew the word out and opened his eyes wide. "She wrote three of them. Wow! She must really be good. Anna illustrated them, huh? Anna's not only beautiful but smart and talented as well."

"Whoa, Mark. Why are you blushing? How long have you thought our sister is beautiful and smart?" Tom grinned as he placed an arm across Mark's shoulders.

"Tom, you may have changed on the outside, but it's obvious you're still the same inside. A real stinker."

"Sorry, Mark. I didn't mean to embarrass you or make you feel badly. You'd be surprised how much I **have** changed. You know how I fought leaving here. Well, I learned to love Alaska and the people. It was hard to leave them."

"Hey guys. Do you want to go for pizza with us?" Anna called as she came out of the house with Janell Morris, Dede Dodd and Michelle Tully.

"Sure."

"Good deal."

They all piled in the Dodd van which Dede was driving. "Buckle up everyone. We're off." she sang out.

"Do you guys drive yet?" Tim asked.

"Yes, I do," Mark answered. Jim and Alex said they knew how but only Mark had a license.

"Anna has her license from Alaska. She'll have to get it transferred or whatever you have to do," Tim explained.

"Dad lets me drive with him on the back roads, but mom would have a fit if she knew," Alex confessed.

"Your dad hides things from your mother?!" Jim was shocked as were all the young people.

"Our dad would never do anything like that. He tells us we must respect both of them and be honest with them. They're honest with us and expect the same in return. Besides, suppose you were involved in an accident. Your mother would sure know then."

"Aw, nothing's gonna happen."

"That's why they're called accidents. Things happen that no one plans or expects."

"Here we are," Dede called out.

"Last one in pays for all the pizza," Janell teased.

"Oh, no. Everyone has to agree to it and we didn't," Anna declared.

There was a pleasant confusion while they ordered. Anna looked fondly around the group thinking. *Dede, Jim, Mark and Michelle have all matured. They used to give each other such grief. The jury is still out on Alex. My brothers have been little brats at time, but all in all, we've gotten along well. I'm proud of how they've grown.*

"Back to driving" Jim said. 'We're all in the same boat as far as age goes. I'm going to lay a, shall we say, a bet on the rest of you guys. That is if you're man enough to take it."

"A bet," Tim spoke hesitantly. "What kind of bet?"

"No betting," Anna said pointing a straight finger at him.

"Oh, money won't be involved," Jim explained. "What I have in mind is for all of us to practice driving until we go for our driver's test. But before we take the test, I suggest we have an adult help us set up an obstacle course and drive through it. We'll compete to see who gets the best score."

"Super!" Tom was excited. "I'm sure our parents would approve of that. But how come the rest of you guys haven't gotten your license? Tom and I didn't need one is the only reason we don't have one. We walked everywhere or went by dog sled or snowmobile."

"My folks wouldn't let me because they thought my grades were too poor."

"I broke my leg in football practice and have been out of action for some time."

The excuses were good and the subject was dropped. They did agree that none of them absolutely had to drive. Everything they needed was either in walking distance or someone would drive them. Being an average teen they liked the idea of driving and getting with friends.

"I have another great idea," Jim continued. "I have an uncle, dad's brother, that is a Virginia State Trooper. I'm sure he would be glad to set up a course and test us. He could even ask us questions and help us practice for the written part of the driver's test."

"Great." All the boys did a high five. "I'm depending on our beautiful, smart, sweet talented sister to work with Tim and me," Tom laughed looking at Mark.

"Tom," Anna snickered, "You really are a stinker. I bet dad will want to be the one teaching you."

"Well he can help so he and mom will feel better, but we'll have practice t when he won't have time or he'll be at work. Please, please, Anna, promise you'll help us get a good start before you leave for college." Tom got on the floor on his knees and begged like a dog.

"Okay, okay. I know when I'm a sucker, but I'll help."

"Yea! With your help we'll be ready for anything," Tim beamed.

"You might as well crown me now, king of the road," Alex bragged. "I've got a good start."

Anna thought to herself how much time she had before she left for college and all she had to do. She was also happy that Michelle was also going to Madison.

Alex scooted his chair closer to Anna and placed a penny on the table in front of her.

"What's that for?"

"I thought it was a penny for them, but maybe the price has escalated with the increase in the economy," Alex grinned.

"Okay, brain. What are you saying to my sister?" Tim bristled with a brother's protective attitude.

"Hold your horses. Don't you talk our language any more? It's a penny for your thoughts. Remember?" Alex sneered.

"Well don't get in a sweat, buddy. I was just checking."

Tom quickly changed the subject asking about former teachers and classmates. He looked puzzled at Tim. *What's wrong with Tim?*

"Anna, would you like to drive into D.C. shopping tomorrow?" Dede asked. "We three are going and it would be perfect if you'd come, too. We'll stop at Seven Corners first. You won't believe how it has changed and grown."

"I'd love to. I can't think of anything that would prevent me from going," she answered. She was thinking, *What's wrong with Tim? He and Tom appear to have exchanged personalities today.*

"It's been great getting together. I sure missed you folks, but I'm glad you had the experience of living in Alaska." Jim lightly punched each twin.

"Yeah, we've waited impatiently for you to come back so we could do things like old times," Mark added.

"Even good things must come to an end," Alex broke in. "I gotta get home before dad does or I'll be in even more hot water."

"More?" Tim raised his eyebrows.

Mark drew a breath of disgust. "Alex couldn't take the car, so he took the riding mower and drove it through his mother's flower bed and vegetable garden. His dad thought it was funny until he discovered that Alex had wrecked his motorcycle. He's supposed to be grounded and under home arrest, but he sneaks out." Mark didn't smile and neither did the others.

"S'truth," Alex laughed. "I'm close to my house, so I'll trot on home. It sure was nice being with all of you."

He has more nerve than I have, and I got into some doozies when I was younger," Tom mused.

The young people crawled back into the van and drove back to the Jacksons. They got out with the boys whooping, yelling and teasing as usual.

"Ho ho. That's too little to be the famous Greatheart. What is it anyway?" Mark teased.

"Hope! Mom must have let her out to meet us. This is Greatheart's daughter." Tom proudly introduced her. Tim had written and kept them all up-to-date on all the dogs.

"I think she's darling," Dede knelt to pick her up. "Aren't you precious."

"Hello, sweetie pie," Michelle reached to take Hope. "We loved your grandmother, but we never got to meet your mother. I hear she was very special, and you look like a very special girl."

"Is she part wolf?" Jim asked.

"She's one-fourth wolf," Tom explained. "Greatheart is half wolf and we bred her to a champion Malamute. So the tubby lady her is half Malamute, one-fourth wolf and one-fourth German Shepherd. That little wagging plume of a tail is from the malamute."

"Let me tell you how we got Greatheart bred and got into trouble." Tim was laughing until he could hardly talk. He told the story amid much laughter and teasing. "And that's how Hope is a dukes mixture."

"Boy, are you lucky. You actually broke the law and it turned out well," Jim observed.

"We paid for it. And the whole town heard about it. We were so embarrassed. It could have turned out bad if Mr. Whitzel had not been such a gentleman."

"Now we have our hands full trying to housebreak her. Come here, Hope. Go potty like a good girl." Tim tried to show how she was learning. They got a charge out of it when she obediently squatted and tried to do something. "See she's learning. She knows the word potty," he bragged.

"But how many nights have we gotten up every two hours and staggered outside with her to teach her to go outside?" Tom rolled his eyes.

"She really wasn't hard to work with. Greatheart helped by taking them out, while they were still nursing, with her when she went. The most trouble we've had is with her chewing on everything," Anna sighed. "Shoes, chair legs, table cloths, you name it and she's tried to make confetti of it."

The girls got ready to leave. "I'll pick you up tomorrow morning at nine-thirty," Dede reminded Anna. "The stores in Seven Corners open at ten."

"I'll be raring to go. I've missed big stores, but I had so much fun today. Thanks for making this afternoon special," Anna told the crowd. "Come on in, Hope. You really are a good girl," she said as she waved to he girls.

As the three children entered the house, Anna turned to the twins coming in behind her. "Tim, would you come into the den with me, please? I'd like to ask you something." Tom went on to his room as Tim and Anna walked into the den. Tim waited for her to sit down before he sat. Herb had taught the boys to hold doors for ladies and let them enter first and to wait to sit until a lady has sat down.

"Tim, I guess I've been too close to you to be observant. You and Tom are growing so fast and I'm proud of both of you. I'm doubly proud that you're both gentlemen, thanks to our parents' teaching."

Tim tilted his head to one side and smiled waiting for her to continue.

"You've always been so kind to people and careful of their feelings that I was surprised this afternoon when you were aggressive to Alex. Would you care to explain that to me?"

Tim sucked in a breath, pursed his lips and hesitated. "Alex was never one of my favorite people. As you say, I hated to hurt his feelings. He was a bully and once I heard two teachers, on the playground, calling him "Little Hitler". When we were talking about Mom's books and you illustrating them, Alex smirked when Mark said you were beautiful. I didn't like his facial expressions. Then in the Pizza Parlor he was playing up to you in a way that an older guy might."

"I wondered why you were bristling. Never fear, brother dear. I know Alex's age and for sure he isn't my type. I'll be careful, but thank you for being protective of me. I don't deserve a great brother like you."

Tim stood up. "I promised Ton I'd beat him in a video game. I have to protect my reputation as the best player. See you later." He started out of the room, wheeled around and came back to hug Anna. "I'm the one that's lucky, having you for a sister. I'm sure going to miss you while you're away in college. Do you realize we've been together all our lives and done just about everything together? I'm happy for you, but I can't help but think how our lives are changing."

As Tim went out the door, Anna heard him yelp. Running out into the hall she put her hand over her mouth as her eyes widened in shock. Tom came bounding down the stairs and Irene ran in from the kitchen.

"Hope. What have you done?" Irene said slowly. "Where were all of you that not one could see what she was doing? I don't blame her. She's little and get bored easily. All of you know to watch her." She hesitated. "Truthfully, I'm just as guilty. I knew she was in the house and all of us know to watch her."

Tim squatted down beside the puppy. Hope turned over on her back and whimpered as if she knew she was going to get punished. "Dad is going to have a fit," he said.

"Fit! He'll kill Hope and us, too for not keeping an eye on her. Girl, if you had to chew on something why did you choose dad's golf bag to destroy?"

"Who left the hall closet door open so she could get to the bag?" Irene questioned.

"We didn't even open the closet, Mom," Anna answered. "But I bet it had been open a sliver and she worked it open to get in. Oh, Hope. You've ruined it. She's even chewed the glove he had in the bag. And this hand towel can't even be used for a rag."

"I've got it!" Tim jumped up. "Dad had a promotion and we need to get him something nice to congratulate him. Let's put our money together and get him a new bag for a gift. How much do we have now? I have sixteen dollars and thirty-one cents."

"I'll leave it to you three. Try to get her interested in a chew toy. Better still, put her leash on and take her for a walk. Maybe she'll wear herself out." Irene waved her hand and went back to making her grocery list.

"We might as well make this a training session," Tim told Hope.

"What are you doing?" Tom asked.

"I'm putting her on my left side with the leash behind my hips and holding the end of the leash in my right hand. Heel, Hope." Each time she tried to run ahead, Tim would puller back and say "Heel". When she was again by his left side, he would say, "Walk."

"Mom, Hope's really smart. We've only been walking her at heel for four days. Today she got on the left side on her own and stayed without pulling." Tom bragged.

"We all know she's smart. That's why she gets into mischief. Galena was unusually intelligent and wolves are very smart. You remember Greatheart learned quickly and did things for us few wolf dogs had been known to do. Koko was very intelligent. He was hyperactive just as Hope is. She has good blood lines and intelligent ancestors." Irene knelt down to rub the fat tummy that was turned up to be rubbed.

CHAPTER TWENTY-SIX

The Jackson family had become accustomed to the cooler climate in Alaska and now felt the July heat in Virginia was uncomfortable. They went swimming or stayed in air-conditioned places as much as possible.

All of them were relieved to be back in Virginia, safely, but it didn't feel right. Their beloved Galena would never greet them again and Greatheart belonged to someone else clear across the U.S. However, Hope's energy and love for them made life easier to bear.

The twins were delighted to find part-time jobs in a sporting goods store and one in a grocery store placing items on the shelves during hours after the store was closed. Herb raised the allowance of the twins to fifteen dollars a week and twenty for Anna because she would need more in college.

The twins still had chores to do. Irene and Herb explained that this home was theirs, also and they lived in it the same as everyone else. Therefore, they were responsible for specific jobs to keep the house running smoothly. Of course herb would come through where extra money was needed.

"You silly girl. You know you're showing off," Tom laughed. He and Tim were walking Hope by a home that had a scrolled iron fence around the property. Two beautiful Alsatian dogs were prancing and barking on their side of the fence. The twins admired the beautiful, long, white coats of the dogs. But Hope's head was held high, eyes straight ahead as she pranced by. "She's pretending she doesn't even see or hear them."

"They are beautiful dogs," Tim acknowledged. "Maybe we can get them together to play sometime."

That night at the dinner table, Tom was overjoyed at Hope's response to her training. He told Herb about her walking by the dogs and not acting up. "She heels well now. When we start out, she automatically walks on our left side, but is very response to a change of commands."

Not to be outdone, Tim contributed by bragging on his own training abilities. "And when we come to a curb, she stops without being asked and waits to be told that she can cross. She's responding to hand signals some now."

Herb laughed. "I'm remembering what a time you had teaching Greatheart to stay. She wanted to run after you and romp."

"That's because Greatheart is smarter than they are," Anna teased her brothers.

"My dear children," Herb changed the subject, "I'm pleased with my new golf bag and can hardly wait to use it. It is a nicer one than I've ever owned and I'll be so proud to show it off. Thank you again."

"Enjoy it, Dad. You deserve it and it'll be a long time before we have enough money to get something like that again." Tom sighed with a mock expression of agony. "That old bag was pretty ratty. And haven't you always told us that pride goes before a fall? Don't get so full of pride that you have a bad day." He laughed.

Herb chuckled. "Go ahead, throw it in my face. You know what I meant."

"Anna, what are you doing in your room so much? We hardly see you except at meals. Do you need our help?" Tim asked.

"You're a good sport for asking, but you can't help with what I have to do. I'm going through my clothes washing, mending and seeing what I might need to take with me. I'm also making a list of person items I'll need so I won't forget something, like a toothbrush and deodorant. Once I start classes, I won't have time to run out to shop. Hi, little Hope. Oh, yes, I'll need towels, wash cloths, tissues and oh-----. I just know I'll forget something. Hope, why don't you come to college with me and take care of me?" Hope wriggled with glee at the soft tone of her beloved human's voice. Anna set her down and she ran around to the others to see if they needed a doggie kiss or a hug.

The next day, Anna met the twins in the hall. "My dear brothers, why haven't you been after me for driving lessons? I'm surprised that you're not more anxious especially after the challenge."

"I can't explain it, but I honestly don't feel as if it's one of the more important things in my life. I can always walk or ride my bike. By the way, may we use your motor bike while you're in college?"

"If I don't take it with me, you sure can. You're going to get a nice surprise soon, but don't think you can get it out of me."

On Tuesday the twins visited Fairfax High to meet the principal, Lloyd Grissom.

"Hello, boys. I see that I'm going to have to get well acquainted in order to tell you apart. Your transcripts are here. I'm pleased to see you're both honor students and I sincerely hope you keep that up. Are you interested in sports? Maybe you'll go out for basketball."

The twins looked at each other and grinned. "Yes, sir. We have been on both basketball and baseball teams." Tom informed him.

"We haven't made hard and fast decision as to what we'll do yet," Tim explained. We're waiting to see what our classes will be like and what we'll be doing outside of school. We're in a youth choir at church and we hope to be involved in city youth programs."

"That's great. You know where my office is and if I can help you with anything, in or outside of school, don't hesitate to talk to me. There's going to be a lot of students eager to see you again and some who want to meet you. Some teachers are working on new teaching equipment in the library and one has been looking forward to seeing you again."

The twins looked puzzled and followed Mr. Grissom out of his office, down the hall and into the library.

"My goodness! It can't be. My boys are tall, handsome young men now." A woman ran to hug them. The top of her head just fit under their raised arms.

"Mrs. Berry!" the twins said as one. "What are you doing here? I planned to call you tonight and see when we could visit." Tim reached to give their much loved sixth grade teacher another hug.

"I've been like a little kid anxiously waiting to see you boys. I want to see your pictures and hear all about your great adventures."

"We have a video of a sled dog race that dad was in with Greatheart and he won. We'll bring that for you to see, and you'll swoon at the beautiful scenery." Tom told her excitedly.

"It also has some of the friends we made in Nome and parts of the town. It was strange at first, but we fell in love with the people and the place," Tim added.

"Boys, how would you like to speak in assembly one day and share with the students about your life in Alaska?" the principal asked.

"Even confess our goofier moments?" Tim laughed.

"Sure. I don't know why not. We'd love to, but what do you want from us?" Tom asked.

"Whatever you want to share with us," the principal answered. "We'd give you about fifteen minutes following your program for the students to ask you about something that interested them."

"I'll get permission to bring my class over so we can hear it, also. They've heard all about you through your letters. The ones that were in school with you are now here in high school," Mrs. Berry said.

"Oh, you're not teaching here in high school?" Tim asked.

"No. I just came today to learn how to work the new equipment."

"Good deal then. We'll talk to you later. I sure did appreciate your letters keeping us in touch with our friends here." Tim hugged her again.

"I was thrilled to hear from you and so glad you had this opportunity." she smiled giving both boys another hug.

"As much as we're enjoying talking to all of you, we have a job we need to get to. It costs a lot of money to furnish things we need in school and for our personal pleasure." Tom said as the twins told everyone goodbye and left.

On the fourth of July Herb took the family to the city park to join friends and neighbors for the celebration. Lots of young people were in the city swimming pool and some were playing soccer. Tim was running after the soccer ball when his attention was diverted to an interesting group entering the park.

"Hey, Tim. Whereya'going?" Tom called to his twin. He looked to see where Tim was staring. A group of people, of all ages, were settling jut a few feet from where the Jackson family was sitting. Tom ran to join Tim.

"Mom. Dad. Did you see all those dogs? Why are they here?" Tim still stared with interest.

Herb looked around. "Humm. I didn't see them. I bet they're from the guide dog training school. The instructors are probably teaching the dogs to work in spite of noisy distractions. The dogs need to bond with their assigned person as long as they're working, so don't bother them."

"May we pet the dogs?" Tom asked.

"I don't think so," Irene answered quickly. "You heard your dad say the dogs need to keep their attention on their assigned person."

A man, who seemed to be in charge of the group overheard the Jackson discussion and came over. "Excuse me. I couldn't help but hear what you were saying. I'm John Middleton. I help train the dogs and people together so they can work safely. We have this group here today because we know there'll be crowds, lots of young children and fireworks. The dogs are being trained to ignore noises and crowds and to take care of their person."

Anna, and some of the girls, had left the pool and joined them. She was curious as to what the group with the dogs was doing. "Oh," she said with a catch in her voice, "look at that precious child in the wheelchair."

"Young lady, please don't say anything where these people can hear you," John Middleton placed a friendly hand on Anna's arm. "We work hard to encourage them to feel good about themselves. They have enough to overcome without self-pity. We teach them that each one has a valuable contribution to make up society. They need to be strong emotionally and --"

"Yes, Mr. Middleton. I'm sorry and I understand. I would never purposely make them feel badly about themselves or demean them. I do feel compassion, however."

"Of course you do. By the way," John said turning to Herb. "Your sons show a lot of interest in the animals and your daughter seems to be naturally caring about people. Do you think they might be interested in being volunteers in our Canine Wonders? Would you object to them working with us and learning how we operate?"

Anna broke in before her father could answer. "Would we! I would be honored to be allowed to help and I'm positive my brothers would be eager to volunteer. In fact, they'll be a lot of help. They learned to train our wolf dog while we lived in Alaska."

"Really!? A wolf dog? I'd like to hear all about it sometime. Right now I need to see about my people." He looked at Anna. "Would you like to meet Marshall and his dog? That's the five year old in the wheelchair. Don't let him throw you. He's a bright little rascal. It's sometimes difficult to remember he's only five."

"I would love to meet Marshall." As Anna walked with John to the child in the wheelchair, she saw a black Labrador lying at the boy's feet.

"Marshall, my man. This is your lucky day. Here's a beautiful girl who wants to meet you." The dog stood up and placed himself in front of Marshall.

"Hi, John." The boy's small face lit with a beautiful smile. Boy! She's be-u-ti-ful." He dragged the word out. "My name's Marshall and his name is Chuckles," he pointed to the dog. His wide grin was contagious. "What's your name?"

"I'm Anna. I love your dog. How did he get the name, Chuckles?"

"Cause when he was little, he'd get so excited he'd make happy sounds like he was laughing. He's a clown, too."

"Well, I love his name, but how is he a clown?"

"He won't let me be sad. He'll do a lot of silly things to make me laugh. He's my bestest buddy."

"I can see that, but what funny things does he do?"

"He rolls on his back and puts his paws over his nose. When he thinks he's done something wrong, he'll lay flat down and put his paws over his eyes. He gets my ball in his mouth and throws it up in the air and chases it. He does a lot of funny things."

"I think he's a handsome dog. Is it okay if I have my lunch with you?"

"Oh, boy, yes. Be careful though. Chuckles will expect you to share."

"I don't mind sharing with you or Chuckles, but I must ask Mr. Middleton if it's all right. I'm not sure I can even touch your dog because he is supposed to be helping you and guarding you."

"Sure you can touch him. If he didn't have his working harness on, he'd roll on his back and beg you to rub his tummy."

Anna looked around. "Where is your lunch, Marshall?"

At that moment John Middleton walked over with a plate for Marshall. "Yummy," Marshall rubbed his stomach. "Hot dogs, potato salad, pickles, deviled eggs, tomatoes and lots of good things. John, can't Anna have some of our lunch?"

"She sure can. We have enough for a small army." Marshall laughed as if it were the funniest thing he'd ever heard.

"I tell you what. I have fried chicken, so why don't I share a piece of chicken with you and I'll eat one of your hot dogs."

"Sounds good to me. Can I have a leg?" Marshall bounced in his chair.

"May I have a leg?" John corrected his grammar.

"You can if Anna has enough," Marshall said and then wondered why John and Anna laughed so hard.

John motioned for Anna to move to one side with him. "Marshall sometimes gets choked because he has trouble swallowing. Don't let him bite off the bone. Maybe you can tactfully offer to tear the meat off for him. After all, we are in the park and it's difficult to get to a sink to wash sticky hands. You can make him think you're just trying to help him keep clean. I'll leave it up to you, but I'll be nearby. He **is** my responsibility. I keep a careful eye on all of folks."

As Herb walked over to them, John said, "Mr. Jackson, your daughter is a wonder. You can observe what good care she is taking of young Marshall and making him feel special."

"It always makes a father proud to hear his child complimented. I have to take a mental step back often and remind myself that she is a mature young lady on her way to college. She'll always be my precious little girl and my sons will be my heart's joy, but we need to let them grow and have a chance to make their own decisions. If they don't make mistakes, they'll never learn how to make sensible decisions."

"I doubt your children will make many mistakes."

Herb threw his head back and laughed loudly. "I'll have to tell you sometime what Tom has put us through, but he's doing well now and he is growing and maturing. By the way, I'm Herb."

"I know what you mean. Mr. Middleton makes me feel old from someone my age. Please call me John."

"I'm glad so many of my children's friends are also interested in volunteering with your group."

"It's great as long as they don't display too much sympathy. These people need to be as strong emotionally as possible. Oh, I don't mean they're to be ignored when they're upset. They just don't need to be encouraged to feel sorry for themselves."

"Knowing my children, and their friends, you won't need to worry."

Four boys and three girls joined the group. "Mr. Middleton, may we speak with you?"

"It'll cost you a nickel, but I guess I can share the time," he grinned.

The young people grinned as Jim spoke. "I guess I've been chosen as spokesperson. We've been discussing the work you're doing. All of us have animals and we sure like working with people. We'd like to volunteer to help any way we can, if you'll have us. We're friend of Tom, Tim and Anna."

Before John could answer, another worker, Jean Worley, faced them. "We could sure use your help. If you're willing to bathe dogs, clean kennels, hug puppies, walk young dogs, talk to nervous people and comfort them and keep cheerful through it all, them we can use you."

John laughed. "I'm not sure how cheerful you'll be after all of that, but it give one a good feeling to know you've helped someone from being a prisoner in a limited world and made an animal happy, also."

"Just give us a chance," Jason Horn urged.

"We don't mind hard work," Mark Tuttle added.

"I have a cousin who is a Downs Syndrome child, so I'm used to having to be patient and careful with a person in need," Miguel informed him.

Chuckles pulled Marshall's wheelchair to the group while Anna walked beside him. "I heard your offers to help, and I'd like to be part of that until I have to leave for college. I can work for a short time and can always work during vacations and holidays, if that's okay."

"Why don't all of you come to the school day after tomorrow and take a walking tour. You can get acquainted with some people who are finishing their training with their dog. It will give you a chance to know what will be required and you can then decide if you still want to be involved."

"I can pick everyone up in the van at nine and we'll go down together," Dede offered.

"Mark, Jason and I will walk to the Jacksons and wait for you there," Jim said.

"Silly. You can ride over with me, or are sisters to be avoided unless you have boys with you?" Dede teased.

"Kookie sis. I love you, but I want to walk with the guys and talk."

"Okay, it's agreed," Tim spoke, "we'll leave from our house at nine. Is there a place to get lunch?" he asked John.

Jean answered. "There's a nice restaurant about two miles from the school, or you can bring a lunch. If you work with us, you'll eat in the cafeteria."

The teens walked around telling the fifteen people that they had enjoyed meeting them and would be visiting the school. Marshall led a cheer for them.

CHAPTER TWENTY-SEVEN

"Attention! Attention!" Mayor Richard Warfield spoke over the sound system. "Welcome to our fourth of July celebration. It's time for the games. Fortunately there are shade trees for spectators and for the contestants to rest without getting too hot. Grab a good spot and let Debbie and Mary explain the rules. Everyone can't win, so I hope you'll all be good sports."

"Hiya! Hiya!" Debbie called pertly as she bounced on the platform. Mary started clapping and getting everyone to join in.

Debbie continued, "The first game is a three-legged race. Partners, come up and get your sack, then go to the starting line and prepare to race. The men will race first, then the women. Winners will receive these gin-u-wine one of a kind silk ribbon." Mary held up a six inch blue ribbon. "Blue is first place, red is second, third is green and fourth is white. Have fun everyone. Play fair and be good sports so that everyone can enjoy the day."

Tom and Jim paired off with one sack. "Come on, Dad. Let's show them how it's done," Time said while claiming a sack. Jason and Miguel Perez lined up beside Mark and Danny, then Benji and Harold Stallard quickly joined the group.

Tim placed his right leg in the sack as Herb placed his left leg in. they put their arms around each other's waist and held the side of the sack with their free hand. Tim whispered, "Dad, let's move out first on our outside leg, then step forward on our inside legs. If we stay in sync, I bet we'll beat them." Herb grinned and nodded.

The Mayor fired a started pistol in the air and the contestants started off. On their third step, Benji and Harold fell. The crowd groaned for them and then cheered the others. Anna and Irene ran beside the runners to watch their three males.

"Yeah! Now what do you have to say about this old man?!" Herb punched the air with his fist when he and Tim came across the finish line in first place. A local news photographer took their picture. Mark and Danny were second, Tom and Jim were third and Jason and Miguel were fourth. All were very close together.

Mary called for the women partners to claim a sack and line up. Anna and Irene moved in place. Dede and Janell, Michelle and Alice Werner, Sue Hall and Patti Benton, Ginger and Jamet Jenson and Sharon and Arlene lined up. The starter pistol was fired and off they went. The crowd laughed and went wild when Anna and Irene collided with Sue and Patti and the four fell before they had taken two steps.

Being good sports, Anna and Irene cheered the others on. Michelle and Alice won with Ginger and Janet right on their heels. Dede and Janell were third and Sharon and Arlene claimed fourth.

What a close race, and so exciting. Too bad folks, I'm sorry that some of you got a rough start, but you're all good sports and this is for a good cause," Mary shouted. "Now we have a game for the oldest to the youngest.

"On this long table beside the stage are twenty stacks of soda crackers; four crackers in each stack. Contestants will run from this line to the table and eat the crackers as quickly as possible. The first one to eat the four crackers and then whistle, 'How Much Is That Doggie in the Window' is the winner. We must be able to recognize the tune. Ready? Get set. Go!"

There was a lot of laughter and suggestions called as each contestant grabbed four crackers. An older woman, Mrs. Mercer and Mark started whistling at the same time. Mark got the giggles and couldn't continue.

Mrs. Mercer won, but Mark was declared second.

People mingled and talked waiting for the next game. Debbie jumped up on the stage. "Okay, listen up. We have fourteen couples signed up for this one. There are fourteen piles of old clothes donated by you good people. The contestants will line up, and when the starter gun is fired, couples will race toward the pile their standing in front of. The couples dress and help each other dress. When all the clothes in the pile have been put on, run back to the starting line. Winner, of course, will be easily recognized."

The contestants took off and struggled to dress in a hurry. The crowd was in stitches at the ridiculous clothing some were putting on. Some had pants way too long. One girl had a pair of men's long john underwear. All were good sports.

Marshall had Chuckles take up to where Anna and Tom were standing. "Why don't they do something chuckles and me can do?" he whined.

"Chuckles and I," Anna corrected him.

"You can borrow him if you want to, but I would like to do one game with him."

While the teens were enjoying Marshall's innocent expressions, Tom ran to the Mayor with a suggestion. "Mr. Warfield, Dad, would you two come here for a moment, please?" He told them of his plan and they agreed.

The Mayor stepped up on the stage and called for attention. "We've just had some good folks offer to sponsor another race. You know that all these games are sponsored as are all classes in the Youth Rodeo. The profits are donated to a worthy charity that the Fourth of July Committee agrees upon. Each year it's a different charity. I don't know which one it will be this year, but keep up with our news. I'll let Tom Jackson tell you about this game because he and his dad, Herb Jackson, are sponsoring it."

"What's Tom doing up there?" Anna asked surprised.

"Because it's his idea," Herb answered coming to stand by them.

"Tom had an idea? When did he develop brains to have an idea?" Alex giggled and walked unsteadily away. His crazy laugh trailed behind him.

"Is Alex drinking?" Irene asked astonished.

"I don't think so," Herb said hesitatingly. "I hope it isn't what I suspect."

Everyone stopped talking to listen to Tom. "We'll call this game, "Fireman". Contestants will start at a given point and carry a cup. Those boys are filling three tubs with water. The contestants will run down there, scoop up a cup of water and run back to these buckets assigned to each one and empty the cup of water into the bucket. They'll make as many runs as they can until the whistle blows. The water will be measured in the buckets. The person who has carried the most water will win. You'll have a few minutes to sign up. OH, yes, only people in wheelchairs can enter." The crowd laughed joyously when Marshall cheered so hard he almost turned his chair over.

Chuckles pulled Marshall's chair to the place he was told to go. Marshall looked anxiously around, because he was by far the youngest. There was one other dog and five adults rolling their own chairs. Marshall was nervous.

The starter gun was fired and Marshall yelled for Chuckles to go. The dog seemed confused, but he took Marshall to a tub as he was told to do. Marshall leaned over and scooped up a cup of water, then yelled for Chuckles to go. Chuckles quickly caught on and dashed happily back and forth three trips before the whistle sounded. Marshall was declared the winner. It was difficult to determine who had the biggest grin, Marshall or Chuckles. He yelled for Anna to give Chuckles a hug, but she hugged them both.

"Don't you dare cry," John admonished Anna.

"I can't help it. Marshall will know these are tears of joy."

"Anna, what's wrong?" Marshall was worried.

"Well, you know how women are, Marshall. We cry at everything, when we're happy as well as when we're sad. I am so happy for you that I am shedding tears of joy."

"Okay. As long as you're happy."

The Youth Rodeo was held in the ball field from three until seven. By then it was dark enough for fireworks that the fire department took care of. Anna stood by Chuckles and Marshall. Tom, Tim, and the other children each stood quietly by a dog in case the animal needed calming.

At seven-thirty the first fireworks were set off. A few of the dogs began to fidget, but fortunately none of them broke training. All had been exposed to all kinds of noises, but this was the first for them to be in a crowd with fireworks causing so much noise.

Chuckles thought he had to protect Marshall. A man leaned over and put his hand on Marshall's shoulder to ask if he was enjoying the fireworks. Chuckles looked as if he were frowning and pushed between the man and his young master. John told Marshall to praise Chuckles.

"I'm so proud of you and Chuckles and especially glad that you're my new friend." Anna told Marshall. At eight John gathered his group and helped them board their bus to go back to the school.

"I'll see you young people when you come down. Don't say anything, but maybe you can surprise this group and come to their graduation a month from now."

The boys said they would be there, but the girls reminded John they would be away in college. The Jackson family stayed to help the clean up crew and put materials away. Tom and Jim were taking the sound system apart.

"Jim, do you know what's wrong with Alex? I can't put my thumb on the problem, but there is definitely a problem. I watched him this afternoon and he didn't appear to be drinking, but ---- I don't know. There's something funny about him. Does he smoke?"

"He's smoking something. I saw him one evening with some unfamiliar kids that looked like a rough bunch to me.

They were dressed okay, but their behavior was not acceptable. Alex was smoking, but when eh saw me looking at him, he tried to hide it. He kept laughing as if he could not control himself. He wasn't steady walking away."

"Well. Something's wrong," Tom grimaced. "Let's play it cook and maybe he'll talk to one of us. Now I want to go home and check on Hope. We don't usually leave her alone this long, and I'm sure she could hear some of the fireworks. She has never heard them before and will be uneasy. Come see me as soon as you can."

At home, the twins asked permission to call Ben in Alaska and ask about Greatheart. They told Ben all about their day and promised to write and tell him their experiences in the dog training school.

"Greatheart is really living up to her name," Ben bragged. A bull elk came into town and got so confused the men couldn't get him turned around and out of town. The poor animal was frightened. Without being told, Greatheart ran toward him and herded him around and out of town. The elk was unharmed and there was no danger or injuries. She was a hero. Are you prepared for a shock? Chief Houmay was there and called everyone's attention to the wonderful dog. He has decided that he likes her and talks to her as if she can converse with him. They have become friends."

"Wow! That's great news. I'm so glad. Is Greatheart near you?" Tim asked.

"Yes. She's right here beside me."

"Hold the phone so she can hear Hope bark. Does she act like she recognizes Hope?"

"No. She's puzzled because she doesn't know where that dog is or why it's barking. She acts as if she might know your voice though. She's turning her head and tilting it and whimpering. No. There she goes. She's over on the couch now. Sorry about that."

They would have talked over an hour, but Herb wanted to talk to Yehat Eskise and hung up when he was finished.

"Hope, that was your mother. I know you don't remember her. You were such a tiny baby when she went to live with Ben and you left with us." Hope looked at Tom and tilted her head from side to side as if she were trying to understand what he was saying.

Tim rubbed her ears and neck. "I just hope to turn out to be as smart as your mother and grandmother. I have a feeling you will. You'll have entirely different experiences that they had though."

"Anna, can you come in here, please?" Tom called Anna to join him and Tim in their room. "We're worried about Alex and wonder what we should do. We'd like to hear what you think."

"What has he done? Tell me what you're worried about and maybe I'll have an idea as to what should be done, or if it's even any concern of yours."

They told her what they had observed and what impressions they had. "He's stopped going anywhere with our crowd. He's running with some kids that are from wealthy homes, just as he is, but they don't seem to have any self-respect and certainly not for others."

"Let me see what I can find out. I'll check with the girls and see if their brothers have told them anything. I'm not inclined to get involved in anything that at don't know at least the basics about it."

Irene was walking by the room and heard part of the conversation. "What's this about Alex?"

"Mom, Alex is not only acting strange, but he has a whole new set of questionable friends. None of us get to talk to him anymore. When one of us happens to run into him, he's evasive or just walks away."

"I'm truly sorry. Alex has not had a family and home life such as you and your friends have had. Both of his parents are attorneys and always busy and away from home. I can't remember them ever attending a school function or a parent teacher meeting. Alex was raised by housekeepers and never had any responsibilities at home. Neither has he felt he needed to take responsibility for his actions. Sometimes children from the well-to-do homes are the true underprivileged." She hesitated and thought a moment. "Don't go anywhere with Alex or with his new group, but be ready to listen if he seeks your attention. He was a good friend when all of you were younger. Be compassionate, and be careful what you say publically."

"Oh, Mom. We wouldn't go anywhere with him now and I'm sure none of our friends would either. I hope he'll come to us. I want to help him," Tim assured her.

The following morning Dede pulled up in the van with Michelle and Janell. Anna and the six boys ran out to make the trip to Canine Wonders Guide and Service Dog Training School.

Jason was excited because his parents had never allowed him to own a pet and he had always loved dogs. He had loads of questions, but the group was patient with him and answered as best they could. Tim finally placed a hand on Jason's shoulder and said, "Jason, we're all going to learn new things today. Just hang loose and all of our questions will be answered."

Dede drove carefully through Fairfax and on route 50 west to Chantilly. On the north side of Chantilly was the forty-seven acre area for the training school. Dede pulled into the parking lot in front of the administration building. They were greeted by a giant, black male Labrador that was friendly and welcoming. Jean came out to meet them. "You've met Baron."

"Hello! I'm glad you came. Come on in out of this heat. There's no air stirring and it feels as if it's 100, but it's only 92," she laughed. "We've been waiting anxiously for you to get here because we could see that all of you were serious about helping."

"When do we see the dogs?" Jason asked eagerly.

"Hi, folks," John Middleton greeted them as they entered the lobby. "I sure am glad you could make it. How was your trip? Did you have trouble finding us?"

"No trouble," Tom answered. "Your directions were very clear. We're just anxious to see everything and learn what we're to do."

Jean motioned for a man to come into the room. "This is Jake Sargeant, one of the best trainers in the world. We're so lucky he's working with us."

"Flattery will get you everywhere," Jake laughed. "Hello everyone. I won't say welcome aboard yet, and I'm relieved to see that you look like young people who will do a great job. I need to know everyone's name and make a name tag for you. That's for us and for the people who board here to know you. Let's start with you," he pointed to Mark who was nearest to him.

"Mark Tully, sir."

"Oh, please. Don't sir me. I'm just Jake. And you?" he pointed to the next one.

"Jim Dodd."

"Dan Baxter."

"Jason Horn."

"Tom Jackson."

"Tim Jackson."

"Oh, boy. We'll have to put a bell on one of you," he laughed.

"Anna Jackson."

"Are you related to these bookends?"

"I'm honored to be their sister."

"Sorry. I don't mean to be smarty, but you have to admit that they are difficult to tell apart. I'm sure that after we get to know them, there will be differences that will be obvious."

"Yes," Anna smiled. "I know, but good luck on that. They can be tricky. I'm serious though. They're great guys even if they are my brothers."

"I'm glad to see brothers and sisters so close. Okay, who're you?"

"Dede Dodd. Actually Delores Dodd."

"I assume you're Jim's sister."

"Yes, sir, and I, too, am proud of my brother."

"I'm Michelle Tully, and I have the greatest brother of all." The girls started laughing and teasing each other.

"While they're settling that, I'm Janell Morris and I'm an only child."

With name tags in place they then went into a room where they saw a video on the history and present work of the school.

"Now may we see the dogs?" Jason pleaded.

"You sure can," Jake laughed and slapped him on the back. "We'll have to walk, or you can ride a golf cart to the opposite side and on the other side of the parking lot."

"Let's walk so we can see more of the campus," Anna suggested. "Jake, I hate to tell you, but we girls will be leaving for college in a couple of weeks. I'm sorry I won't be here full time, but I'll help whenever I'm home."

"For gosh sakes. What can you do part time?" Jason asked.

"Nothing subtle about you, is there buddy?" Dan teased him.

"Huh?"

Talking was set aside as the door was opened and the group faced a long section with cages of dogs on both sides of a very wide aisle. The noise of the welcoming barks and puppy yips made it hard to be heard.

"How precious," Anna knelt by a cage of puppies. "I didn't realize they'd be in such large cages. They're like small rooms."

"Notice that the cage inside has feeding trays and water bowls. They are at least eight feet by eight feet and seven feet tall. We keep four to six puppies, depending on the size, together, but only three or four as they grow. There is an opening leading to an outdoor eight feet by twelve feet cage for exercise time. Animals are changed around so that they learn to get along with other dogs. Volunteers come out several times a week to hug the puppies and play with them so they become sociable with people."

"That's great. I can't get over how clean everything is, even smells nice," Mark observed.

"Yes. Twice a day, or whenever necessary, the cages are hosed out. We use only safe chemicals that clean and deodorize. About three times a day, the dogs are taken into the big field at the back so they can run and get rid of energy. "

"Do the puppies go out with the big dogs?" Tom questioned.

"Not at first. Puppies are hugged and petted until they are from four to six months old, again depending upon the breed and rate of growth. Then they can be turned out with bigger dogs that are a year old or less. You'll be walking the dogs that are past the hugging stage."

They walked on full of excitement and questions. "At about six months of age they'll be loaned to select families who have been thoroughly investigated and approved. The families will keep the dog for about a year, teaching them the basics; sit, stay, lie down, fetch, come, quiet and so forth.

"They'll also take them in cars and expose them to noises like roller skates, sirens, doorbells and others. They'll take them into restaurants, hotels, walking on the sidewalk in a shopping area and crossing the street. The dogs will be taught good manners, but will be loved and treated well."

"Then what happens?" Jason was eager and interested.

"The dogs are brought back here for serious training," Jean explained, "and that's where Jake comes in. they're checked carefully for attitude, aptitude and health. They're given specific training that some person actually needs. This is our clinic. We're fortunate to have nine veterinarians who are good to volunteer their services unless a lot of their time is required; then they're paid. They give shots and do general health checking. Of course when families have the dogs, they're responsible for health care, but they can bring them to us if there's even a suspicion of problems."

John continued, "When the dogs are returned, they are in rigorous, serious training. As soon as a dog is approved, he or she is paired with a person. The person will come to live in our dormitory and bond with their dog by training together. We have a special graduation when the dog and person bond and each learns what their responsibilities are. They then go home together, but the person knows they can call on us at any time."

"Do all dogs finish the training expected of them?" Tim asked. "I've heard that dogs training for police work sometimes don't make the grade."

"You're right," Jake answered. "In rare case a dog has to be taken out of the training program and given to someone who will love it and care for it. We do keep a check on them. It's expensive though. It costs at least ten thousand dollars to train a service dog, a little over six thousand dollars to train a dog for the deaf and several thousands to train others for specialized work."

"Good grief! Where do you get the money? I thought the dogs went to people free of charge," Michelle said.

"Caring people give donations, some put on fund raisers, others remember us in their will and we have endowment funds. The money we invest brings in a good interest to meet daily needs, however, the interest has been low lately." Jean told them. "We always need money for daily needs."

"Where do you get the dogs?" Janell asked.

"It is far too important to have good, healthy dogs with good temperaments, personalities, if you will. We own excellent breedings so that we can breed our own. You met big daddy when you first came in. On rare occasions we might find a good dog in a humane shelter; a qualified breeder might donate one or an individual might give one. The dogs are screened carefully because they will be working with humans who might literally place their lives with the dog," Jake explained.

"Let's move on," John said. "There's too much to see and hear about in one visit. You've seen our puppies, now let's move on to the next room for the next stage. These are the dogs that need walking and are ready to be taken to private homes for a year."

CHAPTER TWENTY-EIGHT

"You're just in time," Jake smiled. "A group of dogs have just been taken to the field to play and relax."

"Wow!" Mark exclaimed. "There must be fifty of them."

"No. I think there's twenty-four. Would you like to go in and throw balls or just romp and play with them?"

They could hardly wait to get in with the frisky dogs. Jason was especially thrilled. After ten minutes John call them to move on with him. "We thought you might like to see the dormitory where our people stay while they have the final training with their assigned dogs."

"Does the dog stay in the room with the people?" Jason asked.

"Of course. That's the idea. The dog and person live together and do everything together that they'll do when the person goes home." The teens met some of the people in their rooms. One blind woman didn't want them to touch her dog or come in her room. They tactfully went on.

The group was subdued when they came back to the lobby of the administration building.

"I had a vague idea of what is done, but I appreciate the work with my whole heart now that I've seen it," Anna spoke quietly. She then turned and grinned broadly. "Marshall! I didn't know you were here."

"I heard you say you'd be here today, so I got daddy to drive me over. You **are** going to work with us, aren't you?"

Anna sat on a chair beside Marshall and explained how the boys would work but the girls would be in college and could only work during vacations. Marshall leaned over to hug Anna. "I'm so glad I got to know you. Can you come to my house and see me?"

"I'd love to, but I won't have time right now. I will never forget you and will expect you to answer letters I'll write to you."

"Sure," he yelled. "Daddy, will you help me write a letter to Anna?"

"I sure will, son and mom will, too. Thank you for being so nice to my big boy. I hate to break up a good thing, but we need to get home."

"Anna, don't you want to give Chuckles a hug? I don't want him to feel left out. He likes you, too."

"I would love to hug Chuckles." The dog threw himself against her chest and gave her doggie kisses. All of the young people hugged Marshall and Chuckles.

Tom turned to John. "Is it possible for you to give us a time schedule as to when you'll need us? Tim and I have paying part-time jobs and we need them for school supplies. We need to schedule our hours."

"I'm working on that," Jake answered. "We need you on Saturdays for sure and any days during the week you can spare. Let us know when you'll be available."

"What will we start doing?"

"Bathing dogs, cleaning kennels and general cleaning. That's on Saturdays. You'll be needed to walk dogs and clean up during the week."

"Great," Jason grinned. "I've never owned a dog so someone will have to show me how to bathe one. I'm willing to work and learn."

"We'll help you." Tom placed an arm across Jason's shoulders. "There'll be times that we'll all need help. We'll help each other."

"I'm sorry that we need to leave. I'm leaving for college this Saturday for an orientation. After that I can help until the first week in August. The others can come whenever they wish, but I'll be thinking of all of you."

Anna smiled and waved to the staff who'd gathered around them.

"The numbers of volunteers vary because of personal appointments and things they have to do. With your group, we have about twenty-five youth volunteers and about twelve adults. We're thankful for all of you."

"By the way, where are the dogs in training?" Janell asked.

Jean answered. "Today they're at a mall learning to go on an escalator and to move among crowds. They've already been on busy streets learning to maneuver through traffic."

"Look. Here comes one of our people and his German Shepherd. Watch what happens," Jake told them. "This man can only see shadows and the difference between light and dark. He needs constant help."

Someone had brought the man in a car and had gotten his wheelchair out of the trunk. A big male Shepherd with a harness on got out of the car and stood by the chair. The man hooked a long leash from the dog's harness to one arm of his chair. The dog guided the chair from the car, up a ramp and toward the door. Reaching the door the man looped a short rope around the door handle and the dog took the rope in his teeth. He backed up pulling the door open. The man said, "hold." As soon as the chair cleared the door, the dog hurried through and left the rope in the man's lap.

"Why didn't he come through the automatic door?" Jason asked puzzled.

"He wants to keep his dog in practice. Hello, Martin." John greeted him.

"Hey, John. Isn't Hercules great?"

"He sure is. The two of you work well together. Martin, I want you to meet some nice young people who are new volunteers. They're on their way home now, but I'm sure they can wait long enough to meet you and Hercules."

Tom walked to Martin and took his hand to shake it. "Hi. I'm Tom Jackson and you're going to be familiar with me real soon because I'm going to tell you about the greatest German Shepherd that ever lived and how she mated with a real wolf."

"I can hardly wait," Martin said. "When will you tell this story?"

"My twin brother and I, and some of our friends, will be here on Saturday. Will you be here?"

"Just try to keep me away."

"Mom, you wouldn't believe what marvelous things these dogs can do," Tom gushed. "They use a lot of German Shepherds, Golden Retrievers, Labradors, Australian Shepherds and Collies. Have you ever seen a smooth coat Collie?" he didn't wait for her answer. "It makes chills go up my spine to see the dogs work. One man has a great Shepherd named Hercules and ----"

"Oh, for heaven's sake, let someone else have a chance. This is only our first day at work. Mom, Dad, did you know that some prisons are letting selected prisoners they can trust keep dogs and teach them?" Tim continued.

"No. this is the first I've heard of it, but I'd like to know more about the program," Herb answered. "Anna, why aren't you giving your impressions of the school?"

"Surely you jest, Dad. How could I get a word in with these two bozos. I can't blame them. It's going to be very rewarding and exciting to know how much your work means to a person who needs you."

"I take it all three of you think it's going to be a worth-while project."

"Yes, sir. I'm sorry I won't have more time before I leave for college, but I'm glad my brothers will have such a delightful experience."

That night Tim leaned against Anna's doorway. "Hey, Anna. Knock. Knock."

"Who's there?"

"Amish."

"Amish who?"

"Amish you already." The three siblings shared laughs and remembrances.

The next day Anna took the twins to an empty lot to start them driving. "First look at everything on the dashboard and learn where everything is so that you can operate the vehicle without having to search while your eyes should be on the road. Ask questions now if you want to know how something works."

The twins carefully looked at everything even how to raise and lower the seats, turn on the lights, the wipers and set the side mirrors. Tim sat in the back while Tom took the first turn. Anna was patient but firm.

"Whoever is in the back seat must keep silent on the pain of death, or at the pain of thirty lashes with a wet noodle. If you get scared, hold your hand over your moth and lie down on the seat, but don't dare to do anything that will distract the one driving. Is--that--clear?"

"Yes, ma'am," Tim saluted, but grinned.

"Sure thing," Tom said, "now can I start?"

"No. My car will not start until you do something very important. That applies in the back seat as well."

"Oh, yeah. Fasten the seat belt." Tom looked pleased with himself. "Okay, now I'm ready."

"Check the rear view mirror and both side mirrors to be sure you can see clearly. Is your seat in a comfortable position?" Tom nodded. "Put the key in the ignition and place your foot on the brake. The brake, in newer cars, serves as a brake and a clutch. Turn the key on, the gear is in P for park. Put your finger on the button on the shift and press down while you shift the lever to D for drive. Place both hands on the wheel and slowly let up on the brake at the same time you press down on the accelerator pedal. Slow is the word today and a safer way to learn."

Tom carefully did as she instructed and surprisingly started without jerking. "Hey! Nothing to it," he chortled.

"Don't get too big for your britches, yet. There's a lot to learn." Anna had him drive forward, turn corners and stop as if he were at a traffic light. Tom practiced for about half an hour and then got in the back seat so Tim could take his turn.

Tim had carefully listened and observed all Tom had done and he did very well.

"In the next lesson, I'll teach you how to pull over to a curb and parallel park. I'm so proud of both of you and mom and dad will be pleased, too. Please don't be tempted to drive someone's car to show what you've learned. A good driver is a cautious one."

"I have a surprise for you. Here it comes now." Anna went to meet a man pulling up in a pickup.

"Isn't that Daniel Hobson?" Tom asked Tim softly. "I hope Anna isn't getting involved with him. He doesn't have a good reputation."

"Cool it," Tim hissed. "We've only heard rumors and you know what dad says about rumors. Make sure you know facts before making comments. Besides, she's never mentioned him, so I don't guess she's involved with him."

"Hi, guys," Daniel called a friendly greeting as he climbed into the bed of his truck. "Is this what you wanted, Anna?"

"Yes, and thank you so much." Anna called to her brothers to come get the orange traffic cones from Daniel's truck. "Daniel was kind enough to borrow these from where he works. We'll take good care of them and return them in good condition."

Daniel left and she showed the twins how to set the cones about thirty feet apart in a straight row. They practiced driving and weaving between the cones. Then they placed them in two rows ten feet apart, six of them on each side and two in the middle at the end making a parking place. Anna had her brothers practice backing between the cones without touching them.

"My goodness. You're doing so well, if I didn't know better, I'd think you'd already been learning. The next time we'll practice parallel parking. Now get the cones in the trunk and let's go home."

They had set up the cones for parallel parking when Daniel pulled up in his truck. "Here comes Daniel. Is he taking the cones?" Tom was worried.

"Hi people," Daniel called happily. "Are you ready?"

"Ready for what?" Tom looked from Anna to Daniel.

"The next stage in your driving practice. When you get on the highway you won't be alone. All drivers are not courteous and careful. You're going to need to learn how to drive defensively," Anna smiled encouragingly.

"Defensively? I hope you don't mean we'll have to fight," Tom spluttered.

Daniel threw his head back and laughed. "No, but sometimes you'll feel as if you are because there are some drivers who really should not be on the road. They'll try your patience and."

"Tom, you first. You're going to drive around this field and practice passing Daniel as if he were in traffic with you. He'll pass you and he might even do something that upsets you. A good driver may fume and fret, but he or she keeps cool and alert."

"Trust me to be careful and not do anything that will put you or your car at risk, but you do need to be alert for many situations. I will pull some stunts that will not be courteous, and in some instances, may be dangerous.

When driving, always keep your eyes, ears and mind on just that -- your driving," Daniel told them.

As Tom was driving, Daniel came up close behind him and suddenly cut around Tom, picked up speed and was well ahead of him. "Very good," Anna praised Tom who had remained calm and alert. "The next time you turn this corner, I want you to pass Daniel the same way. Don't get too close before you cut out to pass. Check all your mirrors to be sure another car is not also passing. Turn your left signal on to show the car behind you that you're pulling out. When you drive back in front of Daniel, use your right signal to show up your pulling in front of him."

After about twenty minutes, Tim took the wheel and did the same things. Suddenly Daniel passed Tim and immediately cut in front of him with no signal and cut him off. Throwing his brake on, Tim looked as if he might faint. Tom shrieked in the back seat. Tim stopped and got out of the car.

"You dumb jerk!" Tim yelled angrily. He looked perplexed when Anna and Daniel laughed. Tom shakily crawled out of the back seat prepared to sail into Daniel and tell him off.

"What's so funny?" Tim frowned. "You could have caused a wreck."

"Tim, I warned you to be careful about careless drivers. Sometimes they're drunk, on drugs or very angry about something. It's better to gain experience here than to be caught unprepared in traffic," Daniel explained. "And something else very important. Never, ever get out of your car to yell or do battle. You might run right into one. You might even get shot and killed. Get the license number and report the incident; where it happened, what happened, what time and day it was and a description of the car. Drivers like that need to be taken off the road."

Tom laughed weakly. "Well I guess we did learn a valuable lesson today. Ah, could we continue on another day? I don't think I'm ready for more of this."

"Daniel and a few others will meet us the next two or three times to practice defensive driving before you practice on the open road," Anna said.

The three thanked Daniel for his help and went home.

Anna had enjoyed orientation day at James Madison University in Harrisonburg, and met her roommate. She and her friends had agreed that they would have other roommates and still be close friends. She was excited to be entering college, but knew she'd miss family and work at the guide dog school.

Jason gave everyone a charge with his enthusiasm in bathing dogs. He usually got more suds and water on himself than on the dog. Each time the group left the school, they counted their blessings.

One morning De had picked everyone up for the girls' last day at the school. Mark looked behind them. "Holy cow. That's Alex driving behind us. He's breaking the law driving alone. He only has a learner's permit."

"Not only that, we don't want him to know where we're going. He might be more trouble than we're prepared to deal with if he brings his gang down." De spoke anxiously as she kept looking in the rear mirror.

"I have an idea," Tom spoke quickly. "Casually turn left at the next corner." De turned as if she meant to drive that way. "Now turn right at the next corner and drive into the parking lot on your left."

"Hey, it's the City Police Building," Jason laughed. They all gave a sigh of relief when Alex drove by and picked up speed to disappear. They waited until he was well out of sight.

"Let's go down the alley and out on Cortez Drive. We can turn right at the next intersection and go our merry way. Keep eagle eyes open. It never would do for Alex to find the school," Mark told them.

"It might do him good," Tom mused. "Maybe if he saw other people's troubles, he would straighten and drop those wild friends. He might even be the old lovable Alex again."

"When was that loser ever lovable?" Tim snapped. "Forget him. The work we're doing is too important to risk hurting innocent people and animals just to give Alex the Horrible another chance. "

CHAPTER TWENTY-NINE

The remainder of the drive was uneventful and they were soon pulling into the school grounds. They all grinned with joy to see fat, happy little puppies wriggling in the arms of older people sitting on benches or walking around the grounds. "The puppy huggers are at work," Janell sang out.

"Isn't it great? The puppies get lots of love and attention and those dear old people, who might be lonely, feel they are needed, and they are." Michelle spoke as she looked lovingly at the people and puppies.

About half an hour later a gentle rain began to fall. The teens hurried to help get the puppies in their clean cages. The cages for the older dogs could be hosed out by leading a few dogs at a time in the walkway, then turn on big fans to dry them so the dogs could go back into a clean, dry cage.

A Veterinarian, Dr. Larry Mason, was just finishing giving shots and checking some dogs. He patiently answered the teens' questions about his work. The young people then made a dash for the dormitory to learn what training was required to help bond people and dogs. They loved talking to the people and learning their personal lives. As they left one room and started walking down the hall toward the lobby, they heard a child's excited voice calling to them.

"It's Marshall."

"Hi sport."

"Whatchadoin pal?"

The teens called a welcome to Marshal. "Go Chuckles." The dog gave a happy bark and came charging toward them.

Anna stepped in front to stop the dog and chair. She leaned over to hug Marshall while the rest took turns hugging Chuckles and Marshall.

Anna had a strange feeling of grief as she took a careful look at the little boy. The pale skin of his face seemed translucent and the violent smudges under his eyes were darker than usual. He looked as if he had lost some weight and got tired easily.

"I asked Mommie to bring me over so I could see everybody." Marshall burbled. "Me'n Chuckles talked it over and he wanted to come, too. Mommie, you haven't met these friends of mine. This is Mommie," he said proudly as he introduced each one, very proud that he had learned to recognize the difference between Tom and Tim.

"Hi, Mommie. I'm Tom. We're certainly glad to know you."

"Mommie is what I am, but you can call me Sharlene. My little man has told me about all of you, especially you, Anna. Thank you all for being so good to my son." Her voice was pleasant, but Anna detected a hint of sadness in her eyes.

While the crowd too Marshall to see the new puppies, Anna visited with Sharlene. "Is Marshall not feeling well? He seems to be more tired than usual and looks pale."

Sharlene put her hands over her face and started crying. "I guess it would help to talk about it, but it's so hard. I blame myself. Brian, my husband, gets impatient with me and denies that I'm to blame."

Anna took Sharlene's hand and led her into the empty conference room. "I know you don't know me, but I'm a good listener, and whatever you say will stay between the two of us. I've noticed that Marshall is not as strong as he was when I first met him."

Sharlene took a deep breath and smiled weakly. "Marshall loves you so much. He loves all of you, but you're special to him. He talks of you so much that I feel I've known you for a long time."

She stood up and started pacing. "I had rheumatic fever when I was a little over a year old. My parents were told that my heart might be weak and to keep alert for symptoms of anything out of the ordinary. Nothing happened, but I was never permitted to participate in sports because I tired too easily. I was told, when I was older, that it might be dangerous for me to have a baby. When I was expecting my baby, my heart did act up a little, but not enough to be serious. I almost lost him during the eighth month and had to stay in bed for five weeks." She sat down and hesitated,

"It was a difficult birth and Marshall was deprived of needed oxygen. The doctors diagnosed his problem as mild spina bifida. He was nine months old before he even tried to sit up. He didn't have water on the brain, but he does have neurological problems. First he had a brace on his back, then had to use the wheelchair. We've taught him to think in a positive manner and enjoy what he has."

"You've done wonderfully well. I am surprised though that such a young child has a service dog. I didn't know they were provided for young children," Anna commented

"They aren't as a general rule. My father is a brain surgeon and he donated a very large sum of money with the stipulation that a dog be provided for his grandson. Not only to help him with the physical condition, but to be a companion and a protector."

"He and Chuckles make a great team," Anna grinned. "Sharlene, I'm not medically trained, but I truly don't think you should blame yourself for Marshall's problems. So what if you were in bed fro several weeks before he was born. That was good. You had excellent care and it was just unfortunate that this happened. **Not. Your. Fault.** "Anna emphasized.

"Yes. That's what my doctor said. Now I have to put on a happy face. I hear Marshall and the thundering herd approaching."

Anna and Sharlene stepped out into the hall to see Chuckles pulling the wheelchair in a run with a happy boy yelling encouragement. "Mommie! You should see the cute puppies. I wanted one, but Tom told me that if I got one, Chuckles might think I didn't love him much any more. I don't want Chuckles to feel bad, so I'll just visit them here."

"That's great," Sharlene hugged him. "Chuckles has been your best friend and we need to think of his feelings."

"Yes, he has been my best friend, but now I have a lot of new friends," he yelled as he hugged Sharlene.

"Marshall," his mother spoke softly, "none of us are hard of hearing. You're practically screaming. I know you're excited, but we can hear you just fine. Do you think you're being good to Chuckles to run him all the time and expect him to pull you and the wheelchair?"

"I'm sorry, Chuckles. I do love you, but I enjoy going fast." The dog wriggled and made his laughing face at Marshall.

The young people looked sadly at each other as Marshall began to have trouble holding his head up. "Mommie, I think I'm tired now. Can we go home and rest?"

"We sure can, darling. I'm sure your friends will be here to see you another time soon."

"Take me to the car, Chuckles," Marshall said wearily.

Chuckles headed for the front door. Tom and Tim asked Marshall if they could have another hug. While they did this, they tactfully lifted him in the back seat into his special seat and buckled him in. They folded his chair and placed it in the back of the car. Chuckles jumped in beside Marshall and waited patiently to go.

After Sharlene drove away, Anna spoke softly. "I don't think Marshall looked well. He seems to get worse each time I see him."

Mark agreed. "We noticed he was tired when we were showing him the puppies. That was one reason we suggested coming back though he wanted to stay. We even took him out of his chair and let him sit on the floor so the puppies could crawl over him and play. He had fun, but he obviously was too tired to enjoy it long."

The told the staff they'd see them next Saturday. "Today is my last day for a while," Anna told them. "I'm going to miss all of you and the animals."

The other girls explained it was their last day also. "We have sure enjoyed doing what we could and we've learned a lot. We can hardly wait to return during vacations. Thank you for this opportunity," Michelle said.

On the way home a tan Lincoln passed at great speed and almost struck them cutting in so close. "Wasn't that Alex?" Mark asked irritated.

"It sure looked like him. Not having a license hasn't stopped him from driving. Those kids with him may be from affluent families, but they act like gutter trash," Jason bluntly stated.

"I hope they don't cause an accident or kill an innocent person. What's worse would be if they crippled someone for life," Janell worried.

That night the news carried the story of a stolen tan Lincoln that had been abandoned miles away. The car had a deep gash along one side. No arrest had been made, but an investigation was underway.

"I hope Alex wasn't involved, but from what you've told me, I'm afraid it was possible that it was him. Thank God no one was hurt or killed. Another day might be a different story." Herb shook his head sadly.

Anna had one more practice session with her brothers.

The next Saturday, the twins took Hope to the school with them. Tom petted Hope and talked to her. "I'm glad we were given permission to bring you, girl. We've told everyone about you, your mother and grandmother. They all want to meet you. Isn't that nice?" She gave him a doggie grin.

The girls went with the boys, not to work, but they'd been invited.

Hope proudly pranced on her leash and stopped right in front of Baron as if to say, "Okay, big boy, this is your lucky day. You get to meet me."

"Be a lady, Hope. That's big daddy there," Tim laughed. "He's sired a lot of good puppies that have helped a lot of people." Baron's sweet personality and big-muscled healthy body made him a valuable breeding dog.

The group laughed when Hope immediately dropped and showed submission as young dogs do to a mature dog. Baron just looked her over, yawned and went back to his spot on the grass.

The staff had a surprise party for the volunteers. Martin and Hercules were right up front. Several people attended with their assigned dog because everyone had learned to love these young people.

"Hi, kids. I'm glad you boys are going to stay and we'll look forward to seeing you girls as often as you can visit. Thank you for telling us about Galena and Greatheart and showing us the pictures. Galena sure must have been something, but I'm happy with Hercules," Martin stated.

The twins looked a little sad. Tom said, "We loved Galena with our whole heart because we grew up with her and grieved a long time when she died. We loved her daughter, Greatheart, and hated to leave her behind in Alaska. We had to do what was best for the dog. Now we have this bundle of joy and are thankful we've had such good, loving dogs."

"Good, loving dogs happen when the owners love and care for them properly," Jake said as he stopped by. Everyone turned to see what was causing the commotion at the door. Marshall and Chuckles burst through with whoops of laughter.

"I was afraid we'd be too late. Ohhh, Is that Hope? Come here you beautiful girl. I love you already just from hearing about you." Hope obediently trotted to Marshall as if she understood. She laid her head in his lap and grinned up at him.

"Look! Hope and Chuckles are going to be friends," Marshall yelled. The two dogs stood side by side looking lovingly at Marshall as if they understood the situation.

Marshall hugged everyone and made Anna promise again to write. After refreshments, some of the boys took Marshall to see the puppies. The group had to leave before the tired little boy would agree to go home.

Anna left for college with mixed feelings. The week crawled by for the boys. They could hardly wait for Saturday to get back to the school. Irene was driving this time.

"A few weeks ago none of you could have convinced me that bathing a dog would be so much fun," Jason laughed. "I don't even mind cleaning cages and picking up the exercise field."

John Middleton came in as the boys were finishing. "Would you mind helping out in the dormitories?"

"No, we'd love it," Tom answered for them snapping his fingers and giving a little dance step.

"We have a new group of students starting this afternoon. I would appreciate it if you would talk to them and share your experiences. In general, just help them relax and feel welcome. I'll tell them about our school and show the video. Jean has refreshments for all of you."

The teens enjoyed getting to know the new group of young people. The best part was when Marshall and Chuckles came breezing in. Marshall wanted to meet all the new people. "Chuckles even smiles at you," Mark told them. Marshall went to the sightless people and offered for them to hug Chuckles so they could look forward to having a dog like him.

Irene and Rita Dodd were standing beside Tim so he introduced them to Sharlene. "I'm so glad I came," Rita said. "Hearing about it and what goes on and seeing it for one's self is a big difference."

Irene spoke to Sharlene. "Forgive me if I seem insensitive. I don't intend to be, but I would like to know how your adorable little boy is in the wheelchair."

Sharlene told the two ladies the same story she had told Anna. "He's getting weaker," she wiped her eyes. "He's lost interest in a lot of activities except visiting with your children."

Mark, Jason, Tom, Tim and Jimmy were standing nearby. Tom quietly turned and knelt in front of Sharlene's chair. "We have learned to love Marshall and we care what happens to him. If any of us can help you, please let us know." the other boys stated they felt the same way. Sharlene leaned over to hug Tom but was too choked to speak.

On the way home, the boys were unusually quiet. "Mom," Jimmy finally spoke, "is it possible Marshall won't live much longer?"

Rita looked at Irene and answered. "Who can say. Only God knows. He has a lot of problems and the little darling has had a rough start in life. He is adorable and I can understand how all of you have come to love him."

"Well," Jimmy went on, "I guess we'll just have to be as good and thoughtful as possible with him. He's an only child, so I guess he feels as if we're big brothers to him. I'm pleased to be one to him."

CHAPTER THIRTY

Anna had been gone a full week when the high school opened. Tom and Tim were eager to meet all their fellow students, especially the ones in their classes, and revive friendship with former friends.

Hope was puzzled. All her life she had the Jackson children with her. Now the boys were gone for a long time during the day and she hadn't seen the girl in a long time. Irene had agreed to walk Hope and continue with her training.

The third week of school the twins gave their talk in assembly and showed pictures on an overhead projector. They student body howled with laughter at some of their escapades in Alaska, but there was a respectful when the twins told about Galena. Most of the students had known and were almost as sad as the Jacksons at her loss. There were a lot of questions about Greatheart and Hope.

"When can we see her?"

"Does she look like a wolf?"

"How big is she?"

"Is she easy going or aggressive?"

The twins happily answered all questions and assured them that Hope was like any other dog. She was a little larger and a little heavier than the usual dog, but she was eager to please and got along with everyone. Tom told them there very few mean dogs, just careless trainers.

Tom then told the students about Canine Wonder and what wonderful work they were doing. He didn't give the location because Alex was in the audience.

Angela Hurley stood up. "Can we donate money to help out at the school? Or maybe we could raise money somehow. They must have huge expenses."

Mr. Grissom jumped up and hurried to the microphone. "What an excellent idea. I'm happy that my students care about other people and want to help. How many of you would be interested in have a school sponsored fund raiser?" A loud round of applause, cheering and whistling answered him.

"Great! May I suggest that you discuss this among you and give your written ideas to Tom and Tim. They can form a committee with as many helpers as needed. I hope several of you will volunteer to be on such a committee." Again there was a loud round of applause and then dismissal.

On Friday the written ideas were given to the twins. They took them home after inviting some friends to join them. It was difficult because there were a surprising number of excellent ideas.

"I really like this idea of a carnival. We can use the football field and the gym," Tom told them.

"I like it, too," Mark was bouncing in excitement. "Marti makes a great Gypsy fortune teller and we can ----"

"Marti?" Tim's voice broke in.

"You know. Margaret Marinacci. She's called Marti now. She played the part of a fortune teller for the Ladies Guild fund raiser and was a big hit."

"Okay," Jimmy cut in, "we have a lot of ideas. Let's go over them all,"

Tim grabbed a legal pad and began to jot down the ideas they thought were good. They began to read out the ideas with such excitement that Tim finally called, "Whoa. Slow down. So far these sound good but we need to consider time and space."

"Break balloons. Ask business people to donate small items such as small toys, inexpensive jewelry, coupons for free pizza or hamburgers--- well, you get the idea. Write on a piece of paper what the prize will be and charge ten cents for each throw of a dart or three darts for a quarter. If they break a balloon, they get the prize that is written inside."

"Have prizes in another booth with a big tub of water. Float apples in the water and charge a quarter to get an apple in the teeth with the hands behind the back. Keep the fruit and a prize. They'll have to be timed; maybe fifteen seconds for a try. How about a face painting booth for kids?"

The twins looked at each other knowing they had the same idea. "I can't promise, but maybe we can get some of the service dogs to demonstrate with their owner, or with the school." Tom told them. "Maybe a couple of police would demonstrate what their specially trained dogs do."

"Here's another great idea," Jim said with excitement. "This suggestion is for a talent show. That's right up my alley. A talent show and a carnival would involve the public. The students can't raise enough money among themselves, but the public can sure help."

"That's great ideas, but can we work them in on the same day?" Mark looked uncertain.

Tim jumped up. "Why not? We could have the talent show -- say between ten and twelve, break an hour for lunch and start the carnival from one to five. The Home Ec. Department would probably be happy to have a booth for food. That way families could bring younger children and we'd have time to clean up the ground afterwards. It gets darker earlier remember."

"Here's one I like," Jacob Beimer spoke shyly. "This person suggests a basketball game between the boys' team and the girls' team. We could even have food there."

"That would mean another day, but it is a good idea," Tom said.

"How about a dance -- a sock hop? Charge five dollars for a couple or three dollars for a single. Students would be happy to loan CDs for the music." Marylea Perkins gave her idea.

"Great! We could have a basketball game during the afternoon and a dance that night." Mark was so pleased with the idea that he stood and danced around. "Students and public would be involved."

Irene came in with a cake she had baked for them and soft drinks. "You people sound as if you need some pick-me-up. How's it going?"

"Marvelous Mrs. J. and thanks." Jimmy reached for a paper plate to get a piece of cake. 'We're going great guns. There's so many good ideas. One is for a horse show which would suit me, but it would be costly and time consuming. Too, we'd need special insurance. It would bring in a lot of money, but a big responsibility, too."

There was a laugh from the doorway. They turned to see Herb leaning against the dog frame. "I think a basketball game or a softball game between students and adults would be the ticket."

"Hi, Dad. Sorry. Wrong time of year for softball." Tim answered. He placed an arm around his mother. "I suggest that we take a list of the better ideas to Mr. Grissom on Monday and ask him to let the students vote on what they think are the best ones. The most popular votes can be considered, but the students would have to know that their help would be needed."

"But the more that get their two cents in, the longer it's going to take to plan," Mark complained.

After a lengthy discussion, they agreed to let the student body vote. "After all, we're depending on them for support," Joella Pierson reminded them.

On Monday, Mr. Grissom allowed Tom to speak to all homerooms on the speaker. "First, we want to thank all of you for such fantastic ideas. It was too hard for us to make a selection. We're going to give your homeroom teachers a list of the suggestions. Discuss them and vote on the two you think will be feasible. Remember, we need to select ideas that the public can be involved because we need the money."

The suggestions were given to the teachers and they were to take a vote and give the results to Mr. Grissom by noon Tuesday. Two school secretaries and a librarian would count the votes.

On Tuesday, after the lunch periods, Mr. Grissom was laughing as he gave the ideas that were accepted by the majority. "Okay, folks. It looks as if we're going to be busy for a couple of months. The majority of you voted for a carnival, talent show, dance and a basketball game between the boys and girls." A loud cheer could be heard all over the building and even out on the field.

Mr. Grissom continued. In addition to Tom and Tim, three girls and three boys are to be the organizing committee. All of the students will be needed in some way. Remember, we're doing this to provide a service dog for a person in need. I know I can count on students from Fairfax High."

After many meetings and much research, plans were made for the last Saturday in September. There would be a talent show in the morning and a carnival in the afternoon. Small prizes, trophies and ribbons would be needed. The basketball game in the afternoon and the dance that night would be held on the Saturday in November before thanksgiving.

One night at dinner, Herb looked at the twins with a twinkle in his eyes. "Boys, I hope you won't be embarrassed, but your mother and I will be in the talent show."

"Great!" the twins spoke as one.

"What will you do?" Tom asked.

"That's for us to know and you to wonder about," Herb laughed.

The September fair days and cool nights were ideal. Dozens of students volunteered to contact people to sponsor a trophy or ribbons. Tara Ellis came bubbling in one morning. "I had an appointment with my doctor last Friday. I asked him to sponsor a trophy and he said he'd let me know. He called me last night and said he and two of his friends would each sponsor a trophy. That's three of them!" she yelled and jumped as if leading a cheer.

"Yea! Way to go." Charlotte gave Tara a high five. "My uncle owns a variety store and he's offered to give us a lot of small prizes."

Terry Anderson broke in. "Dad owns a tack and feed store and he'll give two trophies if we advertise for him."

"At this rate we'd better have a booklet telling about the events and thanking the sponsors by listing them," John Luman added. "Mom works at City Hall and I'm sure she can help us put a booklet together. They have computers that can do anything but cook a meal."

Tim informed them that Anna had said she would see what she could do.

"She's loads of miles from here in college. How can she help?" Bette Spearson asked.

"She didn't say, but knowing Anna if she decided she's going to do something, she'll come up with a doozy." Tom bragged.

"My dad loves to do carpentry. It's his hobby. He can help build booths or whatever we need," Woody Morrison said.

Ellen waved her hand in the air for attention. "I think we should give first through third trophies and first through fourth ribbons, and we need to give them in categories."

"What do you mean categories?" Jacob asked.

"I know what she means," Bonnie stated. "There will be singer, dancers, instrumentals and miscellaneous in the talent show."

"Now what do you mean by miscellaneous?" Jacob asked again.

"Baton twirling, juggling and so forth."

"That would mean about sixteen trophies for just the talent show."

"Everyone will know why we're raising this money and they won't expect us to do more than would be fair," Verta Lynn said. "But I guess we'd better have about twenty trophies in case of a tie. It is a possibility."

"Okay," Ellen stood up, "twenty trophies and if we need more we'll just have to get them later. How about judges?"

"We shouldn't ask teachers from this school. Why don't we ask local church musicians to judge the singing and instrumentals and the drama teacher from Woodlawn High would, I sure, be willing to judge the rest." Bonnie suggested. "I think they'll all be willing to help."

"That's a great idea. The drama coach at Woodlawn High is Mrs. Sherwood and she lives on the same street I do. I'll ask her and maybe she has a friend that can help. That is if it's all right with you for me to ask," Verta offered.

"Sure, go for it."

"I have neighbors, Anthony and Connie Thompson, who are in a theatre group. I bet they'd be willing to help. They don't have kids in school. We need more than one judge for each category," Fred commented.

"I'm so proud of us. We're working better than I hoped," Tom chortled.

"The man knows the truth," Mark grinned. "Why don't we meet next Friday after school with a list of those who are willing to judge and those who will donate a trophy or ribbons."

CHAPTER THIRTY-ONE

"Magnificent! We have three judges for each category," Tom informed the group who immediately cheered. "Uh, did you people notice that Mrs. Alice Morton signed up to sing?"

A loud groan went up. "We'll have to alert the town that they're not hearing an air raid siren." Jimmy laughed.

They were laughing so loudly that they didn't notice the door opening and Mr. Grissom entering. "What's the joke?" he smiled. "I need a laugh. My wife has tickets to an opera for tonight and I'm too bushed to go, but she will insist. I won't enjoy it." he pretended to shiver.

"We're just being goofy. Pressures of planning, school and home responsibilities ---" Jacob was still laughing.

"Here, Mr. Grissom. Look at this list of judges and sponsors. There's also a list of people donating prizes and food." Tim was pleased with the cooperation they were getting. Publix Grocery is donating twenty loaves of bread. Lion King is donating six packages of sliced ham and sic packages of sliced cheese. There'll be more."

"We have a small problem though," Tom told him.

"Lay it on me. It can't be worse than the opera."

"The Old Dominion Bagpipe Band and Drum Corp has volunteered to play. At the same time Tripping the Jig, the Irish dance school has offered to perform. We have K-9 dogs and some of the service dogs from the training school. The talent show will be long enough without these, but we don't want to turn anyone down and discourage them or hurt their feelings."

Mr. Grissom thought a minute. "How do you feel about inviting them to perform on stages during the carnival hours? Then people could listen and watch free. The dancers and bagpipers could have fifteen minutes each. The K-9 dogs probably won't need more than fifteen minutes."

After a lengthy discussion the group agreed to try to work in the groups who were willing to perform. Tom asked for attention. "Maybe the bagpipers would be willing to play for the dancers and they could share a stage. We can ask them."

"Okay, gang," Tom continued. "Here's what we agreed on. Speak now or forever hold your peace. The talent show will be from ten until twelve.

"Fortunato's Nursery as agreed to furnish potted plants and tree roses to decorate the stages. Each person performing will furnish their own music. Any questions or suggestions?" They agreed, but, naturally, they were all nervous as they'd not attempted this before.

Tim took over. "After an hour break for lunch, we'll start the carnival at one. Our Fairfax High Band will march on to the field as soon as the gates are open and lead the first people in. They'll pay a reasonable fee to enter. There'll be a barrel near the entrance for donations. Throughout the day, the band can march through the crowd playing. Around two thirty the K 9 dogs will give a demonstration and the officers will answer questions. A section will be set aside for the service dogs to do as they please. They may decide to demonstrate or just hand out brochures. Tell everyone to ask a runner to tell the announcer when they're ready to perform so the public can be informed over the speakers. Around three thirty the Irish dancers will perform and at three forty-five the bagpipers will perform. There will be at least one student and one parent, or adult, at each booth and each activity. The football and basketball teams have agreed to be runners and take notices around. Everyone will work in two hour shifts."

"What about trash on the field?"

"The Glee Club has volunteered to set up trash barrels and to patrol the grounds as well as help us clean up afterwards."

"Our Safety Patrol will walk the grounds and help to keep order. The city police will come by at different times, but I hope we won't need them. Our Home Economics classes have volunteered to take charge of the food booths. Hopefully we'll have enough donated until we won't have to buy much. Two different pizza restaurants have donated twelve pizzas each and the Burger King has sent us more than one hundred coupons for free variety plates," Jacob announced with pride and glee. "We'll ask other fast food places to donate what they can."

Marshall was his usual exuberant self when he heard the plans. "Dad, can we go? I want to see everything."

"We'll talk abut it with your mother and make a decision as a family."

"Hey everybody. I've had three letters from Anna and one each from Dede and Janell. Mom says I'm poplar with the girls."

"Son, the word is popular. My popular son."

"Why don't we get dates and go ice skating tonight?" Mark suggested. "We'll soon be too busy to do anything."

"Sounds good to me. Why don't we meet at the Pizza Mart and eat before we skate," Tim said.

Alex was at the ice rink with a rowdy group. They were skating fast and cutting around people and in and out, almost causing some adults to fall. Alex laughed at Mark and Doris for waltzing on skates.

"I think they're pretty good," one of Alex's friends said.

"You don't know anything, clown." Alex laughed loudly and skated backward trying to do jumps and twirls. He finally fell and rolled on the ice, still laughing manically.

Tom looked on grimly. "We'd better get the girls out of her and take them home safely. Let's don't let on to Alex that he's bothering us or that we're leaving. What a waste. He's always been a straight A student and now he barely gets by and is failing. He's now on suspension."

For the big Saturday, the day was beautiful, sunny and just cool enough to feel good. The planning committee met early the check on lights, microphones, outside speakers, flowers, stage decorations and booths.

"What great talent are your parents planning to display?" Mark asked.

The twins shrugged. "You know as much as we do," Tim answered.

"Look at that crowd in the auditorium," Dories exclaimed as she peeped through the curtains. At a donation of three dollars each, we ought to make a good sum. Eight hundred fifty can be seated and it looks like a full house. Look. Some boys are bringing in folding chairs and lining them at the back and down the side aisles."

"Close your mouth, Tom. You might catch more flies than you expect," Herb laughed at his son's stunned expression. Herb was wearing a big, fuzzy coat and what was known as a zoot suit. Irene was wearing a silver dress of tiny beads with three long pearl necklaces. She had a hat called a cloche and chunky shoes that were worn in the nineteen twenties.

"What in the world?"Tim muttered as if he didn't know whether to greet them or pretend he didn't know them.

At that moment Herb and Irene's names were called and they ran on stage with some lively Charleston music. Herb threw off his coat and he and Irene started dancing a rousing Charleston. The audience went wild. The twins were both pleased and embarrassed.

Jimmy Dodd hid in a corner when his parents ran on stage dressed as they had in high school. Rita was in a poodle skirt with a white sweater and oxfords. They did a lively jitterbug. There was a gasp when Darrel leaned over and let Rits roll over his back and land on the floor on the other side of him while he reached for her and pulled her through his legs from back to front.

A fourteen year old girl, from Woodlawn High, won the dance trophy for her impressionist ballet danced to 'America the Beautiful'. A black youth, from Oakton, won the instrumental trophy for his violin solo. Twin girls won the singing for dressing as bums and singing and dancing 'Side By Side'. A Fairfax City policeman won the miscellaneous category for juggling knives and other objects.

"Wow! Even taking off the few expenses we had, we made one thousand nine hundred fifty-five dollars for the talent show." Tom punched the air.

"Marshall, my man!" Tim called as he got up from his lunch table and pretended to dance over to Marshall and his parents. He spun Marshall's chair around and pretended they were dancing. Tim asked permission to take Marshall over to introduce him to other students. Before his parents could answer, Marshall said, "Sure. Me'n Chuckles would like to meet your friends."

"Chuckles and I," Tim corrected.

"Can't I go?" Marshall pouted.

His father waved a hand in the air. "Take him if you can stand it." He knew Tim would take good care of Marshall.

"Hi, gang. This is my pal, Marshall, that Tom and I have told you about. He's our favorite new friend."

Marshall beamed. "Everybody come meet my buddy. His name is Chuckles and he's the bestest friend in the world." He gloried in the attention and was upset when everyone had to get back to work.

Tom eased over. "Tim, isn't he getting too excited?"

"Yeah, he looks awfully pale and tired," Mark whispered.

"Marshall, we have to go to work, so I'm going to take you back to your parents. See, they're over there with my parents." Chuckles looked worried because Tim pushed the chair and the dog only walked beside them.

Sharlene looked at her son and sucked in a breath. "We need to get home.

Thank you for giving my little man a good time."

"Mom," he whined. "Can't we stay for the carnival? It isn't fair."

"There's nothing you'll miss at first. Let's take Chuckles home so he can rest and we'll come back to watch the K-9 dogs."

"I guess that's okay. Besides Chuckles might get jealous if he thought I might like those other dogs." Marshall's head was wobbling and he could hardly hold it up.

Irene and Herb had agreed to meet Marshall and his parents at the K-9 area. The two couples enjoyed walking around and seeing everything. Marshall was thrilled when a policeman hid a knotted rope in his wheelchair and one of the K-9 dogs found it. He was extra thrilled when Marti held his hand and told him that he would be famous and everyone would always remember him.

Irene and Sharlene were walking together. Sharlene was worried. "Marshall gets tired more easily, but he's a little trooper. He did take a nap when we went home. I can't keep from worrying."

"It's been exciting for him. This is something unusual even for the students here at the school. If you need to leave, Sharlene, we'll understand, but we must get together soon." Irene hugged Sharlene.

"Promise me that you'll tell Tom and Tim that I loved everything," Marshall told Herb with a hug. Herb had been carrying him and now carefully placed him in the wheelchair.

"I promise. They'll be seeing you soon and you can talk about everything with them. So long."

CHAPTER THIRTY-TWO

The carnival was more of a success than the students imagined. They were all as tired as they'd ever been, but very pleased. With the permission of the Nursery, the potted plants and trees were auctioned off. With a good clean-up crew, the twins were happy to be home by nine.

Hope came rushing to her beloved boys and jumping all over them. "Sweet Hope. You are so forgiving. We've been so busy for several weeks and have given you such a little time," Tom said as he hugged her.

"Mom! Dad! Where are you?" Oh, hi there." Tom was excited as he and the planning committee met at the Jackson home to count the carnival money. Hope was jumping around not sure what the excitement was.

"Hurry. Dump the money so we can count it," Jacob ordered.

"Holy cow! Three thousand four hundred thirty dollars and four cents," Mark shouted.

"Four cents? Where did four cents come from?" a puzzled Jimmy asked.

"You did have a barrel for donations. Maybe someone dropped in whatever change they had or maybe that's all some little child had," Herb reminded them.

"I can't believe it. With the donations from the talent show we now have a total of five thousand three hundred eighty-five dollars, and oh, yes, four cents," Jacob wrinkled his nose and then cheered.

"I hope we more than double that. The money will go a long way to furnishing a dog to someone who needs one,"

Irene ran to answer the phone. "It's Anna," she called. "She wants to know how the day went." The twins took turns telling her of the activities and Marshall.

"I told my dorm mother about what your school is doing. She asked administration if we could hold a fund raising project to help you and we have permission to do so."

"Bless you. And bless all those who'll help," Tom stated. "Let us know what you'll be doing so I can tell everyone here. Here, speak to Hope. She's going crazy. She hears your voice and doesn't know where it's coming from."

"Hope. Can you hear me, Hope? How's my good girl?" Hope sniffed all over the phone and then ran around the house searching for Anna.

Herb took the other students home while the twins took Hope to their room. All over town there was great excitement because the students were thankful for the work everyone had done and the results.

October would bring a big homecoming party; football game and a dance. With school, church, part-time jobs and home responsibilities, the twins were not able to get to Canine Wonders as often as they'd like. They were extra pleased when fifteen students, from other schools, heard about the school at the carnival and had volunteered.

The twins spoke to Marshall every day on the phone and visited when they could. Needless to say, Marshall was not satisfied because he had become accustomed to the attention.

Marshall called one day and Tom answered. He complained that maybe they didn't like him any more because they had not seen him in three days, which is a long time for a little boy. "Ole buddy, you're still our best friend. Honestly, we're so busy with school, our jobs and preparing for exams that we haven't even been down to Canine Wonders. Thanks for telling me what Anna said in her letter. Give Chuckles a hug from us and we'll give Hope one from you. Okay? We'll see you before long."

Reaching down to ruffle Hope's hair he said, "Hope, we must take you to see Marshall and Chuckles soon. Don't you agree?" She sure did.

The weather was much colder. Beautiful multi-colored leaves were falling off the trees which meant more yard work. Herb took the twins for driving practice on the open highway.

The Saturday for the football game and dance was cold, but clear. Fairfax High and the rival school both had bands and cheer leaders who marched in the parade in the city. There were politicians in cars, the Chief of Police, police on motorcycles, floats from businesses as well as school groups, booster groups, baton twirling schools, 4-H horse groups and many more.

The football game started at two. Anna came for a surprise visit. She got permission to announce over the loud speaker that her class of college freshmen was going to have a talent show open to the public. There would be prizes and a door fee of three dollars. "Our college President has a nephew who uses a service dog. That's why he's willing to do all he can to make this work. If the talent show is successful, we'll be able to do more in the future." The crowd cheered and whistled.

The announcement was made that there would be a barrel at the main gate for donations if anyone wanted to help. Tim had explained for the benefit of the visiting team and their sponsors about the plan to buy a service dog. The day was memorable when Fairfax won the game. The barrel held six hundred eighty dollars and thirty-six cents. Jimmy was still going bonkers at the odd change. This made a total, so far, of six thousand sixty-five dollars and forty cents.

The dance started at seven and was a tremendous success. Trina Fuller refused to ride home with her date because he had sneaked out and was drinking.

"Tom, I'm sorry, but I need a favor," Trina looked miserable. "I need a ride home and you live on the same street so--I thought ----" she stopped embarrassed.

Tom looked at his date, Susan Woodson. She smiled and nodded. Susan put an arm around Trina. "I'm glad you had more sense than to get in the car with Garry. It isn't smart to drink and drive. It isn't smart to drink at all."

Tom smiled. "You girls wait here. I need to speak a minute with Mr. Grissom and then we'll leave."

"Susie, I'm sorry to be such a bother. I bet you and Tom had plans after the dance."

"No. Tim and Eileen are with us and we had agreed to go home right after the dance. Church tomorrow and, too, the twins want a visit with their sister before she goes back to college. Relax. You're no bother. We'd rather you go with us than risk your life with someone drinking."

"Thank you, Susie. I'll be right back. I want to tell those girls something." Katrina walked off and in a minute came running back to Susan. "Susie, please tell Tom I appreciate the offer of a ride, but I've found a ride home. Thanks again." She ran off.

"Trina, wait," Susan called but she was already out of sight.

Irene came into the living room where her three children were laughing and visiting. "I don't want to hear groaning this morning. We have church."

"Aw, Mom. It's been a long time since we could have a good talk with Anna. We have a lot of catching up to do," Tom told her.

"Will wonders never cease. I remember, not too long ago, when you boys thought your sister was too bossy and avoided her."

"I guess all little boys feel like that. I hope we've outgrown childish behavior such as that."

After church, Irene had prepared their favorite; chicken and dumplings, raw sliced carrots, cauliflower and pickled beets with deviled eggs and buttermilk biscuits. Groans were heard all around the table when she brought in her delicious pumpkin pies.

While Anna and Irene cleaned the kitchen, Tom and Tim played a video game in their room. Suddenly Herb gave a shout. "Come here, quickly. There's news on television you'll all want to hear."

The reporter looked sad and surprised as he gave the story. "This is a disastrous happening after a great game and a good time at a high school dance. It's unfortunate, but there's usually one who will drink, take drugs, or do something they shouldn't and it is horrendous that innocent people pay for their stupidity. Last night, at about midnight, a student at Fairfax High, Alex Bauman, drove his father's car to and from the high school dance without being licensed. He had two girls with him in the car. Sergeant Larry Thornton, Virginia State Patrolman, has the facts. Sgt. Thornton."

"Well, we got a call from an excited, elderly man who reported that a car just passed his house at a high rate of speed and, instead of making a curve, had run straight on hitting a concrete pole and bounced off to hit a parked car. I arrived on the scene because I was on duty in that area. At first I thought they were all dead. The driver was draped over the steering wheel and his head had made a hole in the windshield. No seatbelt. The passenger, beside him, had her seat belt fastened, but had been thrown forward and snapped back so hard she appeared to have a broken neck. The girl, in the back seat, had no belt and had been thrown forward over the front seat. She was hanging with her head against the dashboard."

"Thank God they were unconscious and not dead, although it is difficult to believe that they survived. I called for ambulances and EMT assistance."

"Sgt. Thornton, was the car badly damaged?"

"The front end was sliced off and the car was crumpled all over. All windows were cracked and the driver's head had made a hole in the windshield. The jaws of life were used to cut the metal enough for the young people to be lifted out without doing further injury to them. The dashboard had been pushed back against the two in the front seat."

"When did you find out who they were and when did you notify families?"

"An ER nurse recognized one of the girls as Trina Fuller. When Trina's parents came they identified the other girl as Meg Dawson and the young man as Alex Bauman. Neither teen had an ID on them."

A doctor gave the report. "As to their injuries, Alex has a spinal injury and some internal damage. Meg has broken ribs, glass cuts and abrasions. Trina has a concussion, glass cuts and minor injuries. I cannot guess what their futures are. Meg and Alex have regained consciousness, but Trina is still unconscious."

"Thank you, doctor. We have Mr. and Mrs. Bauman on live camera. Reporter Raenell Pierson is interviewing them. Raenell, can you hear me?"

"Yes, Quincy. I'm at the home of Alex Bauman and have been talking to his parents." She turned to a distraught couple. "How do you feel about your son's accident, and do you accept any responsibility?"

Mrs. Bauman was crying. "Alex is a good son. He has never given us any trouble. I don't believe he was taking drugs. I'm sure they'll find it was a mistake in the blood testing. Alex knows not to drink or take drugs. We have never allowed any of that." She was so nervous and upset, she kept babbling.

Mr. Bauman gulped audibly. "I don't want to believe that our son was taking drugs, but as an attorney, I've seen it happen in many good families. I want to know more facts before I say more publically. I will say this. If Alex was on drugs, I assure you that I will not rest until I discover who is making drugs available to our young people. That's all. Please respect our grief and let us take care of our son."

Chapter Thirty-Three

"Dear God," Irene breathed on a sob. "Those poor families. Those innocent girls. How dare Alice say her son has never given them trouble and that he isn't taking drugs. She has never paid enough attention to him to know what he's doing."

"Or who he's running around with," Tim spoke softly, obviously shaken.

Herb sat stunned. The twins were in shock and Anna, standing between them, had an arm around each brother.

Hope couldn't understand why her family was sad. She whined and trotted from one to another, finally standing in front of the children to bark.

"Oh, Hope," Anna said, dropping to her knees. "You know we're upset and you don't understand. It's unfortunate that people aren't nicer like dogs, at least like you."

"I need to go to the hospital and visit them," Tom finally was able to talk. "Dad, can you take us, please?"

"Son, I have to see that your sister gets back to college. It's too soon after the accident. I'm sure the doctors won't want anyone but immediate family visiting. They need to gain strength and there may be more injuries that will show up later. I'm surprised the information was given out at all. Wait a few days, at least until after Tuesday."

"But, Dad. We don't expect them to talk to us. We'll just feel better if we can look at them. I know we can't do anything." Tim was gulping and choking on a sob.

Irene said quietly, "I can't help but feel thankful that you boys were not in that wreck. I know that some parents may not know what their children are doing, but that's no excuse for not constantly reminding them of right and wrong. Children need to know that parents check on them because they love them and want the best for them."

"Wait and pray, boys," Herb told them.

"Dad's right," Anna told them. "Trina is still unconscious and Meg and Alex are still in shock and too weak for visiting."

The twins walked sadly to their room. Herb took Anna to the bus and gave her money. He looked at her with moisture in his eyes and hugged her over and over. "I'm so proud of my children and love you so much. It would break my heart if I found either of you were sneaking and doing something you'd be ashamed to tell me about."

"Dad, we love you and mom. You will not find either of us in serious trouble because you've loved us and taught us well." She gave a weak smile. "Except for Tom's experience with the dynamite. Remember, Alex was left with a nanny and housekeepers all of his life. He must have been twelve when he was entirely on his own. His parents have wealth and top jobs, but they haven't shown the love and caring you have for us. Thank you, Dad." She hugged him again and then boarded the bus.

Mr. Grissom called a special assembly on Monday morning. "Students, whether you believe it or not, I care about each and everyone of you and I'm here for you if you need me. I beg you, if you have experimented with drugs, or are drinking alcohol, please come to me or one of the counselors and let us help you break away from something that will destroy you. I never encourage students to tattle, but in this case, I am. If you know of another student who is drinking or taking drugs, please tell me so that I can have a chance to help that person. Your name will never be mentioned. Otherwise we may be burying that student. Go to your homerooms and remember, if you need to talk, I'm here, not to pass judgment, but to help."

Tuesday, after school, the twins went by the hospital. Alex tried to talk, but he was too weak and still unclear as to what happened. They just told Meg they were praying for her and wished her well. They weren't allowed in Trina's room because she had only regained consciousness that day and was very weak. A nurse told them Trina had no memory of the accident. The twins, with heavy hearts, made their way home.

The following Saturday, at Canine Wonders, the group was disappointed that Marshall did not come. For the first time the work was just another job.

"Mom," Tom called as he and Tim entered the house.

"In here, boys. I'm making jelly and can't leave the berries cooking."

"Mom," Tim began as they came into the kitchen, "today is the first day that no one brought Marshall. We're afraid he might be too sick to come."

Herb came in as they were talking and they told him of their fears. "After supper you can call and check on him. He may have had a medical appointment. If he's sick, Sharlene might be upset, so be kind. They might not want Marshall to know how sick he really is, so be careful what you say."

"Sharlene? Hello. It's Tom Jackson. Tim and I missed Marshall today."

"Thank you for calling. The last two days have been bad. He's showing a little more interest today, but he isn't well. Marshall wants to talk."

"Hi. Who's this?"

"It's Tom. And me, Tim, on the extension."

"Oh, goody. Next Saturday is my birthday. Mommie says we'll have a family party, so could you and the others come for cake and ice cream?"

"Anna and the girls won't be here, but we boys sure can. What time is your party?"

"Mommie, what time can they come?"

Sharlene took the phone. "Oh, my. We planned on a quiet time just us, but we'll be glad to have all of you. We hadn't planned a big occasion. You know why. Can you come at five after you leave the kennels?"

"You bet and we insist on bringing the cake and ice cream," Tom told her.

"Oh, thank you, but no. That won't be necessary. I've already planned on what I will serve."

"But you didn't expect a bunch of us. Please, Sharlene. We want to do this for Marshall."

"I'll reluctantly say okay, but Brian won't like it. He'll appreciate it, but he'll feel we should feed our guests."

"We insist. We'll furnish everything, dinner and all. If you want to decorate, that's okay." Tim stated firmly.

As the twins told their parents, Herb and Irene were excited and wanted to help. "I'll make his favorite meatloaf, mashed potatoes and peas. I'll get Rita Dodd to make

315

something and Marsha Tully will want to furnish her delicious rolls and maybe a beverage. I'll talk to them and help you plan."

"I'll give you money for a large sheet cake and about a gallon of ice cream," Herb offered. "Have his name written on the cake with maybe a dog and balloons printed on it. Find out what his favorite ice cream is and get enough for the crowd. Don't forget paper plates, cups, napkins, tableware and whatever is necessary. We want to make it easy for Sharlene so she won't be cleaning up. Tell your friends to bring simple gifts like puzzles, books, so forth."

"Do you know something that we don't?" Tom asked his parent.

"Such as ----" Herb looked puzzled.

"Like you know he may not live much longer." Tim had a choked voice.

"Sharlene does say he's getting weaker by the day. Yes, boys, it could be any time, but we don't know for sure. We'll all grieve when it happens, but you wouldn't want him to linger in pain and misery," Herb spoke haltingly.

"No. No." both boys answered. "We'll do what we can and make this the best birthday party ever. We'll tell the others so they can be prepared and won't let Marshall suspect."

Tom, Tim, Doris and Ellen went to the hospital to visit their friends. A nurse told them that Meg Dawson had been discharged. She was to stay at home for a week, have a doctor's appointment and then be told when she can return to school.

"Hey, guys," Alex spoke weakly. "I am ashamed of myself. I need to apologize to you for ignoring you, my good, true friends. I'm ashamed that I neglected you for those others. Will you forgive me?"

Tom took his hand. "Yes, of course, Alex. You made some bad decisions but you're paying for it. If you learned a lesson from this and will never do it again, it'll be great. If you had only hurt yourself, it would be bad enough, but you hurt two innocent girls."

"That's the worst of it. I didn't mean to harm anyone, but it happened because I was stupid and thought I was being a smarty. Those yo-yos I was running around with didn't help any."

"Blaming someone else is not going to help you," Tim spoke kindly. "Face up to what you did and make a vow that you will never take any more drugs or drink any alcohol. You were always on the first honor roll and you've let yourself down there. You're in danger of failing and not graduating with us this year."

"Alex," Ellen took his hand. "You know drugs and alcohol cook the brains. Thankfully you haven't been on them long enough to have done much damage to your brain, but who knows. Plus they damage your heart, liver and kidneys. You may have more troubles in the future."

"I know what you say is the truth, but you all sound so serious."

"We are serious," Doris told him. "We know how much good you can offer the world and what a great future you could have. You can do something great by warning others what can happen to them."

"I heard you say one time that you wanted to either be a brain surgeon or a college professor of science. You have the ability to do it, but you have to be willing to apply yourself. You can talk to individuals, or groups, and tell them what your bad decision caused," Ellen said.

They talked a few minutes more and wished Alex well. They then went to visit Trina. As they walked down the hall, they met Alex's mother.

"Alex is going to have more trouble than he knows about. When he was thrown over the steering wheel into the windshield, he had an injury to the back of his neck at the top of the spine. The broken bones will heal but the nerve damage is questionable."

Tom hugged her. "We are so sorry this happened, but to tell the truth, we knew for some time that Alex was an accident waiting to happen."

"You kids pretend to be his friends. He went everywhere with you. Why didn't you tell us what he was doing? Why didn't you talk to Alex and stop him?"

Doris touched Alice Bauman's arm. "We did try to talk to Alex. He laughed at us and went off with his new friends. They ganged up and followed us, harassed us and taunted us. One even threatened Tom and Tim because they tried to talk Alex into leaving that gang."

"Surely not. Did Alex know about it? Who are these boys anyway?"

"Yes, Alex knew. He was with them when they threatened us and Alex just laughed." Tom told her the boys' names and she gasped.

"I know those boys and their parents. Surely you're wrong. Why the father of one of those boys is our family doctor. They're all from good homes." she babbled.

"Alex is from a good home, too." Tim reminded her. "He was bored and looking for someone to give him the attention he craved."

"How dare you talk to me like that."

"Mrs. Bauman, I don't mean to be a smart-aleck and add to your troubles, but be honest with yourself. How would you have reacted if we came to tell you that Alex was with a rowdy crowd, skipping school, acting strangely and avoiding old friends? Would you have appreciated us coming to tell you or would you have resented it?" Ellen asked her.

She took a deep breath and choked on a sob. "I don't honestly know."

"If we could see the personality change in Alex, why wouldn't you recognize it at home?" Tim asked gently.

"I guess I was just too busy with my work and social obligations, thinking I was doing so well. Truthfully, we rarely saw Alex. "Now that I look back, I remember that he began to argue with us, sass us, running out of the house and disappearing when we tried to talk to him. I thought it was just teenage years. It was easier to ignore than to make an effort to pin him down. His father has worked with families who have these same problems. Why didn't he see it?" She was becoming hysterical.

"If you had known the boys he was running around with, would you have gone to their families and ask them to talk to their own sons?" Doris asked.

319

"I can't answer that either. I guess truthfully the blame should be laid at mine and my husband's feet. When Alex was born, I was making a name for myself as a prosecuting attorney and my husband already had a well established law practice. We were just too wrapped up in our careers to pay attention to a child we hadn't planned on having," she cried.

Tom put an arm around her. "Forgive us for adding to your heartaches, but it has to be said. We don't think badly of you. You've done what hundreds of parents have done, but it isn't too late to make things right. Alex does love you both and I'm sure you love him. You have to practice tough love and be firm in family rules. Don't be ashamed to share this with the public and maybe save other children."

"Thank you," she said, blowing her nose. "It's pretty sad when children my son's age have to tell me how to raise my own child. I know you mean well and I am grateful. Thank you for being a good friend and telling us the truth."

"We're here if you need us. We've said many prayers for Alex and the two girls, and we'll continue praying for them and for you and your husband." The young people went on to Trina's room.

Trina was pleased to see them. She moved slowly and talked haltingly. "I still am not sure what happened. I know what I've been told, but I don't remember. If I had known Alex was taking drugs, I would never have gotten in his car."

"Don't dwell on it," Ellen patted her shoulder. "You're getting better and we're thankful for that. Just relax, cooperate with the medical staff and concentrate on getting well. We want to see you back at school." They didn't want to tire Trina, so they left promising to return.

CHAPTER THIRTY-FOUR

Rita and Irene had a lot of fun preparing the food for Marshall a surprise party. The twins picked up a large sheet cake after school on Friday that they had ordered. Herb promised to buy the butterscotch ice cream on their way to Marshall's house.

"My goodness, look at all this good food. Marshall, look at this. Doesn't everything smell and look good?" Sharlene was almost in shock. Brian just stood looking as if he would cry.

"Wow! Look at that great cake," Marshall yelled. "Yummy. I can't wait for a piece. And you brought me presents." He was bouncing in his chair with excitement and Chuckles ran around barking trying to decide what was going on and if he was to be included.

"Whoa, sport. We gotta have some good food first before we eat the yummies," Tim gently reminded Marshall. Mom, Mrs. Dodd and Mrs. Tully made your favorites."

Marshall ate slowly because it was difficult for him to swallow. The boys ate and talked to him, taking their time so that Marshall would eat as he should. He went wild over the cake when he discovered the dog on it.

"Now can I open my present?" Marshall was still yelling.

"May I?" his father corrected him.

"You can help if you want to, Dad, but the presents are for me." Even Chuckles tore the wrapping off a beef bone and lay in the corner to enjoy.

"Look! Look! Video games, books, puzzles, drawing pencils and everything. Thanks gang. This is the bestest birthday anyone could ever have." He laughed even louder as they sang "Happy Birthday" to him.

"It wasn't long until it was obvious that Marshall had all he could take. Brian put him to bed while the ladies helped Sharlene clean up. The boys told Marshall good night and he begged for a story. They told him a story until he went to sleep and they tiptoed quietly out.

Brian shook everyone's hand and hugged each of the ladies. "I can't find words to express how grateful we are for the interest you've shown in our son. We love him so much," He choked. "It's obvious he failing, but he's our little ray of sunshine. Thank you is all I can say and God bless you."

"No need to thank us. It's been a pleasure to know Marshall and I, for one, have learned a lot about working with children like him," Tom said.

Sharlene got their attention. "I want to tell you something before you leave. Remember my father is a brain surgeon. A colleague of his told that his daughter has asthma and suffers from sleep apnea. Their son and daughter-in-law rescued an eight months old mutt from the animal shelter. The dog was scheduled to be put to sleep the next day. They took the dog to visit the son's mother who was the colleague's daughter and the dog seemed to really like the older woman. The mother felt tired and stretched out on the couch. Suddenly the dog began jumping at her and barking. When they checked, the mother had stopped breathing. They called 911 and she was resuscitated. To make a long story short, the dog was a natural. Illinois has a phone board in the emergency station that shows the name of the person calling, the phone number and the address. They placed a lever on this woman's phone to make it easier to make an emergency call. The dog had some quick training and then that little scamp quickly learned to press the lever when the woman needed help. He has saved her life two or three times."

"Holy catfish. I'm speechless. Isn't that fantastic?" Tim blurted.

"Well, you said a lot Mr. Speechless," Tom teased. "Seriously, the public needs to know how valuable these dogs are and how much company they can be to an elderly or lonely person." They left and talked of the amazing story all the way home.

Cold rains came down steadily through Wednesday. The students were concerned that it would be raining for the basketball game and dance the following Saturday. Everyone cheered when Friday dawned bright and clear, although chilly, with the promise of the same on Saturday.

Students and townspeople poured into the gym for the game. Two coaches from other schools had volunteered to be referees, but could hardly work the game without laughing so hard. Some of the boys would pick the girls up and move them out of the way. As a boy aimed for a free foul shot, a girl ran over and tickled him. Both teams played well in spite of their tricks on each other. The girls demanded a rematch when the boys were declared winners. The people were laughing and cheering loudly. A barrel was at the door for donations.

Later at the Jacksons Jacob again went into hysterical jubilee when the money was counted. Donations at the door totaled four hundred forty dollars. The money from hot dogs, snacks and sodas came to sixty-four dollars and seven cents," Jacob grunted. "Where are all these odd pennies coming from?"

"Don't gripe. It's all going for a good cause. Who cares as long as people keep donating," Mark said.

"That's a total of six thousand five hundred sixty-nine dollars and forty-seven cents," Tim shouted.

"Okay, gang. Enough time wasted. We've got to get ready for the dance, pick up our dates and go, go, go," Tom cheered

The dance was open to the public and the response was overwhelming. Mr. Grissom thanked everyone for attending and invited them to share in the punch and snacks. "On a more sober note, I hope we don't have to visit the hospital tonight. Have a good time and keep it clean and safe."

Herb could not believe his eyes. Tall, long-legged Tom was pretending to be a puppet while Tim pretended to pull strings and dance him. It was comical and talented. Herb and Irene looked at each other and laughed.

"Remember when we were not sure Tom would survive to this age? He was so careless and into so much trouble. I'm proud of my boys. I could cheerfully stand up and tell this crowd that we are the luckiest parents in town," Irene gushed.

A majority of the students started asking their parents, or a neighbor, to dance with them. Jimmy Dodd's father, Jerry Dodd, did a loose-jointed dance that had the crowd giving him the floor and applauding. Jimmy was surprised at himself. *I must be maturing. I'm not embarrassed at day. In fact, I'm proud to let folks know he is my dad.*

As the crowd was disbursing to leave, Tom announced that they had taken in one thousand seven hundred ninety-five dollars for the evening making a total of eight thousand three hundred sixty-four dollars and forty-seven cents. Everyone was pleased that they had a small part in supplying a dog for a person who needed one.

The students felt let down after all the planning and excitement was over. Tom asked if he and Tim could invite their best friends in Alaska to visit them during the summer.

"We'll discuss it after I've talked to Yokno's parents," Herb answered.

The phone rang and Irene answered giving a small squeak. "What's wrong?" herb jumped up.

"Nothing. It's Anna and she almost broke my eardrum. She's thrilled about something. Yes, dear. Could you lower your volume a little? Wonderful! Wait until your brothers talk to you." Tom went to the phone in the kitchen and Tim took the one his mother was using.

"What is it, Anna?"

"We had a talent show involving students and public. With donations and sponsors you have ---" she screamed "---three thousand nine hundred dollars."

The twins were as thrilled as Anna. "Let's see," Tom quickly worked the math. "That makes a total of twelve thousand two hundred sixty-four dollars and forty-seven cents." His voice increased in volume as he spoke.

"Thank you, Anna. Thank you."

"Thank the people who were willing to help us."

"I'll write a letter to the editor of the newspapers in Harrisonburg and thank everyone who helped," Tim said.

"Maybe you should include an article about the work of the service dogs training and how much they mean to individuals. A human interest story on Marshall would be even greater," Tom encouraged Tim.

Tim wrote his lengthy article and it was published in several newspapers. It even got a note of interest on the television news. Donations came in from all over the state of Virginia and close surrounding states. Now the total was nineteen thousand six hundred eighty-five dollars and, of course, forty-seven cents. Amazingly donations kept coming in from other states.

The twins called Canine Wonders to share the good news. Then they called Marshall. Sharlene answered.

"We're going to present the total to the school next Sunday afternoon. There'll be reporters and a lot of dignitaries. We want to donate the money in honor of Marshall. Could you have him there by two o'clock?"

"I don't see why not, but it will all depend on how Marshall feels."

Chapter Thirty-Five

"I'm proud of all my students," Mr. Grissom said in assembly. "All of you are invited to the presentation ceremony, but dress warmly. It is December. I hope it's just cold and not raining. It's less than three weeks until Christmas. Won't this be a magnificent early Christmas present for the school?" The students cheered and whistled.

"Will Marshall be there?" Bonnie called out.

"Will he?" Mr. Grissom turned to the twins.

"You bet. He can hardly wait," Tim laughed.

The day was bitter cold and windy, but a huge crowd had gathered on the Canine Wonders lawn. "I've never seen so many people outside of a stadium," Jake spoke in awe. "They're standing, so let's get this show on the road. We'll try not to keep them out in the cold too long."

Sharlene and Brian walked beside Marshall's chair as Chuckles pulled him to the area around the microphone. The dog recognized the twins and went straight to them. The twins looked sadly at each other at the sight of Marshall, but put on a big grin for his benefit. Out of the corner of his eye, Tim saw several girls hugging each other and trying not to cry. He glared at them and slightly shook his head.

Jake welcomed everyone and informed them of the pamphlets inside. "We had planned to bring small groups in to see a video and tour the building, but there are many more than we anticipated and we just can't. We also planned on refreshments, but come on folks, we didn't plan on so many. I guess I'll just extend an invitation for you to make reservations to visit. Now I'll turn the program over to the young people whose hearts are bigger than this building. Thanks to them, we're having this day."

Tim took the microphone. "It looks as if I've been elected spokesperson. First I want to welcome the Governor of our great state." The gentleman stood among loud applause and cheering. Tim introduced several politicians and local people of importance.

"I couldn't be more proud than I am right this minute. My heartfelt thanks goes to the people who responded and helped so much. I am blessed to be able to call these people friends," he waved toward the students. "My greatest blessing is my friend right here." he dropped to a knee beside Marshall's chair. Chuckles pushed between Tim and Marshall. "The courage this young man has shown puts us all to shame. Talk about big hearts. Marshall has more love, caring for people in general and just plain intestinal fortitude."

"What's that?" Marshall piped up. His clear little voice ran over the microphone. 'Does it mean I have some bad disease?" he frowned.

"No." Jacob knelt beside Marshall. "It means you got guts, kid, and you're our hero."

"Hero! Me?" Marshall beamed. Daddy, Mommie, did you hear that? I'm a hero."

"You've always been our hero," Sharlene whispered trying to quiet him. Brian choked and got red in the face knowing Marshall's medical problems.

Tom took the microphone. "Let's get to the business we're here for before we all have icicles running down our cheeks. Marshall, my good buddy,---"

Marshall turned his chair with Chuckles determinedly trying to get ahead of him to pull. Tom knelt beside Marshall. "I hope you're ready for a nice, big, big surprise. With the fund raisers we had through the school, and Anna's college friends, we are presenting Canine Wonders with a check for ---" he hesitated for effect - "Are you ready for this?"

"Oh, you meanie. Tell me quick. Is there enough to buy a dog for a little boy or girl?"

"More than enough. The grand total is twenty-four thousand eight hundred fifty dollars, and, oh, yes, forty-seven cents. Enough and more for two dogs."

A gasp rippled through the crowd and then a cheer went up that must have been heard in the next county. John Middleton took the microphone not ashamed of the tears in his eyes. He meant to thank them, but couldn't talk for the lump in his throat.

Marshall had no trouble talking. "Really? Will it buy two dogs?"

"More than enough," John finally said. "It will furnish the dogs, all the training and veterinarian care. I can't find words adequate enough to express my appreciation and love for you folks. You've worked faithfully and all of you have become like my own children," he told the teens. "A speech would spoil the moment so I'll: -- he choked and waved his hand in the air. "I understand there's cookies and punch if anyone's interested."

None wanted cold punch and they wanted to get home because the sky threatened to open and dump snow. Tim thanked everyone again and told them they had planned to make it a yearly even to raise money for a dog. People were quickly going to their cars shivering.

"Can you come home with me and play video games?" Marshall asked the twins even though he was weak and tired.

"We will soon, but not today. We'd better get home before it snows on us," Mark explained. Putting his hand over his heart he said, "I promise we'll come soon. It's just a few days until Christmas. I bet Santa will bring a lot of great things to our hero. We want to be there and see what you get."

Although the snow had spit off and on throughout the afternoon, it didn't snow full blast until seven. "I'm so thankful we made a good sum for the school and hopefully everyone is home safe and warm. We should go to the hospital tomorrow and visit Alex and Trina," Tom yawned.

Herb and Irene looked at each other with warm, gentle expressions of love in their eyes. They were so thankful. Tom had matured at last.

Irene went to answer the phone and turned to the twins with a big grin. "Fans of yours are on the line."

The twins took extension phones. "Hello," Tim spoke hesitantly.

"Hi ya, old buddies."

"Benjamin Yoakno! What a great, nice surprise."

Ben laughed. "There's someone else here."

"Greatheart?" the twins spoke as one.

"Wrong," came another familiar voice.

"Charlie Running Horse."

"You win the prize, but there's others here."

Sam Cramus and Alan Brave Bear also talked some. The boys in Alaska took turns and they talked for some time.

"Let me tell you what happened," Tim broke in.

"That's what we called about. How much did you earn and how is the little boy?"

The boys cheered in Alaska. "We're happy for you. Please write a long letter and tell all the details. We want to know all about Marshall." Ben finished. "We feel as if we've met him."

"Whoopeee," Herb laughed. "I'm glad I'm not paying for that phone bill. Did you wish the boys a Merry Christmas from us?"

Tomorrow's the last day of school before the holidays," Mark said. "How about us planning a skiing trip?"

"I'll have to talk to my parents before I can commit," Jacob frowned.

"Yeah, us too," Tim said. "It sounds great, but we don't know what family plans will be. Besides I'm worried about Marshall. I have a bad feeling that I can't explain. I don't want to go too far away."

Tom explained. "We want to be near if Sharlene calls us with bad news. She promised to contact us if there is a change of any kind."

"We all want to be there for Marshall," Mark agreed.

"I'm heading home now," Jimmy told them. "It looks like more snow. I'll probably see all of you tomorrow. Be careful going home."

The day passed slowly for the students. There was a loud cheer all over the building when the final bell rang. Teachers thanked students for their gifts and drew a breath of relief.

Mr. Grissom spoke over the speakers. "My wishes are for everyone to have a Merry Christmas, Happy Chanukah, Kwanzaa and Happy New Year. See you next year."

Tom, Tim, Mark, Ellen and Doris went to the hospital to visit Alex and Trina.

"Hi, gang," Alex was cheerful.

"How are you doing, pal?"

"I'm not in much pain any more, but, for some reason, I till can't stand. I guess it'll come slowly." they talked a few minutes and then the group left.

"Trina, look at you. You're up and dressed," Doris was pleased.

"My doctor said if I passed all my tests tomorrow and still doing as well as I've been, I can go home tomorrow."

"Hooray!" Tom hugged her.

"We'll see you at home during the holidays," Ellen promised.

Herb got up from the dining table to answer the phone just as the family was finishing dinner. "Oh, no. I'm so sorry. We'll be right there. No, we want to be with you."

"Is it Marshall?" Tom asked softly.

"Yes. He had to be rushed to the hospital and it looks bad."

"Let's hurry and get down there. Sharlene and Brian will need comfort and moral support." Irene reasoned as they hurried to prepare to leave.

"Absolute not. You cannot go in there. That's a mighty sick little boy and you can help him by leaving him alone." A nurse spoke sternly to the twins.

"Only immediate family."

Brian came out of Marshall's room. "What's going on out here?"

"This --- this nurse won't let us in to see Marshall," Tim spluttered. "He'll want to see us."

"Nurse, these boys are like big brothers to my son. I request -- no, I demand they be allowed to visit for a couple of minutes."

A doctor hurried to them. "Mr. Wolverton?"

"I'm Brian Wolverton. That's my son in there."

"Your son is very sick, but you know that or you wouldn't have brought him here tonight. We're doing all we can to make him comfortable and giving his antibiotics for a high fever. I'll be able to tell you more after the results of all the tests arrive. In the meantime, he must be kept quiet and stress free and as happy as possible."

"Thank you, doctor. He'll be happy and stress free if these two boys will be allowed to go in for a couple of minutes. He loves them dearly and expects them."

The doctor dropped his head and thought a moment. "It's not something that is normally done, but if you say so, they can go in for not more than two minutes. Boys, remember, no stress." He shook a finger at them.

When the twins eased into the room Sharlene started crying. She quickly turned her back so Marshall couldn't see her. The twins stood on either side of Marshall's bed.

"Hi, champ," Tom whispered. "How's it going?"

"Tom, Tim," Marshall whispered. He smiled sweetly at them. "Santa won't know where I am."

"Oh yes he will," Tim answered. "We'll phone him and let him know."

"Are you sure?" he asked weakly

"Do dogs bark?" Tom smiled. Marshall tried to smile.

"We have to go and let you get some sleep. Your body will heal quicker if you rest, eat good and take your medicine." Tim patted his arm.

"Yuck," Marshall made a face.

Sharlene walked out with the twins and Brian came in to be with Marshall. Irene and Herb hugged Sharlene. "Is there anything we can do?"

"Not at the moment. Just pray and stand by. Thank you, boys. Your being here is better than medicine for him." She smiled through tears.

"If you and Brian need to go home, we'll be glad to sit with him," Herb said.

"I'll let you know. Saying thank you is not enough. How blessed we are for having good friends like you."

On the way home, Tom asked. "Do you think we should call Anna?"

"Not tonight," Irene answered. "Wait at least for another day and maybe we'll have more information. Besides it's too late for a call to her dorm."

It was difficult for the twins to settle for the night. They called the group that went to Canine Wonders with them. All of them agreed to pray.

"Can I see him?" Mark almost sobbed.

"No. Only immediate family," Tom told him knowing it would not be wise to tell of their visit.

The concerned young people all gathered at the hospital the next day to speak to Brian and Sharlene and just to be together.

Tom answered the phone and hung up with a grin. "That was Sharlene. Marshall's pulled out of this -- again. It was a virus. His immune system is very low because of his medical problems. The doctor said he was lucky this time, but Marshall's body can't take more of this."

Irene hugged Tom. "Our prayers have been answered. Your friends will want to know, but remind them that he is still in a dangerous situation. Love him and make him happy. Always be up beat when you're with him. He knows he'll never be out of the wheelchair, but he doesn't think of death."

Two days before Christmas, Irene and mark's mother went to Marshall's house with Tom, Tim, Mark and Jacob. They dressed Marshall warmly and carried him out to the car to take him and Sharlene to see all the lights and decorations. Marshall was thrilled when they came home with him for hot chocolate. They didn't want to tire him, so didn't stay long.

CHAPTER THIRTY-SIX

"Shhh. Remember, this is a surprise." Tim led sixteen young people quietly to the Wolveton's door. When Brian answered the door, they trooped in. "Surprise!" They had called ahead and got Brian's and Sharlene's permission to visit.

Marshall was lying on the couch ready for bed. "Hey. What are you guys doing here?"

Doris knelt beside Marshall. "It's the magic of Christmas. The first gift to the world was the greatest gift of all and filled with love. We're bringing you lots of love -- and gifts."

"Merry Christmas," they chorused.

"But tomorrow's Christmas," Marshall was delighted.

"We know, but we wanted to beat Santa here," Jacob as he gave Marshall a present. Chuckles bounced around delighted to have them. There were squeals of happiness with each gift Marshall opened. A hug came with each gift and chew toys for Chuckles.

"This is the bestest Christmas I've ever had. Chuckles thinks so, too."

"Chuckles, is that true. I didn't hear you say a word," Tim laughed.

Sharlene walked over. "Son, these friends brought you wonderful gifts. What are you going to give them?"

"Gee," he said quietly, "I don't know."

"How about giving them a song?" Brian suggested.

"Okay, Daddie, will you play for me?" Brian placed a violin on his shoulder while Sharlene ran her fingers on the piano keys. "Let's sing, silent Night," Marshall sang out.

"Yea!" the group cheered.

"I know," Marshall said happily. "I'll sing the first verse and everybody jump in for the other verses."

"Oh. Glory," Tara Ellis whooped. "Stand back. You've never heard Charlotte jump into a song."

There was a lot of good-natured teasing. The sweet tones of the violin rang with a few notes then Sharlene started playing the piano.

Several of the teens wiped tears from their cheeks as the clear, sweet voice of Marshall's drifted through the room. His smile lit the room as he waved his hands for them to join him. They sang several carols in addition to some silly Christmas songs such as Rudolph and Grandma Got Run Over By A Reindeer. Jingle Bells finished the warbling.

At six thirty Tim motioned to the others and they gave hugs and good wishes as they left.

"What a great evening. I don't know when I've enjoyed anything more. Did y'all see how pale and tired Marshall was?" Ellen laid her head on Mark's shoulder and he placed an arm around her.

"Yes. He was very tired, but happy." Mark said and started singing, "What Child Is This."

Tom ran to answer the phone as he and Tim came home. "Sure. We'd love to." he said and hung up. Tears stood in his eyes as he faced his family. "That was Marshall. He asked if we would take Chuckles if he has to go to the hospital again. He said he knows we love Chuckles like he does and if he has to be gone for a long time Chuckles will need exercise and care."

"Oh, my gosh," Tim blurted. "Do you think he suspects he might be dying?"

"Probably not," Tom answered. "He was weak and tired when we left. He has accepted that he will need to go back to the hospital and he knows his parents stay with him. He wanted to be sure Chuckles was okay."

Herb hugged Irene, "We'll gladly take the dog if it's okay with his parents."

Christmas morning came bright and cold with a thin layer of snow. Irene fixed blueberry pancakes, scrambled eggs and sausage links. They ate, cleaned the kitchen and went to the living room to open the presents under the tree.

"You know, it's funny," Tim mused. "When I was little I couldn't wait to see what Santa brought."

"I went for the stockings first," Tom laughed.

"Now we eat a leisure breakfast, clean up and then come in to open gifts. This is the one part of growing up that I don't like. I miss that thrill and excitement that I had as a little boy," Tim finished.

"Son, you are growing up. The years will pass faster than you think and some morning you're going to be drug out of bed before daylight so that you can enjoy the excitement of your own little boy. Here, open this one."

As they were in the middle of unwrapping gifts, the front door burst open and a blast of cold air swept in. "Hey family," a cheery voice called.

"Anna! I thought you were going home with your roommate," Irene ran to hug her followed by the three men.

"You'll think I'm a baby, but I've always been with family for Christmas. Buffy and her dad took me to the bus station and I came home. I took a taxi from the depot. **Merry Christmas everyone**. Come on. Group hug."

"This is probably the best Christmas I'll remember because I realize that no matter how old you get, or how far from home you are, family is still the best. I have a special gift for Marshall. I hope we can go over this afternoon to visit with him."They all talked as Anna ate. Herb got up to answer the phone. "Dear God, we're on our way," they heard him say.

"No! Don't tell me it's Marshall. It's Christmas." Tom choked

Herb nodded. "He's in the hospital and Brian and Sharlene are very upset. They need us there." They quickly dressed and left.

Running into the hospital, they were met by a white-faced Brian who staggered. He looked old and sad. "He's gone," he sobbed. "He's with the angels, no longer in a wheelchair, but dancing and singing as he's always loved to do." He sat down crying uncontrollably.

"Where's Sharlene?" Irene asked rubbing Brian's back.

"She collapsed. Dr. Martin gave her a sedative and put her to bed."

"What can we do? What do you need done?" Herb put an arm around Brian.

"Nothing now. No, you can call our minister, friends and relatives. I'm not up to being on the phone. The list is on the kitchen table. We were too upset to go to bed, so we stayed up and made the list because we felt it would be soon." He handed Herb a set of keys. "Here. I'm going to stay until Sharlene is ready to go home."

"Brian, why don't you go home with Herb and the boys? Anna and I will stay with Sharlene. Go home. We'll be with you both as long as you need us." Irene urged him.

"I'm too late," Anna sobbed. "I should have come home instead of going to the Hoover's last night. I didn't get to see him and I had a gift for him."

"Honey, you wrote to Marshall and called him. He was so proud to have a big sister in college. He loved you and knew you loved him."

"You're right, Mom. I'm being selfish. I'm only thinking of my own grief. Sharlene and Brian need us now. How sad Christmas will always be for them after this."

At the Wolverton's Tom called a few of his friends and asked each one to call others. Everyone was grieving. Next he called Mr. Grissom. Six hours later Irene brought Sharlene home.

Three days later the church was packed with students, church members, relatives, people from Canine Wonders and loads of friends. The minister choked when he started speaking.

"The body that Marshall's soul used is in front of you, but the Marshall we knew is no longer there. He is a spirit in heaven." The minister explained so that the small children, Marshall's friends, could understand. "Marshall left something that we all need. He left the ability to accept what life offers and make the best of what we have. He was so full of love that he glowed. Even in pain he was always smiling and he sincerely cared about other people. He loved animals and made provisions for his dog companion to be cared for in a new home. We would all be a better person if we would emulate him." A huge crowd followed to the grave site.

Brian and Sharlene were surprised and touched when they were contacted by the staff of Canine Wonders. They had requested no flowers, but instead that donations could be made to either Canine Wonder or the Children's Hospital. Donations were pouring in at the school in Marshall's memory.

Chuckles now lived with the Jacksons to the delight of Hope. Chuckles would whine and search all over the place. "He misses Marshall," Tim observed. Hope was at chuckle's side wherever he went. She seemed to know he needed comforting. When he would give up and lie down, Hope was beside him as close as she could get.

"Look at that," Irene smiled. "Hope is being a little mother to him. Mother! No! Boys, I absolute forbid Hope being allowed to mate. I refuse to be as accepting as I was with Greatheart. And I ---- why are you laughing?"

"Mom, don't get bent out of shape. Chuckles can't be a mate to Hope. He's fixed. Poor guy," Tom laughed. "Although he's content to be with Hope, he still misses Marshall and he will for a long time. He'll get bored with no work to do. He's used to being needed. We need to exercise him often."

Irene reminded them that Sharlene and Brian would be in Indiana with her parents for two weeks. "That's what I meant to ask," Tom snapped his fingers. "How come her parents didn't attend the funeral? Brian's parents were there, but they live closer."

"Sharlene's parents are both elderly and have medical problems even though her father putters around the house and yard. When Brian and Sharlene return, we'll invite them over for dinner. Boys, it's time for you and your dad to take Anna to college. She had permission to miss a few classes, but she can't be gone longer. I'll stay here with the dogs and have supper ready for you when you get home. Anna, do you have money and your new clothes?"

"I have it all, Mom. Calm down. I'm not going to Outer Mongolia. I'm only a couple of hours away. If I need something I can call." Anna hugged her mother and kissed her cheek, then ran out in tears to the car.

January winds were bitter cold, but everyone had their work and activities. Fairfax High students were changing and maturing. The loss of Marshall and the wreck that Alex, Meg and Trina had, caused loads of them to take stock of their own lives with more seriousness than they had. They were also more appreciative and respectful of adults.

In addition to school, volunteering at Canine Wonders, part-time jobs, church and sports activities, the twins were going to the Children's Hospital one day a week to entertain the children. Hope and Chuckles happily went with them to greet the children and to make everyone feel good.

"Some of these sweet, little characters have been abused, some have no families and some are from privileged homes. Still they all, without exception, need love and attention" A nurse told the twins one day as they were observing activities through a plate glass window.

CHAPTER THIRTY-SEVEN

As the twins were waiting to enter the huge rectangular shaped room, Tom knelt with one arm around Chuckles and one around Hope. He looked at the nurse with them. "Will you take the children out who are afraid of dogs?"

"No. I'll keep them to one side away from the activity. That way they can see without feeling threatened."

"Good idea," Tim praised her. "Maybe they'll be won over when they see how kind and gentle these dogs are. Both dogs have been with children all of their lives and have been carefully trained."

"Several people have brought in a variety of pets. Some children have had a bad experience, or nervous parents who didn't want them exposed, or have never been around animals. Let's go in now. Just walk slowly around and let the children see you. Allow them to come to you."

The twins walked slowly around the room chatting with any child who came near them. "Tom," Tim whispered, "Chuckles keeps looking at the little boy lying on the blanket."

"I noticed that. The boy has dark hair and is about the same size that Marshall was. Maybe Chuckles feels he's found Marshall."

"No, I don't think so. He was accustomed to Marshall's odor. He can smell that the boy is not Marshall. He's picking up vibes of some kind from the child though."

"Mrs. Hawkins," Tom called softly to a nurse. "Why is that child lying on the blanket? He hasn't moved since we've been in here. He acts as if he doesn't even see us or know we're here."

"That's a very sad case. His name is Donald Heyl. He was in a car with his parents when a drunken driver ran into their car and forced them over a cliff. The parents were killed and David was brought in unconscious. He had a broken leg, two cracked ribs and several abrasions." She sighed deeply. "Physically he's healing, but we haven't found any relatives yet. He doesn't talk or take an interest in anything, and he refuses to try to sit up or walk. He's just in his own little world."

Chuckles gently pulled away from Tim and walked over to David. He calmly walked on the blanket and sat down. Finally he stretched out full length by David but still not touching the boy.

"David didn't even turn his head. He acts as if he doesn't know the dog is there. Was David's eyesight damaged?" Tim was concerned.

"There's nothing wrong with his eyesight and his brain wave tests are good. He's just so sad and probably confused." A man spoke softly behind them. They had not seen Dr. Martin walk quietly in the room. He stood between the twins with a hand on each shoulder.

"David knows the dog is there. He's lost the will to help himself. I know that dog. He was with Marshall for a long time. He was used to Marshall's mood swings and took excellent care of the boy. My opinion is that the dog senses the boy's despondence, and in his own way, is trying to take care of David."

Fifteen minutes later, as the twins were leaving, Tom walked to the nurses' station. "Is it all right if we bring the dogs more often? I'm betting Chuckles will eventually reach David."

"I don't know why you can't come more often. You've been approved and cleared. I've heard of animals being used as therapy and maybe it will work with David. Thank you, boys. Both dogs are well behaved and we do appreciate them."

Each time, after that visit, Chuckles will go straight to David and lie quietly beside him. On the third time, David turned his head to look at chuckles. Boy and dog lay quietly looking into each other's eyes.

Hope began to make low crooning sounds and would stand over David looking down at him. She and Chuckles would touch noses across the child as if they were talking about him. Hope would then walk around to others.

"I believe both dogs are sensing something inside David that we can't observe," Tim said.

On the fourth time, David reached for Chuckles and kept a hand on the dog. The next time, David turned toward Chuckles and put an arm across the dog. Three more visits went by with David lightly hugging Chuckles.

"Look," a nurse caught their attention with tears standing in her eyes. David had placed an arm and a leg over Chuckles. His cheek was on the back of the dog's head. The nurses were motioning for others to look. Someone had gone to get Dr. Martin. He looked with a big smile, turned quickly and left before they could see his tears.

The next visit David got farther on Chuckles' back. The dog raised himself leaving his rear end on the floor. Hope came and stood on the other side of David. David wobbled but did push himself up to sit between the dogs. "I knew it," Tom whispered happily.

Two more visits and Chuckles stood pulling David up. "It's obvious Chuckles knows what he's doing," Tim stated. The next two days the twins had semester exams and wasn't able to go to the hospital. Irene offered to take the dogs to the hospital.

"Thanks, Mom. I imagine David is missing Chuckles and wondering if he's lost another friend. Call it selfish, but we've come this far with David and I want to be there as David progresses," Tom said.

When the twins walked in with the dogs, David smiled and reached out an arm. "Hello, doggie," he giggled. Chuckles gave a happy bark and rushed to the boy. David rolled with Chuckles and laughed. Hope tilted her head from side to side and seemed to be smiling. Chuckles stood and allowed David to pull up on him. David staggered slightly when Chuckles slowly and carefully took a step forward. David was forced to move with the dog or fall. They took four halting steps before David sat down with a thump. The little boy was startled when nurses applauded. He smiled shyly.

"What happens now?" Tim asked disturbed. "Have you found relatives to take David?"

"Yes," the nurse hesitated. "We found his mother's parents living in Kentucky. They haven't spoken to her since she married David's father. He was a different religion to

347

them. Now in their late seventies, the man has emphysema and the woman is crippled with arthritis. They can't take care of him and don't want to be bothered since they've never seen him."

"What will happen to him?" Tom was upset.

"If the grandparents can't suggest another relative, then David will become a ward of the state and will be put up for adoption. He'll be harder to place than a younger child and his emotional problems will go against him being adopted. In the meantime he'll be placed in a foster home."

"How old is he?" Tim asked.

"He's just turned six. He'll have a birthday in May."

"Our birthday is in May," Tom smiled.

The twins were sad when David cried as they left. "Bye, bye, doggie," he sobbed.

"David, we'll be back. You know we do come back. Chuckles and Hope have to go home but they'll be back real soon to see you." Tom choked.

Hope went to David and licked his face. She then stood with her head against his chest until he hugged her. Both dogs left looking back.

Outside the hospital, the twins were delighted to see Trina arriving with her mother. At the same time a girl, their age, walked by with a giant harlequin Great Dane. The Dane excitedly ran after Hope and Chuckles thrilled to find doggie friends.

Suddenly the Dane ran around making strange shrieking sounds while circling Trina. Hope walked to Trina and stood staring up at her. "What's wrong with your dog?" Tom asked the girl.

"I have no idea. She's only eight months old and probably just going silly to see your dogs."

"She's beautiful, but isn't she too strong for you?" Tim asked.

Before the girl could answer, Tom heard Tim make a sound of alarm and turned to see that Tim had caught Trina's head just in time to keep her from cracking it on the sidewalk as she fell backward. Trina was making gurgling sounds and began to thrash around.

"Run inside and get help," Tim yelled at Tom. "Thank God we're in front of a hospital." Hope stood across Trina's legs. An intern came running out with two nurses. Hope growled and had to be ordered away before they could get to Trina.

"She's having a seizure of some kind. Let's get her inside quickly."

Two orderlies had run out with a gurney and gently lifted Trina to take her into the hospital.

Trina's mother had let her out and had gone to park the car. She came running toward them. "What happened?" she asked worriedly. The twins and the girl with the Dane walked into the waiting room with Mrs. Fuller telling her on the way what had happened.

"That's why I brought her in to be checked. She had a seizure last night and then went into a deep sleep. That's never happened before."

Tom smiled at the girl with the Dane. "My name is Tom Jackson and this is my twin, Tim. This is Mrs. Fuller, the mother of the girl who fell."

"My name is Hillary Coramex. We're new in town. We live two blocks over on Hershey St. this is Millie," she proudly patted the dog. "I'm trying to teach her to walk beside me."

Tom grinned. "She'll learn. It takes patience and consistent training. We've trained several dogs. One was half wolf."

"Wolf?" Hillary looked frightened. "Weren't you scared?"

"No. She was the daughter of a dog we'd had all our lives. We'll tell you about it some time. You'll be going to the same school we do. I bet we'll become friends."

"I hope so. Excuse me, but I need to get this monster home. Mrs. Fuller, I sincerely hope your daughter will be well."

"Thank you, Hillary. You must come for a visit soon."

The twins stayed with Mrs. Fuller until Dr. Hamilton came to talk to her. "I know you're frightened for your daughter, but you must go home and rest. I'm keeping her overnight for observation and try to find what caused the seizure. I'm sorry but I can't tell you anything about her condition this soon. It will take time."

"May I see my daughter, doctor?"

"Certainly. She's sleeping, so don't be upset. We're keeping her quiet and we're experimenting with medications to find what will help her."

The next afternoon Dr. Hamilton met with Mrs. Fuller. "Apparently the injuries Trina received in the automobile accident caused some form of nerve damage. We don't know all we'd like to know about the brain. It is vitally important that she take the medications exactly as recommended. Please contact me if you have concerns or questions. I know this can be confusing to you and to Trina. I want to see her once a week until she is stabilized. Needless to say, she must stay home tomorrow."

"Are you telling me that my daughter will have these seizures for the rest of her life?" Mrs. Fuller asked anxiously.

"I wish I could give you a definite answer, but I can't. Time will tell. In the meantime, don't hover over her and make an invalid out of her. Be as normal as possible. Treat her as usual making sure she understands the importance of taking the medication as prescribed."

Hillary enrolled in school the next day, but Trina didn't get to meet her. The twins were pleased that Hillary was in a couple of their classes. They introduced her to other students and made her feel welcome.

On Saturday the twins went to visit Hillary and meet her family. "Let's go see Trina. It's time you two got acquainted." Trina and Hillary became instant friends. They told Hillary about Canine Wonders and were so excited and interested to visit and learn more about the school.

The following week Mr. Coramex drove the twins, Trina and Hillary to Canine Wonders. They were impressed. "I want to be a volunteer, too," Hillary told John. "I'm willing to work hard and follow directions."

"Come with the boys next Saturday and give it a try to see if you're still willing to help us. We'll be happy to have you."

Several days later, when Trina was visiting Hillary, the two girls were listening to music and dancing around. Suddenly Millie began to moan and run around Trina. "You silly clown,' Hillary spoke sharply to her. She turned to laugh with Trina and gasped in horror as Trina fell with a seizure. "Mom. Dad. Come quickly."

Mr. Coramex gently held Trina to keep her from banging her head while Mrs. Coramex called Mrs. Fuller. "We'll take her to the hospital and meet you there," she told Mrs. Fuller.

Again Dr. Hamilton was on duty. "The medication absolutely must be taken on schedule. I know it's a horrible thing to happen to a young girl, but it has happened, and we have to deal with it. Trina, you probably won't like what I'm going to say next. You must wear a special helmet anytime you're away from your home. Then if you fall you won't cause further injury to your head."

Trina started to cry. "I'll look like a monster. None of the kids will want to be around me. Some of them will make fun of me."

"If they're really your friends, they'll want you to be safe and take care of yourself." Dr. Hamilton hugged her. "Do this now because there's a real good chance you'll outgrow the seizures, or medication will stop them. I know you feel this isn't fair, and it isn't. Let's work together and take good care of you so that you'll be healthy and happy as an adult."

The next day Trina reluctantly wore the helmet to school and told some of the students why she was wearing it. "Well look at it this way," Tim laughed. "You won't need to worry about a bad hair day because no one will see your hair." He felt badly when Trina began to sob. Dori and Ellen rushed to her side.

"Shame on you, Tim. Don't you have any compassion?" Doris glared. "Just remember it can happen to you, too."

"Trina, I'm so sorry. I was trying to make you laugh and feel better." Tim put an arm across her shoulders. "I'll punch anyone in the nose who bothers you."

Trina gulped and smiled. "It isn't you, Tim. It's this whole miserable situation. I don't think I'll ever get used to it. How long am I going to have to pay for the mistake of getting in the car with the wrong person? Pay no attention to me. Just call me Weeping Willow," she tried to giggle.

The bell rang signaling classes were starting. Tim put his arm around Trina as they walked through the mass of hurrying, pushing students.

CHAPTER THIRTY-EIGHT

The next visit with David was so successful that the twins hated to leave. David not only walked on his own beside Chuckles, but attempted to run a few steps. Hope had kept a small group of children occupied, but she kept an eye on David. The children laughed as they threw a ball and Hope ran to get it. A few times Hope slung her head and threw the ball in the air and then jumped to catch it.

"Bye, Chuckles. See you later." David sang out. He now knew that this friend would return. He hugged both Hope and Chuckles.

"Look at the dogs," Tom laughed. "They're acting like little kids, hanging back and hating to leave."

A nurse hurried to talk to the twins. "We don't know how much longer David will be with us. He's well enough now to be moved. Thanks to you and the dogs he's much happier."

That night after dinner, Tom and Tim told their parents about David's progress and their fears about his adoption. "I wish we could take him," Tom said. "I want to know who adopts him so that I can tell them to get him a dog and sing with him." After the twins went to bed, Herb and Irene talked for over an hour about David.

The day was free for the students because it was a teachers' work day. The gang had planned to meet in City Park and play the girls against the boys in soccer. As Trina ran down one side, Hillary's dog suddenly took off after her moaning and carrying on. Hope ran beside her, not making a sound, but not taking here eyes off Trina. Tom had a brainstorm.

"Trina. Sit Down." She looked perplexed at him. "Sit. Down. Now!" She sat and Hope positioned herself across Trina's legs and kept staring into her face. Millie ran circles around her. Suddenly Trina sunk over and started to twitch. Hope wouldn't even let the twins near Trina. She growled at all of them if they came near.

Mark was spluttering in his anxiety. "Tom, how in the world did you know to tell her to sit down? How did you know she was going to have a seizure? What's wrong with Millie and why is Hope so defensive?" Questions came from all the teens.

"Whoa. I can answer only one question at a time. I've been thinking about the two times the dogs were with Trina when she had a seizure. Remember? Millie made moaning sounds and ran around her. I think the dogs are picking up nerve stimulus of some kind or maybe there's a chemical change in her body that they smell. You know there are dogs that can detect cancer by the smell. I've been reading about this, but don't have answers. I can't explain it, but I want to talk to John."

As Trina became aware of where she was, she tried to get up. Hope kept pushing her back and wouldn't let her stand. After a few minutes two of the girls helped Trina up, but Hope stayed beside her.

"I think Hope feels Trina got up too quickly," Tim smiled.

"Come on, Tim. Let's get Trina home." Tom put a supporting arm around her and Hope pranced right by her side.

When the twins were back at their house, Tom called John and told him all that had happened. "How extraordinary. I'd like to see both Millie and Hope and talk to the owner of Millie."

Hillary and her parents brought Millie to Canine Wonders. Millie ran happily in the fenced-in yard with Hope and a couple of school dogs. Trina and her parents soon followed. The young people told John what had happened all three times when Trina had a seizure and the dogs were near.

"I'd like permission to keep both dogs at the school and give evaluate them. They could be given special training as alert dogs. I've never trained an alert dog, but I have friends who can do the job. I've learned they're being used all over the United States."

"But she's my dog," Hillary wailed. "You can't just take my dog."

"Of course not," John soothed her. "I assumed you'd be willing for the dog to have training that would make her useful to someone. Forgive me. I got excited, but don't intend to force you to give up your dog."

"Hillary," Mr. Coramex said firmly, "if your dog can help a person in need, wouldn't you be proud of her and want to help that person?" She kept her head down with tears running down her cheeks, but said nothing.

The atmosphere grew lighter when Hope ran through a doggie door, but Millie couldn't make it. Tom walked over and opened the door for Millie to walk through. "Hey, old lady. You're just too long-legged for that hole." Millie grinned at him and slapped Tom's legs with her muscular tail.

"Please, Hillary," Trina begged. "I don't know what it is, but your dog seems to know when I'm going to --uh-be sick. Hope is quieter because she's older, but she's a big help, too. Daddy will buy you another dog, won't you, Daddy."

"You are so selfish, just thinking of yourself." Hillary almost screamed. "It's **my** dog and I've had her since she was weaned."

"Hillary," her father spoke sharply. "We're not going to force you to give up your dog. We just felt that you are mature enough to make the choice to help others. Besides, you'd get her back. I am so embarrassed," he said to the group. "Let's go home, Hillary, and talk it over."

The Fullers left thanking everyone for their time and concern.

Mr. Coramex stood at the door. "Thank you for inviting me to hear about the training school. I'm impressed. I've heard of service dogs and guide dogs, but I've never thought much about them. I'd like to visit again, Mr. Middleton, and learn more about your work."

"My name is John and you're welcome to visit at any time."

"Thank you. My name is Joe, actually Jose. Come on dear," Mr. Coramex put an arm around his wife and reached a hand to Hillary. He looked at the Jacksons. "It was a pleasure meeting all of you. Thank you."

"Our pleasure," Herb smiled and they shook hands.

"I'm intrigued with your dog. I understand that you had a wolf dog at one time. I'd like to hear all about that. Hope shows promise of helping Trina, but Millie is stronger. She could lean on her if necessary. She's young, but she does show a strong reaction to seizures. She could be a lifesaver." Hillary hung her head, and, without looking at anyone, ran out to the car.

"What an interesting evening," Irene said thoughtfully. "Jane Coramex only spoke when I spoke directly to her. Joe is certainly in control in that family. It's obvious Hillary has been spoiled."

"Anna will be here in a few days," Tom reminded them. 'She has a talent for talking to people who are distressed. Maybe she can get through to Hillary."

"Gee, family. I'm happy to be home even for a few days. I've been homesick, but I've never studied so hard in my life. College is sure different, but fun. I love it. My heart still aches when I think of Marshall. Such a sweet, little, loving boy. I'm glad we have Chuckles."

'Wait until you meet David," Tim grinned. "He's something like Marshall in that he has a lot of guts and so loving and accepting."

Anna listened carefully when the twins told her of Hillary, Trina and the dogs. "My dear, darling brothers. You shouldn't be too hard on Hillary. Now be honest. If someone had suggested that you give Galena to them, I know you wouldn't have been any happier than Hillary is."

"Yeah, but ---" Tim started

"We would have if she was needed for someone as sick as Trina," Tom exploded.

"Would you honestly have been willing to loan her to someone else?"

The twins looked solemnly at each other and then at Anna. "Well --- maybe not at first," Tim spoke softly.

"Promise me you'll be nice to Hillary and don't let others be ugly to her. It's hard enough to be the new kid on the block and make a lot of changes, and then be asked to give up a pet you've loved all its life. She hasn't known any of you long enough to have bonded or developed a loyal friendship. Let her parents handle the situation. Think how you would feel in her place."

"I guess you're right," Tom muttered. Tim nodded

"Now that you've settled that, let's have a family conference," Herb told them. He and Irene sat on the couch. Anna was in a lounge chair and both boys were on the floor, knees raised and arms clasped around their legs.

"Your mother and I have been discussing David's situation."

"David! How so?" Tom was surprised.

"You know that David was in the car when it wrecked and he knows his parents are dead. Thanks to you boys and Chuckles and Hope, he fought through his medical and emotional troubles. You helped pull him out of a depression. The hospital is discharging him tomorrow. Their idea is to send him to a foster home where he doesn't know anyone and he'll have another shock in his little life. Too, there may not be anyone willing to adopt him which would mean he'd be in there for at least another twelve years."

"Dad, are you taking a round about way of telling us that David can come live with us?" Tim was hopeful.

"Give that boy a blue ribbon," Herb teased. "Yes, we've talked it over and talked to the proper authorities. We thought that since he knows you and the dogs, and is comfortable with you, he might adjust better if he lived here for a while."

"But, Dad," Anna said with a serious expression. "Won't it be just as hard on him when he has to leave us to go live with strangers? He'll be adjusted to living here and it'll seem to him as if we don't want him or care about him when he's handed off." Anna was almost out of breath in her concern.

Irene smiled and reached to take Herb's hand. "We're wondering how you'd feel about us adopting him. It will take time. We'll have to be investigated and ---"

"Investigated? Us? But everybody knows we're a good family. We'd love him and be good for him." Tim argued.

"It's the law, Tim," Tom explained with a look of disgust. "Any ole body can have a child, sometimes one they don't even want, and be abusive. But when someone, out of the love and goodness of their heart, wants to give a good, loving home to a child, they're investigated and watched and have to prove themselves to jillions of people and __"

"Wind down, Tom. One thing at a time. Do you object to David living with us? He's six and we'll need to handle him lovingly but firmly. If we let him go, he might be sent from foster home to foster home until he's eighteen. Then he'd be turned loose on his own to get along the best he can."

"No. Never that," Tom was emphatic. "We grew up with you and look how we turned out."

Anna burst out laughing. "That might not be much of an endorsement," she teased. She turned with a graceful swing. "Go for it, parents."

"Holy cow. A little brother. Not one who torments me and makes life embarrassing," Tim said softly.

"Yeah a little brother which means you'll have to clean up your act and not set a bad example for the little guy." The twins started wrestling on the floor while Hope and Chuckles gleefully joined in.

Irene then told them the rest of the news. "We've talked to hospital administration and county social workers. I'll call tomorrow early and tell them we'll pick David up when they're ready to release him. Dad and I are proud of you three, but we didn't expect anything different. We were sure you'd be willing to take David into your hearts. We'll make him feel as if he's truly one of the family."

The twins stood, high-fived and hugged Anna. "Group hug," Herb laughed and stood up. "Then everyone to bed."

Anna and the twins stayed at home while their parents went to get David. They ran out to meet the car as Herb drove in. Chuckles and Hope ran with them feeling the rejoicing. When David stumbled out of the car, Chuckles gave a joyous bark and ran to him.

"Oh, boy. Am I really going to live here? Is Chuckles going to be my dog?" He turned a happy, smiling face to the twins. "Are you really going to be my big brothers?" He jumped up to climb up Tim and reached to Tom so that he was hanging between the twins. They hugged David.

"You sure are going to live here and yes, Chuckles will be your dog. Hope lives here, too. But we have to let them make other people happy when they're needed. But they'll never be taken away from you for good."

Tim turned holding David in his arms. "There's one more even better surprise. This is your new big sister, and she's the best sister in the world. David, meet your sister, Anna."

David sobbed with joy. Anna reached and took them. "I'm the lucky one. I've had these two great brothers and now I have a great little brother. Welcome home, David. Why are you crying?" Anna's tender heart melted.

"My mommy and daddy are dead and there's no one else. I was afraid nobody wanted me and I'd not have a family again." Hope looked on with sympathy. Anna turned and ran into the house making David.

CHAPTER THIRTY-NINE

"What'er you doing?" David was puzzled as they sat down at the dinner table. "We're asking a blessing before we eat. We need to thank God for being so good to us and giving us a new son," Irene explained.

"I'm really your son," David said in awe.

"You sure are, son," Herb rubbed noses with David.

"Don't forget to thank God for Chuckles, David bounced in his seat as he looked at the dog at his feet. The then turned puzzled. "Who's God?"

There was momentary silence and then Tom spoke. "Tim and I will tell you all about it later."

During the school break, Anna drove the twins and David to Canine Wonders so they could visit and show off their new brother. David was thrilled with all the dogs and the loving attention he received from the staff.

The night before Anna was to return to college, the phone rang as they finished dinner. Tom answered and turned to face his family with a big grin on his face. "Yes! Great! We'll see you tomorrow." He hung up with a satisfied expression.

"Apparently it's good news," Irene remarked.

"Quit grinning like a monkey and tell us, Tim urged.

"Yeah monkey, tell us," David stood up in his chair he was so excited. Anna reached and got him to sit down.

"You were right, Anna. Things did work out. That was Trina," he hesitated.

"Talk," Tim jumped up and pretended to choke Tom.

"Hillary has agreed to allow her dog to be trained." Everyone cheered and stood to hug each other.

"Me, too," David insisted. They had to explain what a high-five was.

"I want to go back to college, but right now I want to stay and be a part of whatever works out. I won't get to see Trina and meet Hillary and Millie until school is out for the summer. I had thought of continuing summer classes, but now I'm not so sure. Maybe I'll come home and work at Canine Wonders," Anna seemed to be thinking out loud.

"I just got you and now I'm losing you," David pouted.

Anna reached to hug him. "You haven't lost me. I'll write to you and call and I'll be home before you can miss me. I bet dad and mom will bring you to college to see where I live."

"Will you?" David danced around anxiously.

"I guess that can be arranged," Herb smiled as David climbed on his lap.

"Hooray!" David cheered.

"I think we should visit Hillary and tell her how proud we are of her," Tim suggested.

"Let's do that and then go by to see Alex. I know how I'd feel if I was in a wheelchair and my life had changed so radically even if he did bring it on himself," Tim mused. "We'll do that tomorrow early."

"Mom, may we take David with us to visit some friends? We want to show him off." Tom grabbed a couple of cookies hot from the oven, and put his arm around his mother.

"If he wants to go. Please, please keep a close eye on him and bring him home before he gets too tired. Remember, he's still recuperating."

"David, would you like to go with us and visit some friends of ours?"

Tom called to him. David ran into the kitchen.

"Yeah!" he shrieked. "I'd like to go with the big boys."

"Ho, David. We aren't deaf, but we soon will be at this rate," Tom laughed.

"Big boys," Irene laughed. "That's debatable."

"What does batable mean?" David frowned.

"The word's debatable," Tim answered, "and it means you when you ask too many questions."

"No it doesn't, David," Tom knelt by him. "It means a lot of questions should be asked to prove something is true."

"Huh?"

"Never mind, squirt. Get you coat and let's go. Put your cap on, too. It's windy and cool. Mom, keep the dogs in, please."

The twins walked with David between them, taking his hands and lifting him off the ground. "Run, Tim. We have to get away from this monster." They ran laughing and swinging David between them.

"Tom, you silly goose. How can we run from the monster when he's right here between us?"

"No! I'm not no monster," David protested.

"I'm not a monster," Tom corrected him.

"He didn't say you were a monster. He said me."

"Oh, ho. Who does that remind you of?" Tim smiled sadly.

Alex was glad to see them. "Let's go into the den and play with my new video games. Hey, little guy. Do you want to ride on my horse?" Alex patted his lap offering David to sit and ride in the wheelchair. David immediately liked Alex.

"Alex, who's the woman who answered the door and let us in?" Tom asked.

"She's one of the nurses my parents hired to stay with me. They still go their own way and leave me as they've always done." Alex looked depressed and the twins felt sorry for him.

"Boys, you'd better be glad my mother is not home. She still blames everybody else but me for the accident. She said you told her you're my friends, but didn't do anything to stop me from driving. She'll probably never admit that I was neglected and bored. Oh, well. There's no need to go down that old road."

They played a few games with Alex and then excused themselves to visit with Hillary and get David home.

"Thank you for letting me ride your horse," David hugged Alex. "I'm glad I know you now, too."

"Any time, sport. You're a great guy and I know Tom and Tim feel lucky to have such a great brother. Come see me again." Alex followed them to the door. "Come back soon, guys. I have a tutor who comes in to help me keep up with my studies, but believe it or not, I miss being at school with all of you. I wish I'd never gotten mixed up with that other crowd. Never again. I only hope others can learn from my mistake."

"We're sorry, too, but that's all in the past. Let's hope we all learn from our mistakes and go forward," Speaking firmly Tim raised his closed fist. "We'll see you, pal. When you feel adventurous make sure we're home and roll up the streets for a visit."

Hillary was at Trina's house. Tim looked thoughtful as Tom was telling the girls about the visit to Alex. "I have an idea. Let's talk to John before we mention it to Alex, but let's see if Alex is eligible for a service dog. You know to pick up dropped items, go with him, carry things and mostly be a companion."

"I want so much to learn all I can about these service dogs," Hillary said. She looked sheepish. "I'm truly sorry that I acted like such a jerk before."

"We understand," Tim comforted her. 'We'll have to tell you about Galena and Greatheart when we can show you pictures at the same time. We know you were just being human. Forget it. You're headed in the right direction now."

"Come see my dog. His name's Chuckles," David shouted.

"Oooo little brother. My ears will be so happy when you learn to talk a little more quietly," Tom ruffled David's hair. "Where's your cap? Let's go see if Chuckles and Hope have missed us." He looked at Tim. "I wonder if I was ever like that."

Tim burst out laughing. "Oh, how soon they forget. Tom, you gave our parents more grey hairs than they would have had and, yes, you used to holler when you talked. I remember because I was so good and quiet and shy," Tim grinned.

Tom hooked an arm around Tim's neck. "Oh, yes, you were so good."

"See I knew you'd remember," Tim laughed.

David's lower lip pouted and his voice trembled. "Don't hurt Tim."

"We're playing. He's not hurting me," Tim explained.

"Well, it looked like you's a hurting." He looked perplexed when everyone laughed at his vocabulary.

"That's part of pretending to make a lot of noise and sound like the real thing." Tom grabbed David and swung him up. "Wanna pony ride?" He slipped David on to his back and put an arm under David's bottom to hold him up. Pretending to gallop out the door, Tom had David laughing.

Hillary went to Canine Wonders the next three times the group went. One day, as they were preparing to leave, Hillary walked to John. "Would you please tell me more about how I can be a puppy raiser?" She listened intently, asking intelligent questions. "Do you think I can take a puppy home with me?" She asked timidly.

"Let me talk to your parents and we'll get the ball rolling if they approve." John patted her shoulder

"Could we bring a puppy home, too?" Tom asked eagerly as he overheard Hillary's request. "John, you know how well we have trained dogs and how good we are to them."

John laughed. "I'm not sure your house can take another dog. We'll see."

CHAPTER FORTY

That night the Jacksons were watching a special on opportunities for people with special needs. They were delighted to learn that miniature horses were doing so well as guide animals. The tiny, white shoes on them were delightful. The announcer told that the shoes were to protect the tiny hooves from hot pavement, broken glass and anything that would harm them. The horses were favored because the dogs were usually good for only eight years whereas a horse lived to be at least forty years and some of them for fifty years. These little cuties could be housebroken. They would crawl up on a couch beside people and would even sit in laps. The twins became very excited.

"Dad! Dad! May we go to Fredericksburg to see these miniature horses and learn how they're used by blind people?"

"Calmer and quieter, please. I'd like to see them and learn more also. I'll need to check and find an address and a phone number. Too, it all depends on my work schedule. The owners would appreciate a call asking permission to visit. I'm not sure they want the public trooping in on them."

"Why wouldn't they want the public? They're doing a good service and I bet they accept donations." Tom was as excited as he had been as a younger child. Tim was on the floor with David and looked eager, also.

"Leave it for now," Irene cautioned. "Dad promised he'd look into it and we'll all go as soon as it can be planned."

"Oh, you precious little darling, Hillary gushed as she hugged a wiggly Golden Retriever puppy. "I'm sure going to enjoy working with you. I'm going to call the gang and invite them to visit."

"Isn't she sweet?" Trina laughed as she got a doggie kiss on her nose.

"You beautiful girl," Tom admired her.

"Hillary, you have a big job ahead of you, but you're going to love every minute of it." Tim stated.

"Her name is Joy, and she's sure living up to her name."

"Hey, gang. Good news." Tom said. "I, or rather, we" he bowed to Tim, "talked to Jake and John about Alex. They were willing if Alex and his parents would come to the school and talk to them. A doctor would have to submit the required medical forms and Alex would require detailed training. If everything went well, he could graduate with his own companion dog."

Hillary's mother had come into the room and heard the news. "Tell me about the training for these dogs. Will we need to do any of that with this dog?" The twins told her about the process from puppy handlers to school training to bonding with a chosen person.

"The volunteer who takes the puppy home for training, teaches the dog not to beg at the table, to walk willingly and quietly as well as being alert beside their person. They do all the basic training such as sit, stay, lie down, come and so on. The volunteer will take them in cars where they'll be exposed to various noises such as kids on skates and sirens. The dog will learn to go on elevators, escalators, revolving doors and through crowds of people as well as ignoring other animals. They go into restaurants, movies and anywhere a person might want to take them. Hillary, don't you have a cape for Joy so that people will know she's in training?"

"I sure do." She jumped up and ran out of the room returning with a small, red blanket with gold letters reading, "Guide dog in training."

"That's cute," Trina said fastening the blanket around Joy.

"Then what happens?" Mrs. Coramex asked.

"It's also important that the dog gets lots of time to run and play. They need to be bathed and brushed and have regular check-ups."

"What comes under specialized training?" Mrs. Coramex was interested.

"How to pull a wheelchair, open doors, guide the person across a street, alert the person to any danger, turn on lights, pick up dropped items, pick up a ringing phone and give it to their person. Too, if a person falls, the dogs needs to stand quietly and allow the person to brace on their back to get up."

"Are they also trained to be a guard dog?"

"Not specifically. However, as the dog bonds with the person, I'm sure they would guard."

"Is that why Hope and Millie are at the school now?" Trina asked.

"Sure. Hope won't need a lot of training because we have given her a lot. When she's ready you'll have to go stay at the school and live with her so you can get final training together."

The following week Hillary answered the phone to hear an excited Trina. "I'm so excited, I'm not sure I even know who I am."

"Tell me, quickly. You're killing me with the suspense," Hillary laughed.

"We heard from Canine Wonders and I'm to go in and live for the final training. I don't have to attend as long as others do because my case is different."

"Hurray! I'm so happy for you. When do you leave?"

"I'm not sure. My parents have to talk to Mr. Grissom and make plans for me to have my school work."

"He's a great guy. He'll work with you. Everyone will be so happy for you."

Later Trina told the twins that she felt blessed to have friends like them. "I can't thank you enough. I'm going to succeed and I'll need strong support from all my friends."

"You'll have all of us," Herb told her. "You're the important one now. Don't forget. It's possible you'll outgrow the seizures or a medication can be found that will help completely. Keep strong in heart. Always remember, God is in control."

Trina, come here, please." Mr. Grissom called to her. "I talked to our teachers and they're all eager to help. You're an excellent student and it should be no trouble for you to take studies with you. When you return, you may have to take a test in some classes."

"That's okay. I'll do whatever is required. Thank you so much. I'll thank the teachers later."

On Friday Trina went to the office and got a folder of assignments. Four boys and six girls took her to a pizza place for a get-together. "This is not good bye. It's good luck and hurry back," Mark raised his soft drink to toast.

"We'll probably see you tomorrow at Canine Wonders," Tom smiled.

Tim placed an arm across the back of her chair. "We might not be allowed to visit with you while you're in training, but just know we're nearby and will do what we can for you."

Hillary was delighted when John led Millie in. "Millie, my baby, you've learned so much. You're not running around like a crazy dog."

'She's a real lady. She was just young and had not been trained," John smiled. "She still likes to run around and play, especially with the puppies, but she's learned when to play and when to work. While we were out on a trail she walked sedately on a leash. She even looked both ways before crossing a street, and acted like the cats, on the steps of a house, were not even there."

John turned to the twins. "Hope is a real gem. She is a little older and settled, and you have trained her beautifully. I can hardly believe how quickly she picked up what she's to do. She seems to read my mind."

The days rolled by and Trina was released to take Hope home with her. John gave Trina a last 'look-over'. "You and Hope make a great team. Don't ever be too proud, or embarrassed, to listen when she warns you. If you're walking on Main Street, in a large crowd, and she pushes in front of you, sit down and lean against a building. If you have a chance to go into a store, don't be ashamed to explain your situation and ask to sit down. Business people are used to seeing our dogs and will understand."

"I'll remember everything, I promise. I won't let pride get in my way."

Herb had investigated and found a school for training miniature horses to be service animals. Early one Saturday, he took his family to visit the farm.

The owners, Gerald and Phylis Warwick, couldn't have been nicer. David had to be held down because he thought they were just the right size for him to ride. Gerald did kindly place David on the back of one of his regular-sized horses and lead him around. He explained that the little horses were not for riding, only for taking care of people.

"Can I have one, Dad? Oh, I would love to have one," David jumped around.

The twins reminded him that they had the dogs, and the horse would require a much bigger yard as well as being a lot of work. Furthermore the tiny horses could not hold the weight on their backs.

"When you get bigger, we'll find a horse school and see about riding lessons for you, if you're still interested," Herb promised.

The family told Gerald and Phylis about the dog training business. The couple had heard about it, but didn't know much. The twins were delighted when a blind man visited with his little gelding, named Napoleon. They appreciated the opportunity to ask how he felt about having a horse instead of a dog. He told them of the daily care needed.

The children reluctantly left, wishing they lived closer so they could be involved. Herb left a generous donation and asked for bulletins that he could share with others. They loved the pictures of the little fellows in cute sneakers. The sneakers are provided by Sabre Sneakers and by Supreme Equine Designs.

"Anna would have loved this," Tom said. "Maybe this summer she can come with us and see for herself."

"Can I come, too?" David demanded.

"May I come? Tim corrected him.

"Sure you can come, too."

CHAPTER FORTY-ONE

Mr. Grissom walked to the microphone. "Good morning, students. I trust everyone had a great weekend and now you're raring to go." He laughed at the moans and boos. "I want to introduce someone to you and tell you about her. Come, Hope."

There was a loud gasp as the large dog trotted obediently to Mr. Grissom. "Trina, you come, too." He clapped his hands. "Come, Trina." Laughter.

Mr. Grissom explained why Trina would have Hope with her in classes. "This is a working dog and you must be careful not to interfere with her working relationship with Trina. When you see her stand in front of Trina and lean against her, or if she puts her head on Trina's lap when she's seated, you'll know the dog senses a seizure. Trina must put on her helmet and sit down on the floor."

"Why does she have to sit on the floor?" Sharon Peterson asked.

"So she'll be down and won't fall down and hurt herself, stupid," Roger Watkins answered with a sneer.

"Hey, none of that. It isn't nice to call someone a name that will hurt them. Sharon has probably not heard of service dogs. Or maybe she hasn't met Trina and is not aware of her illness."

"Sorry, Chief," Roger said cockily, but Mr. Grissom ignored him,

"Just remember," Mr. Grissom continued. "Any of you could have had an accident that left you with the same problem Trina has. Thank your lucky stars and try to be understanding and helpful."

"How does the dog help you, Trina?" Boyd Mullins asked.

Trina looked at Mr. Grissom and he nodded. She stepped to the microphone with Hope beside her. "Two nights ago Hope woke me by jumping on my bed, whining and licking my face. I was able to get out of bed and lie on the floor before the seizure started. If I had stayed on the bed, I might have fallen off and been hurt or broke bones. This beautiful, sweet animal has more common sense than a lot of people I know. I can never thank Tom and Tim Jackson enough for loaning me their dog."

Several students whipped around to look at the twins. "Man, that's your dog? Why are you loaning her to Trina? She's intelligent and can help people." Jordon Kirk exclaimed.

Tom stood and spoke loudly so he could be heard around the auditorium. "That's why we're loaning her to Trina. She **is** intelligent and is helping Trina."

Hope, hearing Tom's familiar voice, looked out at him and wagged her tail, but she stayed where she had been trained to stay.

"How long did it take to train her?" Marcie Ditmar asked.

"An animal can not be trained to smell chemical changes or sense changes. That's why these dogs are so rare. They are born with the skill and we just enlarge it with training. Hope had the same basic training that any dog has. Her basic instinct is fine-tuned to sense something that's going to

377

happen and take care of the person. No one has been able to fully explain it." Mr. Grissom told them.

"Will she lead a blind person?" Greg Faulkner asked.

"If she were trained to do so. Dogs are carefully chosen to do what they show an inborn sense to do. They can lead the blind, help a deaf person, pull a wheelchair and be a companion and many areas of skill."

"Do all the dogs, uh, I mean are they all successful and good for the job?" Sheila Tritt asked.

"No. Very few fail," Tim explained. "If they do, they're trained to do something else. Some go to the police for specialized work or to guard a business. A rare few turn out to be just good family pets."

"Sorry, but that's all the time we have," Mr. Grissom interrupted. "Thank you all for being so attentive and remember, **don't pet the dog unless Trina says you can. She is working and can not be distracted.**"

That afternoon in Algebra class, Mr. Orr happened to see Hope place her head on Trina's lap. "Trina, get your helmet on and get on the floor." Trina quickly followed orders and sat with her back against the wall. Hope stood across Trina's legs and leaned gently against her chest. The seizure was not as severe as some had been. Trina soon focused her eyes and was embarrassed, but her classmates cheered and told Hope what a good dog she was.

Ted Groden went to Trina and reached down to help her up. Hope growled at him and refused to let Trina get up. "Thank you, Ted, but I'll get up as soon as my legs don't feel like wet spaghetti," she laughed. The class laughed with her. She used Hope's back to pull herself up.

"Let's get the show on the road," Mr. Orr called for their attention. "This is the first time you've seen this happen. From now on I don't expect any interruptions in class. Just go about your business and let Trina go about hers. Trina, don't be embarrassed. You can't help what has happened to you. Just be thankful for that great dog."

A few nights later Tom answered the phone and gave a yell when he heard the message. As Tim ran in and asked what was happening, Tom waved his hand in the air for silence. "Thanks for calling, Jim and I am going to beat you so bad."

"What? What?" Tim was impatient as Tom hung up.

"What's all the racket about?" Herb and Irene came into the room.

"That was Jimmy. His uncle, the state policeman, is going to give us a driving test this weekend. Tom danced around with David and Chuckles being so excited they were under foot.

"I am now so ready for my license," Tim agreed. "I haven't been interested, but we're going to college soon and I'll want to drive."

"Okay boys, here's the deal." Jimmy's uncle, Sergeant Earl Dodd, told them. "Corporal Thurbow, down there, is going to help us. We have an imaginary street laid out with deep curves, dead ends and all kinds of obstacles. You'll drive through the course. Be alert for Cpl. Thurbow to change what is there. You'll have to make an instant decision. After you've finished, you'll pull beside the cones and do parallel parking. Any questions? No. then who is first?"

Tim and Tom, Dan Baxter, James Horn and Jimmy Dodd looked at each other and each one stepped back. They jerked around at someone laughing out loud at them. Alex sat in a wheelchair. "Hey, guys. We've all mouthed off for weeks. I put myself here and can't do what I dreamed of doing, but all of you can. Now get to it."

"Alex, there are specially built, but very expensive, cars built for the handicapped. You might not do exactly what you would like, but you'll be surprised at what you can do with a little effort," Anna stepped behind him and put her hands on the chair. "Let's you and I wait over here and let these chickens do their stuff." Anna was a pleasant surprise to the twins.

"Okay," Tom gulped. "I'll go first."

Sgt. Dodd watched as Tom got in the car, clicked the seatbelt, checked all mirrors and the position of his seat. Dodd wrote on his clipboard.

"Wait," Tom called. "You didn't tell us at what speed we're to drive."

Sgt. Dodd smiled. "There are signs at various points. However, at all times, use your common sense. The road conditions may be such that a driver cannot safely drive the posted speed limit."

Tom looked behind him to make sure it was safe for him to pull out. He turned on the signal light to show he was moving out in that direction. As he came around a curve, Cpl. Thurbow kicked some cones in front of him to represent a child running out or an obstruction of some sort. Later he piled things up to represent a wreck. Tom reacted quickly and safely. Cpl. Hooked up a fireman's powerful water hose and suddenly turned in on the windshield to represent a storm. Tom finished the course and pulled up to park. He looked to make sure it was safe to back. He suddenly braked and looked around.

"Something wrong?" Sgt. Dodd called out.

"Yes, sir. I was looking in my right side mirror and saw a cat run behind me. I didn't want to hit it."

Everyone looked to see a big yellow tom cat strolling across the field. Tom finished backing in smoothly and correctly. Sgt. Wrote on his pad and then called for the next driver.

The others took their turn with Cpl. Thurbow pulling different kind of surprises and testing them.

"Gather around, fellows. As soon as I confer with Cpl. Thurbow, I'll tell you the scores." the boys stood nervously beside Alex's chair and talked.

"I wanted to be with y'all so badly," Alex moaned. "I bet I'd uh done the best. Face it. I brought this on myself. In a childish way, I guess I was trying to get at my parents for not being like yours." He looked at the twins. "I used to be so jealous that you could talk to your parents about anything and that they were always there for you. They might punish you for something, but they loved you and proved they cared."

"Believe me, Alex. We do understand." Tim put a hand on Alex's shoulder. "I'm sorry that everyone in the world doesn't have parents like ours."

"Hey, pal." Tom knelt down in front of Alex. "You said you wanted a different crowd to buddy with, why don't you attend our Youth Bible Training with us? You won't find anyone there that's trying to get you into trouble."

"I don't know," Alex said slowly. "I've never been in church."

"You're never too old or too late," Tom grinned.

Anna put an arm across Alex's shoulders. "I am so proud of you for taking the blame for your own decisions. It's a rotten shame that you had to pay the price like this, but who knows? In the meantime, talk to younger children, and your peers, and tell them what can happen. Some youngster might need a nice big brother like you, and you can help in many ways."

"Okay, gang, this is it." Sgt. Dodd and Cpl Thurbow walked to the group. "Tom, since you were first, we'll start with you. You didn't have a chance to observe what others were doing, so you did extra well. I was impressed that you checked everything carefully before starting. Even though you had a 45 speed limit at one point, you slowed to make the curve. You checked all three mirrors before you acked and saw the cat. It could have been a child that ran out or an elderly person moving slowly. If you do as well on the written test, you'll make a top score."

"Jason, I realize you were nervous, but never get behind the wheel of a car unless you feel alert and good about yourself. You didn't check mirrors or anything before you started. When the 'child' ran in front of you bouncing a ball, you did stop in time, but you braked so hard, you turned sideways in traffic. All in all you're not doing badly, but you need more practice."

"Tim, I thought I was watching Tom again. Whoever taught you two did a superb job." Tim hugged Anna and grinned.

"Did you teach these rascals, young lady?"

"Yes, sir. I did and it was a lot of fun. I'm proud of my brothers."

"Rightly you should be. They're both doing extremely well."

"Dan, my man, you did well, but you did drag on the speed. Apparently you were unsure. I would far rather that you start like that and then pick up speed with experience and confidence than be a speed demon and have an accident. You did well."

"Jimmy, you didn't check anything before you pulled out. Otherwise, you were good. All of you are going to do well when you go for your test. The written part will be first. If you pass it, then you'll be taken on the street by a designated state police. Just be yourself. I'm pleased that you boys waited until you were old enough, and mature enough, to do the job well. Too many youngsters start too early and aren't mentally or emotionally ready. I'm giving each of you the notes I made. Good luck to all of you."

"Thanks a million, Uncle Earl and Cpl. Thurbow. This started out as a bet as to who could do the best."

"Jimmy, driving is a big responsibility. You're not only responsible for your vehicle, your passengers, but also other drivers on the road. It isn't smart to try to outdo others. A car can be a dangerous weapon if not handled correctly. I have a Virginia State Highway Manuel for each of you to study for your test. Keep it in the glove compartment after you have a license."

"Excuse me, sir,"Alex spoke to Sgt. Dodd. "Do you have an extra copy of the manual I might have? I'd like to learn what is required. I drove illegally and carelessly, and now two innocent girls and I are paying for it, I caused trouble and heartache for other families. I'm honestly sorry for that, but it's too late to be sorry. The damage is done."

"It's never too late to be sorry and recognize our mistakes. Don't give up. Keep exercising. You're young yet and you don't know what might be in your future. There are special built cars for your needs."

They were interrupted by a figure yelling and running into the group. "Am I too late? Don't tell me I'm too late. I wanted to watch."

Tom squatted in front of David, looking at him in surprise. "Where's mom and dad?"

"Oh, I guess they're at home. I'm big enough to come by myself."

"David," Anna spoke firmly, did you tell mom and dad where you would be?"

"No. Cause they wouldn't uh let me come," he pouted.

Tim glared at the others for giggling. Sgt. Dodd quickly caught on and squatted down in front of David.

"Young man, did you cross streets and traffic to get here?"

"Yes," David said softly, hanging his head and hunching his shoulders.

"And you didn't ask your parents' permission?"

"No, I didn't" David said loudly. "I didn't ask cause they'd uh said no."

"My goodness. They're probably crying their eyes out wondering what happened to you. They must feel awfully bad. Do you know why they worry?"

"They don't need to worry. I'm big enough to cross the street." David now looked defiantly at the officer, but there was a hint of tears. He held up his arms for Tim to pick him up. "I just wanted to be with you."

Sgt. Dodd quickly stood and took David's hand. "Come on. I'm taking you home."

"No!" David yelled. "I go with my sister and brothers."

"Not this time, son. You did something wrong, so you have to go with me to talk to your parents. You know I could put you in jail. Or if your parents are not caring about you, I can put them in jail, son."

"Not your son," David stamped his foot.

"David," Anna spoke. "Go with the policeman and mind your manners. If we had done something wrong, we would have to go with him. We'll meet you at the house." David stood still. "NOW David."

"I thought you loved me," David sobbed.

"Don't start that," Tom said. "You know we love you but when we make a mistake we have to face it. You said you were big enough to cross the street, well, be big enough to go with the policeman."

David crawled in the seat of the officer's car and slumped down. As the car pulled away the Jacksons had to turn away so David wouldn't see their sad faces.

"It breaks my heart," Alex said with a catch in his throat. "How could you stand there and do that to the little fellow?"

"He won't learn any younger," Anna answered. "If we always let him get by with what he wants, he'll get into serious trouble because he'll never learn to analyze a situation and maybe he would endanger many lives with his thoughtlessness. I'm sorry, Alex, but you, of all people, should know what we're doing."

Alex hung his head. "Yeah. I know. I wouldn't be in the shape I'm in if someone had loved me enough to lay down the law when I was younger. You're right." He turned to push his chair away.

"Thanks for coming to give us support, Alex." Tom said. "We appreciate it. We'll pick you up next Wednesday at six for church." Alex nodded and left.

Irene was sitting with tears in her eyes but not speaking. Herb looked sadly at David. "Son, why did you run away? We thought you loved us and were happy here. We were so afraid you wouldn't come home again. Suppose Chuckles had followed you and got hit by a car. How would that make you feel?"

David hung his head and cried. "I'm sorry. I just wanted to see the boys drive for the policeman."

Sgt. Dodd put an arm around David. "I think David now knows what he did was wrong and caused you a lot of worry. I bet he'll tell you from now on where he's going. Won't you, David?"

David nodded. "I am sorry." He sobbed louder. Irene opened her arms and ran into them. Anna and the twins walked in.

Sgt. Dodd stood up. "I have to go. I told my brother that my partner and I would be joining them for dinner. Thank you for including me in your driver training. You're wise to want to be safe, courteous drivers."

"You boys are going to be excellent drivers," Cpl Thurbow said and left.

David," Herb looked at him, "go to your room and stay there until I come up. You need to think about what you've done and I need to think what I'm going to do about it."

"But I said I'm sorry," David protested. Slapping his feet on the stairs he went on up to his room mumbling to himself.

"I don't know whether to hug him or yell at him," Tom sighed. "We explained to him how busy we would be and that there wouldn't be anything for him to enjoy, but he did as he pleased. What do you do with a kid who does as he pleases without thinking?"

Herb threw his head back and laughed loudly. "I remember a boy who climbed out his bedroom window before daylight and scared the stuffing out of all of us."

"Don't forget the walrus and the exploding shed," Tim grinned. "Oh, yes, and the scare at the Grand Canyon."

Tom blushed and stammered. He smiled weakly as the family laughed and prepared for bed.

CHAPTER FORTY-TWO

The next morning, after breakfast, the family gathered in the den. Herb took David on his lap and hugged him. "David, you must always remember this that we love you and we think we're lucky to have you. You've been going with the boys when they take chuckles to the hospital and nursing home. To make sure you remember your mistake of yesterday, you cannot go with them all next week."

"That's not fair," David yelled.

"Was it fair that you left without permission and worried us so much and placed yourself in danger?"

Pouting, David slowly shook his head.

A few days later David came skipping into the kitchen. "How much longer, Mom?"

She knew what he meant. "Just a couple more days and you can go with your brothers. I'm sure you've learned to tell us before you do something." He grinned and kissed her cheek.

"Can I have some cookies and milk?"

"May I?"

"Sure, you can. You're big and can have what you want."

Irene bit back a smile. "Being big doesn't mean you get what you want."

The twins celebrated their birthday by receiving their driver's license. As David's birthday was the next week, the twins planned a surprise for him. Herb and Irene smiled at each other. The twins were doing for David what had been done for them over the years.

Tom and Tim were delighted to meet new students at their school. Twins Michelle and Martin Winfield had moved to Fairfax from Indiana. Their father had been transferred to Washington, D.C. to work for the government after he came home from Iraq.

"Do you have a room together?" Martin asked the twins in surprise.

"No. We did when we were smaller, but after we returned from Alaska, dad had a big room built downstairs and two bedrooms over it upstairs. David has our old room." Tim explained

"None of my business. I just thought it might be inconvenient to have any privacy if two grown boys roomed together. Naturally, my twin being a girl necessitates us having two rooms."

"We figured we'd have roommates when we go to college and we decided not to room together so we could meet more people," Tom explained.

A few days later the twins talked to David about celebrating his first birthday with them. He would be a big seven. "David, would you like for us to drive you to a park where there are a lot of rides and fun things?"

"Just you and Tim and me?" he asked excitedly.

"You know Tim and I will be going to college soon and you need to have buddies your own age. Why don't you invite some friends from school to go with us?"

"We'll see," David copied Herb.

On Thursday evening Tim called to David. He ran into the room and climbed on Tim's lap. "Why don't you call

Eddie and Chuck and invite them to go with you for your birthday in the park?"

"They wouldn't be interested."

"You won't know until you ask them."

David finally agreed to call them. He turned from the phone with wide, happy eyes. "They want to go. They want to be my friend," he said as if he couldn't believe it.

"Well, why wouldn't they want a great guy like you for a friend?" Irene asked him hugging him.

"I never had a friend before," he said excited.

"Never? None at all?" Tom was surprised.

"No. My real daddy said me and him were friends and that's all we'd need."

The twins and Irene looked at each other. "David, why don't you go get an ice cream bar," Irene suggested and he ran off. "That explains his immature social skills. Why would a man do that to a bright, little boy?"

"Mom, remember we were told that the parents shunned David's parents after they were married. Apparently it hurt his father to the point he rejected everyone except his own family." Tom surmised.

Tim brightened up. "We'll see that he has friends of his own age and learns to socialize. That explains why he clings to us. I thought it was just because he met us first, but he's used to one adult." David came in eating the ice cream and Irene asked him to take it to the kitchen.

David, Eddie and Chuck had a whopping good time. Tim staggered into the house that evening. "I don't think I'll be able to walk straight for a week. We rode so many rides that my brain hasn't caught up yet."

Tom dropped to the couch with a groan. "Dad, Mom, how did you stand us growing up? Keeping up with three little energetic boys was a major effort. I'm really tired trying to keep up with them."

"You learn fast," Herb smiled at the twins. "Think how we felt after having a well-behaved little girl and then two energetic boys came along. You're getting practice for your own little boys in the future. Far in the future, I hope."

"Oh, no," Tom groaned. "Right now I feel as if I'll never get married. I'm afraid I'd half kill a kid of mine if he acted like I did," He collapsed on the couch and his parents laughed loudly.

The remainder of the school year passed quickly and summer vacation started. The phone rang and Tim reached it first. He listened. "Thank you for calling, Mrs. Fuller." He hung up and looked sad.

"What is it?" Irene asked.

"Trina went into a violent seizure and is in the hospital. Her mother thought we would want to know."

David surprised them by saying, "Why don't we ask God to take care of her?"

"Excellent idea, son," Herb said as the family gathered for prayer.

The next day the twins went to the hospital. Mrs. Fuller was in Trina's room. The boys were disturbed seeing so many tubes and gurgling machines on Trina and her head wrapped in a bandage.

"What's happened now?" Tom whispered. At that moment the doctor slipped in.

"Why don't you folks come out in the hall and I'll try to explain." they quietly followed him. "We found a blood clot forming on the brain. Another result of that senseless accident. We drilled in and drained it. All we can do now is wait."

"Did everything look good to you after the surgery?" Tim asked.

"It sure did. I have a good feeling that little lady will have some good news after this." His pager sounded. "Sorry, I have to run."

The twins kept checking on Trina even though only family was allowed in the room with her. A week later, when they went to the hospital, they were pleasantly surprised to meet Trina walking shakily in the hall with her hand on Hope's back.

"Guess what," Trina was thrilled. "The doctors think I'll not have any more seizures unless something unexpected happens." His expression changed to sadness. "I guess you'll want Hope back. I've learned to love her and would like to keep her."

"We know how you feel, but we never intended to give her up for good."

"I understand, but I do love her."

"We won't separate you. Visit her any time you want."

The people at Canine Wonders rejoiced with Trina at her good news. John talked to the twins. "Boys, would you consider donating Hope to our program? We need more like her."

"No." Both boys answered quickly. Tom looked thoughtful. "Do you know of a healthy, registered Malamute that could be bred with Hope? Our mother will be upset, but we'll talk to her about donating the puppies to your program. They could be trained from the beginning."

Two weeks later John called them. "I found a dog like you wanted and we approve of him. Keep a check on Hope and when she's ready to be bred, bring her in."

Chuckles and Hope both continued to visit the Children's Hospital. They never forgot how to deal with the children.

"David, come here," Tom called. David ran from the back yard with Chuckles and Hope in hot pursuit. He stopped to stare at the two strange boys. "David, these are our good friends from Alaska. This is Benjamin Yoakno Eskise and he's a real Eskimo. This is Charles Running Horse and he's a real Indian. We just picked them up at the airport. They've come all the way from Alaska to see us and meet you." David just stared.

All through dinner David sat unusually silent. After dinner Tom and Tim excused themselves to take Ben and Charlie to visit Alex. Friends in Alaska had been told all about the friends and problems here in Virginia. Everyone looked puzzled when David didn't beg to go with them.

David took his bath, brushed his teeth, said his prayers and got into bed.

Irene and Herb sat on the bed to read to him. They grew concerned because this was not like David to be so quiet and still. Was he sick?

"Why are you so quiet, son. Don't you feel well?" Herb gathered David in his arms. David still said nothing.

Irene put a hand on his forehead and then stroked his cheek. "Sweetie, we can't help you if we don't know why you're upset."

"Are those boys going to stay here?"

"They're just here for a visit, then they'll go back to Alaska. Why? Don't you like them? They came to meet you."

"Tom and Tim like them better than they like me."

"Where did you get that idea? Of course the boys like their friends, but they love you. You're their brother."

"They went off with those guys and didn't even ask me to go."

"Oh, darling," Irene reached to take him in her arms. "Tom and Tim are a lot older than you and those boys are their age. When you get as big as they are, you can stay up later and go out with your friends."

"Is that all?"

"You betcha bottom dollar, cowboy," Herb grinned. "I'm going to read a story and you're going to scoot down, close your eyes and have beautiful dreams." Chuckles whined and put his head on the bed, then sighed and lay down on the floor.

"Chuckles doesn't understand why you're upset. He thinks there's something wrong with you. Calm down. This story is about a dog and a cat who became good friends and protected each other."

The twins invited Mark and Jimmy to go to a theme park with them. The six boys had a great day. It was the first time Ben and Charlie had ridden a roller coaster.

Ben had brought a video of Greatheart. It included the town and some of the people. The best part was Chief Houmay kneeling with his arm around Greatheart and grinning widely. The boys' visit went by much too quickly.

Charlie and Ben won David's friendship by telling him about their exciting times when the twins lived in Alaska. They told him about Galena and Greatheart. He was very proud when they bragged on Chuckles. Charlie and Ben were thrilled with the hospital visit and the one to Canine Wonders.

When Ben and Charlie were taken to the airport, David hugged them and told them he wanted them to come back. "I'm glad you came."

"We loved meeting you, sport. Wouldn't you like to visit us in Alaska? You could see Greatheart and a sled dog race and a lot of fun things."

The twins had a summer job which helped them earn money for college. Their volunteer work and church work went on as usual. Anna worked every day at Canine Wonders.

One night, after David was in bed, the family was enjoying a quiet time. Tom stirred. "Mom, I've been thinking over what's happened since we returned to Virginia. You could write another book about Alex learning the hard way and Trina's and Meg's misfortunes. Hillary learning to share and open her heart to others and how Hope worked with Trina. Millie is making a great therapy dog. Knowing Marshall was special. David coming to be part of our family and Hope having babies to donate to help people.

Tim was playing with the two little puppies they had brought home to train. "Boomer and Chopsticks should be in that book," Tim added. "Did Tom tell you what his plans for the future might be?"

Tom sat up and beamed. "I know you'll approve. I've decided that I want to study child psychology and child therapy. I want to work with children like Marshall and David."

Irene and Herb swelled with pride and thankfulness that Tom was, at last, becoming a mature adult.

The next evening Anna came dancing into the room. "Attention. I heard some great news today at the school. Alex has been assigned a companion dog of his own. He will be down there in training." Everyone was enthused.

They smiled watching Chuckles patiently allowing the two guide puppies in training to crawl over him and chew on his ears. He looked over his shoulder and made funny noises as if he were trying to talk.

"Whad he say?" David asked innocently.

"I bet he said he's happy he has a good boy of his own named David, and he's sure glad Tom and Tim found him." Herb picked David up and started out of the room.

"I bet he said it's time we were in bed and maybe those two ornery little pups will go to sleep and leave him alone." Anna stood and stretched.

Doors were locked; windows were checked and everyone went to their rooms. The lights were off, except a night light in the upstairs hall. A black dog made soft chuckling sounds as he padded round making sure everything was all right for his family.

THE RAINBOW BRIDGE

There is a bridge connecting Heaven and Earth. It's called the Rainbow Bridge because of its many colors. Just this side of the Rainbow Bridge there is a meadow filled with sweet grass and wild flowers and a stream of fresh, sweet, clear water. When a beloved pet dies, the pet goes to this place. There is always food, water, spring weather and companions. The old and frail animals are young again. Those who were maimed are made whole. They play all day and get along. There is only one thing missing. They are not with their special person they loved on Earth and who loved them. So, each day they run and play until the day comes when one of them suddenly stops and looks up expectantly. The nose twitches, the ears are up and the eyes are sparkling. This one runs from the group with joyful noises. You have been seen and when you and your pet meet, there is a loving embrace. Your face is kissed again and again and you look once more into the eyes of your trusting pet. Then you cross the bridge together into Heaven never to be separated again.

A VERY SPECIAL WELCOME

This is about some of the animals who were waiting when the terrorist flew into the New York Towers, the Pentagon and attempted to crash into the White House.

On the morning of September 11, 2001, there was an unexpected amount of activity at the Rainbow Bridge. Decisions had to be made quickly. There were issues not often addressed here in the fact that many animal residents had no loving person to wait on.

Think of the puppies who lived and died in hideous puppy mills. No person on Earth had ever had the chance to love and protect them. What about those who spent many unhappy hours tied in hot, dusty yards with no water or shelter and those who were abused and neglected? There was no one for them. We don't talk about that up here because we share loved ones arriving. We all know there is nothing like your very own person who thinks you are the most wonderful animal in the universe.

On that Tuesday morning, a request rang out for pups, who had no special person, to volunteer for an extra special assignment. An eager, curious crowd surged forward. Each one wondering what the assignment would be.

A solemn voice told them that unexpectedly, and all at once, over 5,000 loving people had been forced from Earth. The pups, as all pups do, felt the humans' pain deep in their own hearts. Without hearing more, there was a clamoring among them as they shouted out.

MAY I HAVE ONE TO COMFORT?

I'LL TAKE TWO. I HAVE A BIG HEART AND I'VE BEEN SAVING KISSES.

One after another they came forward for an assignment. One cozy-looking, fluffy puppy hesitantly asked, "Are there any children coming? I would be very comforting for a child and I've always wanted a child to cuddle."

A group of Dalmatians surged forward. "We'll take the firemen and comfort them." Large working breeds called out, "We'll take the police officers and love them."

Father Mike got a special Yorkie all his own. It was difficult to determine for whom the joy was complete. Dogs, who on Earth had never had a kind word or a pet on the head, ran forward and said, "I will love any humans."

Then all dogs wherever on Earth they had originally come from, rushed to the Rainbow Bridge and stood waiting eagerly to share their love.

Horses, cats, birds and all kinds of animals ran to meet the humans to make them feel welcome and loved.

Of course, these Rainbow stories are just sweet stories. I do urge you to love and take care of any animal you have or meet. Spaying and neutering all pets will prevent little ones that are not wanted and will not be cared for.

Over 10,000 adoptable dogs were euthanized in this country during 2008-2009 because no one offered to give them a home. Spaying and neutering will keep this from happening. Be a responsible owner.